# Schooled in Magic

Christopher G. Nuttall

Twilight Times Books
Kingsport Tennessee

**Schooled in Magic**

*This is a work of fiction. All concepts, characters and events portrayed in this book are used fictitiously and any resemblance to real people or events is purely coincidental.*



Paladin Timeless Books, an imprint of
Twilight Times Books
P O Box 3340
Kingsport TN 37664
http://twilighttimesbooks.com/

First Edition, August 2014

Library of Congress Control Number: 2014907100

ISBN: 978-1-60619-298-6

Cover art by Brad Fraunfelter

Printed in the United States of America.

Dedicated to Emily Martha Sorensen, who inspired the core idea behind this series and gave her name to the heroine.

# Chapter One

"IT'S TIME TO CLOSE, MY DEAR."

Emily Sanderson nodded reluctantly as the librarian stepped past her seat and headed to the handful of other occupied chairs. This late at night, only a handful of people remained in the library, either intent on reading or simply because they had nowhere else to go. The library was small and rarely more than half-full even at the best of times. Emily loved it because it was her refuge. She too had nowhere else to go.

She stood and gathered her books, returning them to the trolley for re-shelving. The librarian was a kindly old man–he'd certainly not asked any questions when the younger Emily had started to read well above her grade level–but he got grumpy when visitors tried to return books to the shelves themselves. Not that she could really blame him. Readers had a habit of returning the books to the wrong places, causing mistakes that tended to snowball until the entire shelf was out of order. And Emily hated to see poor Rupert grumpy. He was one of the few people she felt she could rely on.

Most teenage girls her age would never crack open a history book, unless they were looking for the answers to some test. Emily had fallen in love with history from a very early age, taking refuge in it from the trials and tribulations of her life. Reading about the lives of famous people–their struggles to change the world–made her feel her universe had a past, even if it didn't have a future. Perhaps she would have made a good historian one day, if she'd known where to start working towards a history degree. But she already knew she would never find a proper life. She knew what happened to most graduates these days. They graduated from college, they celebrated, and then they couldn't find a job.

Her stepfather had certainly made it clear to her, after an endless series of arguments about what she wanted to do with her life, that she would never do anything worthwhile with her life.

"You'll never amount to anything," he'd told Emily, one drunken night. "You won't even be able to flip burgers at McDonald's!"

Her mother should never have married again–but she'd been lonely after Emily's father had vanished from their lives, so long ago that Emily barely remembered him. Emily's stepfather–she refused to call him *father*–had never laid a finger on her, yet he hadn't hesitated to tear down her confidence every chance he could, or to verbally rip her to shreds. He resented Emily and Emily had no idea why. She didn't even know why he stayed with a woman he clearly didn't love.

Emily caught sight of her own reflection in one of the windows and winced inwardly. She didn't really recognize the girl looking back at her. Long brown hair framed a face too narrow to be classically pretty, with pale skin and dark eyes that looked somehow mournful against her skin. Her clothes were shapeless, hiding her figure; she rarely bothered with makeup, or indeed any other form of cosmetics, not when there was no point. They wouldn't improve her life.

Nothing would.

And they might attract unwanted attention too.

The librarian waved to her as she took one last look at the bookshelves and headed for the counter. "No books today?"

"No, sorry," Emily said. She had a library ticket—it said a great deal about her life that it was her most treasured possession—but she'd filled it over the week. There would be no more books until she returned some old ones. "I'll see you tomorrow."

The familiar sense of despondency and hopelessness fell back over her as she stepped out and walked down the street. There was no future for her, not even if she went to college; her life would become consumed by a boring job, or an unsatisfactory relationship. No, the very thought was laughable. She was neither pretty nor outgoing; indeed, she spent most of her life isolated from her peers. Even when there were groups that might have attracted her—she did occasionally take part in role-playing games—part of her never wanted to stay with them for very long. She wanted friendship and companionship and yet she knew she wouldn't know what to do with them if she had either.

In fact, she'd been to a game earlier, before coming to the library. And she'd left early.

But now she didn't want to go home. Her stepfather might be there, or he might be out drinking with his buddies, swapping lies about their days. The former was preferable to the latter, she knew; when he was out drinking, he tended to come home drunk, demanding service from Emily's mother. And then he shouted at Emily, or threatened her.

Or *looked* at her. That was the worst of all.

She wished to go somewhere—anywhere—other than home. But there was nowhere else she could go.

Her stomach rumbled, unpleasantly. She would have to prepare a TV dinner for herself, or perhaps beans on toast. It was a given that her mother wouldn't cook. She'd barely bothered to cook for her daughter since Emily had mastered the microwave. If she hadn't been fed at school, Emily suspected that she would have starved to death by now.

As she trudged home, she realized something with a crystalline clarity that shocked her; she wanted *out*. She wanted out of her life, wanted out so badly that she would have left without a backward glance, if only someone made her an offer.

And then she shook herself into sense. No one had made her an offer and no one would. Her life was over. No matter what it looked like on the outside, she knew her life was over. She was sixteen years old and her life was over. And yet it felt as if it would never end.

*A fatal disease would have been preferable,* she thought, morbidly.

The wave of dizziness struck without warning. Emily screwed her eyes tightly shut as the world spun around her, wondering if she'd drunk something she shouldn't have during the role-playing session with the nerds and geeks. She had thought that they were too shy to *ever* spike her drink, but perhaps one of them had brought in alcohol and she'd drunk it by mistake. The sound of giggling–faint, but unmistakable–echoed in the air as her senses swam. And then she fell ... or at least it *felt* like falling, but from where and to what?

And then the strange sensation simply faded away.

When she opened her eyes, she was standing in a very different place.

Emily recoiled in shock. She was standing in the middle of a stone-walled cell, staring at a door that seemed to be made of solid iron. Half-convinced she was hallucinating–perhaps it had been something worse than alcohol that she'd drunk, after all–she stumbled forward until her fingers were pressed against the door. It felt cold and alarmingly real to her senses. There was no handle in the door, no place for her to try to force the door open and escape. The room felt depressingly like a prison cell.

Swallowing hard, Emily ran her fingers over the stonework, feeling faint tingles as her fingertips touched the mortar binding the wall together. It felt like the castles she'd read about, the buildings that had been constructed long before concrete or other modern building materials had enabled the artists to use their imagination properly. There was a faint sense of *age* pervading through the stone, as if it was hundreds of years old. It certainly *felt* hundreds of years old.

Where was she?

Desperately, Emily looked from wall to wall, seeking a way out of the cell. But there was nothing, not even a window; the only source of light was a tiny lantern hanging from the ceiling. There was no bed, no place for her to lay her head; not even a pallet of straw like she'd seen in the historical recreations she'd attended with her drama group. And how had she come to be here? Had she been arrested? Impatiently, she dismissed the thought as silly. The police wouldn't have put her in a stone cell and they wouldn't have had to spike her drink to arrest her.

A hundred scenarios her mother had warned her about ran through her mind; her captor could be a rapist, a serial killer, or a kidnapper intent on using her to extort money from her parents. Emily would have laughed at the thought a day ago–her stepfather wouldn't have paid *anything* to recover her from a kidnapper–but it wasn't so funny now. What would a kidnapper do when he discovered that he'd kidnapped a worthless girl?

A clatter that came from outside the iron door rang through the cell and Emily looked up sharply. She would have sworn that the iron door was solid, but all of a sudden a tiny hatch appeared in the metal and a pair of bright red eyes peered in at her. There was something so utterly inhuman about them that Emily recoiled, convinced that they belonged to a monster. Or a devil. There was a second rattle at the door, which then blurred into a set of iron bars, revealing a hooded figure standing outside the cell. His eyes, half-hidden under his hood, weren't just red; they were *glowing.* The rest of his face was obscured in darkness.

Behind him, there were more stone walls. A pair of skeletons stood against the wall as if they'd been left there to rot. Something about them caught Emily's attention before she saw the first skeleton begin to move, walking forward as if it were still flesh and blood. The second skeleton turned its head until it was looking directly at Emily, the sightless eye-sockets seeming to peer deeply into her soul. Emily felt her blood running cold, suddenly convinced, right to the very core of her being, that this was no ordinary kidnapping. She must be a very long way from home.

"Welcome," the hooded figure said. There was something cracked and broken about his voice, almost as if he hadn't spoken for a very long time and had lost the knack. "You may call me Shadye."

He spoke his name as if Emily should know it, but it meant nothing to her. She tried to speak, but discovered that her mouth was so dry that speaking was impossible.

Shadye stepped forward, up against the bars, and studied her thoughtfully. His red eyes flickered over her body, before meeting her eyes and holding them for a long chilling moment.

Emily forced herself to speak. All the novels she'd read about kidnapped heroines suggested that she should try to get the kidnapper to see her as a human being–although she was far from convinced that Shadye himself was a human being. The fantasy books she'd devoured in an attempt to ignore her father's departure and her mother's desperate search for a second husband seemed to be mocking her inside her skull. All of this could be a trick, perhaps a reality TV show, but something in her mind was convinced that what she saw and sensed was real. But what? She couldn't have put it into words.

Besides, she couldn't see any TV cameras anywhere.

"How...?" She broke into coughs and had to swallow, again. "How did you bring me here?"

Shadye seemed oddly pleased by the question. "They said that there would be a Child of Destiny who would lead the forces of light against the Harrowing," he said. Emily realized suddenly that he wanted to gloat, to show off his own cleverness. "But I knew that every prophecy has a loophole. I knew that if I could catch that Child of Destiny before it was her time, I could use her against the cursed Alliance and defeat them utterly."

Emily felt a sinking sensation in her stomach. "But I am not that person..."

"No Child of Destiny knows who she is until her time has come," Shadye informed her. "But the Faerie know, oh yes *they* know. And I called for them to bring me the Child of Destiny and they have brought me you." He rubbed his hands together in glee. "And now I have you in my hands. The Harrowing will be pleased."

"Right," Emily said. Her, a Child of Destiny? Only in the literal sense...and she doubted that Shadye would believe her if she tried to explain it. What did her mother's name have to do with anything? She fought desperately for something to say that might distract him. "And I guess I'm not in Kansas any longer?"

"You are in the Blighted Lands of the Dead, on the southern face of the Craggy Mountains," Shadye said. Her words seemed to mean nothing to him, which was more disconcerting than anything else. "Wherever this *Kansas* place is, I assure you that it is far away."

Emily started to answer, and then stopped herself. "If you don't know where Kansas is," she said, trying to keep her growing fear under control, "I really am no longer in Kansas."

Shadye shrugged, the motion stirring his robe. Emily frowned as she saw the way the cloth moved over his body, disturbed in a manner she found almost impossible to describe. She couldn't see what lay beneath his robe, but there was something about the way he moved that suggested he was no longer entirely human. A very faint shimmer of light seemed to surround him, half-seen forms flickering in and out of existence ...

Somehow, that was all the more disturbing to her imagination.

*This is real,* Emily told herself. It was no longer possible to believe that she was standing in the middle of a TV studio, with hidden cameras recording everything she said and did. There was something so *real* about the scene that it terrified her. Shadye believed that she was the person he'd been searching for and nothing she could say, or do, could convince him otherwise. She thought of all the fictional heroes she'd known and loved, asking herself what they would do. But they had the writer on their side. *She* had nothing but her own wits.

Shadye snapped his fingers. The iron bars melted away into dust.

Fresh shock ran through Emily's body at the impossible sight, but before she could do anything, the skeletons stepped forward and marched into the cell, their eyeless sockets firmly locked on Emily's face. She cringed back as the bony hands, so eerie without flesh and blood, caught her shoulders. The skeletons propelled her forward, no matter how she struggled. The sorcerer's servants didn't seem to notice, or care. Oddly, their bones were held together without touching, as if their flesh was invisible. Like magic.

"You don't have to do this," she said, as she was marched out of the cell. Was she even on *Earth* any longer? "I..."

Shadye cackled, a high-pitched sound that chilled her to the bone. "Your death will bring me all the power I could desire," he said. Emily redoubled her struggles, but the skeletons never loosened their grip. "Why should I let you live when I would remain like *this?*"

He pulled his hood away from his face in one convulsive motion. Emily stared, horrified. Shadye's skin was pulled so tightly around his skull that she could see the bones underneath, his nose cut away, replaced by a melted mass of burned flesh. His eyes were burning coals of red light, shining in the darkened chamber, utterly inhuman. She saw his hand as he lifted it to stroke his hairless chin and winced at the cuts that criss-crossed his flesh.

Emily had seen all sorts of movies, ones where the directors strived to outdo themselves in creating new horrors, but this was different. This was *real.* She took a deep breath and smelled dead flesh in the atmosphere surrounding him. It was suddenly easy to believe that his body was dying, animated only by his will—and magic.

"There is always a price for power," Shadye said. His voice darkened, unpleasantly. "But there are always ways to escape the price. And when I offer you to the

Harrowing...oh, they will rebuild my burned frame and grant me power eternal."

He turned and strode off down the corridor, pulling his hood back up to cover his head. Emily stared at his retreating back, just before the skeletons started to push her down the corridor after him. Resistance seemed utterly futile, but she struggled anyway, panic giving her extra strength. Just for a moment, she broke free of their grip and turned to run, but then there was a flash of blue light and her muscles locked, sending her falling to the floor. No matter how she struggled, she couldn't move anything below the neck. She watched helplessly as the skeletons picked her up and carried her after Shadye.

The sorcerer started to laugh. "I told you where you are," he said, mockingly. "Even if you escaped my dungeons, where would you go?"

He was right, Emily realized. She'd never heard of the Craggy Mountains, let alone the Blighted Land of the Dead. And *he* had never heard of Kansas. No matter how she wanted to avoid it, she had to accept the fact that she had somehow been transported from her own world to one where magic worked, where *skeletons* could be used as servants and an evil sorcerer could sacrifice her for power. She was utterly alone, ignorant of even something as basic as local geography.

Shadye was right; even if she did escape, where would she go?

They reached a stairwell leading up into the darkness. Shadye seemed unbothered by the lack of illumination, as did the skeletons, but Emily found it hard to restrain her panic as they climbed onward and upward, while she was unable to see anything. Her legs bumped against the walls from time to time, the spell binding her holding her body as firmly as ever, just before they finally walked out into the open air. The ground below their feet was mud...no, she realized suddenly, it was ash. She sniffed and then shuddered at the stench of burned flesh in the air. In the distance, she caught sight of what had once been a forest. Now, it looked as if something had killed the trees, leaving their dead remains standing in the midst of the darkness.

"The Necromancer Kings faced the assembled might of the Empire not too far from here," Shadye said with heavy satisfaction. He seemed to like the sound of his own voice. "They say that the skies were black with dragons and terrible lizards as they fought for forty days and forty nights. In the end, so much magic was released that the land was permanently warped by chaos. Those who stray into these lands without protection find themselves twisted and transformed into horrors. Few dare to visit my fortress, even though they believe that they have powers that can match my own."

Emily found her voice. "Why did they fight?"

"The Necromancer Kings wished to enjoy their powers without restraint, to create a world where their whims and wishes would be the whole of the law," Shadye said. "But the Empire and their wizards believed the necromancers to be an abomination. The wizards believed that they had won, yet the Harrowing can never be stopped. All they could do was delay it, for a time."

He stopped and muttered a series of words under his breath. There was a brilliant flash of light, bright enough to make Emily squeeze her eyes closed against the glare.

When she reopened her eyes, she saw a large building made out of dark stone right in front of them, as if it had been there all along. Perhaps it had been invisible, she told herself, taking some measure of comfort from the thought. If Shadye had needed to hide his dark temple, or whatever it was, it suggested that someone was watching for him. Maybe he'd been lying when he'd claimed that no one came into the Blighted Lands of the Dead.

The skeletons carried her into an opening that appeared out of nowhere, an instant before her head would have slammed into the stone. Inside, there was a sense of overpowering *vastness*, as if the building was much larger than she could comprehend. The smell of blood assailed her nostrils; a moment later, as she looked around, she saw great waves of red blood washing down the walls and pooling on the ground. Shadye seemed unbothered by walking through the blood, bowing from time to time towards statues that appeared out of nowhere, only to vanish again when Shadye walked past. They were disturbing. Oddly, the ones that looked most human were the most disquieting. One of them, a stone carving of a handsome man with sharp pointy ears, was impossible to look at directly. Another, an eldritch horror out of nightmares, seemed almost friendly by contrast.

And yet she couldn't understand why one scared her more than the other.

"There," Shadye said. He reached into his robe and produced a sharp black knife, carved from stone, before addressing the skeletons for the first time. "Place her on the altar."

The altar was a simple stone block, easily large enough to accommodate her—or any other sacrificial victim. Emily opened her mouth to protest, but it was futile; the skeletons picked her up and carried her forward with implacable strength. Somehow, the simple lack of carvings on the altar was even more terrifying than the horrors she could see in the distance. It struck her, suddenly, that there was no doubt to whom the altar was dedicated. This place belonged to Satan. It was a place beyond the sight of God.

She tried to recall the prayers she'd learned as a child, but nothing came to mind. Instead, she kept trying to struggle, but the force holding her refused to surrender. The skeletons placed her on the stone and stepped backwards, almost as if they were admiring their work.

"We begin," Shadye said. He started to chant as he waved the knife in the air. Emily couldn't understand a single word, but she *felt* the gathering power in the chamber, as if someone—or *something*—was slowly pressing itself into existence. Brilliant tingles of light danced over her head, slowly fading into a darkness so complete that it sucked up the light. In the last moments of gloom, she saw new statues—savage-faced angels—appear at the edge of the chamber.

Shadye stopped chanting. Absolute silence fell, as if unseen watchers were waiting for a final command. The summoned presence hung on the air, its mere existence twisting reality around it.

Emily saw *something* within the darkness, a hidden movement that seemed to be only present within the corner of her eye. A strange lassitude fell over her, as if there was no longer any point in fighting and it was time to accept her fate. Shadye stepped forward, one hand holding the knife as he raised it up and over Emily's heart...

And then, suddenly, there was a brilliant flash of light. The summoned presence simply vanished.

Shadye bit out a word that was probably a curse and ducked as a bolt of lightning sliced through the air over his head, before smashing into the far wall. She twisted her neck as another flash of light lit up the chamber, revealing another dark-clad form standing at the far end of the room. Darkness fell for a second before the third flash of light showed the figure much closer, followed by the monstrous angel statues, which had moved when Emily wasn't looking. Her savior? It was obvious that he didn't want Shadye to have her.

"No," Shadye snapped. He lifted his hand, somehow plucked a fireball out of empty air and threw it at the newcomer, who lifted a staff and deflected it into the darkened reaches of the chamber. There was a deafening explosion as it struck one of the angel statues, which appeared undamaged. "You will not cheat me!"

A second later, the newcomer tossed a spell of his own. Shadye vanished in a flash of light.

The spell holding Emily to the altar snapped at the same instant, allowing her to move again. She sat up, only to see the newcomer race toward her. Another flash of light revealed that his face was hidden behind a wooden mask. He reached for her and she drew back, suddenly unsure of what this new man wanted. Shadye had wanted to sacrifice her. What would this man want?

"Take my hand if you want to live," the newcomer said, when Emily balked. The darkness was flooding in from all sides, pushing in around them as if it were a living thing. "Come with me or die!"

Emily didn't hesitate any longer. She took his hand.

And then the dark chamber vanished in a final blinding flash of white light.

## Chapter Two

Once the brilliant light faded away, she was standing in the middle of a very different room.

"Welcome to my Tower," her rescuer said. His face was still hidden behind a wooden mask, but his voice was kind. "Don't worry. Shadye can't get you here."

Emily nodded, trying to keep her body from shaking. Her knees threatened to buckle, but she did her best to look around this very strange new place. The room in which she stood was large, but crammed with strange devices and boiling pots of liquid that looked as if they were about to bubble over and spill on the ground. Dark lines had been drawn on the floor, creating patterns that changed every time she looked at them. Light steamed in from a massive window, bright enough to suggest high noon. But it had been dark just a moment ago...

"Here," her rescuer said, as she started to shake again. He passed her a glass of clear liquid. "You may need this to calm yourself."

Emily hesitated. All her life, she'd been told that she shouldn't take gifts from strangers–but she did need a drink. Besides, if he wanted to poison her, he could probably have done it without forcing her to drink anything. That decided, she drank the water. It was cold, almost tasteless, but refreshing. Afterwards, a strange calm descended on her mind.

The man nodded to a pair of wooden seats below the window and Emily walked over to them, peering out of the window overlooking a green and pleasant landscape. Everywhere she looked, there were forests and lakes–but no sign of human life at all. The ground seemed to shimmer with magic.

She caught herself and looked back at the newcomer. "Who are you?"

"You need to know one rule right from the start," the man said slowly, as he removed his mask and pulled back his hood. "Do not *ever* ask a sorcerer his name. Ask instead what he would like to be called."

Emily sucked in her breath as he looked up at her. He looked surprisingly young, with a handsome face and a shock of brown hair, but there was something in the way he moved that nagged at her mind. It took her several seconds to realize that he wore a young body, yet walked in the manner of an older man. His lanky body seemed almost as strange to him as it did to her.

He smiled at her and she suddenly felt reassured. "You may call me Void, if you like," he said. "Please, be seated. You must have many questions."

"Yes," Emily said. Hundreds were tumbling through her mind. One question seemed very important. "Why...why did you rescue me?"

Void seemed oddly surprised by the question. "Why not?"

Emily studied him, trying to understand. He'd risked his life to save a girl he didn't know? Why would the question surprise him? Or maybe he'd jumped in to prevent Shadye from sacrificing her and thought that Emily would be able to deduce that for herself...

She cleared her throat. "What...what did you do to him?"

"Shadye?" Void seemed to smile. "I stunned him, rather badly." His smile faded away into a grim expression that seemed more natural to him. "Sadly, I fear that he will get better."

Emily stared at him. "Why didn't you kill him while you had the chance?"

"His protective wards wouldn't have slipped that far," Void said. "I couldn't have sneaked the attack in at all if he hadn't been in the Inverse Shadow. He had to lower part of his guard just to enter the building."

Emily felt a wave of confusion. What had been so special about the Inverse Shadow?

"But I got you out," Void added, with a childish grin of triumph. "My old master would be turning in his grave. If he were in his grave."

Emily had to smile back, and then collected herself. "Right," she said. "Where am I?"

Void didn't seem surprised at *that* question. "You're in my Tower, located on the edge of the Greenwood, in the Southern Marches of Barcia." He studied her face for a long moment, thoughtfully. "But that means nothing to you, unless I miss my guess."

"No," Emily said. Despite the calm, she felt her thoughts starting to spin. Where *was* she? "Shadye said he brought me here."

"He did," Void confirmed. He paused, just for a second. "Actually, he ordered creatures from the realm between the worlds to deliver him a person fitting specific criteria. They brought him you."

Emily shook her head in disbelief. "And why me? What makes me so special?"

A third question appeared in her mind a second later. "And how can I get home?"

Void hesitated. "I only sensed your arrival in this world, so I confess that I don't know why Shadye thought that you were important," he admitted. For the first time, he seemed rather unsure of himself. "As to getting you home...it may not be possible. It may never be possible."

There was something in the way he said it that kept her from realizing his true meaning for almost a minute. "I can *never* go home?"

The thought staggered her. Her life hadn't been good; she'd watched her mother drink herself close to death while her stepfather had been unpleasant and abusive whenever he cared to remember that he had a stepdaughter. But it had been her life. She'd had her books, the company of the nerds and geeks whenever she wanted to play games, and a bright future ahead of her...

...Or had she?

Her teenage years would have ended with her going to college, and then perhaps searching for a job. She would never really be able to live her own life, nor find a position that suited her. She knew from older acquaintances that it wasn't easy to find a job, let alone make ends meet in the adult world. One day, all the skills she'd learned at school would be utterly unimportant. The only consolation was that those who had ruled the school through being popular, pretty or athletic would be even less important.

And it was hard to escape the thought that no one would miss her now that she was gone.

"The problem is locating the world that birthed you," Void admitted, breaking into her thoughts. "If we were to open a gateway into the worlds beyond to locate your home world, the necromancers would have their chance to interfere with the magic, perhaps killing you or the conjurers. Even if they didn't, searching for your world might attract attention from beings that live outside the normal walls of our reality."

Emily remembered the dark presence in what Void had called the Inverse Shadow and shuddered. "So I can never go home," she said softly. In some ways, having no choice made it easier. "Why did Shadye think that I was a Child of Destiny?"

Void's eyes went very wide. "He thought that you were a Child of Destiny?"

"He said I was," Emily confessed. "But my mother was called Destiny."

Void stared at her for a long moment, then burst out laughing. "Shadye would have been in for a shock when he finished sacrificing you. The Dark Gods would not have thanked him for your soul."

Emily didn't understand the joke at first—and when it dawned on her, it didn't seem very funny. "But he would have killed me!"

Void nodded. "My guess is that one of the criteria I mentioned was that you would be a Child of Destiny. But the creatures that inhabit the worlds beyond are mischievous, prone to reinterpreting orders if they're not very specific. A Child of Destiny... if he didn't bother to clarify what that actually *meant*, they might have gone after you instead. But you'd still meet the other criteria."

He studied her for a long moment. "Wizards have been attempting to use magic to foretell the future for thousands of years," he added. "It rarely works very well, because the future is constantly in flux. Sometimes knowing about a possible future destroys it; sometimes knowing what is in store makes it inevitable. Even the best of wizards will leave the future to take care of itself.

"But we do know that some people are born to be at the heart of history. Those people will make decisions that reshape destiny, that completely alter the future. If Shadye had offered you to his dark lords, they would have rewarded him with power beyond imagination." His smile flickered back into existence. "But Shadye has a great deal of imagination."

Emily rubbed her eyes, trying to comprehend what he was telling her. "But I don't have any say in what happens," she said, finally. "Back home, I was nothing."

"No one is ever nothing," Void said cryptically. "The Children of Destiny are rarely seen and recognized in advance. Sometimes, we only ever realize that they were there in hindsight. Who would have thought that the lowly goatherd Avon would become the linchpin of an alliance that would push the necromancers back into the dark lands? In hindsight, we know that he was living at the crux point—and if they'd killed him before his time, the necromancers would have had the world."

"Or if they'd convinced him to join them," Emily guessed.

Void nodded.

Emily remembered the history she'd studied, very taken by the thought. "Or if he'd fled from the battlefield..."

"Precisely," Void said. He stood up and looked up, out of the window. "Do you know that there are more necromancers in this world than there are powerful sorcerers?"

Emily rolled her eyes. She'd barely been in the new world for more than an hour, maybe two. How could she have hoped to learn anything about its history, culture or geography? Shadye certainly hadn't been interested in educating her. How did Void expect her to know anything?

"The only thing that keeps them from crushing us is that we can work together and the necromancers are unable to cooperate very well," Void explained, without looking back at her. "Every one of them believes that his rivals would stick a knife in his back the moment he looked away. They have good reason not to trust one another..."

He turned and looked down at her. "They are still gaining in power," he said. "Three years ago, the Kingdom of Gondar was overrun by their forces and the population was enslaved."

Emily stared at him. "And you could do nothing? With all your power, couldn't you do something to keep it from happening?"

Void looked down at his hands. For the first time, Emily realized that they were scarred, as if he'd been cutting himself time and time again. "All our efforts could do little more than hold back hell long enough to get a tiny percentage of the country's population out before it was too late. With Gondar in their hands, they have a land route through to Chirico, which now needs to pull back its troops from the border defenses and see to its own defense."

"Forcing you to split your forces," Emily said. She'd played enough games with the nerds to know how it worked, even if *Command and Conquer* logic never worked in the real world. "But I don't even come *from* this world. Why me?"

Void smiled. "Shadye may have asked for a Child of Destiny without specifying that she—or he—had to come from this world," he said, wryly. "Or the entities might have deliberately misunderstood the instructions. Or...he may have had a reason for summoning one from a different world."

His expression darkened. "But right now, a Child of Destiny is far more likely to swing the odds in our favor than against us. Shadye may simply have been intending to ensure that one never appeared, or to remove him from the world before he reached his time."

Emily felt her head spinning again. This was too much. Void was talking calmly about matters that hadn't meant anything to her before she'd arrived in this world, before her life had turned upside down. And Shadye had not only brought her here against her will; he'd marked her for death, long before she could have done anything to him. Her lips cracked into a bitter smile. Shadye should have known that if he'd left her in her world she would never have grown into a threat to him.

And yet, how could she *ever* be a threat to him? She'd seen the sorcerer work magic casually, without any effort at all. She had no magic, not even an understanding of modern technology that could be used to alter the balance of power. Her teachers hadn't taught her anything useful; she had no idea how to produce gunpowder, or steam engines, or even the basics of modern medicine. Shadye had probably targeted her because she would be helpless even if she did manage to escape his grasp.

"You will be assured of my protection for as long as you are forced to remain in this world," Void said, when she asked. "This world is not always safe for the unwary, or the weak, and Shadye's interest in you may attract attention from others."

Emily looked down at the floor, watching the strange patterns as they shifted from place to place. She'd read countless fantasy novels where the heroine was a chosen one, picked from all others to save the world, normally wearing a chainmail bikini as she hacked and slashed her way to slay the dark lord, or banish the demon back to hell. Offhand, she couldn't recall *any* novel where the chosen one had simply been a case of mistaken identity. And in the books where there was no tinge of destiny, the heroine was almost always supremely competent. What was *she* going to do? Impress Shadye by her masterful grasp of role-playing games, creative writing, and wasting time browsing the internet and reading web-comics? She didn't even have a homicidal rabbit with a switchblade on her side.

"I..." She stopped and swallowed hard. "I think Shadye might have chosen me deliberately."

Void lifted an eyebrow, politely. "You think he might have seen something in you that everyone else missed?"

Emily flushed. She hated it when people tried to be snide. "I mean that he targeted me to force you to waste your time with me," she said. "He might be doing something else while you're helping me to fit into this world..."

"I'd hate to think that Shadye could calculate so precisely the time it took me to slip into the Inverse Shadow," Void murmured. "Or even that I would have risked my life saving yours. A necromancer would expect me to kill you before you could be sacrificed, not try to save you. Besides, he couldn't have counted on me realizing what was going on in time to intervene."

His face twisted into a manic grin. "But we can easily test that theory. Follow me."

He walked across the room and out of the door before Emily could even stand up. Shrugging, she followed him through the door and into a network of corridors that glowed with a pearly white light. Void stepped through another door into a room crammed with old books, a handful scattered on chairs as if their reader had just taken a break to find a bite to eat, and paused outside a second door. When Emily caught up with him, he opened the door and motioned for her to precede him into the room. Inside, there was a small table, with a handful of objects scattered on the wooden surface and little else. The walls were bare stone.

The moment she stepped inside, she felt a muffling fall over her mind and stopped dead in her tracks. "You have some sensitivity," Void noted. He didn't seem to have felt anything. "This room is designed to contain unexpected discharges of magic. I haven't used it since my last apprentice left me."

There was an odd note in his voice that left her feeling it would be unwise to pry too far into his affairs. "Look down at the table," he instructed, "and take an item."

Emily frowned. "Which item?"

"Use your instincts," Void said seriously. "Pick up the one that feels *right* to you."

"Oh," Emily said. It was a test, then. She'd never tested well. "How long do I have?"

"As long as you feel you need," Void said. He moved over to the wall and leaned against it, adopting an insolent pose. "Pick the one that feels *right* to you."

Emily nodded, staring down at the objects on the table. One was a large hammer, marked with runes that seemed to have been etched into the metal; a second was a long black cane that appeared to be made of shadow. A third looked to be a magic wand, right out of *Harry Potter*; a fourth seemed to be a fairy wand, complete with a glowing star on the tip. There was a bracelet with solid metal runes, a green ring that seemed to glow with its own light, a sword that gave off a sense of being incredibly old, a dark statuette of a falcon and a key marked with a Greek letter. The Omega letter, if she recalled correctly. A book that looked almost as old as the sword, with yellowing pages and a brittle cover, marked in dark letters she didn't recognize...

Finally, there was a piece of wire that twisted in ways that went outside normal reality. She tried to follow the wire with her eyes and felt the world spinning around her until she tore her gaze away from the object.

Shaking her head, trying to escape the sense of being *muffled*, she looked from object to object. The hammer glowed with electric power; the cane looked almost translucent, as if it wasn't really there. Something about the key warned her not to even *think* of touching it.

*Pick the one that seems right to you*, Void had said. Emily tried to think about it logically, and then realized that magic—and she was dealing with magic—might not follow the rules of logic and reason. She might as well assume that she was in a role-playing game and act accordingly. Her hand drifted from item to item, never quite touching anything until it settled on the book. She'd always loved books, right from the day her mother had shoved a kid's comic under her nose and gone off to drink herself into a stupor. Books had been her companions throughout her entire life.

Carefully, she picked up the book and held it out to Void. "I choose this," she said. "Is this the right choice?"

Void snorted. "*Is* it the right choice?"

"Yes," Emily said, suddenly tired of the game. "It is the right choice."

"You have a talent," Void said. "Every would-be apprentice is offered the chance to choose something from a similar table. Choosing the book..."

He smiled, thinly. "We shall expect great things from you, I think." He took the book from her hands and studied it thoughtfully, before passing it back to her. "Far too many take the wands, or the hammer, or the sword. They would make poor magicians."

"I can be a magician?" Emily asked, stunned. "But -"

"You have the talent," Void confirmed. He turned and led her out of the room. "The book is yours now, although it may be a long time before you know how to use it. My master gave it to me and promised to teach me all of his dangerously-won knowledge if I learned to read it in less than a year. It took me ten years to learn."

Emily stared down at the book. Ten *years* for someone to learn how to read it? The letters seemed to twist and turn in front of her eyes, as if the meaning constantly changed into something else. Emily had never tried to learn a foreign language in her life, unless one counted the codes they'd invented for their games. How could she even make a start on reading the book?

"I need to make some arrangements for your future," Void added. "We shall eat and then you can rest while I speak to the rest of the council. They will need to be informed of your appearance. And then we can decide what to do with you."

# Chapter Three

Emily lay in bed, unwilling to open her eyes. It had all been a dream. It had to have been a dream. Because being transported to a land of magic and wonder, so different from the dull mundane world that had given birth to her, was a dream come true. No; it was too good to be true. When she opened her eyes, she knew that she would be back home...

But the bed felt uncomfortable and unfamiliar - and the air was too hot - and someone was in the room. Someone *else*?

Her eyes snapped open. She was lying on her back, staring up at an elaborately crafted ceiling decorated with gold and silver leaf. A young woman stood by the foot of the bed, holding out a robe for Emily to wear. Her original clothes had been taken away to be cleaned - or so she thought. It wasn't as if she wanted them back.

It hadn't been a dream, Emily realized. She found herself smiling brightly as she pulled herself out of the huge bed.

The serving girl passed her the robe–there was a curious blankness in her eyes that bothered Emily on a very primal level–and stepped back, heading for the door. She was young, with long blonde hair and blue eyes, wearing a uniform that managed to combine elegance and practicality. The girl didn't seem curious about Emily, or what she was doing in her master's bed, but she worked for a magician. No doubt she was used to all kinds of wonder and magic.

The robe was long and shapeless, hiding her figure more completely than her own clothes. Emily let out a sigh of relief as she donned the robe - it felt surprisingly soft and warm against her skin–and she headed to the bathroom to splash water on her face. One thing that *hadn't* been mentioned in any of the role-playing campaigns she'd fought was that medieval plumbing left a great deal to be desired. There was no hot running water, let alone a device to flush the toilet. Magic clearly didn't provide a substitute for such basic technology... Maybe, she told herself, she could convince Void to install running water in his tower. It might make the environment healthier.

Chuckling at herself, she washed then stopped in front of a mirror, studying her face. A moment later, the image rotated around, showing her what she looked like from behind. Emily started backwards in surprise, then realized that the mirror image was due to magic, exactly what *she* would have created if she'd had the power and the talent. She found herself casting a glance at the book Void had given her, wondering if it would teach her how to create a magic mirror or other useful tricks.

She couldn't resist. "Mirror, mirror, on the wall," she said, "who's the fairest of them all?"

"Silly question," a voice said. Emily nearly jumped out of her skin. "*Fairest* is a subjective measure. One man's *fairest* woman might be another man's ugly cow."

Emily started to laugh. "Don't you have any opinions on the subject?"

The mirror's voice deepened. "I'm just a mirror," it pointed out, rather snidely. "I am really nothing more than a reflection of yourself."

"I see," Emily said, although she wasn't sure that she did. Her body image had never been very good. Surely the mirror would have mocked her as comprehensively as her stepfather. "Thank you."

She stepped away from the mirror, towards the heavy wooden door. The serving girl had left it open and was waiting outside with an expression that suggested that she was prepared to wait forever.

Emily stepped out of the door and wasn't entirely surprised when it closed behind her, slamming shut with a faintly ominous thump. Void had promised that she would be safe in his tower; it was, he'd bragged, protected by countless security spells.

Emily could feel *something* in the air as the serving girl bowed to her and led the way down the stone corridor, past a giant window looking out over the forest. Something huge hung in the air, something with giant bat-shaped wings ... Emily stopped and stared. It couldn't really be a live dragon, could it? How could something that big even *fly*?

*Magic*, she reminded herself. She had to remember that magic really worked here.

The dragon flapped its wings slowly; the next moment, it was gone. Emily felt a sense of loss, as if all the magic in the world had drained away into nothingness. Tears prickled at her eyes, but she wiped them away impatiently. There would be more wonders to come.

The serving girl led her the rest of the way into the dining hall. Void's hall was large enough to seat a small army, but there was only one table, set up in front of a roaring fire that flickered with eerie green and blue lights. The sorcerer himself was seated at one end of the table, devouring a plate of sausages and bread. A pair of serving girls stood behind him, silently waiting for his orders. There was only one other seat at the table.

"Come in," Void called.

Emily hesitated. Something about the sheer size of the hall stuck her as faintly ridiculous. She'd certainly never had the impression that Void liked to entertain outsiders in his hall ... she stopped and laughed inwardly at herself. Since she had only known Void for less than a day, how could she claim to be an authority on him?

She walked over to the table and sat down facing him. "The kitchen staff was quite pleased to hear that you were staying with us," Void said. "They want to cook something a little different from time to time, but I'm rather set in my ways. I don't want anything more than meat and bread for breakfast."

He smiled, as if he expected her to share in a joke. Emily, who normally ate only corn flakes and coffee for breakfast, didn't understand it. Her parents might like the thought of devouring eggs and bacon for breakfast, but *she* had never been able to endure eating a large breakfast–it always left her feeling slightly unwell.

One of the serving girls placed a jug of water beside Emily, while another gave her a mug of hot black liquid that smelled faintly of ground earth and sand. Emily hesitated, before picking it up and taking a sip. It managed to taste almost, but not completely unlike coffee. On the other hand, it seemed to contain enough caffeine to give her system a morning jolt.

"The water was safely boiled by my staff," Void assured her, as she eyed the jug doubtfully. "Anywhere else, ask them if the water has been boiled. Some of the common folk don't believe in the invisible devils in the liquid."

Of course, Emily told herself; humans hadn't *always* known that water had to be boiled to ensure that it was safe to drink. Her reading had told her that unsafe water had been the cause of countless epidemics throughout history. *Invisible devils* was as good a way as any to describe germs, even if it wasn't very scientific. But to a world built on magic rather than science, it might make perfect sense. Hell, the germs might be *real* devils.

"Thank you," she said, as she poured a glass and took a sip. The water tasted sweet to her lips. "What are we going to do today?"

Void lifted a hand. "Wait until you've eaten," he said, firmly. The serving girl returned and placed a platter of meat, eggs and bread in front of Emily. "A good meal will make it much easier for us to talk properly."

Emily had no idea how he expected her to eat so much, but as she dug into the meal she found that she was far hungrier than she had realized. The meat tasted a little like beef, yet there was something in the taste that she didn't recognize. And, of course, she had no idea what kind of creature had laid the eggs. Only the bread tasted remotely familiar, rather like the bread they had cooked in home economics class. But it tasted much better than the bread thirty schoolchildren had produced while they were watched by a nervous teacher worried about what might happen to her career if her students poisoned themselves. Perhaps it was her imagination, but the food seemed healthier than anything she'd eaten back home.

"I have been summoning Beings and making enquiries," Void informed her as the serving girl removed the platter after Emily had finished. "It seems that you have been the victim of ... imprecise specifications."

He'd said much the same thing yesterday, Emily knew. "Shadye was very specific in his demands," Void continued. "He ordered certain entities to bring him a Child of Destiny, with great magical powers, yet no real *awareness* of those powers. Unfortunately for him, he failed to specify what a Child of Destiny actually *was*, or where he or she should actually come *from*. Had he specified that the entities should concentrate their search on *this* world, you wouldn't be in this mess."

Emily nodded thoughtfully. She hadn't known that she had magical powers, but then there was no such thing as magic in her world. Unless, of course, Arthur C. Clarke had been right when he pointed out that a sufficiently advanced technology was no different from magic. Or perhaps mental powers–assuming that *they* existed–were really no different from magic, either.

*Or maybe you should just go with whatever Void says,* a voice at the back of her head said. *The laws governing magic in this place might be very different from anything you've ever read about.*

Void's eyes twinkled. "Necromancers rarely bother to consult with others, if they can even bring themselves to recognize that outsiders might bring a new perspective to their problem. No doubt he believed that the entities would obey orders...which, to be fair, they did. He just wasn't specific enough to get them to do what he wanted."

"And so they picked me up instead," Emily mused.

"If nothing else," Void added, "think of it as a lesson in the requirement for absolute precision when dealing with magic and magical entities."

He shook his head. "But that leaves the problem of deciding what to do with you. Shadye may not have realized that his summoning failed–indeed, given that I plucked you out of his grasp before he could sacrifice you, he may believe that he succeeded, only to lose you to me. He will certainly be looking for you; he may even try to remove you from my Tower and take you back to his territory."

Emily shivered. It was easy to feel safe inside the tower, but suddenly that safety felt like an illusion. She'd seen both Shadye and Void do things that she would have sworn were impossible only a day ago. What could she do if Shadye captured her for the second time? He certainly wouldn't make the same mistake twice.

"There's also the fact that you need to be trained, and trained properly," Void said. His voice was mild, but there was a force behind it that made her sit up and take a good look at him. "Right now, you're a potential source of magic for any untrustworthy mage out there; Shadye won't be the only one who wants to capture you once word gets out. Shadye wanted to use your power and your status–your *presumed* status–as a Child of Destiny; others will have far darker ambitions. You need training and I can't train you."

Emily felt her heart twist. She had expected, she realized now, that Void would train her. He was odd, but she was coming to like him. The thought of leaving his tower and going out into the wider world beyond chilled her, particularly with hostile wizards out there intent on capturing her and taking her power–the power she hadn't even known she possessed–for themselves. She certainly didn't want to think about what they might do to get their hands on her power.

"I'm a bad teacher," Void admitted, when she pressed him. "I've had seven apprentices in my time. Three of them had to be dismissed for disobedience, two died in magical accidents, one went rogue and became a necromancer ..."

There was a long pause. Emily finally broke it. "And the last apprentice?"

"I had to kill him," Void said flatly. Emily wanted to ask, but she had the feeling that it might be unwise to press him any further. "Suffice it to say that my history of tutoring apprentices is not good."

He hesitated, as if he was unwilling to admit to anything else. "There's also the fact that you need a far wider field of study than I can provide for you in my tower. You've only met myself and Shadye–and there are plenty of other types of magician out there. I would just limit you if you studied under me. You deserve better than that."

There was a second pause. "I'm sending you to Whitehall," he said. "You'll be safe there."

Emily blinked, trying not to feel abandoned. "Whitehall?"

"There are only a handful of places where new wizards are trained," Void explained. "Of all of them, Whitehall is the oldest, constructed back in the days of the Old Empire. Politically, it's unaligned in the power struggles between the Allied Lands—and it is a bastion against the necromancers. Your presence elsewhere may"—he paused, as if he were selecting his next word carefully—"upset people."

"I don't understand," Emily said. "Why am I so special?"

Void snorted. "Luck." He shook his head, ruefully. "If word gets out to the Allied Lands that you are a Child of Destiny—even if you're *not* a Child of Destiny in anything other than the literal sense—there will be repercussions. And once they realize just how much power is welling up inside of you, they will either try to co-opt you or kill you."

He shrugged. "It won't surprise you to know that the Allied Lands spend as much time fighting each other as they do fighting the necromancers. We mock them for their disunity, but ours is just as bad."

Emily frowned. "So which side are you on?"

Void gave her a sharp look, and then nodded in understanding. "I'm a graduate of Whitehall myself. As such, I owe overall fealty to the Allied Lands as a whole, not to any single country. Those of us who are on the sharp end in dealing with the necromancers have no time for power struggles between the Allied Lands. Maybe Princess Samira didn't actually *want* to marry Prince Davit ... whatever really happened, it's not an excuse to start a war that creates openings for the necromancers to break into the Allied Lands."

"You said that the necromancers were tightening the screws," she said. "Can't the Allied Lands see that they're in trouble?"

"I'm sure they can," Void said. "They just don't bother to actually *think* about what they're doing."

He looked at her, directly. "Whitehall sits in the mountains, at a crossroads of power where two ley lines intersect. That gives the school's wards incredible power. No necromancer can enter the school, or its grounds, and no one from the Allied Lands would dare to breach its walls without permission. The Grandmaster's will is absolute within the school."

Emily found herself smiling. "His name wouldn't be Dumbledore, would it?"

"I wouldn't know," Void reminded her, archly. "Those of us who seek great power keep our names secret, remember?"

Emily flushed at his tone.

"I have made arrangements for you to go there today and be enrolled at the school, before anyone apart from Shadye and I learns of your true nature," Void continued. "You don't need to worry about payment; the Grandmaster owes me a favor or two, so he has agreed to waive the tuition fees in your case. Besides, I think that if you have proper training, you will be formidable indeed. I rather doubt that Whitehall is anything like the schooling you had back home, but it will provide you with the grounding you so desperately need."

"Thank you," Emily said. It was hard to escape the conviction that she was being abandoned, but it was clear that Void was doing his best for her. Going back to school ... well, she would actually be learning something more fascinating than sanitized facts and pointless nonsense. Besides, if Void was right and other magicians would be seeking her out, she'd better learn to defend herself as quickly as possible. Shadye had overpowered her with contemptuous ease.

Void smiled. "You're welcome," he said. "If you become a defender of the Allied Lands, standing beside us, I will be more than repaid."

He stood up. "I have also made arrangements for your transport. The kitchen staff will provide you with food for the journey."

Emily blinked as she stood up herself. "You won't be coming with me?"

"I'm afraid not," Void said. "Don't worry. Your transport"—he grinned, as if he were smiling at a private joke—"trust me, no necromancer is going to want to risk drawing the attention of your transport."

"Right," Emily said. All of a sudden she felt as if Void had given her a red shirt to wear, perhaps complete with a targeting circle. But then, he *had* lived in this world for his entire life. No doubt he knew what he was doing. "I meant to ask you something."

Void lifted a single eyebrow, patiently.

"Your servants," Emily said, quietly. "Why do they all look so ..."

She couldn't think of a suitable word, but Void understood. "They have pledged themselves to me for the duration of their services. In order that they might live here, they have accepted powerful loyalty spells, ones that prevent them from doing anything contrary to my interests." He gave her a reassuring smile. "You're starting to sense magic properly, my dear."

Emily winced. She had no way to be sure, but she would have bet good money that the spells went a great deal further than simply ensuring the loyalty of his servants. The blank stare in the girl's eyes chilled her. Perhaps she no longer had any real free will of her own, or perhaps Emily was just imagining it. She *hoped* that she was imagining it.

She shook her head. This world might be more exciting than her old world, but it had dangers of its own. And Shadye wasn't the only one who misused magic.

## Chapter Four

"How big is this tower?" Emily asked.

Void smiled as they kept walking up stairs that seemed to reach all the way to heaven. "It's as big as it needs to be."

"That isn't an answer," Emily said, irritably. The knapsack of food and drink Void's servants had given her was dragging at her shoulder. This world had clearly not invented comfortable rucksacks - at least, not yet. Absently, she wondered what–if anything–she could introduce from her world to make lives easier here. "How big is the tower?"

Void's smile grew wider. "The tower is far larger on the inside than on the outside. Each successive owner has added more to the interior, creating a mass of passageways and compartments that run for miles underground. Even I couldn't tell you just how big the tower is on the inside."

A gust of cold air struck her as they finally reached the top and out onto the battlements. Emily felt a wave of vertigo as she realized just how long a drop it was to the ground far below, and just how small the battlements were. A child could climb on them and then be blown off by a sudden change in the wind. They didn't look very secure to her eyes, but as far as she could tell the true defense of the tower rested in Void's magic. A small army of men could climb over the battlements if they could get past the wards.

"He comes," Void said, pointing towards the sun. "Look!"

For a moment, Emily saw nothing. Then, out of the sun's glare, a dark winged shape dropped down towards the tower. It was so large that she had problems trying to take it all in; its green scales flashed in the sunlight, while its brilliant golden eyes and wings were so immense that they seemed to stretch for miles. Giant claws, each one larger than Emily's entire body, glinted with light as the dragon dropped to the battlements, landing with a gentle thump. It seemed impossible that the tower could even hold up under its weight.

Emily shrank behind Void as the dragon opened its mouth, a wisp of smoke emerging from its nostrils. Inside, there were razor-sharp teeth and a long tongue that licked at its lips, as if it had decided that the two humans would be a pleasant snack. For a being that large, the rational part of Emily's mind insisted, two humans would be nowhere near enough to sate its hunger.

And then she caught the golden eye and froze, transfixed.

Somehow, she *knew* that the dragon was *old.* The magic field surrounding the creature bombarded her with impressions and sensations, piling them into her mind. It was old enough to have seen eons pass while it drifted through the skies, heedless of the scurrying humans on the world below. She no longer felt any sense of threat from it, merely a sense of ancient knowledge and amusement.

Void seemed equally stunned by the dragon, even though they had to be a fact of life in his world. But how many magicians, Emily asked herself, knew dragons personally?

"It has been a long time," the dragon rumbled. Emily shuddered at the thought of what a dragon might consider a *long* time. All of the fantasy books she'd read had claimed that dragons had *very* long lives. "Do you finally wish to call upon the debt I owe you?"

"I do," Void said. His voice sounded tinny in comparison to the dragon's deep rumble. "This girl needs transport to Whitehall."

Emily suddenly felt very small as the dragon's great golden eyes peered down at her. "A traveler from another world," the dragon stated. It wasn't a question. "How strange. We have not seen one like you for many years."

It bent its head down towards the ground. "You may ride on my back. None will dare harm you while I am here."

Void nodded to Emily. "You can trust him to take you to Whitehall," he said. "And I will see you again, soon enough."

Emily hugged him, suddenly, and then turned to face the dragon. She'd always had the impression that dragons were romantic, but there was nothing romantic about *this* dragon. Up close, there was a faintly disconcerting smell—sulfur, she guessed—and the scales felt uncomfortably hot to the touch. Years ago, at a petting zoo, she'd touched a snake, but this was very different. Touching the dragon was like touching an armored tank that had been out in the sun.

"Use the scales to climb on my back," the dragon said. It sounded vastly amused at her struggles. "You cannot hurt me."

Emily hesitated, and then scrambled up, half-expecting to feel scales giving way under her weight. But nothing happened. She reached the dragon's back and swung her legs over the side, clutching a scaly hump that rose up in front of her. A moment later, there was a sudden gust of wind and the dragon threw itself upwards, into the air. The ground dropped away with terrifying speed. Emily yelped and clutched the hump tighter, trying not to look at the ground, or at the wings as they flexed against the air. She'd flown in airplanes before, of course, but this was different. She knew there was nothing between her and the ground. If she fell, she would plummet to her death.

The airflow seemed remarkably mild as the dragon twisted in midair, rather like a rollercoaster, and snapped at a bird with its sharp teeth. There was a brief explosion of feathers and nothing else, apart from a dragonish gulp. Emily shivered again as the dragon leveled out and started to fly away from the tower; somehow, she managed to turn just long enough to see Void's tower as it receded into the distance. It looked like a giant chess piece, standing alone in the middle of the forest.

There was a wave of heat as the dragon blew fire into the air, its entire body flexing underneath her. Emily told herself firmly not to be scared, trying to convince her eyes to look back down at the ground. If she'd had any doubts that she was in a different world, they would have faded away when she saw the villages below. They were primitive, utterly untouched by the modern world. The only genuine road she saw reminded her of the stone roads the Romans had built when they'd conquered most of Europe; the remainder were little more than muddy paths traversed by horses and carts. Most of the fields were tiny compared to the ones she'd seen back home, worked by hand rather than by combine harvesters. If she recalled correctly, medieval farming had never been very efficient. It had taken the development of modern technology to make farming on a vast scale profitable.

Down below, she caught sight of people working in the fields. It was hard to be certain, but they looked to have been beaten down, as if they knew that they weren't working for themselves. Perhaps they weren't, she told herself, as she saw a handful of others who were clearly standing guard, watching the workers. Armed guards, she guessed, as the dragon flew over a small castle-like building at the centre of a number of villages. The local baron probably lived there, exploiting the peasants and taking all of their crops for himself. Perhaps he didn't even leave them enough to live on.

The dragon blew more fire into the air as it flew over a colossal lake sailed by hundreds of tiny fishing boats. Emily glanced to the other side and saw that the lake was actually a giant inlet linked to the sea, allowing sailors to dock their boats on the shore where they were sheltered from storms and powerful waves. None of the boats looked particularly advanced either. The largest she could see was not much bigger than a fishing boat from back home. Perhaps they didn't bring the bigger sailing ships into the lake, or perhaps they simply didn't exist. Void hadn't said much about local geography, but he'd hinted that the necromancers were pushing in on the Allied Lands. Perhaps the Allied Lands had no time to explore the rest of their world. Coming to think of it, she asked herself, did they even know that their world was a sphere?

*If this world is a sphere*, she thought, after a moment. If magic was real, why couldn't there be a flat world?

In the distance, a wall of mountains rose up in front of them, covered with hardy green plants that seemed to provide food and shelter for a tiny human population. The dragon roared and lunged forward, diving between the peaks and dancing through the mountains, playing chicken with the rocky walls. A long valley opened up in front of them and the dragon flew down it, heedless of the small village hidden away from the rest of the world. Emily winced in horror as she caught sight of people staring at the dragon, then running away in terror. They had to think that the dragon was intent on eating them, or on eating their animals. A woman stood up at the edge of the village, shouting at the dragon, only to be ignored. The dragon was too high for Emily to make out even a single word.

But how could she understand *anyone* in this world?

The dragon chuckled as he lifted up above a mountain peak, and then dived down into another valley. This one seemed to be completely deserted, nothing more than trees and flowers hidden away by mountain peaks. The dragon jinked right and left, before flying up and over a giant statue that someone had carved into the side of the mountain. Even *looking* at that statue gave Emily a chill. She'd seen pictures of giant statues that had been destroyed in Afghanistan, but this one was larger–and clearly not human. Giant pointed ears dominated a face so cruel and calculating as to be completely alien, with eyes made black gemstones that glowed in the shadow cast by the statue. Beyond it, there were a row of seats looking out over a depression in the rock. It took her a moment to realize that she was looking at a sporting arena. The entire area seemed completely deserted ... ... yet she felt the hackles rising on her neck as the dragon lifted up into the air. It felt as if they were being watched by unfriendly eyes.

Helplessly, she glanced around, feeling the sensation growing stronger and stronger with every second. There was nothing that *looked* threatening, apart from the statue itself, but it was just a statue. Wasn't it?

But this was a world where magic worked, she reminded herself. A statue might come to life and fight the dragon in a world like this, for all she knew.

The sensation fell away as the dragon lifted even higher into the air, leaving the eerie statue and arena behind. Emily allowed herself a sigh of relief as the mountains became foothills, revealing a ruined city on the other side. It looked as if someone had bombed it to hell and then the citizens had abandoned it. There were hundreds of damaged buildings, along with dozens of statues that had been knocked to the ground. One towering building had been left intact, right in the centre of the city; the remainder had simply been wrecked by whatever force had torn the city apart. Emily wondered absently if Hiroshima had looked like that, before trying to deduce what magicians would use in place of a mundane atomic bomb. Maybe they enslaved dragons and used them to wage war on entire cities ... again, there was no way to know.

She shivered as the dragon flew away from the city and over the desolate, barren wasteland. There were hundreds of towns and villages, all abandoned and left to rot. In places, there were only a handful of signs that there had ever been a village or town there at all. There were no living humans. The inhabitants had fled or had been killed by the forces that had destroyed their homes.

Puzzled, Emily stared at the wreckage, trying to work out just how long it had been since the city and the surrounding countryside had been destroyed. Surely, a medieval village wouldn't last very long if it had been completely abandoned ... but then, some European cities had structures dating back over two thousand years. She shook her head, dismissing the problem as insoluble. It would have to be answered at Whitehall.

Carefully, keeping one hand holding on to the dragon's skin, she opened her knapsack and found a roll of bread with some meat, a very makeshift sandwich. Void's kitchen staff had produced enough food to last her for several days, along with four bottles of water–Void had told her that the bottles were spelled to keep the water cool - and one of a green liquid that smelled vaguely like lime. She ate the sandwich thoughtfully, washing it down with more of the pure boiled water. There was no way to know how long it would be until she reached Whitehall, or what might happen before she was admitted to the school. She might need to save the rest of the sandwiches for later.

Emily shook her head, wondering at herself. Yesterday, she had been bored of life, desperate to escape her family. Today, she was flying on a dragon ... and somehow she'd come to accept it without any real quibbles. She was in deep trouble–Shadye wanted her dead, others might want to keep her alive, draining her power into themselves–and yet she felt excited, delighted to be here.

Maybe, after being so long in the shadows, her real life could begin. Or maybe, coming here meant she would finally have a chance to be someone important.

The ground changed so rapidly that she missed the moment when overgrown towns and villages became nothing more than charred ash on the ground. It looked to have been consumed with fire, burned to the ground until there was literally nothing left. She took a breath and tasted wet ashes floating on the air. The wasteland stretched as far as the eye could see, broken only by faint hints that the firestorm had raged over cities too well-built to be completely reduced to ash.

Emily took another breath and felt the tint of magic in the air, sparking against the magic field that kept the dragon aloft. She glanced towards the massive wings and saw blue-green sparks dancing along the scaly surface, moving with an eerie silence that chilled her to the bone.

And then they were suddenly back in the mountains. The sparks faded away into nothingness. Emily breathed a long sigh of relief and tried to relax. It didn't work. The sight below the dragon chilled her to the bone.

These mountains were different from the previous mountain range. The firestorm that had scorched the countryside to ash had raged through these mountains too. There were no plants or trees growing on the craggy stone; everything had been wiped away, leaving nothing, but naked stone.

Emily shivered again.

Then the air suddenly grew colder, just before the dragon twisted and headed towards a towering building perched atop a mountain. As they flew closer, she realized that the mountain was actually *part* of the building and that it was sitting alone, surrounded by another hidden valley of greenery. Unlike the creepy alien city, there were humans in the valley, some staring up at the dragon. Others seemed intent on ignoring it.

Up close, the giant castle appeared to be built from pure marble. It glowed white in the sunlight, a beacon of hope against the darkness pressing in from the other side of the mountains.

Emily remembered what Void had said about the lack of entangling alliances and realized, in dismay, that Whitehall was right on the border between the Allied Lands and the necromancers. The necromancers would have to push their way through Whitehall to fall on the Allied Lands beyond.

The castle blurred into the mountain, hinting that the interior had been completely hollowed out and converted into living space for the students and their tutors. Given what Void had said about the Allied Lands not cooperating very well, it was possible that many of the forces gathered to fight the necromancers were *also* based at Whitehall. Or perhaps she was wrong.

She braced herself as the dragon came to a halt, hovering in the air like a giant hummingbird, before dropping down towards the ground, claws extended for a safe landing. The giant creature touched the ground so lightly that, for a moment, Emily didn't even realize that they *had* landed.

"You may disembark," the dragon rumbled. Emily hastened to obey. "I will consider the debt between myself and your master settled."

Emily wanted to point out that Void was hardly her master, that he'd actually refused to consider taking her as his apprentice, but she doubted that the dragon would care.

"Thank you," she said. Her legs felt weak and unstable after the flight, forcing her to lean against the dragon's hot scales until she felt able to walk on her own. "I -"

The dragon spoke over her. "You should be aware that your master is playing a very dangerous game," he said.

Emily looked up in surprise. She'd thought that the dragons were largely uninterested in humanity.

It was impossible to read any expression on the scaly face. "His plan may cost your world dearly."

Emily hesitated, and then asked. "What do you mean?"

The dragon said nothing. Instead, he flexed its wings and launched himself upwards into the sky.

Emily watched as he rapidly dwindled into a tiny dot that vanished in the sunlight. Then, she sensed someone standing behind her. When she turned around, she saw a little man whose head barely came up to her chest, wearing a red robe and carrying a staff that was taller than he was. His head, completely bald, reminded her of a Japanese warrior monk from some of the bad films she'd watched as a teenager.

He wore a cloth over his eyes, but she had the sense that he could see her, somehow. "I am the Grandmaster," he said. His voice was stilted, as if he couldn't be bothered to speak naturally. "You are welcome to Whitehall."

"Thank you," Emily said, falling back on politeness. The towering castle was awe-inspiring, taking her breath away. "It's good to be here."

The Grandmaster snorted. "They all say that," he said. "If you'll follow me?"

He turned and started to walk towards the castle, his staff tapping against the ground.

After a moment, Emily followed him, sensing other students looking at her as she entered Whitehall. How many others, she asked herself, had arrived on a *dragon*? Somehow, she doubted that many others had made such a spectacular entrance.

# Chapter Five

ONCE SHE STEPPED THROUGH THE LARGE STONE DOORS THAT LED INTO WHITEHALL, SHE felt a rushing, tingling sensation in the air, followed by a faint shimmer that seemed to dance over her body before fading away into nothingness. Her mind felt oddly muffled, as if her ears had been blocked by some outside force, as she walked past a long line of statues wearing armor. The effect felt like the sensation she'd experienced at Void's tower, but it was much more pronounced. She knew that this must be what magic felt like.

The Grandmaster looked up at her and smiled. "There are powerful wards in Whitehall," he said, by way of explanation. "Some to keep outsiders from breaking in, others to stop you and your fellow students from harming yourselves."

Emily nodded.

The rows of immobile armor gave way to a series of paintings of wizards, almost all of them men. There were only a handful of pictures of women, including one of a blonde girl who seemed to be staring at the painter, daring him to do his worst. She couldn't read the names under the paintings. None of the pictures were moving openly, but every time she looked away and then looked back the pose in each picture was different.

They passed a handful of students waiting in the corridor, who stepped to one side to allow the Grandmaster to pass, as they reached a flight of stairs and walked up to a higher floor. The sense of magic in the air was only growing stronger. Like Void's tower, Emily realized, Whitehall was far larger on the inside than the outside. It made her wonder what else might be hidden inside the building: secret passageways, hidden bases, perhaps even a place for the tutors to hide and rest away from their pupils. It made sense; human nature probably didn't change even if magic was involved.

She followed the Grandmaster into a long corridor and blinked in surprise as she saw a line of students standing with their backs to the wall and their hands on their heads. None of them looked her in the eye as she walked past, which made her realize that they must be in trouble. It didn't surprise her. The students she had known back home had been quite capable of getting into trouble without magic, so who knew what mischief someone with magic could do?

At the head of the corridor a harassed-looking man wearing a black robe was talking to one of the students, a young girl with a faintly ill expression.

"But he *hexed* me, Master," she said as they passed. "I didn't actually *mean* to turn his skin blue!"

"And how many times," the tutor inquired sarcastically, "have you been warned *never* to feed anyone a potion without testing it first?"

Before Emily could reflect on this, the Grandmaster led her onwards again, past a pair of statues of wizards carrying wands and a strange creature with a human head and goat's body. After that odd display, they stepped through a wooden door into a large room dominated by a massive wooden desk and a throne-like chair. It was decorated sparsely, with only a pair of pictures and a couple of parchments Emily guessed to be certificates. They certainly looked like the certificates on the principal's walls back on Earth. The desk itself appeared hand-carved, covered in little sigils that had been cut into the wood, but it was barren, without the computer or telephone that she would have seen back home.

"Stand there," the Grandmaster ordered, as he walked around the table and took his seat, facing her. Emily somehow forced herself to stand still, despite the oddities of the day. "Void wishes for you to learn magic."

"Yes, sir," Emily said nervously. She had the feeling that she needed to be very polite to the Grandmaster. He might be small and slight, but he could probably turn her into a toad with a snap of his fingers. Back home, there were laws against mistreating students, even if they were the sort of kids who deserved a sound spanking rather than love and understanding. Those laws might not exist here.

"You have the potential to be a proper sorceress, he says." The Grandmaster looked down at the table, as if he couldn't be bothered looking at her. "We will have to verify that, of course, and in doing so we must ensure that you receive a proper grounding in all forms of magic. There will be several days of testing before we start assigning you to classes, as well as exercises and other tricks to hone your powers in the proper direction."

Emily nodded, feeling her head spinning. There were more forms of magic than just two?

The Grandmaster looked up at her, sharply. "Have you worked magic already?"

Emily hesitated. "I ... I don't think so," she said, finally. "I sensed magic, but..."

He shook his head. "We'll have to show you how to unlock your powers. I'll have Mistress Irene work with you, at least at first."

He studied her for a long moment. "Void wasn't entirely clear on where you came from," he said. "Would you care to enlighten me?"

It wasn't a request, Emily realized. Quickly, she ran through the entire story, from when she'd been kidnapped by Shadye to the moment Void had put her on the dragon and sent her to Whitehall. Uniquely, at least in the adults she had met, he had the ability to listen without interrupting. The Grandmaster listened until she had finished, and then asked her a couple of questions for clarification. Emily answered the first one easily, but the second was impossible. There was no magic in her world, as far as she knew.

"Interesting," the Grandmaster said. He looked down at the table again. "First things first; Void or Shadye gave you a translation spell, probably Shadye. There is something about it that suggests that it was designed for use on someone who might not want it. You can understand us, but I suspect you won't be able to read our writing."

Emily shook her head, remembering the painting. She'd wondered how she could talk to the locals; neither Shadye nor Void would know English. Of course they'd used magic to translate their words into something she could understand! Under the circumstances, it bothered her; one of them had cast a spell on her and she hadn't even realized it until the Grandmaster had pointed it out. What else might they have done to her?

But the Grandmaster pressed onwards before she had enough time to ponder that thought.

"I will have Mistress Irene teach you a basic translation spell for written words," he said. "Beyond that, you may be well advised to study the language and learn it as quickly as possible. A proper understanding will make it easier to take your studies forward to the highest levels."

It wasn't a request, Emily realized. Part of her wanted to chaff at the requirement–no one had ever forced her to learn another language–but the practical part of her mind told her that she had no choice. Besides, she had never studied outside the country before. The rules were probably different for exchange students. They *had* to be able to communicate with their hosts.

He smiled, thinly. "You're not from this world, but I'll give you the standard lecture anyway. The Allied Lands may have countless disputes, ancient and modern, but they are not tolerated in this school. Students who pick fights with other students over such divisive issues are punished; those who remain here long enough to enter the advanced classes are expected to swear an oath to the White Council and abandon their nationalist beliefs. There are too many necromancers out there for us to be distracted by infighting."

"Yes, sir," Emily said. Questions filled her mind, demanding answers. What was the White Council? And what were the advanced classes? She pushed them aside, knowing that there would be time to find out later. She needed to get her bearings first.

The Grandmaster shrugged. "You should be able to rise above it, as whatever disputes there were on your world are unlikely to matter here. However, in the event that you *don't* rise above it, you *will* be punished. It's astonishing how many students refuse to believe the warning until it is too late."

His unseen eyes, hidden behind the cloth, seemed to fix on her face. "There is a great temptation to misuse magic in this school. We allow a certain degree of latitude for youngsters, because it helps them to learn to control their powers, but there are limits. You'll hear more specific warnings later, but–in particular–anything that risks a fellow student's life is grounds for immediate expulsion from the school. Those who actually manage to *kill* a fellow student will have to face that student's family."

Emily gulped. What had she gotten herself into? "Does ... does that happen very often?"

"Too often," the Grandmaster said. His voice was grim, suggesting that he was recalling dark days when students under his care had been hurt–or worse. "If there is *any* doubt at all over what happened, everyone involved will be interrogated under truth spells until the truth comes out into the light, after which punishments will be assigned."

He stood up, suddenly. "We hope that you will enjoy your years here, and that you will live up to the potential Void sensed in you, but there are limits to what we can tolerate," he concluded. "But you're not from here. You should be able to ignore the political scrabbling and infighting between different factions."

"I'll do my best, sir," Emily promised.

The Grandmaster's lips twitched. "The proper title is *Grandmaster*, young lady," he said, drolly. "I suggest that you listen to how tutors introduce themselves and remember it. They take it *so* personally when someone gives them the wrong title."

He smiled, more naturally. "If you will come with me...?"

The line of students standing against the wall had grown longer in the few minutes they'd been in the Grandmaster's office. A pair of them glanced at Emily as she passed; the remainder ignored her, seemingly reluctant to risk catching the Grandmaster's attention. Absently, she wondered what sorts of punishments were assigned in a magical school. Did they have to write lines, or do detentions? Or were they simply turned into frogs for a few hours? She shook her head, dismissing the thought. No doubt she would find out soon enough.

They stopped in front of a blank wall that the Grandmaster tapped it with his staff. It opened, revealing another corridor leading away into the distance. The stone walls were interrupted, every few meters, by wooden doors. A short fat woman waddled out of a side door and looked up at the Grandmaster, before taking a long and thoughtful look at Emily.

"This is Madame Razz," the Grandmaster said. "She is your housemother for your first two years at the school. I suggest that you listen to her very carefully."

"Thank you, Grandmaster," Madame Razz said. She had a tart voice that suggested that she wouldn't stand for any nonsense. "What time is her first class?"

"Mistress Irene will arrange that," the Grandmaster informed her. "Until then, she is free to be outfitted with everything she needs for her first term."

He nodded to Emily, then turned and strode out of the concealed door.

Emily turned back in time to see Madame Razz study her with a faintly disapproving expression. But before Emily could start to worry about it, she beckoned Emily to follow her down the corridor into a large storeroom, which was crammed with everything from clothes to bedding and toilet supplies. Madame Razz studied her for another long moment before producing a white robe from a pile of clothing and thrusting it at her. Emily held it up against her body and realized that it would fit, although it would also conceal the shape of her body from prying eyes.

"The white robes are assigned to newcomers to Whitehall," Madame Razz informed her, coldly. She plucked what looked like an oversized pair of panties off a railing, followed by an undershirt and a pair of socks, passing them all to Emily. "You are not permitted to wear anything else outside your room, particularly anything that may cause divisiveness among the students. You will be assigned five pairs of everything, which you will be responsible for. You will make sure that it is put out for wash, and then collected from the laundry room. If you lose anything, you will be charged for it."

*I love you too*, Emily thought. The Grandmaster had seemed a decent guy, even if he had issued heavy-handed warnings. Madame Razz, on the other hand, appeared to be inclined to assume the worst of any of the girls. She had to have stepped right out of a boarding school from hell.

"You will change your bedding once every week," Madame Razz continued, thrusting more packets of cloth at her. "Once changed, you will place the bedding to be washed along with your clothes. Luckily, the beds are standard, so we can interchange bedding if necessary. However, you are also responsible for removing any protective charms that you might have placed on the sheets. Accidentally leaving one in place to attack the laundry room staff will result in you being assigned to help them for at least a week."

She picked a small amulet out of a bag and passed it over to Emily. "This is a guide to the interior of the building, which changes regularly," she explained. "In the event that you need to go anywhere, hold the amulet in your left hand and speak the name of the place aloud. A ball of light will appear in the air and guide you to your destination. If it refuses to work, you don't have permission to enter that part of the building yet. Certain parts will remain off-limits until you reach a particular level. Wear the amulet until you learn how to ask the school for directions using your own magic."

Emily glanced down at the amulet, and then put it around her neck.

"Toothbrush, toothpaste, washing powder, watch, medical potions," Madame Razz continued, piling bottles of liquid on top of the clothes Emily was already carrying. "During that time of the month, take one swig of this liquid per day and the effects will be much reduced. Be careful not to leave samples of your blood lying around; it maintains a link to you and someone with bad intentions can use it to hex you, or worse. There are charms to cut the link; until you learn them, hand any bloodstained items over to me for disposal."

The watch was odd, seemingly out of place. Emily looked at it and realized, finally, that it was actually designed for someone to wear around their neck, or carried within their jacket, rather than worn on their wrist. It used clockwork, she decided, rather than anything electronic. She'd have to wind it regularly to keep it working.

Madame Razz finally picked a book up from one end of the room, then led Emily back into the corridor. Emily followed her, staggering slightly under the weight, until they reached a single door, no different from any of the others. Madame Razz rapped on it sharply, then opened it by tapping a finger against a rune that had been cut directly into the stone. Inside, there were three beds, two of them already made up and surrounded by piles of books and devices that Emily didn't recognize. The third bed was nothing more than an uncomfortable looking mattress.

"Place the bedding on the bed," Madame Razz ordered. "I assume you know how to make up your own bed?"

She sounded as if she didn't expect Emily to be capable of tying her shoelaces without assistance, but Emily nodded. The last thing she'd wanted was her mother or stepfather coming into her room back home, so she'd taken care of everything from a very early age. It wasn't actually hard to change a bed; it had always amused her that boys—and a number of girls—complained about how unfair it was that their parents made them do their own beds. They spent longer complaining than it took to make the bed.

"Yes," Emily said.

"That's *yes, Madame*," Madame Razz snapped. She scowled at Emily then nodded towards the door in the rear of the room. "Toilet, washbasin and bath are in there. You'll have to come to an agreement with your roommates about rotas for using the bath; I'd prefer not to have to enforce one. The water basin over in that corner contains drinking water; if you happen to want food or anything else to drink, wait until morning. As a new student, you are not allowed to wander the building after lights out."

She turned and nodded towards the other beds. "I've put you in with Aloha and Imaiqah; Imaiqah is a first year student, like yourself, while Aloha is a second year student. As such, she is expected to take charge of the room. Should you keep the room clean and tidy, with a minimum of noise, fighting and bother, you will be rewarded with room points that can be exchanged for decorations, books or even sweets. I would strongly prefer *not* to have to intervene in disputes between you. In the event that it becomes unavoidable, you will *all* be punished. Do you understand me?"

"Yes, Madame," Emily said, trying not to roll her eyes. "I understand."

"Good," Madame Razz said. "I understand that Mistress Irene will contact you; in the event of her not doing so before dinner time, one of your roommates will take you down to the dining hall. Or use the amulet to find the hall."

She marched over to the door and looked back at Emily. "This school is very different than anywhere else in the Allied Lands," she added, her tone becoming almost compassionate. "It can be hard to adjust, particularly if you came from an aristocratic family. If you need help or advice, you can talk to me at any time."

"Thank you," Emily said.

Madame Razz left, quickly closing the door behind her.

Emily looked around the room, her gaze settling on a pile of books beside one of the beds. Her first impulse was to pick them up, but then she felt the magic haze surrounding them and realized that picking them up—at least without permission—would be a very bad idea. Instead, she sorted through the pile of clothing and bedding, before placing the clothing in the empty cupboard nearest her bed. The bottles of medicine went into the smaller cabinet beside the bed, followed by the amulet; finally, she started to make the bed. It was even easier than she had expected, although the mattress felt rough and uncomfortable once she'd tested it out.

Lying back on the bed, she stared up at the ceiling and shook her head. Her life had turned upside down, yet she found some aspects easier to deal with than she had expected. What was strangest of all was how she felt about her old world. It seemed almost dreamlike now. And she knew that she would never want to go home.

For a moment, she concentrated on her roommates. She'd never shared a room with someone else before, not even a sleepover with girlfriends. Whatever her roommates were like, she prayed that she could get on with them. Friends—or at least allies - would make her life here complete.

And was one of them really named *Aloha?* Or was that just a translation glitch?

Shaking her head, she picked up Void's book and started to leaf through the pages, wishing that she could read and understand the words. But, even though Void had promised her that understanding would come in time, they were still nothing more than Greek to her. The spidery handwriting seemed impenetrable.

*It's only been a day,* she told herself. *See what you can do in a week.*

# Chapter Six

EMILY WAS STILL FLIPPING THROUGH VOID'S BOOK WHEN THE DOOR CLICKED OPEN AND THE first of her roommates walked in. She was a short, mousey girl, with long dark hair, a freckled face and a tired expression, cute rather than beautiful. Emily found it impossible to estimate her age; she could have passed for fourteen back home, but she had a feeling that people aged faster in this world, considering that it had no technology. The girl looked surprised to see Emily, one hand coming up in a defensive stance, before realizing that Emily had to be a third roommate.

"You can call me Imaiqah," she said. Her voice was low, almost as if she didn't want to attract attention. "What would you like to be called?"

Emily blinked in surprise as she realized what she'd been missing; names! The Grandmaster–that wasn't a name, that was a title. And he had never asked her name, which was quite odd, once she came to think of it. Neither had anyone else, not even Shadye. Or Void.

She wracked her brain, thinking hard. Void had told her that it wasn't a good idea to ask for a sorcerer's name, which made her wonder if she shouldn't tell anyone else her name either, for fear it could be used against her. She couldn't understand how an entire school operated without anyone knowing their real names, but this was a whole different universe. Things worked differently here.

"Call me ..." She stopped, shaking her head. What *could* they call her? Could they call her Emily, without her surname? Or should she pick a nickname ... surely, Madame Razz had to be a nickname too. And Imaiqah sounded vaguely Arabic. "I'm honestly not sure."

Imaiqah smiled, brightly. "Your tutor will help you decide what you want to be called. First day?"

"First day," Emily admitted. Madame Razz had said that Imaiqah was a first year student too. "How long have you been here?"

"Seven months," Imaiqah said. She stepped over to the bed and held out a hand for Emily to shake. "I'm an herbalist and a mirror magician, or so they tell me. Herbs I understand; mirrored magic isn't working so well. What will you specialize in?"

Specialize? Emily didn't know what, if anything, she *could* specialize in. Void had given her the book of spells, but he hadn't said *anything* about specializing. Remembering some of the role-playing she'd done before being transported to a different world, it was easy to see that Void had probably taken it for granted that she would specialize in something–and that she would know more than she did about magical talents. He might not have understood that her world had no magic at all and therefore also had no specialized magicians as this world knew them.

Imaiqah saw the book on the bed before Emily could answer, her eyes going wide. "You're a sorceress," she said, astonished. "How many spells do you know?"

Emily hesitated, and then admitted the truth. "None." She knew nothing about casting spells, let alone tapping her magic, the magic she didn't quite believe she had. "I only just discovered that I was a sorceress."

Imaiqah stared at her, as if she suspected that Emily was lying. "How is that even possible?" The surprise in her voice was obvious. "I thought that all students were tested for magic."

And then her eyes narrowed. "Where do you even come from? I can't place your accent."

"A long way away," Emily said, unsure how much she should admit to Imaiqah. The truth, that she came from another universe, or a vague statement that wasn't quite a lie? "It's my first day at Whitehall."

Imaiqah nodded in sympathy. "I remember my first day too," she said, turning away and walking over to her bed. "Mistress Irene will see that you are properly set up for your studies, then assign you to classes. Maybe we'll share a class or two."

The door opened again before Emily could say a word, revealing a tall, dark-skinned girl with a scowl on her face. "I swear I will turn that fool into a toad," the newcomer said, one hand clutching a wand as if she intended to start firing off spells in every direction. "How *dare* he try to ask me to walk out with him on the grounds?"

Imaiqah ignored the question as the door banged closed. "Aloha, this is our new roommate," she said. "She doesn't have a name yet."

Emily heard her tone and understood, instantly, that Aloha considered herself the Alpha female in the room. She *was* a second year, whatever that meant. The mushy girls boarding school books her mother had owned had suggested that senior girls could punish younger girls at will. They'd also included suggestions of lesbian affairs among the girls.

"Right," Aloha said. Up close, she *reeked* of magic ... and of something Emily couldn't identify. "I would prefer not to be bothered by any junior students. Keep to your side of the room and I will keep to mine–and don't even *think* about touching my books."

She dumped a bag onto her bed and stalked past them, into the bathroom. Emily watched the door close and then glanced at Imaiqah, who looked a little frightened. No doubt her roommate bullied her, she decided, or at the very least considered associating with a first year to be undesirable. Aloha might have magic, but she was still very human.

"She means it," Imaiqah said. She sounded as if she were trying to make light of it, but couldn't quite pull it off. "Everything she owns is covered in protective charms. I once picked up one of her books and ended up frozen to the floor until she came back and released me."

Emily stared at her, and then looked down at the stone floor. If she'd touched any of the books ...

A dull gong echoed through the building and she looked up. "Dinner," Imaiqah said, with some relief. "Do you want to come with me to eat?"

Emily wanted to say no. She wanted to stay and hide in the room until the sense of weirdness - of being out of place - faded away, but she was hungry. Besides, the world wouldn't change if she hid herself under the blankets. She nodded once, pushing the book of spells Void had given her under the bed, and then picked up her new robes, pulling them over the robes she already wore, even though Madame Razz had effectively stated that non-school clothes were forbidden. But there was no time to change.

She should have changed while waiting for her roommates, but the sense of weirdness had just grown stronger and stronger.

Imaiqah picked up a book from her bedside table, then led the way back out into the corridor. There were dozens of students outside, all wearing robes of different colors, several old enough to be adults. In fact, Emily realized as she looked from face to face, some students looked to be barely entering their teens, while others seemed to be in their twenties. A handful of them carried wands, or staffs; a couple carried broomsticks and one carried what looked like a gnarled club of wood. Their chatter didn't fade away when they saw Emily; they didn't seem to be surprised by an unfamiliar face.

Or maybe there were so many pupils at the school that no one could hope to know them all. Emily had spent two years at her last school and she'd barely known anyone outside her grade.

"That's Marcus," Imaiqah said, pointing to a taller male student wearing a green robe and a red badge that seemed to glow with an eerie light. "He's one of the prefects assigned to keep us all in line; he isn't a bad person, but he takes his responsibilities seriously. Don't go running in the corridors in front of him."

They walked out of the dorm and down a long flight of stairs. Emily said nothing, staring around her. Every time the castle seemed to make sense, something happened to confuse her again. The corridors seemed to be rearranging themselves at will; worse yet, some of the students didn't even look human. One of them had pointy ears like an elf, reminding her of one of the *Star Trek* characters she'd watched as a younger girl. Another seemed to be a living plant, with green skin and twigs in place of hair. And a third ... Emily realized in shock that the strange girl's head was surrounded by living snakes that moved of their own accord. She looked like the pictures of Medusa from the role-playing games, the ones that had been modeled on the legends of Ancient Greece.

"She's a Gorgon," Imaiqah explained, when Emily asked. "It's very rare for a Gorgon to attend Whitehall, or so we've been told. Their society prefers to have nothing to do with the Allied Lands."

Emily actually felt her head spin as she tried to wrap her mind around the concept. Classes with a Gorgon? Could she turn people into stone? Wouldn't her classmates be afraid of her?

They left the Gorgon behind and, eventually, reached a huge doorway which led into a massive dining room. There were tables everywhere, all crammed with students who were stuffing their faces with all sorts of food, served on giant platters. Bright balls of fire hung high overhead, casting warm light over the dining hall. Emily looked towards the raised table at the front of the room and saw a dozen tutors—they had to be tutors—eating with more dignity, looking up between every bite to make sure that their students weren't getting into mischief. They seemed a varied lot; a handful looked like traditional wizards, complete with robes and pointy hats, while others looked even stranger. One even looked like a wicked witch, gimlet eyes flashing as she stroked her cat and eyed her students sardonically. Another looked alarmingly like Red Sonja.

*At least none of them look like Professor Snape,* Emily told herself.

Imaiqah pointed her towards the line of pupils waiting for food, jostling one another as the line slowly advanced towards a hole in the wall. A pair of cooks were serving plates of food, something that looked like a hot stew with boiled potatoes and some vegetables she didn't recognize. One of the cooks smiled at Emily, reminding her of one of her stepfather's favorite sayings. Never trust a thin cook, he'd said; the cook was fat enough to pass for two people. Clearly, she'd been eating her own cooking.

"This way," Imaiqah said, once they had been served. The food smelled strange to Emily, but it *was* from another universe. "The first-years sit at the rear of the room..."

"So, the mouse has found a friend," a new voice said, interrupting Imaiqah.

Emily looked around and saw a tall girl sneering at them. The speaker had long white-blonde hair, surrounding a china doll face that could only be described as patrician.

Before she could think of anything to say, the strange new girl went on. "I trust that you will soon learn the folly of your choice."

Emily had endured school psychologists and far too many cheerleaders who were ridiculously full of themselves, but she'd never been spoken to in such a condescending manner. But because she was new here, she swallowed the response that came to mind and attempted to ignore the newcomer. It wasn't easy.

Finally, she ventured a question. "Umm...who are you?"

"We are Alassa, Heir to the Throne of Zangaria," the girl replied. She had the regal dignity act down pat, Emily had to admit, even if she did seem a little surprised. Had she thought that Emily would *know* her? "You will give us due honor, as we deserve."

Emily stared at her—and then started to laugh. She couldn't help it. Maybe a genuine monarch, with years on the throne of her country, could have pulled off the regal act, but Alassa sounded more like she was posturing rather than actually being dignified.

Alassa's face clouded rapidly and one hand reached for the wand at her belt. But before she could do anything, Imaiqah caught Emily's hand and dragged her off towards the tables. Emily would have preferred to stay and exchange barbs—it was her experience that bullies needed to be fought—but her new roommate didn't give her any choice. Besides, the self-styled Heir to the Throne of Zangaria probably knew much more magic than Emily.

"She's a pain in the posterior," Imaiqah muttered, as soon as they were out of earshot. "If you're not one of her cronies, you're her target."

"I've met the type before," Emily agreed. "Is she really royalty?"

"Where *do* you come from?" Imaiqah asked. "Zangaria is one of the Allied Lands–one of the most powerful states in the West. Alassa is their royal princess and will be Queen one day, may the gods help them."

Emily had to smile. "So why is she here?"

"Their Royal Family has a long tradition of magic." Imaiqah snorted. "So they send their heirs out to Whitehall to learn magic–and, just incidentally, to make contacts among their fellow nobility in the Allied Lands. But she is the social queen of the school and is not inclined to actually make friends ..."

"But she has a small following of cronies," Emily guessed. Oddly, she found it reassuring, even if she *was* in a very different world, to find the behavior she'd seen before had continued to manifest. The people were *definitely* human, regardless of their magic or their odd appearance. "People who keep telling her how wonderful she is, in the hopes that the glamour of royalty will rub off on them."

Imaiqah nodded.

Emily smiled, and then asked the obvious question. "Why doesn't she like you?"

Imaiqah hesitated, then tried to answer. "I don't have strong magic. And I'm a tradesman's daughter."

*That can't be it*, Emily thought. *Or maybe the Royal Brat really is that shallow.*

Before she could ask, Imaiqah went on. "I made the mistake of refusing to do her homework several months ago and now she ..."

She shook her head. "Well," Imaiqah added, "you know."

Emily didn't know what to say. Commiseration wouldn't help, she knew, it had never helped back on Earth. So she sat there, silent. Helpless.

"I really *don't* have strong magic," Imaiqah added, a moment later. "You won't want to associate with me ..."

There was something in her tone that made Emily's heart twinge in pain. *She'd* been a social outcast too, even though she'd lived in a world that should have known better. It wasn't a bearable life; kids could be cruel...and those who might be decent otherwise chose to have nothing to do with the outcast, for fear that the popular kids–and the bullies–might turn on them next. Emily knew the unspoken truth behind every kid who took a gun to school and opened fire at random. They'd been knocked down so hard that they believed themselves to be at war with the entire establishment.

"I can associate with whoever I like," she growled. The Grandmaster had warned her about political factions, but it wasn't as if Emily was going to be socially important. It was rather unlikely that a prince would want to marry her, and she had no family here. "I don't care what anyone else thinks of me."

Imaiqah stared at her, and then started to protect. "But you're a sorceress..."

"I'm still learning," Emily interrupted. It *was* technically true, although–more practically–she hadn't even started learning. "And I can be friends with whoever I like."

She started to eat the stew while studying the other students. They were definitely diverse, far more diverse than any crowd she'd seen back home. Apart from white, black, brown and yellow skins, there were students who were green-skinned, or blue, one so bright a blue that it *had* to have been a magical accident of some kind. And a number of students seemed to be the products of mixed-race marriages, as she knew them from back home, and others seemed to be part-human hybrids. One older student looked to be part-Orc, not unlike the characters from the role-playing games. Another was a dark-skinned elf-like humanoid who looked far too thin to be human.

The stew tasted surprisingly nice, certainly better than anything she'd ever eaten at her old school. There were herbs that sent odd tingling sensations running down her tongue; the meat itself tasted like a vague cross between beef and pork. Servants moved from table to table, pouring glasses of fruit juice and water for the students; Emily couldn't help, but notice that the servants flinched away from some of the tables. She wondered if they were targeted by the magical students for practical jokes on a regular basis.

Imaiqah pointed out some of the tutors as they ate. "Professor Thande is the Head of Alchemy," she said, nodding towards a short professor who was arguing with one of the other tutors. "He prefers research rather than actually teaching, so don't get on his bad side or he'll use you as a test subject for his concoctions. Professor Torquemada, beside him, is the Head of Healing; they've been squabbling for years over something that happened when they were both students. Or so I've been told."

She grinned at Emily, as if she couldn't quite believe that she was actually getting a chance to talk to someone and show off. "Professor Lombardi is Head of Charms; you'll probably have a private session with him before you formally join his classes. He prefers to measure everyone's potential first, before they join the other students. The man beside him is General Kip; he teaches combat magic and battle strategy. Don't ever forget to call him *General*. He assigns the worst detentions in the school."

Emily jumped as a hand fell on her shoulder. "Welcome to Whitehall," a voice said. She turned to see a stern woman looking down at her from a great height. Her face could have been carved from stone, seeming as if it were permanently fixed in a disapproving expression. "I am Mistress Irene. You will report to me in my office tomorrow at nine bells."

"Yes, Mistress," Emily stammered. There was something about Irene that warned her to be careful. In some ways, she reminded her of Madame Razz, but with far more power. "I'll be there."

Irene's gaze switched to Imaiqah. "You will ensure that she finds my office tomorrow morning," she added sharply. "Make sure that she goes to bed early and has a proper sleep. Tomorrow she starts studying in earnest."

She stalked off towards the end of the table to deliver a reprimand to another student, leaving Emily staring after her. "Don't take it personally," Imaiqah advised. "She's like that with everyone. She's meant to supervise all first year students and keep them from killing themselves or each other."

"Oh," Emily said.

Imaiqah smiled. "And she dislikes Alassa. That's one point in her favor."

"Yeah," Emily agreed. "But what will she think of me?"

Imaiqah shrugged and changed the subject. But the thought continued to bother Emily as they returned to their room and prepared for bed. If Irene was so severe, how was Emily ever going to relax in her presence?

*But then*, she thought slowly, *she probably doesn't want me to relax.*

It made sense. She knew magic was dangerous; quite aside from Shadye and Void's barely-leashed power, several of the students bore scars from what Emily assumed were magical accidents. And the Grandmaster had warned Emily that students could die in Whitehall. It was obvious that Irene didn't have an easy job at all.

On that thought, she climbed into bed and fell asleep.

## Chapter Seven

THE FOLLOWING MORNING, EMILY STOOD IN FRONT OF MISTRESS IRENE'S OFFICE, WONDERing if she dared knock. Imaiqah had escorted her to the office after breakfast and then left, pleading an early class. Emily lifted her hand to the door and then hesitated. Mistress Irene's door alone looked intimidating and the woman herself, according to Imaiqah, was formidable. Mistress Irene apparently faced down a necromancer with nothing more than a sharp tongue and a complete refusal to surrender to the dark wizard. After meeting Shadye, Emily had an idea of just how much courage that had to have taken.

Bracing herself, she tapped on the door. There was a long pause, just long enough for her to wonder if Mistress Irene was somewhere else, and then the door swung open, silently. Emily stepped inside and saw a simple office, with walls lined by shelves crammed with books. It was smaller than the Grandmaster's office and far more down-to-earth.

Mistress Irene was seated at her desk, studying a sheet of parchment. She pointed one long finger at a chair and motioned for Emily to sit. Emily obeyed, trying to resist the temptation to glance at the devices on the tutor's desk. Some of them shimmered with brilliant magic.

"You are an odd pupil," Mistress Irene said, without preamble. "You are ignorant, yet powerful. That makes you dangerous."

Emily swallowed.

Mistress Irene's voice was cold, rapping out the points one by one. "Magic can kill the ignorant. You must learn to control your magic as quickly as possible. Losing control could be disastrous. Do you understand me?"

"Yes, Mistress," Emily said.

"Good," Mistress Irene said. There was a pause. "It is possible to use a sorcerer's real name against them, but it requires their complete name to work. You may go by your first name, if you wish, or you may select something else you wish to be called. Choose."

Emily hesitated. She'd wondered, last night, about changing her name completely, but she wanted to cling onto the name she'd been given at birth. Emily alone, it seemed, would be safe to use. Her surname had never been spoken in this new world.

"Emily," she said, finally. Judging from the other names she'd heard–at dinner and breakfast–it wouldn't be *too* strange to local ears. Or so she thought, although she still wasn't entirely sure of what the translation spell was actually doing. Besides, it *was* her name. "You can call me Emily."

"Very well," Mistress Irene said. She looked up, her dark eyes fixed firmly on Emily's face. "*Mana* exists throughout the world. Magic is powered by *mana*. Your body produces *mana*. Do you understand me?"

Emily stared at her. "I think so," she said, finally. Inwardly, she wasn't so sure. Did her body produce *mana* itself, or was she drawing on an energy field surrounding the new world? Or both? Perhaps the human race *produced* the power that kept dragons aloft ... there was no way for her to know. Maybe she'd have a chance later on to apply the methods of rationality to magic and deduce its underlying rules. "That's what makes me a sorceress?"

"A *potential* sorceress," Mistress Irene snapped. "When you cast a spell, you power it with *mana* from your reserves. Learning how to power spells is the single most important lesson you'll learn at this school. Overpowering your spells will result in disaster."

There was a long pause. "There are other forms of magic, but you have to master your own first or you'll never be anything more than a journeyman," she added, in a gentler voice. She picked up a piece of paper and passed it over to Emily, who looked down at it, puzzled. "The relationship between magic and spells is both simple and complex. Simple, because the spells help steer the magic in the right direction; complex, because you have to tie the two together in your mind."

Emily nodded, carefully. "You mean...pouring magic into a given shape, like pouring clay into a mould," she hazarded. "Or do smaller spells work as building blocks for larger spells?"

"As good an analogy as any," Mistress Irene said. "Can you read the word on the paper?"

"No," Emily said, after a moment. She'd half-expected a recognizable alphabet, but in hindsight that had been foolish. The letters she was looking at seemed a cross between Arabic and Chinese. "I can't read them."

"Good," Mistress Irene said. Emily blinked in surprise as her tutor continued. "Had you been familiar with the language, we would have had to find another one for you to use. It is vitally important that you never relax while casting spells, even when you become proficient enough to cast them without verbalizing. A single mistake can be disastrous. Using a different language forces you to *think*."

Emily had to smile. Mistress Irene seemed to like warning her about potential dangers.

"This is a charged wand," Mistress Irene said, picking up a wand from her desk and passing it to Emily. "Wands are normally used for focusing magic; this one has spells inside it, already primed. Can you feel the spells?"

The wand seemed to sparkle in her hand, as if it were alive. Emily *felt* it twisting like a snake, even though she could see no sign of independent movement. Holding onto the wand was tricky, but the more she held it, the more she was aware of ... *spells* waiting for her. And as she became aware of them, she became aware of the *mana* inside her, waiting to be released. Her magic seemed to be crackling with life.

"Try to cast one of the spells," Mistress Irene said. "Focus your mind on it and trigger the spell."

Emily reached out with her mind, unsure of what she was doing. The spell glittered in her mind, but it seemed frustratingly insubstantial, as if the spell existed only in potential. An engine, she reasoned, but one that required fuel to run. The trick was to draw the *mana* from inside her body and use it to power the spell. But she wasn't sure how to form the link between her mind and the wand, let alone the spells waiting for her power. Her power seemed to stop at her skin ...

"*Abracadabra*," she muttered, in frustration.

Something *clicked* in her mind. Power shimmered out of her and into the wand; a moment later, the spell blazed with light in her mind and vanished. Emily opened her eyes, unsure of just when she had closed them, and saw a shimmering image of herself hanging in the air. She let out a yelp in shock, just before the image vanished into nothingness.

"Did ..." Emily swallowed and started again. "Did I do that?"

"You powered the spell," Mistress Irene said sardonically. "Everyone has their own way to tap their *mana*."

Emily put it together, slowly. There was a muscle for magic in her mind and she had to learn how to use it, but–like every other muscle–she didn't really issue precise instructions to her body and mind. The trick was learning how to issue basic orders. When she'd spoken the magic word aloud, her subconscious mind had done the hard work–and now that she knew what she was doing, she could do it again.

"Try the second spell," Mistress Irene said. "See if you can figure out how to make this one work."

"Right," Emily said. She closed her eyes and reached out with her mind, right into the wand. The spell was just waiting for her ... this time, there was no need to struggle to channel power into the spell. It flared to life in her mind and, when she opened her eyes, she saw a second image of herself. This one seemed alarmingly substantial. Her head started to spin a moment later as it glowed brighter. Something was draining the *mana* out of her body. "I ..."

Mistress Irene muttered a word. The image snapped out of existence. A moment later, the sense of being drained faded away.

Emily rocked back on her chair. The spell ... the spell hadn't *stopped*, she realized in alarm. It had just kept draining power from her until Mistress Irene had cancelled it. What would have happened if the spell had *kept* draining her? Would it have killed her outright, or merely knocked her out for a few hours?

"Something else to remember at all times," Mistress Irene said. "*Never* let a spell demand unlimited power. Magicians, even sorcerers, have been known to kill themselves through trying to use a spell before checking it carefully. *Do not* try to use *any* spell until you see how it goes together."

She stood up and picked a book off the shelves. "I'm going to give you a basic translation spell. It will only last a couple of months, but by then you should be capable of renewing it for yourself. Sit still and *don't* resist."

Emily shifted uncomfortably as Mistress Irene muttered several words into the air, moving her hand in a complicated gesture. She felt ... *something* gossamer-thin shimmering into existence around her, as insubstantial as a spider's nest, before it fell down and over her body, embedding itself in her mind. It was all she could do to remain still until the spell was completed. The spell was so uncomfortable that it could *never* be a permanent solution.

The Grandmaster had been right. She *would* have to learn to read the local language, just as soon as she possibly could.

"Now," Mistress Irene said, once the translation spell had been completed. "It's time to start looking at how spells go together."

The next hour passed very slowly as Emily puzzled over the building blocks of magic. Spells, Mistress Irene explained carefully, were made up of smaller spells; it was possible to memorize a more advanced spell, but without an understanding of the underpinning spells it would be impossible to progress any further. Looking at the magic words, Emily was reminded of a simple computer language, one that ran in her brain. One of her nerdy friends had bought an ancient computer and experimented with one of the earliest computer languages, before graduating to more complex systems. She was sure that *he* would have had little difficulty in learning to cast spells because of how familiar he was with arcane computer languages.

"Keep them in your mind," Mistress Irene said, again and again. "Concentrate on breaking down spells into their smallest components."

Emily scowled, feeling her head starting to pound. A computer language didn't actually *do* anything unless it was in a computer; writing a line of computer code on blank paper didn't automatically alter the coding inside the computer. Logically, she had to consider herself a magical computer and run the coding–the spells–inside her own head, but sometimes it didn't seem to work out that simply. Writing down a magic spell was sometimes exactly the same as casting it, sometimes not. Worse yet, it took several tries before she managed to learn how *not* to infuse power into the spells.

And then there were spells–natural and unnatural–infused into people, objects or even the empty air. According to Mistress Irene, *mana* was everywhere, allowing creatures to evolve into forms that could draw on it for themselves. She didn't want to even guess at what sort of evolutionary history might have produced dragons, gorgons or elves, but it made a certain kind of sense. Maybe, just maybe, orcs and goblins were humans who had been warped into something inhuman by exposure to the magic field.

"It's a very good idea to test everything for infused magic before you touch it," Mistress Irene said. "Your fellow students *love* playing practical jokes. One of them even managed to rig his friend's textbook so that it would turn him into a frog when he opened the book. Most of them won't be skilled enough to *hide* a spell-trap from basic detection spells directly, but there are plenty of tricks they can pull to make it harder to detect a hidden trap."

Emily looked down at the spell and nodded, before carefully casting it out loud. The room seemed to dim for a moment, just before a number of objects started to shimmer with an eerie red glow. She looked around, noticing the spells on the desk, the bookshelves, the globe and crystal ball in the corner ... and there were dozens clustered around the door. Some of them looked harmless, even in the red light, but a number looked downright ominous. She had the distant feeling that trying to take a book off the shelves without permission would be very dangerous.

"Good," Mistress Irene said. "Now, a second spell ..."

It didn't seem to do anything, at least at first, until Mistress Irene passed her a small goblet and invited her to repeat the spell. The red glow surrounding the goblet faded away into nothingness, leaving her looking down at a harmless object.

"The simple spell for dispelling trap spells has a much shorter range," Mistress Irene explained. "Should you be unable to remove a spell someone might have left on your property, bring it to me or one of the other tutors. Naturally, removing the more complex trap spells is a great deal harder."

Emily nodded. There would be no point in using any sort of spell to keep her property private if it could simply be dispelled. The spells crawling over Mistress Irene's door looked a great deal more complex, suggesting that cracking them would be difficult, if not impossible. She wondered, absently, what they actually *did* to intruders. Freeze them in place, transform them into something else ... or kill them outright?

*No*, she thought, *that couldn't be possible.* Whitehall might take a more relaxed attitude to students injuring themselves and others than any school she knew back home, but there had to be limits.

The second hour passed far more quickly than the first as Mistress Irene pushed her into memorizing and practicing a dozen different spells. One of them was a very simple defensive spell, enough to deflect many hexes and charms away from her body and soul. Emily shivered at the implications of students needing to know *that* spell as quickly as possible, forcing herself to keep it firmly in her mind. Another spell checked to ensure that a potion was safe to drink, although Mistress Irene warned her that it only picked up on potions that were lethal; she could still become very ill from drinking the wrong potion.

A more complex spell, one that Emily couldn't master in the first session, was designed to analyze other spells, allowing the caster to see how they had been put together by the original magician. Mistress Irene made it work with ease, but Emily couldn't quite keep all the different variables straight in her head. Finally, Mistress Irene told her to leave the spell for now; they'd return to it in two days.

"I'm going to permit you to enter the library and borrow books suitable for a first year student," Mistress Irene said. "I know that students practice spells with or without our permission, so I'd just like to remind you that hurting another student will leave you—at the very least—unable to sit comfortably for several days. If you manage to hurt yourself, you'll have us laughing at you as well."

Her eyes narrowed. "Every student has a different level of power," she added, a moment later. "Push your limits, but don't push too far, too fast. If you feel unwell, or headachy, stop casting spells and rest; eat something sweet to replenish your energy. The kitchen staff will provide you with something to eat if necessary."

"Thank you, Mistress," Emily said, finally. Her head already felt uncomfortable; when she stood up, her legs suddenly weakened and she had to grab the chair to keep herself from falling over. "I ..."

"You're going to the dining hall, where you will eat a large meal," Mistress Irene said,. "This afternoon"–she produced a sheet of paper, which Emily took automatically–"you will be joining the History of Magic class, followed by a free period during which you are expected to study. You'll begin proper classes tomorrow.

"Fortunately, we start basic classes throughout the year, as we never know when someone knew is going to come to the school. But you have to test out of them before you can proceed."

Emily glanced down at the paper. It was a class schedule, written out in a neat, precise hand. The school day was divided up into eight periods, seven of them assigned to actual studies and one assigned for lunch. There were thirty minutes between classes, either to keep the students from becoming exhausted by giving them a chance to get something to eat, or to ensure that if one class ran late there would be no delay for the second class. Being tardy, she suspected, would earn one a detention at Whitehall–or worse.

"I shall assign your roommates to assist you, as you are unfamiliar with our world," Mistress Irene added. Emily gulped; she liked Imaiqah, but she had the feeling that Aloha would be much less willing to help a newcomer explore the school. "Imaiqah needs to retake two classes, so she will accompany you to Transfiguration and Mentalist Magic. Depending on how you progress, you may be moved up to a more advanced class within the next two months."

Emily nodded. The schedule listed a dozen different classes for a first year, including Alchemy, Charms, Cryptozoology, Divination and Ethics. A number of periods had been left blank, but she wasn't sure if they were free periods for private study or if Mistress Irene hadn't assigned her to specific classes for those times yet. Two periods on Tuesday and Thursday had simply been marked sport. Emily scowled at the thought. She'd moved to a completely new world and she was *still* forced to attend gym class.

Mistress Irene smiled. "You haven't done that badly," she said. "Void was right. You do have potential."

Emily flushed. "But I couldn't master the analysis spell. I ..."

The tutor laughed. "I'd be embarrassed if you mastered it without weeks of practicing. Do you know how long it took me to master it?"

Mistress Irene shook her head. "Go to the dining hall and eat," she ordered. "And then let your amulet guide you to History of Magic."

Emily nodded and left the office, thinking–as she left–that Mistress Irene wasn't so bad after all. Perhaps she even had a heart of gold.

# Chapter Eight

"History is nothing more than a series of opinions about the past," Professor Locke informed his class. He was a short, elderly man with long white hair, wearing a pair of spectacles through which he peered suspiciously at his students. "Who, I might ask you, won the Battle of Janus?"

A male student raised his hand. "We did, sir."

Another student jumped up almost before the first speaker had finished. "No, *we* won!"

Professor Locke smiled. "A perfect demonstration of the essential truth of my statement. The Battle of Janus was fought out between Umbria and Holm for domination of the city of Janus, and the trade routes that ran through the Janus mountain range. While Umbria was pushed back, allowing Holm to claim a victory, the battle was so costly that reinforcements from Umbria were able to push Holm back out of the city within the month."

His smile grew wider. "So tell me. Who *really* won the battle?"

Emily considered the question while the more nationalistic of her classmates argued the point. Destroying an empire to win a battle was no victory, as she'd learned playing computer games; a victory that cost an army could be fatal if there was no time to produce a second army. There had been a Greek King who'd fought the Roman Republic, she recalled, who had bemoaned his exceedingly costly victory in one battle—and lost the war.

"The Allied Lands may have united to fight the necromancers," the Professor said, "but they still disagree on many things. One of them is on history. No Kingdom or City-State shares the same view of history, which can be irritating if one happens to be a historian. And yet our history, which is shared even if they don't want to admit it, explains why we ended up facing the necromancers today."

There was a long pause. "Thousands of years ago, the human race warred with the elves. The elves were magic, the elves were formidable ... but there were *millions* of humans. It was *our* time, we believed, and we no longer wanted to be dominated by the Fair Folk. So we warred with them until they were driven back into their hidden settlements and built the First Empire in the rubble of *their* empire.

"But we made a dreadful mistake. We could have reached out to the orcs and goblins, offshoots of humanity created by the elves. Instead, also we warred with them, forcing them into an alliance with the remaining elves. Many years later, they returned and waged war on the First Empire itself. They destroyed the First Empire."

Emily shivered, remembering what she'd seen as the dragon had carried her from Void's tower to Whitehall. Destroyed cities, including structures she was convinced hadn't been produced by human beings; their populations slaughtered or driven away to starve. Had that been the result of the war against the elves, or had it had a far darker cause?

"Those were terrible days," Professor Locke said. "The elves raised countless monsters to lay waste to our lands. Millions died as fire-drakes blew their poisonous breath over human settlements, and giant crabs emerged from the seas to destroy harbors while mermen sank ships in the ocean. The only solution seemed to be to reach for far greater magic and so we did. We discovered that we could use murder to power our spells and use them to strike back against the elves. Eventually, we rallied and drove the elves to the brink of extinction.

"But, as so often happens, the weapon we used to win the war turned in our hands. The necromancers were unable to channel the vast power they possessed without going mad, becoming monsters in human form. They didn't want to stop drinking in the *mana* from thousands of slaughtered humans, or basking in the sheer joy of power. Eventually, they attempted to take over the Second Empire. The battle to stop them also shattered any hope of establishing a new human unity."

Emily considered it, wondering–absently–why *murder* was required. Why not a willing sacrifice? Would it have made any difference if the sacrifices had *volunteered* themselves to the necromancers?

But Shadye had definitely been insane. No matter how genteel he'd acted, he'd planned to sacrifice Emily to the Harrowing, whatever *that* was. And his plan would have exploded in his face if Void hadn't intervened.

Professor Locke nodded towards the map on the wall. Emily studied it with interest; the continents bore little resemblance to anything she remembered from her own world. One vast continent was roughly the size of Europe, Asia and America put together, while a smaller continent to the south was little bigger than Australia. A network of islands–Japan and Britain put together, she decided–dominated the final part of the globe. They *did* know that their world was a sphere.

But it didn't seem to have a *name*.

Thirty-two states were part of the Allied Lands, if she was reading the map correctly. Most of them were grouped to the north of the largest continent, with a handful in the smaller continent and islands. Below them, there was a wasteland; it had to have been where Shadye had attempted to sacrifice her, after she'd been kidnapped from her world. She remembered the barren lands she'd flown over and shivered. The battle to stop the necromancers might as well have been fought with atomic bombs. It might even have been kinder in the long run.

"The necromancers fled into the dead lands to the south," the Professor said. "There, they built their strongholds, grew their slaves and eventually mounted a new assault on the Allied Lands. Their threat is overwhelming; given enough time, they will produce more armies of monsters to turn against us and crush the Allied Lands. The only thing that has saved us so far is their disunity. We cannot expect them to remain disunited forever."

*Their disunity?* Emily wondered. She'd had the impression that Shadye was acting independently of the other necromancers. He'd certainly not summoned any others to join him in sacrificing her for power ...

One of the students stuck up his hand, interrupting Emily's thoughts. "Can we not *keep* them disunited, Professor? We could offer to dicker with them if they fought each other ..."

"It has been tried," Professor Locke said. He tapped a darkened patch on the map. "The King of Halers believed that he could buy off one of the necromancers, an unpleasant fellow called Gower. Gower was sent hundreds of the king's subjects as sacrifices in the hope that it would buy the king's independence. But Gower wormed his way into the kingdom's power structure and turned the nobles against the king, the peasants against the nobles and the army against everyone. Eventually, Halers was so badly wracked by civil war that the necromancer was able to walk in and take over.

"Gower destroyed the kingdom. His monsters wiped out the remaining nobles, before killing enough of the peasants to keep the rest thoroughly cowed, those that didn't flee in time. Now, it is a source of monsters and magical sacrifices for the necromancers, all because a king was foolish enough to believe that a necromancer could be bribed into good behavior. We cannot negotiate with the necromancers. All we can do is muster our own power and prepare for the coming struggle."

Emily knew–looking at the map–that it would be difficult. Void had told her that the necromancers were slowly outflanking the Allied Lands, but he hadn't managed to convey just how desperate the situation was. If the necromancers managed to cooperate long enough to mount a major offensive, they could drive up through the mountains and split the Allied Lands in half. They'd then have access to vast resources–and humans for sacrifice–that they could use to crush the rest of the Allied Lands. And then they could turn their attention to the other continents.

"We do have some advantages," Professor Locke said. "Most importantly, necromancers are driven insane by the sheer power they channel through their minds. They have been known to lash out at each other without premeditation, as well as planning betrayals for reasons that only make sense in their own addled minds. Their power levels also slowly kill them as their brains cannot tolerate the pressure they put on them for long. As they grow older, they are forced to channel more and more power to keep themselves alive, slowly becoming undead lich-creatures. The true horror of necromancy is that eventually they will run out of humans to sacrifice and die out, leaving the land behind them a waste."

Emily spoke before she could think better of it. "Did the elves teach the first necromancers how to become necromancers?"

Professor Locke studied her for a long moment, thoughtfully. "And what, young lady, do you mean by that?"

His gaze was disconcerting. Back home, she would rarely have been called to justify herself to anyone at school. Here ...

"If necromancers need a constantly increasing supply of power merely to keep themselves alive," Emily said, hastily formulating her thoughts, "eventually they're going to run out of power."

"As I said," the Professor reminded her, impatiently.

"Well ... yes, but they have to know that," Emily countered. "So why did they even *start*, back when their brains were presumably *not* addled by necromancy? They had to have realized that necromancy would eventually exterminate the entire human race. But the elves might have given them the idea *knowing* that the human race would either have to abandon necromancy or destroy itself. Either way, they would win."

"An interesting theory," Professor Locke said, finally. "And quite possibly accurate." He leaned back, thoughtfully. "But tell me ... how could we have beaten the elves *without* necromancy?"

Emily knew better than to continue the argument. She simply didn't know enough to make a good case one way or the other. And if necromancy had made the difference between victory or defeat, even the alien-minded Fair Folk of fantasy novels would have hesitated before giving such a weapon to humanity. Unless they believed that humanity would discover it for themselves anyway...she shook her head. That way led madness and a lifetime of raving about conspiracy theories on the internet.

"As I said at the start, history is really nothing more than opinions," Locke said, turning back to the class at large. "Can anyone tell me when the Treaty of Umbria was signed?"

A burly-looking male student put up his hand. "Ninety years ago, Professor. It bound the Allied Lands together into a united force to defend us against necromancers."

"True enough," Locke agreed. "Why didn't the rulers of the Allied Lands unite into a Third Empire?"

Emily could guess at the answer, but left another student to try her luck. "Because the bigger kingdoms intended to dominate the little kingdoms," the student said. "The little kingdoms knew better than to subordinate themselves to the bigger kingdoms, which would have more power in a united empire."

"You mean that your puny kingdom didn't want to commit to the united defense," one of the boys muttered. "Your people have always been cowards ..."

"Stay behind after class ends," Locke said. His ears were sharper than Emily had realized; his tone promised an unpleasant experience for the nationalist. "Believing that other kingdoms are inherently better or worse than your own kingdom is asking for trouble."

The Professor looked back at the first speaker. "Interesting answer, but incomplete." He nodded towards the map. "Anyone else want to try flesh out Gwen's answer?"

Several students exchanged glances, before another girl raised her hand. "The necromancers were already working their way into the castles and palaces where the kings lived, weakening their resolve to fight?"

"Possible, but that wasn't such a concern back in those days, not until after Halers fell," Locke said. He pointed towards the map. "The answer should be obvious."

Emily remembered Alexander the Great, and what had happened after his death in Babylon. His Companions, once his loyal followers, had divided his colossal empire up amongst themselves and tried to create their own dynasties. An empire that had spanned much of the known world had been reduced to a handful of squabbling kingdoms, which had eventually been absorbed by the Roman Empire. They'd moved from globalists to men unable to see beyond their own borders.

"They were all more concerned with their local politics than they were with the entire world," she said slowly. Now she had said it out loud, she was confident that it was the right answer. "They worried more about the kingdom next to them than the expanding necromantic empire, at least until it was too late to nip the necromancers in the bud."

"A good answer," Locke said, "and one that is *barely* enough to save you from the consequences of speaking without holding up your hand."

He looked around the classroom, leaving Emily flushing in embarrassment. "She is quite right," he said, addressing them all. "The necromancers were allowed to become such a problem because no one, not even those who were trained at Whitehall, attempted to do something about it before it was too late. Right now, we have a major problem: we have to hold the line at multiple different points, knowing that if we lose one we may well lose everything."

Emily nodded to herself. It was possible—probable, even—that some parties were evacuating as many people as they could from the big continent, but she knew that they couldn't evacuate them all before it was too late. Could they surrender the large continent and leave the necromancers to die when they ran out of sacrifices? She doubted it; Void had demonstrated that teleportation was possible, which suggested that the necromancers would be able to teleport entire armies right around the world ...

After a long pause, she realized that couldn't be possible on a large scale. Surely, the Allied Lands would have fallen a long time ago if the necromancers could teleport with impunity.

She took another look at the map. It seemed to her that they must survive through a combination of geography and luck, neither of which would apply if the necromancers could teleport.

Emily shook her head, dragging her attention back to the Professor. She just didn't know enough to make an informed guess.

"In theory, this course is not an elective," Locke said, as he returned to his desk and stood in front of it, looking at the students through his spectacles. "A full grasp of history is important for anyone who intends to practice magic as a graduate of Whitehall, rather than a hedge witch or court wizard. You will need to learn history in order to put our local squabbles in perspective—and to understand why it is vitally important that we unite against the necromancers.

"But I know that many of you feel that history is much less important than actually learning magic and control, and I am too old to teach students who don't want to learn. If you would prefer to spend these periods studying something else, you may choose to withdraw from my class and work quietly in the library. Later, should you change your mind, you may attend classes for younger students."

He smiled, rather ruefully. "Over the next few months, we will cover a wide range of topics. The development of magic from the early days until the basic rules were discovered by the great research sorcerers. How and why magic changed the course of history. The origin of the great wars with the elves, goblins, orcs and the other semi-human races. What happened to build the First Empire—and why it was taken by surprise and destroyed in the second great war. The history of magical artifacts, including legends of invincible wands, swords carried only by true kings and even stranger objects from before the dawn of recorded history.

"I will probably be stretching your preconceptions," he added. "You know your kingdom's own version of history, of course, but you will be surprised to see where it jibes and disagrees with that kept by the History Monks. Many of you will prefer to storm out of the class rather than accept that other versions of history exist. Frankly, that's your problem, not mine."

He glanced at his watch. "There's twenty minutes left, but I've said as much as I want to say right now," he concluded. "Should you decide you want to leave history class for the moment, simply don't attend the next class. You will be marked as absent, but there will be no punishment. Your ignorance will be punishment enough."

Emily understood, although she suspected that few others in the class shared her understanding. *She* knew almost nothing about this world, except what she could pick up from her tutors, her roommates and—now that she had permission—the library. It was easy to see that she had to learn as quickly as possible, if only to ensure that she knew what she was talking about in the future. She didn't even have the basics anyone who grew up in the new world would know.

But the others wouldn't understand their own ignorance. How could they? They'd been told the truth—at least the truth as it was officially sanctioned in their kingdoms—long before they'd been accepted at Whitehall. She could easily see why Professor Locke would prefer not to have to teach students who didn't want to be there. He was quite right, really; their ignorance was likely to cost them dearly in the future.

"Class dismissed," Locke said. "I hope to see some of you on Friday."

Emily rose to her feet and headed towards the door, following the other students. They'd have a plan for making the best use of their extra break between classes, perhaps drinking water or juice—or maybe they'd even badger the kitchen staff into giving them snacks. But Emily wasn't so sure what to do. She didn't have any other classes for the rest of the day and the only other thing she could think of to do was to visit the library ... she didn't even know where Imaiqah was, or if *she* was free right now.

Shaking her head, she walked out of the classroom—and right into a group of girls waiting for her. One of them caught her arm and held it tightly. The others surrounded her, preventing any retreat. It was a trap.

"So tell me," the leader purred. "Where do you come from?"

## Chapter Nine

Emily took a long breath to calm herself. It didn't work very well.

School bullies had been bad enough in her own world, but *these* bullies had magic as well as numbers. She could try to fight, yet she barely knew any magic, hardly enough to face people who had been studying for years. What would happen to her if she tried and failed? She could get hurt here. Or worse.

Fear held her rooted to the spot as two of the girls caught hold of her arms and pulled her down the corridor, into a deserted classroom. If anyone else saw her being hauled away, they did nothing.

But that wasn't a surprise, part of her mind noted. Bullies were the same everywhere; people who could have banded together to fight them preferred to stay out of their way, hoping that the bullies wouldn't turn their attention to them. Hell, many preferred to stay on the bullies' good side by joining in the tormenting, rather than standing up for their fellow victims.

She scowled as she saw Alassa, Heir to the Throne of Zangaria, waiting in the classroom. Why was she not surprised?

"Yes," Alassa said. Her voice was sickly-sweet. "Where *do* you come from?"

Emily rapidly considered her options. In hindsight, she should have realized that someone would ask and come up with a story to tell them. But she didn't want to admit to anyone, particularly the school bullies, that she had been kidnapped by a necromancer and marked for sacrifice. The knowledge couldn't do them any good, as far as she could tell, but still ...

"It doesn't matter," she said, cursing her own ignorance. She could claim to come from anywhere on this world, but she didn't know enough to come up with a convincing lie. "I ..."

The grip on her arm tightened alarmingly, halting her train of thought.

"You came here on a dragon," Alassa said. Her eyes bored into Emily's eyes; they were bright blue, but so very cold. "Do you know just how rare it is to even *see* a dragon?"

There was something ominous in her voice, but it took Emily a moment to realize just what it was. Alassa was *jealous*. She might have been the Crown Princess of a country Emily had never heard of until yesterday, yet *she* had never flown on a dragon—and everyone would be talking about Emily, rather than Alassa herself. Teleporting from her country to Whitehall was so...*mundane* compared to flying on a dragon.

"It was a friend of my Mentor," Emily said, finally. Should she mention Void's name? Or would that make the whole situation worse? She had to force herself to swallow hard, fighting down the fear and rage that threatened to overwhelm her. How *dare* Alassa do this to her? "The dragon gave me a lift here ..."

Alassa studied her as if she were a particularly disgusting slug. "Dragons don't show themselves for just *anyone*," she said, sharply. "What *are* you, that you can fly on a dragon?"

The Princess changed tack with astonishing speed. "And what is your social standing?"

Emily considered the question seriously, knowing that even having to *think* about it would make her look odd to Alassa and her cronies. *They* would know where they stood in the social hierarchy at all times. If she recalled correctly, the Crown Princess of just about any country would be socially superior to nearly everyone else. And Alassa wasn't the sort of person to put her birth aside, even when attending Whitehall. The Grandmaster's warnings about allowing nationalism to disrupt the school had probably fallen on deaf ears.

It was possible, Emily told herself, that she could claim a high social position for herself, but once again her own ignorance made it impossible to tell a convincing lie. Alassa, just like anyone else who considered birth more important than achievement, would know every royal and aristocratic family of importance in the Allied Lands. And she couldn't claim to be an aristocrat from another world without admitting that she *came* from another world.

Imaiqah had said that her father was a tradesman, Emily remembered. "My father is a scholar and a gentleman," she said, and prayed inwardly that Alassa wouldn't ask too many questions. Emily had heard that scholars were considered minor nobility in some societies, although she had no way of knowing if that was true of this world. It should be, she told herself firmly. The scholars in this world would have access to magic. "Does that answer your question?"

"I don't believe you," Alassa said flatly. Her bright eyes sharpened as she stepped closer, until her nose was almost brushing against Emily's face. "What sort of scholar's daughter would ride on a dragon?"

Up close, there was something oddly *wrong* about the bully's face. Emily studied her, trying to keep her fear under control, trying to understand why she felt repulsed. A shiver ran down her spine as she finally realized that Alassa was *too* perfect. Her face was utterly flawless, completely unblemished ... and perfectly symmetrical. But why should *that* have been a surprise? Someone as vain as Alassa would use magic to improve her appearance, even if she'd ended up making herself look too good to be true. And while it was impossible to tell under the shapeless robes they all wore, Emily would have bet good money that her body was as perfect–and as strangely *wrong* - as her face.

*Magic,* she thought, sourly. There had been a girl at her old school who had badgered her parents into paying for plastic surgery. Alassa probably had access to cosmetic sorcerers who could cast spells to shape her face into a vision of female beauty; hell, weren't Princesses *supposed* to be beautiful? Her parents probably intended to marry her off to improve their own social position, or strengthen their kingdom. Emily would have felt sorry for Alassa if she hadn't been such a bully.

"So tell me," Alassa said, lifting one finger and holding it up in front of Emily's face. "Where *do* you come from?"

Emily shook her head, bracing herself for a beating–or worse.

But Alassa merely smiled.

"I see by your face that you are of low birth," she said, her tone twisting into one of wry amusement. "Come! It is nothing to be ashamed of, being born amid the mud and squalor. Serving your betters is your natural function. Come be my friend."

Her mockery dug into Emily's composure. She'd grown up in a democratic society, where even the most arrogant of politicians knew better than to risk raising the ire of too many voters. She'd never really understood what it must be like to be born in a society where birth determined social standing. Alassa seemed so completely comfortable with the idea that inferiors served superiors because she had never had to question it. Her kingdom's peasants and tradesmen existed to obey the orders of her family.

Come be her friend? Emily looked at Alassa and knew what that meant. She'd be nothing more than a crony, singing the praises of Princess Alassa and encouraging her to bully other students–and always fearful that Alassa would turn on her. Or she would be expected to do the Princess's homework for her, or whatever other humiliating tasks Alassa wanted her to do. Being friends with someone like Alassa was like being trapped near a lion, throwing other victims into the beast's mouth in the hopes that it would eat you last. A lion would probably be more honest than someone with more royal blood than sense.

"Thank you, but no," Emily said. Alassa wanted her to crawl–of that, there was no doubt–but Emily had enough pride to refuse to bend. Besides, Emily had nearly been killed by a necromancer the day she'd arrived in this world. Alassa was nothing more than a bully–and a bully was nothing compared to a necromancer. "Now, if you will excuse me..."

The girls holding her didn't let up as Alassa's face turned an alarming shade of red. "You dare refuse me? You dare ... !"

Emily felt another hot flash of rage as she started to struggle. Alassa's hand was touching her wand; magic was starting to shimmer around her, as if she were about to cast a spell. But her cronies were holding Emily too tightly for her to escape ...

But something didn't quite add up. Someone like Alassa would have no qualms about squashing a low-born girl, just as she'd bullied Imaiqah in the past. So why was she even *trying* to turn Emily into an ally?

The answer, when it came, struck with the force of a physical blow. Emily had arrived on a dragon, which suggested that she was *important*–and someone who took birth and social standing too seriously would wonder if Emily was actually more important than her. Or if Emily was the sort of person she ought to convince to join her. Professor Locke had pointed out that the Allied Lands were disunited. Emily suspected that Alassa–and others like her–were a large part of the reason *why* the Allied Lands were unable to unite against a common foe.

Alassa was *scared* of her, Emily realized. The only person Emily knew who had been able to summon a dragon, let alone convince it to give a new student a flight to Whitehall, had been an immensely powerful sorcerer, Void. Alassa had to wonder if Emily was more powerful than her, perhaps even powerful enough to trump her royal birth. No wonder she'd brought so many cronies to the confrontation. If Emily had enough power and skill to beat her, Alassa would have to have her friends to back her up.

"Yes," Emily said, before she could think better of it. "I dare."

The sense of magic grew stronger as Alassa lifted her wand, threateningly. "Crawl," she ordered. The girls holding Emily loosened their grip as Alassa's voice became a croon. "Crawl for me; lick my boots, beg my forgiveness..."

"No," Emily said flatly. She pulled her hands free, bracing herself. How had that protective spell gone again? Panic was making it harder to think properly. "Let me go!"

Alassa moved her wand and a spell shimmered into existence. It sparkled menacingly in front of Emily, just before she managed to perform the counter-charm. Alassa didn't look surprised when the spell dispelled back into nothingness; instead, she lifted her wand again and began a second spell. Emily lunged forward and grabbed at the wand, pulling it away from the bully. Magic spun into existence around them both, sparkling with deadly potential.

And then there was a brilliant flash of light and Emily was thrown bodily across the room into the wall. She gasped in pain as she banged her shoulder against the stone, collapsing to the floor. The cronies laughed, hesitantly. They had to wonder if Alassa had *really* meant for that to happen.

"You touched my *wand*! Alassa snapped, her face red with answer. "You..."

She cast a second spell before Emily could move. This time, Emily was unable to dispel it before it struck her body. She could *feel* it crawling over her, working Alassa's will, even though she couldn't tell what it was doing. Surely Alassa couldn't turn her into a frog, or a slug, or something unable to move and talk. Surely ...

"Come," Alassa snapped. It took Emily a moment to realize that she was talking to her cronies. "Enjoy yourself, *peasant*!"

She watched them go from where she was lying on the floor, allowing them to close the door before she tried to stand up. Almost immediately, her legs jerked of their own accord and she fell back to the ground. Her lower body twitched constantly as the spell wove its way into the magic field surrounding her, making it impossible for her to do more than crawl. She tried to stand up again, holding one of the tables in the hopes that it would wear off quickly, but the sensation spread into her arms and she found herself falling back again.

Emily realized in horror that Alassa's spell would keep her down until the bullies returned, or until someone tried to use the classroom for lessons. It was impossible to stand up, let alone walk, as long as her legs kept jerking of their own accord.

*You've been hexed, you idiot*, Emily thought sharply. She *felt* the spell pressing in around her, constantly sparking with magic as she tried to move. *And you know how to dispel hexes.*

She concentrated, trying to cast the spell that Mistress Irene had taught her. The first time, she failed, feeling the strength draining out of her as she lay on the ground. Hot tears of humiliation and rage stung her cheeks. Angrily, she tried to climb to her feet, only to be knocked down once again. Alassa's spell seemed to be growing stronger, making it impossible to crawl further than a few feet; in some ways, being turned into an inanimate object would be less embarrassing. Her body could no longer be trusted.

Angry thoughts burned through her mind. *And you're going to stay on the ground and take it?* It was a bitter pill to swallow, but in truth she'd never seriously considered trying to convince Void–or anyone else–to send her home. Life in a magical world had seemed more attractive than anything waiting for her in the cold sterile world that had given her birth, but now she wasn't so sure. All she knew was that she had to get up and fight the bullies, or they would win ...

Frustrated, she tried to cast the counter-spell again, and again, but she failed both times. However, casting the spell the second time allowed her to sense how Alassa's spell had blurred into the magic field. Naturally, the bully had mastered a spell intended to be more humiliating than harmful–and improved it to the point where it wasn't so easy to dispel. Emily closed her eyes and reached out with her mind, trying to remember the sensation of touching spells from her first lessons, six hours ago. The spell glittered in her mind's eye, a spinning construction of magic words put together to create something far greater than the sum of its parts. And yet she could see the spell's construction clearly now.

Carefully, she cast the counter-spell one final time, concentrating on the weak points in Alassa's hex. There was a brief moment when she thought that she had failed again, but then, thankfully, the hex simply snapped out of existence.

Emily lay on the floor for a long moment, feeling her heart thumping inside her chest. Them, somehow, she pulled herself to her feet. Her legs still felt wobbly, but at least the unnatural twitching was gone. She staggered over to a chair and collapsed into it, feeling sweat trickling down her back as her head collapsed onto the desk. Happiness and relief warred with fear in her mind. Alassa and her cronies could have beaten Emily half to death while she'd been affected by the spell and she wouldn't have been able to fight them off.

She was exhausted, but her mind refused to rest. She'd thought she'd understood the dangers, yet she hadn't, not really. The Grandmaster wouldn't have issued a warning against nationalism if it hadn't been a major problem–and someone like Alassa would have plenty of enemies from other kingdoms, people who considered themselves to be her social equals, or superiors. Back home, the most popular girls and boys had always had followers, cliques that hoped some of their glamour and popularity would rub off on them. Here, where birth was important ... there had to be more than one major group of bullies, if only because others would need to form gangs of their own merely to survive. And *she* was alone, defenseless. No one would come to her aid. The bullies could do whatever they liked to her.

And then there was Shadye, of course. *He* wanted to kill her.

*You'll have to learn faster,* she thought bitterly. Alassa had beaten her through superior magic skill; Emily would have to learn to beat her, whatever it took. Mistress Irene had unlocked Emily's magic. Now, Emily would have to learn on her own.

There was a library, she'd been told. Surely it would have books that would teach her how to defend herself. Surely...

The door opened and Emily looked up in alarm. If the bullies had come back - no, it was a middle-aged tutor, peering at Emily in some surprise. She looked rather like an older version of Emily's mother, with black hair tied in a bun and a permanently grim expression. The robe she wore was yellow and black, reminding Emily of bees and wasps. Emily had to fight to keep the amusement off her face.

"Is there a reason," the tutor demanded, "why you're in my classroom?"

Emily hesitated. She could tell the truth, but that would be tattling. It wouldn't solve anything in the long run, not really. Besides, Alassa had been at the school for months, perhaps years, and the tutors hadn't yet slapped her down. They might have found it diplomatically impossible to punish a royal princess. For all Emily knew, Alassa had grown up in a kingdom that insisted royal children had to have whipping children, boys and girls from poor families who were whipped whenever their royal charges misbehaved.

"I needed to sit down," she said finally. "I ..."

"You have a bedroom for resting," the tutor snapped, interrupting Emily. She walked over to her desk and produced a box of mirrors. "Seeing as you wish to be here, you can place one of these mirrors on each of the desks. Or you can report to the Hall of Shame for detention."

Emily stood up and took the box. The mirrors were small, barely larger than her hand, yet the moment her fingers touched them she felt a flicker of magic. Looking at her reflection, she nearly jumped out of her skin when her reflection winked at her. A moment later, the image shifted, revealing a dark-skinned woman with deep black eyes.

"Put them on the tables," the tutor ordered impatiently. "Class starts in seven minutes."

Emily flushed. Alassa had intended to humiliate her in front of an entire class of students . If Whitehall was anything like the other schools she'd known, word would have been all over the school in an hour. Everyone would have heard about the new girl who'd arrived on a dragon; they'd hear about how she'd been hexed and waited helplessly until someone arrived to help. But she'd freed herself ...

Shaking her head, she passed out the mirrors, refusing to look into them again. Instead, she passed the box back to the tutor and made her escape into the corridors, heading back to her bedroom. Her head was spinning and she definitely needed to lie down before she went to the library.

## Chapter Ten

"I'M SORRY ABOUT HER," IMAIQAH SAID, TWENTY MINUTES LATER. SHE'D BEEN IN THE BEDroom when Emily had entered and thrown herself down on the bed. "She's a..."

Imaiqah shrugged helplessly, unable to find a suitable word.

Emily smiled, despite the exhaustion crippling her body. "A right royal pain in the bum?"

Imaiqah flushed. "Yes," she agreed finally. "She hasn't managed to test out of half of the basic classes and she's *still* a pain."

Imaiqah had asked Emily what had happened and Emily had told her, although she wasn't entirely sure why she'd told her friend everything. Part of her wanted to keep it to herself.

"Oh," Emily said. A moment later, she realized what Imaiqah had said. "Test out of the basic classes?"

"Everyone has different levels of power and skill," Imaiqah pointed out, as if it was the most normal thing in the world. The teachers Emily had known back home wouldn't have admitted that out loud, even if they'd had to come up with complex explanations for why something that was so evidently true was actually false. "You must have noticed that some of the students in your first class were much older than you."

Emily nodded, slowly. She'd assumed, when she'd thought about it, that Professor Locke's warning about the perils of missing history had eventually convinced older students to return to his class. But it did make sense; why should a genius student from the first year remain in a basic class if they could work at a much higher level?

Her head swam again and she started to retch, then cough. The world began to fade out around her ...

"Eat this," Imaiqah ordered. She was suddenly much closer–had Emily blanked out for a long moment? "You pushed yourself too far."

Emily took the food–it looked like fudge to her–and tasted it, before taking a bite and swallowing it as quickly as possible. There was a sudden surge of energy running through her body, one so powerful that she realized just how far she'd pushed herself–and just how worn she'd been afterwards. She should have gone straight to the kitchens to eat after freeing herself from the hex.

"Keep eating," Imaiqah said. She passed Emily two more packets of food, which Emily devoured greedily. "And relax!"

She cleared her throat, and then returned to the original subject. "The basic classes teach the basics. You have to master them to proceed to the more advanced classes, and then–if you want–to follow a specialist path. If you don't master the basics, you have to stay and repeat the class time and time again until you get it right."

"I see," Emily said. A thought struck her. "So I could move ahead to an advanced class now, without taking the basic class?"

"If you could pass the tests," Imaiqah said. She looked up, her eyes wide. "*Could* you pass the tests?"

"Probably not," Emily admitted. She shook her head, wondering how Imaiqah had managed to remain so sane, stuck in a school where she was very much a social outcast. "I'll just have to learn as quickly as possible."

Imaiqah nodded. "There's a rumor going around that you're a Child of Destiny," she said. "Even *I* heard the rumor. Is that true?"

Emily froze. She thought hard. A dragon ... and now a rumor that she was a Child of Destiny. No *wonder* Alassa had been so interested in her, even though she hadn't mentioned that particular issue to Emily when she'd been trying to bully her into her clique. Alassa's parents would probably trade half of their kingdom for a real Child of Destiny who was willing to work for them. They might even have put pressure on Alassa to try to make friends with Emily.

"Not really," Emily said, finally. She doubted that the literal truth would amuse anyone, least of all Alassa. Absently, she wondered just how much trouble she would have found for herself if her father had been named Fate. "I'm just a normal student -"

"- Who arrived on a dragon," Imaiqah finished, with a grin. "Do you realize just how many social queens you embarrassed just by arriving on a dragon?"

Emily flushed. It hadn't been *her* who'd summoned the dragon, let alone enrolled at Whitehall; indeed, she hardly seemed to do anything. She hadn't chosen her parents, or to be kidnapped by Shadye - and Void had pushed her into attending the school rather than teaching her himself. Her status as a semi-Child of Destiny came from birth, rather than actually achieving it for herself. Alassa gloried in the accident of birth that had made her a Royal Princess; Emily found it rather irritating. Perhaps, if Alassa had been fawned upon from the day of her birth, it explained her vast sense of entitlement. Or perhaps she was just a silly girl with more magic than sense.

"I didn't mean to do anything of the sort," she mumbled. Who was spreading the rumors in the first place? Void? Or the Grandmaster? But why would they tell the students that one of their number was a Child of Destiny? The necromancers wouldn't be the only adults who might want a Child of Destiny dead before she came into her own. "I'll try and come on foot next year."

Imaiqah giggled. "I came in a coach. It was the first time I'd ever left my home."

Emily settled back and started to ask questions, trying to learn as much as she could about her new friend. Imaiqah freely admitted that she'd been born in Zangaria, which was–Emily guessed–at least partly why Alassa thought that she could push Imaiqah into doing her homework and other services. Her father had been a reasonably successful merchant with five children, enough that he'd been happy to allow Imaiqah to go to Whitehall when a travelling magician spotted her talent and offered her a scholarship. The description of life as a merchant's daughter didn't sound appealing, although Emily suspected that Imaiqah's family were far more prosperous than the peasants in the kingdom. As far as she could tell, Zangaria was a near-absolute monarchy. That didn't bode well for the Kingdom's future, or for Imaiqah herself.

The door banged open and Aloha marched in, followed by two of her friends. One of them, Emily was surprised to see, was a teenage boy with an oddly freakish body, as if he'd tried to force himself to grow up faster and bungled the spell. His arms and legs were the size of a mature man, while his chest was still small and ill-proportioned. The other was a girl with hair so black that it seemed to absorb light, carrying a small cat in her arms. Emily was charmed until she saw the cat's eyes. They were glowing with an eerie green light.

"You two - get out, now," Aloha ordered. "Go play in the common room or something."

Emily opened her mouth to protest, but Imaiqah caught her arm and tugged her out of the room before she could say a word. "She's in charge of the room," Imaiqah explained, as soon as they were outside the door. "She can order us out if she likes."

"Huh," Emily said. Alassa had been bad enough. This ... frustration burned through her mind, making it hard to think clearly. Humiliation warred with rage in her soul. Was everyone in the school a self-obsessed fool with magic to burn? "What gives her the right to do that?"

"She's senior to us," Imaiqah explained simply. "Where do you want to go?"

"The library," Emily said. It was where she had meant to go before she'd become sidetracked talking to Imaiqah. "I want to see it for myself."

"You should get something to eat first, something *proper*," Imaiqah warned. "Those sugar bars don't last very long."

"And let Alassa have a chance to take another shot at us?" Emily asked. "We'd better go to the library first."

The amulet glowed as they walked out of the sleeping compartment and into the main corridors. Emily allowed the light to guide them while she stared at the students thronging about. They still seemed to be busy, even though classes had officially ended for the day. But then, there was homework for some of the classes and probably activities that were carried out after regular hours. No doubt there were clubs and other such arrangements for students who might have gotten into mischief if they were left alone for too long.

A male student looked up and caught her eye, his stare boring into her skull. Uncomfortable with male attention, Emily looked away. Thankfully, he didn't appear to want to follow them. She breathed a silent sigh of relief and forced herself to relax. This wasn't Earth and those she feared were countless worlds away.

She could *feel* the building reconfiguring itself as they entered a new corridor, walking down towards a simple stone door at the far end. It slid open as they approached, revealing a massive room utterly crammed with bookshelves and books. Some of the books were chained to the shelves, with a handful of students standing and flicking through them, making notes on sheets of parchment. This world probably hadn't invented the printing press: Emily wondered if she could deduce how to make one. It would reshape this world.

"Ah, the lady who came on a dragon," a voice said. Emily turned to see a tall bald man, inhumanly thin, standing behind a desk. "We shall be expecting great things from you, young lady."

"Thank you," Emily said, flushing. Odd waves of magic seemed to shimmer just inside the library. "I ..."

Her voice tailed off as she realized that she didn't have the faintest idea what to say next.

"Every book we have on dragons has been signed out," the librarian informed her. "I haven't seen so many books taken out since Professor Novus insisted that everyone read his autobiography before attending his classes. Those who actually wanted to attend his classes, that was. I think that most of them changed their minds after ploughing their way through the first two chapters."

His gaze sharpened. "Books that rest freely on the shelves can be taken out for a week," he added, in tones that suggested that he gave the same lecture to every student who entered his domain. "You may take out a maximum of six books at any time, although they must be returned at once upon demand. Books chained to the shelves may be consulted, but not borrowed without a signed permission slip from the Grandmaster. Books in the restricted section may only be consulted with a signed permission slip from a senior tutor. Talking too loudly, fighting, or attempting to remove books from the library without signing them out will result in an hour's petrification."

Emily blinked. "What?"

Imaiqah pointed a finger behind her.

Emily turned around and saw five statues standing there, all composed of grainy grey stone. She shivered as she realized that the statues were simply *too* perfect to be anything, but humans turned briefly into stone. As punishments went, it was terrifying. Were the victims aware of their own immobility inside their stony prisons? Could they still think, even as they waited helplessly for the spell to wear off?

"This is a library, not a place to pick fights," the librarian said. "I suggest that you bear it in mind at all times."

Emily nodded tightly and walked away from the desk, then headed towards the bookshelves.

Imaiqah and Emily passed through a second line of magic - a ward, she guessed–and silence fell immediately. Hardly any of the other students were talking; none of the talkers were speaking in anything above a whisper, even the ones who were poring over textbooks and trying to complete their homework. Having seen the statues, Emily could understand a certain reluctance to speak too loudly. She didn't want to know what it felt like to be stone from the inside–and she was sure that none of the other students did either.

As a young child in school, she'd spent a term working as a volunteer in the library. She'd picked up enough to know that she didn't want to spend the rest of her life as a librarian, although she'd had the impression that it wouldn't be a bad job if she'd been allowed to bar all readers from her library. The system governing Whitehall's library, however, seemed far more complex than the Dewey Decimal System she'd had to learn as a child. If indeed there *was* a system. None of the books seemed to be in any kind of order.

Imaiqah leaned close to her, close enough to whisper in her ear. "What are you looking for?"

Emily wasn't sure herself. Half of the books didn't have a title on the spine; half of the ones that did have a displayed title were so badly blurred that she couldn't tell if it was simply the age of the manuscripts, or if some other magic was refusing to allow her to read them. For all she knew, Mistress Irene's translation spell might not be working either. And those that were readable often didn't make sense. *Blood and Guts and Magic. Charms for the Charming. Basic Mist and Misting. Madame Goatherd's Basic Guide to Animal Magic. The Prisoner of Magic ...*

"Self-defense spells," Emily whispered back, finally. She didn't dare speak any louder. "Something I–we–can use against Alassa."

Imaiqah stared at her. "But ..."

"But nothing," Emily whispered. She could understand why Imaiqah might not want to go looking for a fight–Alassa's family literally ruled her country–but a fight might find Imaiqah anyway, whatever she did to avoid it. "We need to learn how to defend ourselves."

Imaiqah nodded reluctantly and led her towards a different set of bookshelves. A number of books were clearly missing–there were gaps in the shelves–and the remainder were very well thumbed, suggesting that every student in Whitehall studied them from time to time. Picking up one of the unmarked books, Emily opened it and saw the title, *Basic Charms for Imbeciles*. She had to fight down a laugh, remembering the "whatever for dummies" books from back home, before turning to the next page. The first charm was one she already knew–the counter-charm that Mistress Irene had taught her–but the second was something new, designed to repel insects from the caster's vicinity. Emily wondered, looking at the diagram, if the spell couldn't be altered to sic insects on an unsuspecting victim.

There was no contents page or index, forcing her to thumb through it to look for interesting and useful spells. Some seemed completely pointless, unless she intended to take up hierology for a career, others appeared to be more adapted for domestic work than fighting enemies. She leaned over to ask Imaiqah if she could see any books that might be more practical. Imaiqah hesitated, then passed her another well-thumbed volume. The title, *Practical Jokes*, made Emily feel doubtful until she opened it to a random page and saw a spell for making an unwitting victim speak only in rhyme. She checked a second page and discovered a hex that caused its victim to lose control of their bladder. *That* was a terrifying thought.

"Pity it isn't written in fake Latin," she muttered to herself. Imaiqah shot her an enquiring look. "Never mind."

The next book she discovered that interested her was entitled *A Fence Against Magic* and appeared to concentrate on defensive spells. Again, she knew the first one already from Mistress Irene, but the others were more complex and powerful, allowing the caster to shield herself or place defenses in a room or even an entire building. The more powerful spells seemed hideously complex, too much for her to cast at once. Indeed, one of them involved so many elements that she wondered if *anyone* could cast it properly.

"You might want this one," Imaiqah whispered, passing her a fourth volume. It focused on countering other magic, ranging from simple hexes to outright dark magic. Emily opened it and saw an illustration that made her feel sick. The picture—a man warped into a monster by black magic—was horrifying. Back home, no one would have allowed such an illustration into a school library.

She'd thought that Alassa's hex was bad, but it was nothing more than a practical joke compared to outright dark magic.

"Or this one ..." Imaiqah suggested.

The fifth book was an overview of the Allied Lands, written by a historian who called himself a History Monk. Professor Locke had mentioned them, although Emily couldn't quite remember what he'd said. Something about them being the only ones who recorded history without the nationalist bias? Absently, she flicked to the chapter covering Zangaria and skimmed the first section. She'd been right; Alassa's father was the absolute monarch of his country, but the Barons seemed to keep a tight grasp of their own powers. The writer noted that the failure to share power with anyone else, even the growing middle class of tradesmen, was likely to cause problems in the future, particularly when the next monarch took the throne. Emily didn't doubt it for a second.

She picked up a sixth book on different magical types and then glanced around at the other shelves, finally stopping to peer at a solid metal gate that led into another room. The sense of protective magic surrounding the gate was almost overwhelming, as if the spells were alive and constantly searching for possible intruders. She didn't need Imaiqah to tell her that it was the restricted section. Two students, both older boys, were standing inside the room, reading chained books. Emily hoped that they weren't secretly planning to become necromancers.

Picking up all six books, she started to walk towards the desk.

Then she saw Alassa sitting at a desk, reading a book. The princess was alone; her cronies nowhere to be seen; Emily blinked in surprise before she realized that Alassa probably needed to study alone if she wanted to pass her basic classes. It was odd—surely her family could have afforded a tutor for their royal daughter—but maybe Alassa was just lazy. Considering the spells Mistress Irene had taught her, Emily suspected that someone could learn a great deal of magic simply by memorizing spells, *without* ever grasping the underlying principles that allowed them to work, which might be Alassa's problem. That would account for the fact that Alassa knew how to hex someone, yet be unable to graduate.

The bully looked up and glowered at Emily.

Quickly, before she could think better of it, Emily made a rude face at Alassa. The bully opened her mouth to deliver a scathing retort, but she only got two words out before there was a flash of light. Alassa's entire body turned to stone. A moment later, the newly-made statue lifted up into the air and drifted towards the front of the room, where it was dumped among the other statues. Emily had to fight down the urge to giggle, if only out of fear of ending up with a stony personality herself, and winked at Imaiqah. Her friend was staring back at her with a mixture of horror and awe.

Emily passed the books to the librarian and had them stamped out to her, before glancing over at the statue Alassa had become. It had seemed funny–it had *been* funny –but at the same time it was horrifying. There would be no permanent damage from the spell, she told herself firmly, yet did even the spoilt princess deserve to spend an hour as a statue? Who knew *what* it would do to her personality?

"I can't believe you did that," Imaiqah said, once they were outside the library. "Don't you know what she will do to us?"

Truthfully, the thought hadn't crossed Emily's mind. "The worst thing you can do with a person like that is let them walk all over you," she said simply. She held up one of the books meaningfully. "We'd better start studying quickly."

## Chapter Eleven

"But why can't I go on to advanced class?" a familiar voice protested as Emily reached Professor Lombardi's office door. She paused outside to listen. "I've taken your class three times already!"

"You can't go on because I have caught you cheating *five* times already," a male voice said. The speaker was clearly on the verge of losing his temper. "The purpose of Basic Charms, Alassa, is to demonstrate that you understand the building blocks of spells before you move on to a more advanced class. While you have memorized countless advanced spells, you haven't actually mastered the underlying principles at all."

"But ... but I can do the spells," Alassa protested. She sounded as if she were pleading for her life, rather than just a chance to move ahead. Emily leaned against the wall out of sight and listened carefully as Alassa went on. "But ... "

"But you don't know what you're doing," the speaker–Professor Lombardi, Emily guessed–interrupted. "Until you understand the basic principles, young lady, you will learn nothing from the advanced class. All you will do is waste my time." He cleared his throat in a manner that cut off a renewed bleating from Alassa. "I suggest that you sit down in class this afternoon and actually concentrate on learning something. You can retake the test in a month if you feel confident ..."

Alassa rudely interrupted him. "But my parents..."

"Would not be happy if their daughter was so incapable as to allow even a weaker mage to hack through the weaknesses in her spells and overwhelm her," Professor Lombardi snapped. "You can report to the Hall of Shame at sixteen bells." There was a gasp from Alassa. "Now, get out of my office and don't bother me again until you've decided to study."

Emily slipped backwards as Alassa stormed out of the Professor's office and down the corridor, muttering to herself in a language that Shadye's spell refused to translate. The princess didn't *look* happy at all.

After she was gone, Emily hesitated, then stepped into the doorway, tapping on the opened door.

Professor Lombardi looked up at her. He nodded, thoughtfully.

"Take a seat," he said, returning his attention to his desk.

Emily nodded, taking advantage of the delay to study the Professor. He was a short man, with lightly-tanned skin and a bushy afro hairstyle that seemed to move of its own accord. It also seemed to change color, although she was honestly not sure if it was magic or if she was merely imagining it. His fingers, long and thin, shaped gestures and invocations of their own accord, as if he were constantly casting spells. She couldn't help noticing that his right arm had a rather nasty scar.

His desk was completely empty and the walls of his office were bare, apart from a single painting of a cute blonde witch hanging behind his chair. And yet Emily could sense magic flickering through the room, focused on Lombardi himself. He'd cast countless protective charms into the air to safeguard his possessions, or to protect his students as they came into their magic.

The Professor wrote out a short note on a piece of parchment that vanished as soon as he had signed it, then looked back at Emily. "The Grandmaster informs me that you are from another world."

"Yes, sir," Emily said.

"And Mistress Irene has already taught you a handful of basic spells," Professor Lombardi continued. "And a full-fledged sorcerer says that you have *potential*."

His eyes narrowed, suddenly. "Whitehall is about developing magical potential. Charms is one course you cannot afford to flunk. If you fail to master the building blocks of magic, you will be forever crippled as a magician and never advance to become a sorceress in your own right. I advise you to bear that in mind at all times."

Emily nodded, then asked a question that had been puzzling her ever since she'd entered Whitehall. "When do I get my wand?"

Lombardi eyed her in some surprise. "A wand serves as a focusing tool for a practicing magician," he said. "A sorcerer needs to learn to cast spells *without* a focusing tool of any kind. You would be well advised never to use a wand unless you wish to become dependent upon it."

Emily frowned. *Alassa* used a wand...did that mean that she couldn't perform spells without waving it in the air? Or did she simply need to use it until she mastered casting spells in her own mind? Emily made a mental note to try to remove Alassa's wand and then see how well she performed without it.

"I've seen some people using wands," she said, careful not to mention Alassa's name. "Why would they use them if they were useless?"

Lombardi gave her a hard look. "There are certain forms of spell work that can be made easier by using a wand. It is also possible—as you already know—to embed spells in wands for later activation. And there are wands that have come to us out of legend and have been passed from master to master, learning more and more from each owner ... but it is unwise to depend too much upon them. There's no such thing as an invincible wand."

He peered into Emily's eyes. "Do *not* try to use one until you have your magic firmly under control," he added. "You run the risk of crippling your development."

*Like the Royal Brat*, Emily thought.

The Professor stood up. "You have already memorized some spells. What you are going to do now is see how they go together"—he eyed her for a moment—"if you haven't already mastered that technique. You have *potential*, do you not?"

Emily flushed. Everywhere she went, it seemed as if people paid attention to her—and never for anything she'd done on her own. Shadye had believed her to be a Child of Destiny, Void had said that she had potential—and sent her to school riding a dragon. Were all the teachers at Whitehall expecting her to be an instant super-magician? Or were they just setting her up to fail?

Lombardi cast a simple spell into the air, which created a glowing ball of light, and then followed up with the analysis charm Mistress Irene had tried to teach

Emily. The first spell's components flickered to life in front of them, four separate components in all. Lombardi pointed to each of them in turn and started to explain what they did.

"The first section–the startpoint - informs the magic that you're crafting a spell," Lombardi said. "Most magicians in training will train themselves to ensure that they cannot use magic without a specific starting impetus and then leave that part of the spell out while they're parsing the rest of the spell. As always, you need to charge magic words with *mana* to actually make them work; mastering the act of devising words without accidentally triggering them is the first step towards mastering charms.

"The second section sets the first set of parameters for a spell. In this case light, no heat, not particularly large ... leaving any of those variables to random chance can produce surprising or unpleasant results. I've seen young magicians burn themselves severely because they forget that they have to ensure there isn't any heat, or blind themselves because they make the light too bright. It is far too easy to forget about setting the parameters once you become used to casting a spell all at once."

Emily nodded, understanding Alassa's frustration with Basic Charms. It was the difference, she decided, between using a computer program someone had designed for the world and one you had built for yourself. The former might be convenient, but the latter would be far more flexible. In fact, continuing the analogy, if someone managed to figure out how to hack into and defeat a publicly-available charm, he or she might be able to do the same thing to everyone who used that charm. But a charm created by a single magician for her own use would be much harder to break.

"The third section," Lombardi continued, giving Emily a long look when she said nothing, "is the second set of parameters; specifically, time and key. Time determines just how long the spell remains in existence before fading away; key specifies just how the spell may be unlocked–and by whom. *This* spell, as you will notice, can be dispelled by anyone. A more complex spell might be keyed to a specific user. It doesn't make it *completely* impossible for another magician to crack, but it can make it incredibly difficult."

His voice sharpened. "I must warn you that creating a locked spell can, in certain circumstances, be grounds for immediate expulsion from Whitehall. Two years ago, a student was expelled for using a locked spell to turn his worst enemy into a pig, then refusing to undo it. It took two trained sorcerers to undo the spell he'd created." He shrugged. "Pity, really. That young man had potential."

Emily gulped. "What happened to him?"

"Good question," Lombardi said. "I'll let you know if we ever find out the answer."

Emily opened her mouth, but then realized that it might not be a wise subject to discuss, at least not yet. Instead, she considered what she'd just been told. She'd wondered why Alassa and others like her were allowed to bully at will, but now it seemed that there *were* limits, ones harshly enforced by the staff. No *permanent* harm, the Grandmaster had stipulated. As a way to encourage learning among students, it was hard to see how it could be beaten.

But Alassa had a gang of cronies...how could one magician beat them all?

*Through knowledge*, she thought, and looked back at the professor.

"The final section of this spell is the endpoint," Lombardi concluded. "It locks the spell structure firmly in place, preventing it from mutating out of control and becoming something very different from what you might have intended. Spells can shift very rapidly when *mana* is pouring through them, even if you set the variables with extreme care. *This* spell might well start to generate heat if it was allowed to mutate, or interact with other spells in the general area. Unlike the startpoint, the endpoint does nothing on its own, so don't forget to place it at the end of any spell, even if you don't intend to charge it with *mana*. Accidents happen, particularly when young magicians are involved."

He paused, significantly. "Did you understand all that?"

Emily hesitated, and then nodded slowly. A computer geek would probably become the most powerful–or at least capable–magician in existence, if he were transported from Earth to her new home, but she knew enough to at least concentrate on the basic principles. Besides, Alassa would want revenge for Emily's trick in the library. She'd just have to keep studying as hard as possible.

"Good," Lombardi said. He grinned, evilly. "Because we're now going to start practicing writing out spells."

He opened a drawer and produced a sheet of parchments and an odd-looking pencil. It took Emily a moment to realize that it had been hand-carved, rather than looking like the mass-produced pencils she was used to from back home.

She took the strange pencil when it was passed to her and examined it thoughtfully. Judging from the marks, it had been sharpened with a knife rather than a pencil sharpener. Making a mental note to import proper pens and pencils if she ever managed to open up a permanent link to Earth, she took the parchment and wrote her name on the top of the page.

Lombardi chuckled, then produced a sheet of paper for himself, with a list of different spell components. He ran his eye down it before passing the sheet to Emily. She studied it, feeling something nagging at the back of her mind. It wasn't until she skimmed through the third component that she realized what it was.

"These components are complete spells in their own right," she said, aloud. Or were they? None of them had a startpoint, *or* an endpoint. "You can string several different spells into one large spell ..."

"That's the advanced class," Lombardi said, seriously. "But seeing that students can't resist experimenting, make sure you test each strand of the spell carefully before you try to activate the entire chain of spells. A single mistake when so many components are strung together can cause rapid mutation, followed by either collapse or disaster. Most magical accidents are caused when some idiot didn't check his work carefully before proceeding."

Emily nodded, thinking back to webpage design. It was easy enough to take something–from a JPEG picture to an embedded video or game–and insert it into a webpage, but the webpage designer wouldn't actually have designed the component himself. Picking the wrong spell to insert into a combined spell could be disastrous if they didn't go well together, just like the wrong piece of embedded programming could cause a webpage to crash, or simply refuse to display properly.

"You'll note that they have nothing to say as to where they start or end," the Professor pointed out. "Adding a second startpoint would almost certainly cause the combined spell to separate into two different components, which would promptly start working against one another. I'll demonstrate that in class later for you and your classmates. An endpoint would bring the combined spell to a screeching halt at that point, leaving the rest of the spell inactive—or doing something you don't want it to do. Could be harmless, could be disastrous; again, I'll demonstrate it for you in class."

"And if someone were to bury an endpoint inside a spell, which was then used as a component for someone else's spell, it might wreck all of their work," Emily mused. It seemed absurd to think that anyone would create a combined spell without checking it carefully, but if there had been magical accidents ... well, she'd always thought that there was no shortage of fools in the world. "Can you do that?"

"You're learning," Lombardi said. He tapped the parchment meaningfully. "I want ... let's see. I want you to devise a spell that will pick up the pencil and then move it over to the table in the corner. Take your time; *don't* try to form the spell in your mind. Write it all down on the parchment, step by step."

Emily looked at the list of spell components, trying to see how they all went together. It should have been simple, yet every component had its own sub-components, with their own variables. She felt an odd flash of sympathy for Alassa as she stared at the parchment. Right now, she was doubting her own capabilities too. A single spell ...

... But it *wasn't* a single spell; she had to build it up out of building blocks that were themselves spells.

Taking the pencil in hand, she started to write out what she wanted the spell to do, section by section. The starting point, the first set of variables, the second set of variables ... each of them had to be altered, but once she had a roadmap of the entire spell she could start to put it together. Looking back at the list of components, she wrote out the first two on the parchment.

"Ah," Lombardi said. He'd been watching her like a hawk. "Hold out your hand, palm upwards."

Emily blinked.

"Hold out your hand, palm upwards," Lombardi repeated. "Now, if you please."

She hesitated, and then obeyed. A second later, he snapped a ruler across her palm, causing her to cry out in pain and shock. "It is an extremely bad idea to write a startpoint before you are ready to cast the spell," he said. He didn't sound angry, but Emily still flinched at his tone. She'd been warned, if not very clearly, and she'd done it anyway. The whole thing had been a test to see how closely she was following him. "*Very* bad habit. Try to get rid of it."

Emily glanced at her palm—and the angry red mark where he'd struck her—and felt herself flushing in embarrassment. Angrily, she scored out the starting point and started again, writing out the variables one by one. A third set of variables was required, it seemed; she added it to the spell and checked through it as carefully as she could. Balancing so many variables was hard enough on paper; doing it in her head, she suspected, would be a great deal worse. How had Shadye and Void managed to master their talents without driving themselves crazy?

Or crazier, in Shadye's case.

"Here," she said, finally. Her palm still stung with dull pain. "How does this look?"

Lombardi cast his eyes down it, thoughtfully. "No startpoint," he said dryly. "I would prefer not to have to repeat that point again. How many pencils do you want to lift?"

Emily looked up from where she was rubbing her hand. "Just one. I thought..."

"There's more than one pencil in this room," Lombardi interrupted. "Next time, specify that you only want *one* pencil to be affected. Depending on how much *mana* you pump into the spell, you could accidentally cause havoc in the classroom."

"... Because every pencil would be affected," Emily said, thoughtfully. She cursed herself under her breath. How had she missed *that*? "I'll change that..."

"Not yet," Lombardi said. He tapped the next spell component. "How high do you want the pencil to go?"

Emily realized her mistake and winced before he could point out her second mistake.

"The pencil is going to crack into the ceiling," he informed her. "Oh, and it's going to rise up fast enough to shatter when it hits. Next time, specify both height and speed—unless you intend to use it in combat. A very fast-moving stone can be a terrifying weapon."

"You wouldn't even need to set a target," Emily guessed. "You could just throw it in the right direction and wait for it to hit."

"Correct," Lombardi agreed. He reached the third section. "Interesting approach to the problem, but tell me; why didn't you simply designate the table as the destination, rather than carefully writing out a movement pattern?"

"I didn't think of it," Emily admitted. At school, she'd had to program a tiny robot to move from one part of the room to the other. They'd had to be very specific—drive forward two meters, turn ninety degrees to the left, drive forward one meter, turn ninety degrees to the right, etc—and she'd assumed that she had to program the pencil's course in the same way. But she could just add the table as another variable ...

"It can be worth exploring different angles," Lombardi said. He rubbed his hands together cheerfully. "You never know *what* you might learn."

He returned to his desk, reached into his drawer and produced a large leather-bound book with a golden eagle inscribed into its cover. "This is your personal grimoire. The charm on the book is such that no one will be able to read it without your permission, at least until after your death. You are expected to write your own spells and note them down in the book for future reference. If you run out of paper, I will provide you with a second book."

Emily took it, staring down at the golden writing. It was *hers,* hers in a way that Void's gift would never be able to match. The blank pages just seemed to be waiting for her to start writing down ideas, and her own personal thoughts and schemes. And thankfully no one else would be able to read it. She'd known girls who had been dreadfully embarrassed when their blogs, Facebook pages and Live Journals had been exposed to the world.

"And if you lose it," Lombardi added, "you'll regret it until the day you die."

## Chapter Twelve

"HE DOES THAT ALL THE TIME, I'M AFRAID," IMAIQAH SAID, AT LUNCH TIME. SHE WAS seated with Emily, eating something that tasted suspiciously like curry. "The last time someone left out a crucial part of a spell, it nearly killed the four people who were standing close to the caster."

"Oh," Emily said. The mark on her palm hadn't faded and it was still throbbing with a dull ache. She'd never been struck like that in her entire life. "I ... I thought that getting hit like that was child abuse."

Imaiqah gave her an odd look. "And nearly killing someone because you didn't check the spell very carefully *isn't*?"

Emily shrugged, then shook her head. For all she knew, Imaiqah might regard corporal punishment as just another part of life.

She hadn't known many people from different cultures, at least before Shadye had kidnapped her, but the ones she had known had often been subtly different from the rest of her former classmates. They'd been brought up to have different ideas about how the world worked, or what was acceptable in modern society–and rarely questioned those ideas. She couldn't imagine how any girl could simply marry a boy selected by her parents, but she'd known girls who calmly expected that it would happen in their future.

So perhaps Imaiqah's attitude wasn't so different after all.

Emily had to admit that Imaiqah–and Lombardi–had a point. Magic was *dangerous*. Emily had been warned time and time again. She still thought of it as something akin to a computer language, but maybe it was more like playing with a loaded gun; you *had* to know what you were doing before you picked up the weapon. And yet Alassa clearly *didn't* know what she was doing before casting *her* spells ...

...But Alassa did know what the spells were meant to do. Perhaps that was enough, at least in the short run.

She tossed the idea around and around in her head as they ate. If a magician cast a spell without knowing what the spell was meant to do, would the spell work? Logically, it should work–but magic didn't appear to be very logical. But a computer language wasn't randomized; it would work even if the user didn't know what it was meant to do. The user might simply be unable to realize the full potential of the language.

"No computers here," she mused. The trick to actually working magic was to cast the spell in your mind and charge it with *mana*, maybe comparable to calculating a formula in your head. But what if someone invented the magical equivalent of a pocket calculator, or a computer? There were limits, she suspected, to spells that could be cast by human magicians. But a computer, on the other hand, should have no difficulty in casting a spell composed of thousands of different components. "I wonder if a computer would actually work?"

She'd read of any number of fantasy universes where technology had simply refused to work, either because the author had determined that technology was incompatible with the laws of her universe or because the author in question been a great believer in the evils of technology. Clearly, those authors had never had to live in a world with lousy plumbing, much less a world with antibiotics and modern sewage. But their concept made no sense at all. The basic laws of the universe had to be identical to Earth's laws or it was quite possible that the human race wouldn't be able to exist at all. Changing a universal constant might kill the entire planet.

But universal constants *were* changed. People could be turned into statues, or frogs–so what happened to the rest of their mass? Even the smallest student at Whitehall would have far more mass than a frog; logically, that mass had to go somewhere else. And yet if it was permanently separated from the spell's victim, wouldn't that be the same as killing her?

*Unless magic is grafted on*, Emily thought.

Maybe all the universal laws worked as they did back home, but magic–*mana*–also existed. How could she test that theory?

A finger nudged her. "You were staring off into space," Imaiqah said, concerned. "And you were muttering. Are you all right?"

"I was thinking," Emily said. She shook her head. If she'd paid more attention to her classes at her old school, she might have been better prepared for scientific experiments. She didn't have the slightest idea where to even *start* building a computer, or a car, or pretty much anything else that she'd taken for granted back home. A thought struck her and she smiled. "Do you know if there are engines that run on steam?"

Imaiqah blinked in surprise. "What do you mean?"

Putting it into words was harder than Emily had expected. The basic concept behind steam engines wasn't *that* difficult to understand, once she had worked out the gaps in her knowledge and deduced the solutions. Build a tank of water and heat it until the water became steam, then push the steam through pipes at force, using the pressure to produce motive power. That power could be used to run a very basic railway engine. Logically, it could be used to run a car too, but she'd never heard of a steam-powered car in real life. Maybe the engine had to be larger than a certain size to actually work properly.

"I've never heard of anything like it," Imaiqah said, finally. "People just use the roads to get from city to town, if they get to travel at all."

"Right," Emily said. Of course, people who lived in a medieval society wouldn't go halfway around the world for a holiday. They might not even recognize the concept of taking a holiday, not when their world was still under the delusion that aristocrats had a right to rule and the lower classes were there to serve. "How far does your father travel in his job?"

Imaiqah gave her an odd look. "He doesn't. He owns a shop in a city."

Emily shook her head ruefully. No big multinational corporations in this world, thankfully. Everything was on a much smaller scale. For all she knew, the necromancers hadn't managed to match Hitler or Stalin in slaughtering helpless victims. And to think that Imaiqah's father was actually one of the most successful businessmen in the world, at least according to Imaiqah. On Earth, he would have been considered nothing more than the owner of a "Mom and Pop" grocery store.

An idea struck her and she smiled. "If I was to send your father ideas for products, would he try to market them?"

"Maybe," Imaiqah said. She frowned, thoughtfully. "But he wouldn't want to gamble everything on one product."

It took Emily a moment to realize what she meant. Building a steam engine would be difficult in this world, as producing advanced metals was much harder. She'd already realized that aluminum was rarer than gold; now, she saw that there would be no steel or metal composites either. Even a small steam engine to test the concept would be incredibly expensive.

*I should have brought a few good scientific textbooks with me,* she thought, sourly. But Shadye hadn't exactly given her time to pack. *Something that would tell me the practical background that I never learned at school.*

She bounced another question at Imaiqah. "What sort of money do you use in your kingdom?"

Imaiqah *looked* at her. "Where *do* you come from? Gold, silver and bronze coins, of course."

Emily thought about trying to explain the concept of paper money, or credit cards, before realizing that it would be a waste of time. "And those coins are actually made out of real gold?"

"Well, of *course,*" Imaiqah said. "What *else* would they be made of?"

"So I could take a gold coin from Umbria and spend it in Cayce?" Emily asked. "Or could I transfigure a bronze coin into gold?"

"You could spend a gold coin anywhere," Imaiqah said, slowly. "My father would weigh the coin to calculate how much it is actually worth, but gold is gold. Transfiguring something into gold ... there are *laws* against that everywhere. You could be *hung*!"

Emily wasn't surprised. If one lived in a world where magicians could use magic to turn lead into gold, surely the value of gold would plummet through the floor. But if they had a way of testing the gold to ensure that it was *real* gold ... they'd *have* to have such a method, or their economy would have collapsed long ago. Or perhaps changing more than a tiny amount of lead into gold was incredibly difficult. Maybe that explained why the economy was on such a small scale.

She'd need money, both for experiments and to keep herself fed and clothed. And she had no particular compunction about stealing ideas from her world and claiming that they were her original inventions. But what could she introduce that she actually knew how to produce?

It struck her—not for the first time—that she was terrifyingly ignorant. Back home, she hadn't had to know anything about how technology worked in order to use it. Now, she was trapped in a world that knew nothing about the scientific method—and she didn't know enough to introduce it herself. Or maybe this world knew a method that involved magic, rather than science, because magic twisted the very structure of the world.

The next period was a free period, so she went back to her bedroom and cracked open the first of the library books. One glance was enough to show her how Alassa could cast so many spells and yet know almost nothing about how they worked. There was no explanation of the variables, or how they went together, merely a formula for the magician to run through her mind. A very simple hex—the book claimed that it gave its intended target a nasty pinch—used only three components. The designer had crammed all of the actual formula into a single component.

Carefully, Emily copied the spell down into her own book—being careful to leave out the startpoint—and broke the spell down to see how it went together. It was surprisingly simple, but looking at the variables convinced her that she'd better be very careful if—*when*—she started modifying them. Altering the variable that governed how hard the target was pinched might be enough to crush bones and kill outright. Another spell seemed to give hypnotic suggestions to its target, suggestions that could cause considerable embarrassment before they wore off.

And to think they gave these mental manipulation spells to kids!

She opened the book of protective spells and found a handful that provided basic protection against charms and hexes. Working out how to cast them was trickier than it seemed; unlike the pinching spell, the protective spells had to be run constantly in her mind. Emily couldn't see how to cast two spells at once until she realized that she'd taken the computer analogy too far. She could cast the spell and leave it fixed in place until she dismantled it.

*Not too powerful, though,* she realized, as she leafed through the book. A protective spell could be hacked by another magician, one who knew what she was doing, or it could simply be overpowered by force. Some simple wards were actually tougher than the more complex wards, but they could still be broken. And if she happened to be knocked out, it was quite possible that most of her protections would collapse.

Finally, she cast two protective spells on herself and tried to figure out a way of testing them. Perhaps she should talk loudly in the library.

She was still considering the possibilities when the door opened and Aloha stormed into the room. Her roommate looked angry; when she saw Emily, she glared at her in a manner that left Emily in no doubt that she was being blamed for whatever had upset Aloha.

But what had she done to her roommate? They merely shared the same room.

"What have you done?" Aloha demanded, echoing Emily's own thoughts. Magic seemed to crackle around her, as if she were on the verge of losing control. "What were you thinking?"

Emily blinked, completely confused. "What are you talking about?"

"Martial Magic," Aloha snapped. "How in the name of all the gods did you even get into the class?"

Aloha raged on before Emily could say a word. "Do you know how hard I had to study to get into that class? Do you know how hard it was to convince the General and the Sergeants that I could handle the pressure? I spent months practicing for the chance to enter the class—and *you* are just given it on a silver platter!"

Emily held up a hand. "I don't know what you're talking about," she said, as evenly as she could. Aloha had to be much more capable—and dangerous—than Alassa. "What is Martial Magic?"

"You should be learning like the rest of us, but no," Aloha snapped. "You're a freaking Child of Destiny and so you are given something that normal students have to study hard to even hope to achieve!"

"I don't know what you're talking about," Emily repeated, more sharply this time. What was all this about? "I spent the day learning about Charms..."

"You haven't even passed Basic Charms," Aloha said. "How *can* they consider you for Martial Magic?"

Emily took a breath and repeated her question. "What is Martial Magic?"

Something in her tone got through to Aloha. "You don't know?"

"No," Emily snapped. "I don't even know why you're so angry!"

Aloha stepped backwards and sat down on her bed, staring at Emily with unblinking eyes. "I want to be a combat sorceress. And to be a combat magician of any kind you have to pass Martial Magic. It's an advanced class focusing on magic in military operations. Students have to know what they're doing, but they also have to have the maturity to handle spells that are deadly, intended to kill."

Emily doubted that. The *Harry Potter* books might have deemed killing and torturing spells to be unforgivable—never mind that Harry himself had used both types of spells on occasion—but *that* magical world suffered from a shortage of imagination. It was easy to use a simple lifting charm to kill someone—either by dropping them from a great height or hurling them into orbit—and the intention of murder would be the same. There was no reason why Alassa couldn't kill with magic, at least not once she passed Basic Charms and learned how to modify a practical joke spell to kill.

"And I applied for the position and was finally accepted after six months of slaving to convince the Sergeants that I could handle it," Aloha added. "Do you know how few second-years get to even try out for the class? And here you are, *a first-year*, and someone just hands it to you on a platter? They wouldn't allow Alassa, a freaking Royal Princess, to take the course without testing her ... when were *you* ever tested?"

Aloha's face twisted. "I was so proud of what I'd done ... "

Emily felt awkward. Back home, it wouldn't have happened. Or maybe it would; perhaps a long-serving cheerleader would be kicked off the squad to open a space for a newcomer who happened to be incredibly talented, or whose father enjoyed political power. But cheerleading was a role for girls who thought that bouncing around wearing skimpy clothes constituted academic achievement and Martial Magic—she assumed—was something a great deal tougher. There hadn't been *any* classes that picked and chose their students so carefully at her old school.

But she could understand why Aloha was so angry. She'd earned her place—and Emily, the unskilled and untutored newcomer, had been given what she had worked so hard to achieve.

"I didn't put my name into the hat," Emily said, quietly. "I don't know why it happened."

"I do," Aloha said flatly. "They're expecting you to save the world."

Emily wondered if she could find a spell that would allow her to do something humiliating—or painful—to Void. He *had* to have told the Grandmaster that Emily was a Child of Destiny, *without* bothering to explain that while it might be literally true, it *wasn't* true in any useful sense. No doubt he'd sworn a magical oath that it was true and had a good snigger afterwards at how easily his words had been misunderstood. Why not? The mishap that had brought Emily to this world would have given him the idea.

"I'm not a Child of Destiny," Emily said, finally. "I ... "

But she couldn't explain the truth.

Aloha just looked at her. "I think that you're not going to embarrass me on the field. If I have to kick you to keep you going, I *will* kick you to keep you going. Do you understand me?"

"No," Emily said. "Why do you care if I succeed or not?"

Her roommate stared at her. "You really don't know?"

Emily shook her head.

"In Martial Magic," Aloha said, "the class is divided up into squads. The squads either pass or fail as a group. If too many squads fail, the entire class fails. You know next to nothing about magic and yet *my* grade will be dependent upon yours!"

Emily felt a cold chill wafting through her body. "You'd better start learning *fast*," Aloha snapped. She produced a book from her cupboard and tossed it at Emily, who caught it awkwardly. "That's the basic textbook for the pre-class studies and trials. I know it all by heart. And if you think that you're going to pass the class ..."

"I didn't ask to be put into this class," Emily protested.

"... You'll have to know it all too," Aloha continued, ignoring her. "And I swear to you, upon my mother's life, that if you ruin this class for me I will turn you into a piece of underwear and leave you out for the boys to wear."

The threat would have been laughable—or disgusting—if it hadn't been deadly serious.

Emily watched as Aloha stormed out, leaving Emily alone in the room. She stared down at the book she'd been given, cursing both Void and Shadye in her mind. What had they gotten her into now?

# Chapter Thirteen

PROFESSOR THANDE LOOKED LIKE A MAD SCIENTIST.

Or so Emily thought, the moment she walked into his large classroom. He was a tall lanky man with unkempt hair and a slightly manic grin, reminding her of David Tennant, the actor who had played the Tenth Doctor from *Doctor Who.* Thande was leaning over a cauldron perched on top of something that looked like a Bunsen Burner, dropping a handful of ingredients into the liquid. It smelled very faintly of spice, and boiling alcohol.

Unlike the other tutors she'd seen, Professor Thande wore a shirt and trousers instead of robes, as well as a belt that carried several different tools for his work. When he turned slightly to study his class, Emily saw a nasty burn mark on his cheek. A second accident–at least, she hoped that it had been an accident - seemed to have left his left hand badly scarred. He wasn't the first teacher she'd seen with a damaged hand, she recalled. It seemed to be a common magical injury.

"Be seated," Thande said, as he returned his attention to the boiling caldron in front of him. "I won't be a minute."

Emily sat down at one of the desks and forced herself to compose her mind. She'd been accosted by five different older pupils on the way to Alchemy Class, all of whom shared Aloha's fears about what a first-year student would do to their shared grade in Martial Magic and had even more inventive threats for what would happen if she let the class down. Emily had seriously considered going to Mistress Irene to ask to be removed from the class, then her natural stubbornness had kicked in. Now, she was determined to do her very best.

Besides, part of her mind whispered, Shadye had marked her for death. Martial Magic might provide her with the knowledge she needed to live a full life rather than remain a prisoner at Whitehall for the rest of her life.

The desk itself was odd, rather like one from an old-time school - a box on legs. When she opened the lid, she saw a dozen cloth bags, each one smelling of something different. Sniffing one of them made her head spin and she put it down quickly, trying to resist the urge to take tight hold of her desk and never let go. The sensation faded quickly, but the lesson wasn't lost on her. Sniffing something when she didn't know what it was could be dangerous.

Looking around the classroom, she saw stained and blackened walls, the result–she assumed - of previous experiments. Thande didn't look as if he was inclined to follow the scientific method. Instead, he looked as if he'd be happy to mix two liquids together and strike a match, just to see what would happen. The walls were completely bare, apart from the one ahead of her, where Thande had placed a green-gold object that looked oddly familiar. She couldn't remember where she'd seen something like it, but she was confident that she had. The thought nagged at her as the classroom slowly filled up with her fellow pupils, until it finally clicked. She was looking at a single dragon scale.

Thande moved to the front of the classroom and clapped his hands together for attention. "I am Professor Thande, Head of Alchemy. You're here for Basic Alchemy, a required class for studying Advanced Alchemy, followed by various specialist departments of Alchemy. Are all those facts correct?"

Emily nodded automatically. There was no sign of Alassa in this class, which suggested that she'd managed to pass it - or that she'd never taken it at all. Emily had expected all students to take the same classes at first, but chatting to the handful of students who would talk to her had confirmed that there were hundreds of different paths through Whitehall. Only a handful of the classes were truly mandatory for all of the students. Unfortunately for Alassa, that included Basic Charms.

"Good," Thande said. He clapped his hands together again. "For those of you who haven't bothered to read your textbooks–a fairly common problem, it seems–you will find that you are lacking in basic knowledge. Can anyone tell me the fundamental difference between Alchemy and Charms?"

There was a pause, and then one of the boys raised his hand. "Alchemy involves brewing things, sir?"

"A very incomplete answer–and nowhere near accurate enough," Thande said briskly. He didn't seem angry, more like he was amused. "Would anyone care to take another guess?"

A girl with skin so white that she had to be an albino raised her hand. "Alchemy involves using natural magic, sir, and Charms involves using your own magic?"

"Much better," Thande said, approvingly. He rubbed his hands together as he started to lecture. "You are aware, of course, that *mana* is everywhere in the world. High levels of *mana* cause unpredictable changes in plants, animals and even the very air itself. What that means, for those of us who are ruthlessly practical, is that *mana* creates magical qualities in natural material."

He picked up a glass decanter from his table and held it up in front of him. "Eye of newt," he said, as he rotated it so that they could see the eyes. Emily felt sick and, judging from the sounds behind her, she wasn't the only one. "What magical uses do these eyes have for the Alchemist?"

There was another pause, broken by the albino girl. "They help you to see, sir?"

"I'm afraid not," Thande said. His gaze swept the room. "The *mana* in eye of newt is useless for any practical purpose, at least as far as we have been able to determine. Perhaps one of you will become an Alchemy Researcher and discover a use, but right now eyes of newt are useless. Completely useless, unless you want to separate a qualified alchemist from someone who merely brags of his own skills."

He put the decanter down and picked up a small glass jar. This one, as far as Emily could tell, held hair. "Shaved hamster hair," Thande informed them. The sounds of disgust grew louder. "And what sort of magical powers do they possess?"

This time, no one dared answer. "In their natural form, they are poisonous," Thande said, answering his own question. "But when boiled in water for seventeen hours and combined with a drop of the patient's blood, they provide an excellent energy boost for a magician who has pushed himself to the limit."

Emily stared at him. What sort of person would shave a hamster and then boil the poor creature's hair for hours, just to see what would happen? Coming to think of it, how had they even *known* that *something* would happen? Her mind spun, making her wish that she'd borrowed a book on Alchemy from the library as well as the spellbooks for self-defense and practical jokes.

No *wonder* science was so badly retarded in this world!

"Those of you who are familiar with Basic Charms will know that spells can mutate if they are not defined perfectly," Thande continued. "The magic in the natural world *has* mutated, twisted in ways that are difficult to imagine. You may consider Alchemy to be partly about mixing different spells together, but that tends to limit your imagination. Which"–he held up his scarred hand–"can be no bad thing."

His voice sharpened. "There are rules for learning Alchemy and I expect them to be followed to the letter. Those of you who break these rules will be used as test subjects for my experiments, experiments that have been known to get out of control and"–he showed them his hand again–"cause unexpected injury. Anyone who continues to mess around after that clearly has the right attitude to become a Master Alchemist, but you can do your research on top of a mountain or in the middle of a desert. It will be safer for everyone else.

"First rule: learn everything you can about Alchemy." He pointed a scarred finger at Emily. "What happens if you mix cornflower with icing sugar and blow it into a candle?"

Emily hesitated. "I don't know," she admitted finally.

"A very good answer," Thande said. "Should you ever be in doubt about what will happen when you carry out an experiment, try and look up the answer first. Which, by the way, is a small explosion." He moved his finger to another boy. "What happens if you mix cat and dog hair together in water and then drink it?"

The boy looked around, desperately. "You turn someone into a cat or a dog?"

"Wrong," Thande said. His face darkened. "You make them bark and meow helplessly for several minutes. And, incidentally, it doesn't work if you *only* use hair from one animal."

He looked up, glancing from student to student. "Ignorance can kill. If you are in doubt about anything, look it up or ask a trained alchemist.

"Second rule: *always* carry out your experiments behind wards to provide safety. Yes, there are any number of alchemists who lower the wards for more contact with the experiments–and most of them come to regret it, sooner or later. You are all students and while you are studying here you *will* keep experimental wards up at all times.

"In addition to that, you will also confine any experimentation to the warded alchemy rooms. Anyone caught practicing alchemy elsewhere in Whitehall will be severely punished.

"Third rule: *always* cast a testing charm before drinking anything you have produced for yourself. A single mistake can kill you outright. If you're not confident with the charm, ask one of your classmates to cast it for you. Refusing to cast the charm for one of your fellows, if asked, will also result in severe punishment."

He paused for a moment to allow that to sink in, then continued. "Also, when drinking other potions, it's a good idea to cast the charm anyway. Some of the newer potion recipes are still producing odd effects if left alone too long. A charm will ensure that it won't kill you outright.

Thande gave them all a commanding stare. "If you are in doubt, ask me or another alchemist. I will not punish anyone for making mistakes, or asking questions, merely for placing their own lives–or that of others–in danger.

"Fourth rule: check everything. Alchemy is, in its own way, as precise as anything you might learn in Charms. Now, open your desks."

Emily obeyed, looking down at the small collection of ingredients.

"You will see a seal on each of the bags," Thande said. "That seal belongs to Elmer, one of the apothecaries who works under me. Apothecaries produce materials for alchemists and, once they verify that they are whatever they claim to be, they bag them up and place their seal on them. The seal will vanish if something else is left in the bag for an unwary alchemist, so make sure that it is still there every time you take something from the bag. If the seal vanishes, take the bag to the disposal chamber and throw it out, along with the entire remaining contents. You're not ready to experiment with materials that may be compromised.

"If you don't use material from an apothecary, check everything; where it comes from, how it was harvested, how it was stored ... everything. A single mistake can prove fatal." He smiled, thinly. "An apothecary who provides bad materials can be executed, if the buyer doesn't kill him first. Murdering someone who conned an alchemist is perfectly legal throughout the Allied Lands."

Thande snorted. "Oh, and *always* use natural materials. If you transfigure grass into mandrake root, just because you cannot afford mandrake, the transfigured grass will still have a magical signature that will throw a stone into the alchemical process. That's a good way to get yourself killed if you're not careful.

"Finally: always–and I mean *always*–write down what you plan to do beforehand. There are notebooks in your desks; write down the planned experiment and stick to it. While carrying out the experiment, write down what happens; once the experiment is complete, write down what happened afterwards. Do *not* leave anything out, or someone trying to reproduce your experiment might run into trouble. Far too many alchemical developments have been discovered, lost and then had to be rediscovered because some damned fool of an alchemist didn't write down what he was doing."

Thande leaned back against his desk and grinned. "That's enough of the boring part. Open your desks again and empty them out onto the top. Now, if you please." He waited until the students had finished sorting out everything and then allowed his smile to widen, waving a hand in the air as he cast a spell. A recipe appeared in front of them, written in glowing letters that burned silently in the air. "Follow that recipe to the letter."

Emily stared at the letters, and then down at the ingredients. If this was what passed for science in this universe ... none of them seemed to be genuine chemicals at all, merely items harvested from plants and animals. She laughed inwardly a moment later; chemicals *could* be harvested from plants, after all. Besides, if alchemists worked to unlock the magical properties of the natural world, it was possible that she was looking at the counterpart of the chemicals she'd been told about in science class at school. If only they'd been allowed to do more practical experiments ...

The first bag contained boiled potatoes. It was so mundane that she found it impossible to take seriously until she cut into the first potato and saw the strange pattern inside. The potato's interior was infested with a purple spider web that sent a tingle though her fingers when she touched it. Wondering if it was a mutated potato—and therefore unsafe to eat—Emily started to cut it up into tiny pieces, following the recipe to the letter.

Thande walked from desk to desk, his eyes missing nothing. "Cut the grains finer than that," he ordered one pupil, before moving on to the next. "The recipe says *one* piece of root."

His voice hardened. "Or can't you read?"

The boy flushed, unpleasantly. "I ..."

"Follow the recipe," Thande snapped, all humor gone. "You can start fiddling with the ingredients when you have a handle on precision."

Slowly, the experiment began to take shape in front of Emily's eyes. Seven ingredients, each one weighed out perfectly ... rather like they'd done in Home Economics class. She almost giggled at the thought. Who would have thought that stupid class was actually useful?

Shaking her head, she wrote out what she'd done and then sat back, unsure what to do next. Nothing actually seemed to be happening in the marble bowl she'd used to mix her ingredients together.

"Now that you have completed your preparation," Thande said, "you may start the experiment itself." He nodded towards the far wall, which slowly lifted upwards to reveal another room beyond the first classroom. "Everyone find a desk with a portable stove, but do not put your mixing bowl on it yet."

The second room was even more barren than the first; the tables looked as if they were designed to take everything from spills to minor explosions. Emily felt the additional protective wards as soon as she walked into the room and took one of the tables, trying to see how to light the stove. There seemed to be no easy solution until Thande stopped briefly behind her stool and clicked his fingers at the stove, which lit up like a bright candle. It felt surprisingly warm when she held her hand over the heat.

"When you start to heat the bowl, be sure to stir carefully," Thande said, as he reached the head of the classroom. "Keep a close eye on what happens as you stir." He paused. "You may start heating your bowl now."

Emily picked up the bowl and carefully placed it on the stove, taking one of the spoons and using it to stir as heat spread through the mixture. Slowly, some of the ingredients started to melt into a messy puddle, which started to bubble and steam as she stirred. The other ingredients appeared unchanged ... but so did meat in a stew, at least at first. If it took time for food to cook, it might easily take time for an alchemical process to run its course...

Emily jumped as a thunderous crash echoed through the room. Down the table, the albino girl's mixture had just destroyed itself. Emily almost forgot to stir as a second bowl also exploded, the protective wards safeguarding the students from harm. A moment later, her mixture fizzed sharply and turned into a black sticky mass, which hardened with terrifying speed. She soon found it impossible to stir it at all.

"Take it off the stove," Thande ordered. Emily started. How had he managed to appear behind her without her even sensing his presence? "You'll be cleaning the bowls afterwards, all of you."

Emily watched as the final experiments ran their course. Only two students seemed to have successfully produced something, although she wasn't sure what it actually *did.* Thande poured it out onto the table and invited them to look at the grayish material. At first, it seemed completely inert, then–when Thande poked it with a metal prod–it shimmered to life and became a mirror. Thande placed a tiny doll beside the material and they watched as the material slowly became a grey duplicate of the doll.

"Those of you who had an explosion probably added too much spice," Thande said into the silence. "Precision is important. Those of you who created a black sticky mess didn't cut the potato up finely enough. Precision is important. Those of you who managed to have your experiments catch fire unbalanced the bowl on the stove. Precision is important."

There was a long pause, and then he nodded towards a door in the far end of the room. "You will clean your equipment carefully, rinse it with cold water and leave it to dry. Having uncontaminated equipment is *also* important."

Emily followed the other pupils into the washroom, feeling her nervousness return as she tried to wash her bowl and spoon. The sticky mess resisted her best efforts until Thande passed her a soap-like substance that washed the bowl clean. Alchemy was an interesting class, but it wasn't her most alarming class of the day. Her first Martial Magic class was coming up rapidly and she would be the youngest and most ignorant pupil on the field.

God alone knew what would happen to her.

## Chapter Fourteen

Emily felt uncomfortable as she changed into the semi-uniforms they were expected to wear for Martial Magic. It had been hard to get used to wearing robes, but after four days she'd found that they were preferable, in some ways, to her normal clothes. They not only concealed everything, they enforced a certain equality among their wearers. The uniforms, on the other hand, were tight-fitting and itched in embarrassing places. It didn't help that the only thing separating the four girls in the class from the twenty boys was a very thin partition.

But they would keep her warm. Owing to the high level of magic in the air surrounding the castle, Aloha had warned her, the weather could change with terrifying speed. It might be raining one moment and then sunny the next.

"Remember what I said," Aloha muttered as they finished dressing and headed for the doorway leading out into the field. "You mess this up for us and I'll make sure that you suffer."

Emily shivered as the boys ran ahead of her towards the middle of a grassy field where the Sergeants were waiting. She'd asked around, but all she'd been able to find out was that the Sergeants *only* taught one class at Whitehall and never had anything to do with anyone outside their classes. Emily couldn't decide if that was a good sign or not, but as they came into view she had to fight down the urge to swallow hard, or to run.

The first Sergeant looked thoroughly intimidating.

He motioned for them to form a line as he studied them, his one good eye catching Emily's before he looked at the next student. The Sergeant looked like a gym teacher from hell. He was easily the most muscular man Emily had ever seen. His left eye was missing, leaving burned flesh and scars that seemed to have become part of his skin and his right eye kept flickering around the field, as if he expected to be attacked at any moment. There was no hair on his head at all.

The second Sergeant looked rather more reassuring. He was a short man with brown hair, a friendly face and—as far as she could tell—an undamaged body. She met his eyes and realized that, no matter what he looked like, there was a formidable personality in there just waiting to explode.

"Greetings," the first Sergeant said. "My name is Sergeant Harkin. This is Sergeant Miles. I served in the Rangers as a Pathfinder, then as a Sergeant, for twelve years; Miles served as a Combat Sorcerer for nine years. We have both fought the monstrous armies raised by the necromancers, which means, for those of you who care to understand, that we know what we're talking about. Those of you who still think you know everything need to forget that attitude right now.

"Whitehall insists that we give you all a written test. This test will have no bearing upon your potential skill as a soldier of any kind, even if you intend to try to become an officer, so we will be happy to hand out cheat sheets to anyone who wants to pass the exam with a perfect score. The reason we offer these is because the exams are not important to your success. I intend to graduate you all as potential combat sorcerers and we don't have time to waste."

Emily heard gasps from four of the boys. They looked older than her—they *were* older, unless they'd advanced faster than Emily believed to be possible—and they would be coping with endless tests and exams as their studies solidified into specialties. Being told that an exam was useless ... it would be a shock, even though Emily had grown up in a universe where almost all basic exams *were* useless. The Sergeant had merely put it into words.

"There are three sections to Martial Magic: Drill, Tactics and Magical Combat," the Sergeant continued. "Drill is where you young children learn to obey orders, and then how to keep your bodies primed for the fight. You do not want to have an unhealthy mind in an unhealthy body if you intend to follow a military career. Some of you will not be used to the concept of obeying orders. We suggest that you forget that attitude as well. You cannot be trusted to issue orders unless you first understand the need to obey them.

"Tactics studies military combat and operations throughout the ages and how to apply them to the current situation. Instead of a written exam, you will be tested in the field and given practical problems to solve. We will be judging you on how quickly you adapt to a sudden change in the situation, how well your plan works when it actually encounters the enemy and how you manage to convince your classmates to follow orders. Failure need not be a problem as long as you learn from your mistakes.

"Magical Combat involves magic specifically designed for military uses," he concluded. "You may have used charms, hexes and jinxes in your earlier years; they are nothing more than jokes compared to the curses written specifically for military use. A charm intended to make a person's clothes fall off their body is a practical joke; a curse intended to maim or kill an enemy is a lethal weapon.

"As we know that you are young students, we will not move on to Magical Combat for several weeks. This is so that we can run you through Drills and Tactics and teach you little monsters how to obey orders before you start experimenting with military spells. We want you to develop the discipline to *handle* the spells before you blow up yourselves, your classmates or—most importantly—us."

His voice turned to ice. "This is not a place where you can horse around without consequences. The spells you will learn here are not jokes. Seeing that you are young and therefore idiotic students, the first person to misbehave in this class will be stripped naked and horsewhipped from here to the burned oak"—he pointed towards a tree in the far distance—"and back again. If that isn't enough to deter you from misbehavior, any further examples will result in immediate expulsion from the class. This is your first and last warning.

"For the first three weeks, any of you who wish to leave this class may do so without consequences. After that, anyone who leaves—either of their own accord or by being expelled—will have a disastrous effect on their squad-mates. The military is not a place for rogue assassins or lone wolves. The military is a place where you must be able to depend upon your fellows and have them depend upon you in turn. Half of the exercises we will make you do will be impossible to solve without working together. If your fellows are in trouble, help them. If you can't think of a solution, work with them. You never know who will come up with a good idea in the field."

The Sergeant's single eye fell on Emily and she shivered. "For those of you who are of the fairer sex, be aware that we make absolutely no distinction between boys and girls in this class. There are combat sorceresses who have been a credit to the army. They all went through the same course and passed with flying colors. *None* of them found it easy. If you have problems or injuries–if *any* of you have problems or injuries–I expect you to inform us *before* it becomes a major problem. You'd be surprised at just how many famous soldiers swallowed their pride in training and admitted that there was a problem."

His face twisted into an unpleasant smile. "That's enough blather from me," he said, pointing one finger towards the burned oak in the distance. "All of you, when I give the order, run to that oak and back here." There was a pause. "RUN!"

Emily jumped, just as the line of students broke up and started to run towards the oak. Catching herself, she ran straight towards the oak, feeling her heartbeat racing as she ran. Her entire body started to ache a moment later, as if she hadn't run in years ... and she hadn't, apart from a handful of gym classes. The ground felt slippery and unsteady under her feet. Everyone, even the other girls, were ahead of her. She would have cursed Void aloud if she had been able to catch her breath. If she'd known that she would be called upon to do physical exercise, she would have practiced running before the first class.

"MOVE," a voice snapped in her ear. Sergeant Miles was directly behind her, carrying a baton which he used to aim a swat at her rear. Emily somehow managed to avoid the blow and kept running as he lifted his voice. "THE ENEMY IS BEHIND YOU! RUN!"

The burned oak seemed to stink of dark magic as she ran around it and back towards their starting point. Some of the boys were slowing down, although they were all still moving as fast as they could, well ahead of her. Aloha, Emily noted, was doing very well indeed. The girl would have had plenty of time to practice.

Sergeant Harkin was counting out loud as the runners raced past him and screeched to a halt, several skidding and falling backwards onto the grass. Emily barely managed to outrun one of the younger boys in the class to come in second to last.

"Pathetic," Harkin said. He seemed to be condemning all of them, not just the ones who had come in last. "Absolutely pathetic. And to think that you are all the great hope of the future."

His voice sharpened as he pointed into the distance. "Do you know *what* lurks over those peaks?"

Emily followed his finger southwards. Perhaps she was imagining it, but there seemed to be a sensation of doom from where the necromancers were lurking, awaiting their chance to fall upon the Allied Lands like wolves on unsuspecting sheep. It was a reminder that their society was at war, even if the Allied Lands seemed to prefer squabbling amongst themselves for the time being. The book Emily had read, produced by the History Monks, had made it clear that the only thing that had prevented the necromancers from winning already was their own disunity, and their tendency to fight each other from time to time. United, the necromancers would have crushed the Allied Lands a long time ago.

"We are at war," Harkin snapped. "There are monsters out there that could tear you apart with their bare hands. You have to work hard to develop yourselves so you can stand between the Allied Lands and the devastation the necromancers would bring to your friends, your family and everyone else! Follow me!"

He spun around and marched off in the direction of a dark forest, part of Whitehall's grounds. "This forest is off-limits to everyone, unless you happen to be taking Martial Magic," he thundered, still moving. "Do not bring your friends here for fun."

Up close, the forest looked ominously dark and shadowy. Emily could sense ... *something* within the tangled trees, a hint of magic that might manifest into something dangerous for any unwary travelers. After what Professor Thande had told them, it was easy to believe that some of the countryside had been forced to evolve by *mana*, becoming hideously dangerous. Who knew *what* lurked inside the forest?

"You two, work together," Harkin snapped, pointing at two of the boys. "You two ..."

He kept assigning partners, assigning Emily to a boy who looked five years older than her.

"I'm Jade," the boy said, sticking out a hand.

Emily shook it gravely. At least he wasn't spending time checking out her chest, unlike too many boys on Earth—and her stepfather, when he was drunk.

Jade smiled at her. "I hear that you are a Child of Destiny?"

Emily flushed. "Don't believe everything you hear. I am ..."

"Am I interrupting something?" Harkin demanded, appearing right in front of them.

Jade and Emily exchanged glances before Jade spoke up. "No, sir?"

"Good," Harkin snapped. He glared at all twelve pairs. "All you have to do is get from one end of the forest to the other. We will be waiting on the other side to see who comes out first, and who gets so badly stuck that we have to rescue them. Any questions?"

There was a long moment of silence. "First team, then," Harkin said. He jabbed a finger at Jade and Emily. "In you go, carefully."

The interior of the forest was dark, so dark that the temperature dropped sharply the moment they were under the leafy canopy. It looked surprisingly normal, yet Emily couldn't escape the sensation that there were watching eyes all around, following their every move.

When she glanced backwards, the forest seemed to go on forever, with no sign of Whitehall or of their fellow students. She couldn't even hear Harkin's bellow as he prepared to send in the next team.

"This way," Jade said, taking the lead and casting a basic spell into the air. "Watch out for traps."

Emily flushed. She should have thought of that. The Sergeants might have created a magical minefield just to test their prospective students, rather than simply using a *mana*-tainted forest that might behave in an unpredictable manner. They might want to push the students to the limit, as well as weeding out those who couldn't hack it, but she doubted that they wanted to *kill* them.

Their surroundings became eerier as they walked further into the darkness. Strange lights flickered in the distance, tiny flashes of lightning that danced at the corner of her eye.

They crossed a stream that made no sound, as if someone had cast a silencing charm over the entire running water—but they could still hear themselves talk. Emily stopped dead when Jade halted, holding out one hand. A moment later, she sensed a spell waiting for them just ahead.

"Stay very still," Jade whispered. The spell seemed to be moving slightly, as if it were a snake preparing to strike. "We're going to have to dispel it."

Emily blinked at him, keeping her own voice low. "Why can't we just creep backwards?"

"Because any motion will attract it," Jade said. "We stumbled right into it and now we have to either dispel it or let it strike us." He scowled. "Judging from all the warnings, it will probably give us a nasty shock even if it doesn't do anything else. Stay still."

He held up one hand and started casting charms towards the spell. Emily was impressed. One of them was the standard dispelling charm, but the other three were unfamiliar. The spell ahead of them seemed to pause, and then vanished into nothingness.

Jade grinned at her in triumph and walked forward. A moment later, there was a flash of light. His entire body locked solid.

Emily stared in disbelief, slowly realizing what had happened. The Sergeants had hidden a *second* spell behind the first, knowing that anyone who dispelled the first spell would rush onwards without taking the time to check for a second surprise. Carefully, she cast the analysis spell into the air, praying that it would work perfectly this time. Somewhat to her surprise, it did, revealing that the paralysis spell was simple enough that it could be easily dispelled.

She started to cast the dispelling charm, before hesitating and running a detection charm over the entire area. Two more nasty surprises revealed themselves before she accidentally triggered them. And, she realized, they were designed to ensure that anyone who tried to deactivate them in the wrong sequence would trigger the spells instead.

*Devious*, she thought. How much time did they *have* in the forest? Carefully, she picked the spell she thought was the right one and dispelled it. Nothing happened to her, but the next spell was coming to life. Working quickly, she dispelled it too, then removed the paralysis spell gripping Jade.

He stumbled and almost fell to the ground.

"I ... my thanks," he said, flushing awkwardly. "I should have thought to check for other surprises before I dispelled the first spell."

"You would have done it for me," Emily assured him, although she wasn't sure if that were true. Jade might have been one of the students who resented her appearance in Martial Magic, even though he'd never threatened her before class. "Now ... how do we get out of here?"

"This way," Jade said. "Or do you want to go first this time?"

The question proved moot. Three steps later, they found themselves in bright sunlight, right at the edge of the forest. Emily glanced behind them in confusion and saw an impenetrable mass of trees and darkness. The noises of the natural world suddenly blared in her ears and she staggered, hearing birds calling to their mates and horses neighing in the distance. High overhead, she thought she saw—just for a single moment—a dragon.

"We're third," Jade said, in annoyance. "How did they get ahead of us?"

He'd spoken quietly, but Miles had very sharp ears. "They didn't waste so much time dispelling spells after stumbling into obvious traps," he said dryly. "Next time, what are you going to do?"

"Check first," Jade said, finally. He looked embarrassed. "I didn't think to check."

Emily looked over at Aloha, who had managed to emerge from the forest with her partner. Her roommate looked surprised, and then nodded slowly. Emily hoped that meant she'd decided there might be a place for Emily in Martial Magic after all, even though *she* still felt decidedly out of place—and unhealthy.

Sergeant Harkin cleared his throat. "Three teams ended up *stuck* in the forest," he pronounced, rather like a judge passing sentence. "Why, one person didn't even help his partner—and ran straight into another trap!"

His voice darkened. "Remember this experience. Take nothing for granted. Watch your back. And help your partner. The next proper exercise will be a great deal worse."

The Sergeant chuckled. "Everyone who made it through the forest can go wash and then have dinner," he said, with a grim smile. "Everyone else can wait until we free them."

Emily nodded, feeling her body aching after one day of Martial Magic. What would the next day be like?

# Chapter Fifteen

"One whole week of schooling," Mistress Irene said. "You seem to be coping reasonably well."

Emily scowled. Her body ached. Running so fast during Martial Magic class had left her breathless for the rest of the first day. Then, when she'd woken up the following morning, her legs had been aching and her chest hurt. Aloha had been just as exhausted, but her roommate had had several months to prepare herself for Martial Magic, including doing more exercise on a regular basis than Emily had ever done in her life. In hindsight, deciding to avoid sports because most school sports were pointless might not have been the brightest decision of Emily's life.

"Thank you," she said instead. The book on Martial Magic said that there would be pain, pain and more pain, and after that some painful pain. Each class would be harder than the last, pushing the students right to their limits. "I'm trying to learn as quickly as I can."

"Your Basic Charms are coming along nicely," Mistress Irene said. "You seem to have already made the conceptual breakthrough that so many others fail to grasp. Professor Thande says that you need to be more precise with your Alchemical work, but you only just started. You should master it before you start wasting expensive ingredients."

Emily nodded and asked the question that had been bothering her for three days. "Who was it who submitted my name for Martial Magic?"

Mistress Irene gave her a sharp look. "Given your ... *circumstances* you should not refuse to learn how to fight properly. There are rumors about you all over the Allied Lands."

"No," Emily said.

"Yes," Mistress Irene confirmed. "The girl who came to school on a dragon, who may be a Child of Destiny..."

"I'm *not* a Child of Destiny," Emily snapped. "Should I have claimed that I only came on a dragon because it was the quickest way to school?"

"Dragons don't give lifts to every human who summons one of them and asks nicely," Mistress Irene said. She shrugged. "But it works out in your favor. A Child of Destiny is supposed to be a little strange—and more advanced than her years. Your presence in Martial Magic will surprise no one."

Emily shook her head slowly. She'd never wanted to advance through favoritism, even back home when the worst that could happen was failing an exam. Here ... well, there had to be a reason why someone as irritating as Alassa was not permitted to advance in Charms until she had mastered the basics. And what sort of idiot thought that Alassa could fake competence indefinitely anyway?

But Whitehall was hardly a regular school. In this particular place, it was easy to forget that the Allied Lands were under threat, from enemies both within and without, and that they needed every magician they could muster to hold back the necromantic tide. That was why Whitehall taught all new students the basics. Apparently, the second-year classes were optimized for individual success.

Perhaps if more students had started formal study *after* they'd learned to read and write back home, all kids would get a better education.

"I see," Emily said, after a long pause. It was bad enough that everyone glanced at her when they thought she wasn't looking, but if it was part of her cover story ... There were gaps in her knowledge that had to be explained somehow, or else the students would realize that she came from an entirely different world. As it was, she hadn't even realized that she had to turn down her sheet to protect her blanket, as it wasn't something that she'd learned back home. "Would it really matter if they knew that I was from a different world?"

"Bad idea to admit more than you have to admit," Mistress Irene said, after a moment of thought. She looked at Emily and shook her head. "You never know what might wind up being used against you."

A moment passed, before Mistress Irene picked up a metal wand. "Your spell-casting is good, although you have a tendency to slop your *mana* outside the spell structure," she added, looking down at the wand. "That isn't too uncommon in a new magician, but you have to work on minimizing leakage. The results may not be pleasant."

Emily nodded. At best, she'd waste *mana* for no purpose; at worst, she would either ruin her own spell or cause chaotic effects. A sudden change in the local *mana* field–caused by a magician losing control of her powers–might create new alchemical ingredients, or become a hazard to anyone who walked into the field without proper preparation. Her books had warned her that it was better to learn control using small, basic spells before trying to advance to the more advanced parts of the syllabus.

"Keep practicing," Mistress Irene ordered. She put the wand down and smiled at Emily. "Do you have any issues that should be raised?"

Emily hesitated. She needed advice, yet she wasn't sure who she should ask–or could ask. Whitehall might be a *magical* school, but magic didn't seem to have improved human nature or prevented academic backstabbing as well as bullying. What if Mistress Irene decided to mislead her? But she needed advice and she had no idea who else to ask.

"Tell me something," she said slowly. "Can I patent an idea?"

"I'm not sure I understand the question," Mistress Irene said. "What do you mean by *patent*?"

"If I come up with a new way to do something," Emily explained, "I claim it as mine, because I was the first person to think of it, and everyone else who uses it in the future has to pay me a small sum of money."

Mistress Irene chuckled. "Goodness, is *that* how things work on your world? How do you encourage debate and research if people have to pay to use *your* idea?"

Her face sobered as she considered the question. "I hope you are not trying to devise entirely new spells already. You're nowhere near ready to try to do more, right now, than modify a handful of the variables. Even *that* would be chancy until you master the art of precision."

"No," Emily said. She looked around the office for something that would illustrate what she had in mind, eventually pointing to the lamp on the desk. "I mean something physical ..."

"I see, I think," Mistress Irene said. She frowned, deep in thought. "It's very different to prevent someone from using a new magical concept. Once someone invents it, everyone else realizes that it is actually *possible* and starts trying to work out how it was done. If you came up with a new spell and used it in public, your friends could analyze it to see how it went together."

Her frown deepened. "I don't think you could claim a physical design permanently," she added, a moment later. "You might be able to convince one of the Allied Lands to forbid anyone to produce it, apart from yourself, but the rest of the Alliance might refuse to honor the edict. And it would cost thousands of gold coins in bribes."

That, Emily decided, made a certain kind of sense. Ideas *did* spread rapidly–and it would be very hard to prohibit someone else from using your idea, at least without creating laws that would be impossible to enforce. *This* world might have had vampires, werewolves and necromancers, but it didn't seem to have lawyers. Apparently, it *was* possible to claim a trading monopoly; unsurprisingly, smugglers took advantage of it to sell goods to people who didn't want to pay the inflated prices demanded by the monopoly-holder.

"Your sponsor might have left you with some money for ... personal use," Mistress Irene said, "but it isn't enough to bribe even a minor functionary."

Emily blinked. The idea that Void might have given her some pocket money had never occurred to her. "He did?"

"Most students ask about spending allowances within the very first day," Mistress Irene said with a grin. "You are entitled to five silver coins a month, with an additional gold coin for every time you gain an excellent mark on your exams. Should you wish to save them, you may place them in storage or keep them within your room. Any purchase requiring more money than you have will require you to convince your supervisor–me–that it is a *necessary* purchase."

"Five silver coins," Emily said. "And how much are they worth? I mean, how much will they buy me?"

"Depends where you shop," Mistress Irene said. "And what you want. And how much effort it takes to produce it. You can get five or six decent robes for one silver coin, or you can have one made from rare and expensive materials for the same amount."

Emily nodded thoughtfully. Back home, children had wasted their money buying designer clothes that really weren't *that* different from cheap outfits, just because they believed that one brand was intrinsically superior to another. Here, they might have a point; materials like silk would be much more expensive than simple cloth. She had no doubt that Alassa and her cronies would have their robes produced to order and made from the finest materials available.

Mistress Irene shook her head. "What exactly do you have in mind for your first ... *idea*?"

Emily hesitated again. In theory, there were countless ideas from her old world that could be introduced to the new world, but she'd run into problems at once. No one had ever taught her how to construct a computer from scratch, or even something as simple as a radio transmitter or telephone. She was sure that she could eventually deduce some of the basic principles just by reasoning from what she already knew, but she doubted that she could put it into practice. And how did someone produce electric power anyway?

Once, years ago, she'd read a book about a girl who had been stranded on a primitive desert world. The girl had promptly introduced gunpowder to the locals and became a millionaire, as well as winning a war against their enemies. Because of this, Emily had already checked to see if there was anything like gunpowder in her new world and there didn't seem to be anything remotely like it, not even fireworks. But there was one small problem with making gunpowder for herself, she didn't actually know how to make it. The book she'd read had claimed that one person could produce a gunpowder factory from scratch. It might have been possible, but Emily didn't know *how*. Modern schools disapproved of teaching children how to make explosive materials.

Maybe she should have had a paranoid kook for a father.

The first *workable* idea had been simple, so simple that she'd almost discarded it before she'd started taking the concept seriously. Madame Razz had issued her five pairs of knickers, but she hadn't given Emily even one bra. The undershirt provided no support at all for her breasts. She'd wondered in some alarm if everyone would be able to see her nipples before realizing that the white robe hid everything from prying eyes. Eventually, she'd asked Imaiqah and discovered that the closest thing to a bra in the new world was a corset-like outfit worn by aristocratic women who wanted the support. Peasant woman merely bound their breasts with uncomfortable strips of cloth.

"If I tell you," Emily said, finally, "can I ask you to keep it to yourself?"

Mistress Irene gave her a long look, and then smiled. "I am your Guardian," she said. "It is my job to look after you while you're attending Whitehall. I will keep anything you tell me to myself unless it poses a threat to you, your fellow students or the school itself. And I have enough money not to need more."

Emily found herself flushing and cursed inwardly. "I was thinking of something like this," she said, and outlined the concept of a bra. "Do you think that it is workable?"

"I've certainly seen girls who could use it," Mistress Irene said. There was a long pause. "I confess that I have never seen anything like it, certainly not for the common folk. Do you realize just how hard it would be to prevent other tailors from duplicating your work?"

"I was going to sell them the idea," Emily said, then stopped. There were no big multinational corporations here, or clothing factories. Clothes were produced by seamstresses and tailors, who apprenticed themselves to masters until they had learned enough to strike out on their own. She could sell the idea to one or two of them, but it would spread rapidly. There would be no way to hold a monopoly for more than a few weeks. "I ... that isn't entirely workable, is it?"

"No," Mistress Irene said. "You might be able to earn some money that way but I don't think that it would last for very long. Unless...you sold the idea to the right person, who could then establish himself as the premier producer of your...breast-supporting garments. I believe that your roommate's father might be able to help you market the idea. He *would* want a share in the proceeds, however. No one does anything for free."

Emily nodded sourly. Hopefully, selling bras would give her enough money to start experimenting with other concepts.

As it was, the world economy could only really be described as basic, with little concept of actually making *more* money. One of her Home Economics classes had discussed just how the concept of lending money, at a small rate of interest, could boost the overall economy, at least until there was a major panic. Opening a bank might work as a way to make money through interest, but that would have to wait until she had a great deal of money to use as a base.

"But there are other possibilities," Mistress Irene added. "If you happened to come up with something that was very useful, you might be paid a fee by the monarch—or the military."

Emily had thought about that, but she couldn't think of anything that she could produce that the military might want. The Sergeants would love gunpowder, she was sure, yet she didn't know how to produce it. She'd given some thought to producing magical guns—using spells to blast the cannonball towards the enemy with great force—before realizing that they already *had* that concept. Maybe if she used a spell to duplicate gunpowder's effects directly ...

She scowled, remembering what she'd read in her book. Warfare didn't involve tanks and aircraft, not here; it involved iron swords, sorcery and animals that had been modified by magic to be more intelligent and capable. There were horses in this world that could almost speak; cats and dogs that could think almost like a human. Everything she knew about warfare from studying history was either already present or beyond her ability to produce, unless ... a thought struck her and she made a mental note to check to see if they had invented stirrups. Or bicycles.

Bicycles would be interesting, if they could be produced with local metals. She might not understand precisely how and why gears worked, but she knew how they went together. It would be easy to sketch out the concept and see if Imaiqah's father—or someone else—could produce them cheaply enough for commoners to buy. Or maybe rent them, if metal was too expensive for bicycles to be produced in vast numbers.

"I look forward to seeing what you introduce," Mistress Irene said.

After a pause, Mistress Irene picked up a sheet of parchment from her table and passed it to Emily. "Your new class schedule for the coming week. I'm afraid you're going to be busy."

Emily scanned it quickly, feeling a sinking sensation in her chest. Now that she had been introduced to all of her classes, she would be starting the main ones with the other new pupils while being expected to join already-running classes in minor subjects and catch up as quickly as possible. She wondered if she was actually *meant* to do well in all of them, or if the tutors merely wanted her to have a taste of each discipline. Sorcerers, it seemed, were expected to know something about everything.

There were two periods for Martial Magic, she noted numbly, both consisting of two hours of hard physical exercise and tactical theory. Thankfully, the planners had placed them both at the end of the day, so at least she would be able to rest after pushing herself to the limit.

She also had a free period every day, but she already knew that it wasn't really 'free.' Instead, she needed to use it to study. Each of her classes had a long reading list of books that students were expected to read in their own time and she had a feeling that if she didn't do her own research, she would run into trouble sooner or later. Besides, there were points that everyone who grew up here knew–that *she* didn't know - and no one had thought to tell her because they believed that they were obvious. She would just have to keep studying and pray that it was enough to keep her going without any major mishaps.

And there was a black mark on two separate periods.

"What's this?" Emily asked.

"For the moment, you can consider them free periods," Mistress Irene said. "Unlike most of the basic classes, Ancient Writing won't be running a new primer class for several weeks. I'll tell you when the next class has been organized. Just read about the subject if you have time."

Emily groaned, rubbing her forehead. There were the reading lists for the other classes, and then the books she needed to study to learn how to defend herself, and then there were the history books covering the Allied Lands ...

"Students," Mistress Irene commented sardonically. "Just remember that what you don't know *can* hurt you."

"Of course," Emily said. Hadn't there been a joke about what you didn't know being able to hurt you because the original saying had been something about backstabbing you to death? "I'll learn as quickly as I can."

"And go to the playing fields this afternoon," Mistress Irene added. "You should at least see one game of *Ken*."

# Chapter Sixteen

According to a book about the history of Whitehall, a sorcerer of somewhat questionable sanity had set out to create the most complicated game he could for budding sorcerers. In the resulting game, there were twelve players to each team, four different sides and—just to confuse anyone who wasn't already, the rules changed depending on what the players were actually doing. Two players in each team, selected randomly, were actually traitors working for a different team, who could win the game by making their own side lose.

Emily detested all team sports with a passion, but *Ken* was particularly absurd, especially considering where it was played. The Arena was as dimensionally flexible as the rest of Whitehall—and massive, which meant that the players had more room to roam. And roam they did; at times, the players would throw balls from hand to hand as they ran through the marked passageways; at other times, they would jump into tubes and pop up at the other side of the Arena. Being hit by a ball sent a player into the penalty box, where spectators pointed and laughed for ten minutes, unless he happened to be carrying one of the other balls when they were hit. If he had a red ball, he was out of the game completely and was booed as they slouched out of the Arena; a yellow ball meant that he had to surrender the ball they were carrying by throwing it to a player from a different team; a green ball meant that he got a free pass. Naturally, the balls changed color at random. A player might jump for a green ball and discover—too late—that he had caught a red ball.

It seemed to Emily that the designer had meshed soccer, basketball, paintball and dodge ball into a single game, played inside a climbing frame for children.

Points could be scored by either putting a ball into a hoop or knocking other players into the penalty box—or off the field completely. The referee was apparently allowed to award additional points for initiative, which could be as simple as picking up a ball on the ground or jinxing another player, just to force them to compete savagely against one another. No one knew what the purpose of *that* was, according to the history book, because the original rulebook had been lost centuries ago. Emily, who remembered the football jocks from back home, suspected that it was really nothing more than legalizing something that would have happened anyway. It was as good a theory as any.

Having created his rules, the sorcerer had run out of imagination and settled for naming it after himself. *Ken*—in the sense of knowing something, rather than Barbie's boyfriend—had been played in roughly the same way ever since ... and, judging by the number of watching students screaming their approval as the four teams fought for victory, it had remained popular up to now.

"Tedious," Imaiqah announced, from where she was seated on the hillock. "You should read a book instead."

Emily couldn't disagree. "Maybe they should play a game on broomsticks instead," she said. "With balls that knock players off their brooms, a hard place to land and a golden hummingbird thingy that unbalances the game so much that whoever catches it is almost certain to win."

Imaiqah gave her an odd look. "Only an untrained magician would risk flying on a broomstick. A trained magician should know just how many spells could bring a broomstick and its rider crashing out of the sky."

"Oh," Emily said. Maybe she should try to introduce *that* particular sport and see how it worked in real life. "How do they actually tell when a given team has won?"

"In a championship game, they keep playing until only one team remains in the Arena," Imaiqah said. "Here, there's a time limit." She pointed towards a large hourglass on the edge of the playing field. "Whichever team has the most points—after adjustment for losing players and fouls—wins the match. If you manage to pull off a Black Horse *Ken*, you get feted for life."

Emily blinked. "A Black Horse *Ken*?"

"That's when you lose all of your players, but still win on points," Imaiqah said. "It doesn't happen very often."

"I ... see," Emily said. Of course it wouldn't happen very often; a team that had been completely removed from the field would not only lose points for each player they lost, but wouldn't be making up any more points afterwards. "They'd have to amass thousands of points before they were wiped out."

"Yeah," Imaiqah said. "Broomsticks. Did you hear about Broomstick?"

Emily gave her a sharp look. Was that a phallic joke? "No," she said, slowly. "Why...?"

"Third-year student," Imaiqah explained. "She never cleaned her room, even when her roommate reminded her time and time again. They weren't earning any credits for cleanliness because she was sloppy and left clothes and half-eaten food lying everywhere, so the roommate was suffering too. Eventually she snapped and turned Broomstick into a broom."

She giggled. "But the roommate didn't get the spell quite right," she continued. "Broomstick took on some of the characteristics of a broom. She thought she belonged to her roommate, that she should be used to clean the room ... she became completely obsessed with cleaning everything when she was finally turned back into human form. There are people who say they've seen her leaning against a wall, waiting to be used."

Emily shivered. "That doesn't sound very funny," she said, finally. It was a thoroughly gruesome story, with implications that chilled her. "What did the roommate do wrong?"

"We all got a lecture on it when we entered Advanced Charms," Imaiqah said. Unlike Alassa, she had actually worked her way through Basic Charms before Emily had been enrolled at Whitehall. "The roommate didn't specify that her mind should remain unaffected because she didn't think that there would *be* any bad effects, not like being a frog for an hour and then catching yourself trying to snap flies out of the air with your tongue for the next week. So the unexplored variable affected her mind ..."

"Good God," Emily said. "And *that* is considered a harmless prank?"

"No," Imaiqah said, more seriously. "I think that the roommate was punished severely, but Broomstick had to be left to recover on her own. The druids couldn't actually do much for her without making the problem worse."

A cheer rose up from the direction of the stands as one of the players scored a goal, winning ten points for his team. Two other players converged on him and threw balls at the same moment, forcing him to duck and cast a charm to shield himself. The rules stated that shielding charms could not be maintained for longer than ten seconds, every five minutes, or the unfortunate player would spend time in the penalty box. Emily rolled her eyes as the spectators counted upwards gleefully, just before the charm was dispelled with two seconds to spare.

Imaiqah coughed, possibly sensing that Emily found the topic of mental changes caused by transfiguration uncomfortable. "I practiced with your numbers," she said, holding up a sheet of paper. "*And* with your accounting system. My father is going to love them."

Emily took the sheet of paper and scanned it quickly. She had come up with the idea of double-entry bookkeeping when she'd realized that Imaiqah, a merchant's daughter, had never heard of it, but she hadn't realized that her world didn't have Arabic-style numerals until she'd seen Imaiqah's first page of accounts. Her father had given Imaiqah a small allowance and, she'd reluctantly admitted, he expected her to justify everything she bought. Emily had written out the numbers she recalled from her home world and taught Imaiqah how to use them. "23" was a great deal simpler than something comparable to "XXIII"–and *that* was a relatively simple example. Who would have thought that medieval accounting required an entire accounting guild because even the educated classes had trouble with numbers?

"Tell him about them," Emily suggested. It was an idea she couldn't copyright, but it would help convince Imaiqah's father that she was a source of other, more profitable ideas. "And why don't you mention the other idea to him at the same time?"

Imaiqah flushed. "I'll have to see what he says," she said, finally. "He may have to start hiring tailors if he wants to produce clothes for the shop ... "

Emily smiled. The concept of mass production didn't exist in this world either, allowing her a chance to outline it for someone who might listen. Instead of a number of highly-skilled craftsmen, have a larger number of workers producing goods piece by piece, she'd suggested, wishing that she'd listened more carefully when it had been mentioned back home. She was sure that there was more to it than that; no doubt someone with money involved, once he had the basic idea, would expand upon it. Tailors might no longer have to sell their wares directly if they went into partnership with merchants.

There was another roar from the spectators and Emily rolled her eyes. One of the other tricks woven into the Arena was a spell that allowed the watchers to follow the action perfectly, no matter how far they were from the wards that marked the edge of the playing field. (Apparently, leaving the playing field without permission counted as being sent off, leaving players trying to trick their opponents into crossing the wards.) But she had to admit that she wasn't really *interested* in *Ken*—it wasn't something she'd be good at doing.

All the school stories she'd read had always made the main character into a sporting prodigy. But it didn't work that way in real life.

Or maybe there *was* a point to Ken that hadn't been mentioned in the book. Players of the game tended to think very quickly, and to react and cast spells without needing to pause and concentrate. The Allied Lands were at war—as hard as it was to imagine, with the sun shining down from high overhead, casting long rays of light over the nearby mountain peaks—and they needed fighting magicians more than they needed sports stars.

"Come on," Emily said. She stood. "Let's go visit the animals."

Whitehall's grounds changed without warning; every time she looked out of the windows she saw something different. There was so much magic soaked into the castle that it had a remarkable effect on its surroundings. If it hadn't been for the amulet Madame Razz had given her, Emily knew that she wouldn't have been able to find her way around at all.

"What would happen," she asked as they walked, "if the spells keeping the school stable were to collapse?"

Imaiqah considered it. "A pocket dimension would either snap out of existence or explode everything inside it back into the normal world," she said. "I wanted a chance to study dimensional engineering; Professor Theta said that a trained dimensional wizard could earn a living almost anywhere, but I would have to undertake three years of study first. He also said that if you knew the coordinates of the dimension, you could open and close the gateway at will without anchoring it to something in our world."

Emily sorted it out in her mind. Whitehall was so vast—bigger than the TARDIS, she suspected—that if the spells *did* collapse, the entire surrounding countryside would be completely wrecked. She'd wondered why Whitehall was so isolated from the rest of the Allied Lands—and would still have been isolated even if the necromancers didn't exist—but perhaps that was the reason. If the school were to be destroyed, the danger to innocent bystanders would be minimized.

They walked through a miniature village—without any discernible purpose, as far as Emily could tell—and into the Garden of the Stoned Philosophers. Emily had been told that students who *kept* talking in the library, despite spending an hour as a statue for each offense, were eventually transfigured permanently and placed in the garden as a warning to their successors. She really hoped that it was a joke. Looking at the statues, they all seemed to be of older men rather than the students she knew. It was *probably* a joke.

"That statue always gives me the creeps," Imaiqah admitted, pointing to one that stood on its own in the centre of the garden. It was a statue of an angel, with hands covering its face. Emily looked at it and recalled the entities she'd seen as Shadye's prisoner and helpless sacrifice. There was something about the statue that made her reluctant to look away from it.

She found her voice. "What is it?"

"No one knows," Imaiqah said. She looked down at the grass below their feet. "They say that there are magical creatures out there that we have never catalogued, because no one ever returns to report their existence."

"You," a voice snapped. Emily glanced up sharply. Alassa was walking out of the trees that had concealed her presence, accompanied by two of her cronies. All three of them were holding wands. "Do you know what you did to me?"

Emily glared at her, feeling rage burning through her mind. "Do you know what you did to *me*?"

Alassa brandished her wand, threateningly. Emily hesitated. Using a wand was a sign that the carrier was not a skilled magician, but it didn't mean that the carrier wasn't a *strong* magician. And *she* had never been allowed to use a wand. She hadn't seen Aloha use one either–and her roommate was aiming to become a combat sorceress. Sparks snapped out of the tip of Alassa's wand, but Emily held her ground. There was no way that she was going to back down in front of the royal bully.

"I gave you what you deserved, you insufferable *commoner*," Alassa snapped. "You..."

Words failed her as Emily stared at her in disbelief, followed by slow-burning horror. Alassa would have been raised to *know*, with every inch of her being, that she was born to rule–and that those who happened to be common-born were her servants. She wasn't allowed to doubt that, not even slightly–and it would provide a justification for anything she wanted to do. No, she wouldn't even *bother* with a justification. The sense of her own superiority was too strong to need to convince herself of the rightness of her own actions.

It was wrong. It was completely wrong. It was so wrong as to be unquestionably wrong. And it was so fundamentally wrong that Emily had difficulty in coming up with an explanation of *why* it was wrong.

Alassa's hand moved and a spell lashed out towards Emily. It struck Emily's protective wards and bounced off, magic crackling around her skin before it faded away into the background *mana*.

Emily started to cast a spell of her own–a freeze charm she'd memorized for emergencies - only to see it deflected away by one of Alassa's cronies.

A second later, Alassa hit her with a second spell. Emily's wards were torn away.

Alassa's third spell slammed into Emily's unprotected body.

She tried to open her mouth, but an eerie tingle spread over her body and the world began to blur. Alassa's spell seemed to grow stronger as the world shrank, somehow dislocating Emily's mind from her body. It was suddenly very hard to hear anything ... it struck her, in a flash of pure terror, that Alassa had transfigured her into something small and immobile.

Imaiqah's words came back to her and she wondered if she was about to become convinced that she was a broom, or something worse. But Alassa could only cast spells she'd memorized. No one would have taught her a flawed spell ...

At least, Emily hoped that was the case. Someone might have given Alassa a useless spell in the hopes it would give her bad habits. But that thought was too terrifying to contemplate ...

The world had faded into a confused mass of impressions. Perhaps she no longer had eyes, so how could she see? But Emily definitely saw something ... Alassa and her cronies were advancing on Imaiqah, intending to teach the common-born girl a nasty lesson for daring to befriend someone who might help her to stand up for herself. Words came to her as though she was hearing them through water: Alassa threatening, Imaiqah pleading ... she sounded terrified. Alassa would tease and torment Imaiqah and then Alassa would do whatever she wanted to a helpless girl.

Pure rage boiled through Emily's mind as she struggled with the spell Alassa had cast on her. It should have been easy to shape a dispelling charm, but it was so hard to think clearly with her thoughts slowly blurring into a daze. A human mind *had* to be dislocated if its body were to be transformed, she realized, as she struggled to counter Alassa's spell. The alternative was what had happened to poor Broomstick.

Imaiqah screamed.

Emily threw caution to the winds, blasting Alassa's spell with all the *mana* she could summon and direct. The spell simply melted away while the world spun crazily around Emily as she snapped back into her human form. Somehow, the rage made it easier to hold onto her magic.

Her eyes returned to normal. She clearly saw that Imaiqah's face was bruised; she'd been slapped, hard. And she'd been so terrified that she hadn't even tried to defend herself.

Alassa turned, raising her wand even as her face was twisted by horrified disbelief.

Emily's rage was making it hard to think. She found two spells in her mind, spells she'd memorized that were both intended to stop a bully in her tracks. She hesitated, just for a second too long–which one should she pick?

Alassa started to cast another spell ...

Emily sensed the surge of magic and knew that her time had run out. Frantically, she tried to cast both spells at once. *Mana* flared through her body, sending her staggering to her knees. She heard, very dimly, someone screaming in pain. Alassa? Or was Emily screaming herself? She squeezed her eyes shut as blinding light burned at her eyelids. Her head hurt, as if she'd been violently sick inside her own mind, or taken something that had intoxicated her.

She managed to open her eyes, then recoiled in horror.

Alassa lay, stunned on the ground in front of her ...

... And her lower jaw was warped and twisted into eerie yellow stone.

## Chapter Seventeen

WHAT HAD SHE *DONE*?

Emily heard someone scream in the distance, but she couldn't take her eyes off Alassa's face. What had she done?

Alassa seemed trapped midway through transformations, as if the transformation had proceeded only so far, then stopped. The morbid part of Emily's mind pointed out that it was lucky that Alassa had been knocked out, or she would have been in terrible pain; the rest of her wondered if she'd *killed* the bully outright. What if she had? She'd been so happy at Whitehall, so happy that she'd never seriously *considered* going home. They'd expel her, and then Alassa's royal parents would kill her...

A hand caught her and shook her, roughly.

Emily turned to see one of the tutors, an elderly man she didn't recognize. Another tutor, with dirty black hair and an unpleasantly jaundiced face, used magic to pick up Alassa, then they both vanished in a flash of light. To the school's infirmary, Emily hoped, and prayed inwardly that they weren't going to the morgue.

What had she done?

*Mixed magic*, part of her mind answered. Two spells. She'd tried to cast two spells at once and they'd interacted.

How *could* she have been so stupid? Broomstick's roommate had been a genius compared to Emily. Emily had let rage and hatred trick her into losing control. She could have protected herself and Imaiqah, *then* cast a single spell on Alassa, or she could have simply thrown a punch right at the bully's face. In a world where magic was exalted above all else, Alassa might not have thought to shield herself against physical blows.

Her head spun again. Emily felt as if she were about to vomit. What had she done? Alassa might not recover at all, or ... she might have permanently mutilated the girl, or ... too many horrific possibilities ran through her mind. She might as well have been playing with a gun, unaware that it had been loaded until the moment she pulled the trigger ... no, she'd *known* that magic could be very dangerous.

She had no excuse.

The tutor's face showed nothing but grim anger. Emily couldn't blame him.

There was a crowd gathering to witness her shame and humiliation. Emily wanted to hide, but where could she go? They would all know that she'd almost killed Alassa, even if the royal princess had thoroughly deserved punishment for her bullying. What would they think of her now that she actually *cared* about the opinions of her peers?

Maybe she should kill herself. She'd thought about ending her life years ago, when she'd realized just how little she had to look forward to, but what she'd done now was far worse than merely having had enough of a pointless life. A girl had been badly injured, left on the verge of death, and it was all Emily's fault. There was no escaping her responsibility for losing control of her own magic. A few seconds of actual *thought* would have allowed her to teach Alassa a lesson without nearly killing her.

She swallowed hard and looked up at the tutor. "Go to the Hall of Shame," he said, in a voice that refused to brook disobedience. "Now!"

Emily nodded, very slowly. Somehow—her legs felt wobbly, unwilling to obey orders—she managed to walk forwards, towards the nearest entrance to the castle. The crowd of students drew back, as if she were carrying a contagious disease and they were afraid of catching it. None of the tutors looked happy; no doubt anyone who spoke out of turn would regret it for a very long time.

She felt eyes boring into her back as she reached the doorway and entered the castle. Somehow—maybe not surprisingly—the door led her right into the Hall of Shame.

She'd seen it before, the first time she'd entered the castle. Students who had broken the rules were sent there to wait for sentence to be passed, although she wasn't sure who did the sentencing. Somehow, she doubted that just anyone would decide her fate. By now, the Grandmaster probably knew and was discussing her future with Void. She could just imagine what the sorcerer who had risked his own life to save hers would say once he heard that she'd ruined her own future. And Alassa's parents would want her dead ...

... Emily shivered, unsure of what to do. Maybe she could just run.

"Hi," a voice said.

She looked up to see Jade standing there. She blinked hard to clear her eyes. They'd expel her from Martial Magic for sure, even if they allowed her to remain in the school.

His voice was surprisingly soft, almost gentle. But he didn't know what she'd done. "What are *you* doing here?"

Emily shook her head. She didn't want to talk about it. "What are *you* doing here?"

"I'm a Prefect," Jade reminded her. "It's my turn to monitor the Hall of Shame."

Of course he would be, Emily realized. They'd want a potential combat sorcerer like him to have leadership experience if he had to go to war.

Jade made a show of glancing up and down the corridor. "You seem to be alone," he said, after a moment. "No one *ever* gets in trouble when there's a *Ken* match on."

Emily flushed, fighting down the urge to cry. She'd definitely go down in the school's history, perhaps under the heading of "what not to do." And to think that it had something to do with sport ...

She looked down, unwilling to let him see her eyes filled with tears. "Am I the worst pupil in the school?"

Jade caught her shoulder and shook it, gently. "You've only been here a week. Do you think you're worse than the idiot who thought that a shark would make a good pet? She transformed it into a cat and used it as a familiar. The monster scratched everyone until it vanished into the kitchen and was never seen again."

Emily stared at him, wondering why his touch was actually reassuring. "Did the shark kill people?

"No, but some of them wished they were dead," Jade said, with droll amusement. "Did they say how long you were to stay here?"

"No," Emily admitted. The tears were still falling. He passed her a handkerchief, allowing her to try to dry her eyes. "I don't know how long to stay here."

"That's a bad sign," Jade said. He looked as if he wanted to pry, particularly after she'd asked if the shark-cat had killed someone, but held his tongue. "You see the marks on the floor? Go stand there, as still as you can, with your hands on your head. Someone will eventually call you into the Warden's office, where ..."

*Sentence will be passed*, Emily thought, numbly. "What happens if I move?"

"The Warden will know and he will take it into account," Jade said. "Don't annoy him, whatever else you do."

Emily almost giggled. As if that would matter!

"Thank you," she said, finally. She dabbed her eyes and then passed the handkerchief back to him. "I ... thank you."

The Hall of Shame seemed larger than she remembered, but then she was the only pupil there. She stopped at the glowing marks, hesitated, then stepped onto them, realizing that everyone who walked by would see her and know that she was being punished. They would probably have heard rumors already, she thought bitterly. The Child of Destiny, who had arrived on a dragon, had almost killed a fellow pupil. She might even *have* killed a fellow pupil.

"Hands on your head," Jade called. "Now, if you please."

Emily hesitated, and then slowly obeyed. The pose was humiliating as hell, intended to make it clear that she was *definitely* being punished. No wonder it was such an effective punishment ... her stomach churned rapidly as she remembered what she'd done, and the horror-struck looks on the faces of Alassa's cronies. They might have been *encouraged* by the princess's parents to guard her. If so, Alassa had been badly injured on their watch. But they could have been encouraged to show her a better way to live ...

But none of that mattered, she reminded herself dully. *She* was responsible for her own actions, including a failure to think before acting. All the excuses in the world wouldn't change that simple fact. What had happened to Alassa *was* her fault and her fault alone.

Time ticked by slowly, to the point where she felt that she'd waited in the corridor for hours. She somehow managed to hold still, apart from twitching, but her arms were starting to ache from the uncomfortable posture. Her eyes flickered from side to side.

Jade was seated at his desk, reading a book. How could he read at a time like this?

The butterflies in her stomach were mating and having children. God alone knew what was keeping them from summoning her to face judgment. How long had she even been standing in the Hall of Shame?

A voice echoed through the corridor. "Emily. Enter the office."

Emily's arms creaked as she managed to make her body move, cramping slightly when she walked towards the heavy wooden door. It didn't open at her approach, forcing her to open it with her bare hands. Yet another twist of the knife. Her arms hurt as she pulled open the door, but it hardly mattered. She felt as if she were walking to her own execution.

She stepped inside and looked around. The Warden's office was completely bare, apart from a desk, a pair of chairs pushed against the far wall and a locked cabinet. There were no personal touches at all. A single glowing ball of light hung in the air, casting a cold radiance over the entire chamber. The effect it created was very much like a prison cell.

The Warden—at least, she assumed he was the Warden—was seated behind his desk, wearing a monk's cowl that had been charmed to shroud his face in darkness. Emily tried to look into the shadow and saw nothing, not even a hint of human features under the hood. A chill ran down her spine as she came to a halt in front of his desk, wondering if he was even *human*. There had to be a reason why he was hiding his identity.

"Emily," the Warden said. His voice was almost completely toneless, leaving her to wonder if he was using a spell to disguise his voice as well as his face. "What exactly happened today?"

Emily swallowed hard and started to explain. The Warden listened carefully. Like the Grandmaster, he seemed capable of listening without interrupting and asking stupid questions. Alassa hated her and her friend, Alassa had transfigured her and hurt Imaiqah - and Emily had lashed out at her without thinking. She admitted that it had been her fault at the end and then stopped, waiting to hear what the Warden said. Whatever it was, she told herself, she could take it.

"Your two spells merged to produce an unexpected effect," the Warden said. "You turned her lower jaw into stone."

He paused, as if inviting comment. Emily said nothing, although inwardly she was relieved. At least she hadn't killed *Alassa* ...

"An inch higher and you would have killed her," the Warden added. His voice was still toneless, but she thought she detected cold anger behind the mask. "You did not focus either spell very well, so there was effectively no focus at all. It could have transfigured part of her brain into stone while the rest remained flesh and blood. The result would have been fatal."

Emily blanched. A person could be a variable in a spell; she'd learned that much from Professor Lombardi. Turning Alassa's entire body into stone wouldn't have been fatal—it certainly wasn't fatal when it happened to noisy students—but if half of her brain had simply stopped working properly, the rest of her brain wouldn't work. Emily knew very little about how brains functioned, yet she could see how the spell would have been lethal. And she hadn't even bothered to aim properly!

"As it was, Alassa was shocked into unconsciousness," the Warden said. "Which is lucky; the Healers had to dismantle what you did carefully and her thrashing about trying to cast healing spells on herself would quite possibly have made the problem worse. Even so, you could easily have mutilated her permanently."

Emily gulped. One of the books she had read for Charms covered healing spells—and the very first page had warned students *never* to try to heal themselves unless there was no one else within shouting distance. There was too much chance of the spell going badly wrong if the caster was in pain, causing additional damage that would need a trained healer to fix.

"You didn't, thankfully, but you may well have caused additional problems for her in the future." The Warden's voice grew stronger, darker. "Partial transfigurations are *always* dangerous. The spell for turning a person's hand into stone should be on the banned list, if you ask me. The only thing that keeps it *off* the banned list was the simple fact that it was only targeted on the victim's hand, with safeguards that your botched spells managed to bypass. We will have to reconsider that position.

"You could have inflicted mental trauma on her," he continued. "If you'd aimed *lower* you could have suffocated her to death, or permanently damaged her reproductive system. Do you have any idea, any idea at all, of just how politically disastrous it would be to have the Crown Princess of *any* Kingdom rendered infertile?"

His voice hardened. "The first duty of any Monarch, be they male or female, is to have a child of their body who can be linked into the spells they use for keeping their thrones in their bloodlines. If Alassa was unable to bear children, the throne would have to be passed to the next person in line–and that person happens to be married to the Crown Prince of a neighboring Kingdom. The political shockwaves would have been bad enough if *anyone* had done it, but everyone seems to think that you are a Child of Destiny. They would be wondering if your *destiny* was to destroy her Kingdom."

Emily found herself speaking before she could stop herself. "Why do you let her bully anyone who doesn't suck up to her?"

The Warden seemed to look at her, but it was impossible to be sure. "Excuse me?"

"The first time I met her, she acted like a bully," Emily said. "The second time, she and her cronies stuck a jinx on me that I had to fight to remove. The third time, she deliberately picked a fight and then tormented my friend! Why do you tolerate it in a place where an accident could *kill* someone, even if it didn't unleash such political repercussions?"

There was a long chilling pause. "We are preparing children to fight in a war," the Warden said. "It is important that we teach them the skills they need to defend themselves, or the wisdom to understand their place in the Allied Lands. You developed defensive skills very quickly, did you not? Alassa needs them too. When she becomes Queen of her land, she will have no one that she can trust completely. Students need *incentive* to learn."

Emily tried to fight down her rising anger and failed. "I suppose that being turned into a frog from time to time does encourage someone to learn how to prevent it from happening again. Does that even work?"

"There are rules," the Warden said. "Rules which are largely unspoken; rules that you have broken, if accidentally. We do not seek to pit untrained first-years against sixth-years who should be qualified magicians. Those we allow to ... *bully* are stronger than their victims, but not insurmountably strong. You could have bested her after little more than a week of training.

"But you acted badly–worse, foolishly - and you must be punished.

"Some of the Senior Tutors wanted to expel you," he added. "They said that you might never learn discipline, or that you now posed a demonstrable threat to other students, or even that your *mana* might be permanently slopping around you. Others wondered about the political issues. Should we throw you to the wolves, just to prevent a major political struggle in the Allied Lands? And several remembered who sent you here and asked if we should risk annoying him."

Emily flinched.

"The Grandmaster concluded that you were a new student, that you were provoked badly and that Alassa had been allowed to get too far out of hand," the Warden said. "She was learning nothing from her actions and indeed the only one of her victims who can be said to have learned anything is you. The lesson may have convinced her that there are limits to how far she can go, *whatever* she may have been taught by her parents. If not, it is unlikely that she will master enough magic to be secure on her throne."

*Or,* Emily thought, *now that she has been publicly beaten, all of her old victims will be lining up to take shots at her.*

"There will be three punishments for you," the Warden said. "First, you will be assigned to assist Alassa in passing Basic Charms. Your grade will be dependent upon how well *she* does on her next exam. Should she *still* fail to pass, you will keep tutoring her until she does. It is fortunate indeed"–his voice dripped irony–"that we are forced to run new Basic Charms classes constantly."

Emily shuddered. Trying to teach someone something when they didn't want to learn - that was always horrific. And somehow she doubted that it would lead to friendship, whatever those dorky parenting manuals claimed.

"Second, you will write a three thousand word essay, due in next Sunday, about just how many things could have gone horrifically wrong when you mixed two different spells together.

Emily winced. Three thousand words! Writing all that out would be a nightmare without computers, or even typewriters.

"Should your essay, which will be marked by Professor Lombardi personally, not reach a sufficient grade, we will have to talk again."

He stood up and walked around the desk, one hand holding a long thin stick. "Third," he said, as Emily stared at the cane in horror, "bend over and place your hands on the desk."

"But ..."

"*Now,*" the Warden ordered. Emily couldn't believe what was happening, even though her hand had been struck to remind her to be careful with her spells. "I won't ask you a third time."

Trembling, Emily obeyed, silently praying that her robe would offer some protection. The first stroke proved that it provided no protection at all. Pain flared across her rear as she yelled. She started to move backwards, only to discover that her hands were stuck to the desk. Five more strokes followed in quick succession, before the Warden stepped back and nodded for her to leave the room.

Clutching her bottom, Emily fled. All she wanted now was to reach her room and cry.

## Chapter Eighteen

"HOW ARE YOU FEELING?"

Emily didn't want to talk to anyone, least of all Aloha. Her roommate didn't seem to like her—and resented her for being included in the Martial Magic class, even though that hadn't been Emily's own choice. And Emily hurt. The red-hot pain in her posterior had faded to a dull burning ache that made it impossible to do anything but lie on her chest and hope that it healed before she had to return to classes.

Part of her mind insisted that it wasn't *fair*! Alassa was a brat, plain and simple, and she'd provoked Emily too far.

The rest of her pointed out that Alassa didn't deserve to be killed—or nearly killed—just for being a brat. A better-trained magician could have slapped Alassa down without risking permanent side effects that would have destroyed Alassa's future in a moment of hot anger. The world wasn't fair ... but then, Emily had known that since she was a kid.

"Go away," she told Aloha, finally. She wanted to read, or to start thinking about the essay that the Warden had ordered her to write, but she couldn't think straight. Pain and humiliation warred with the knowledge that she'd almost killed someone, and that the Warden had caned her buttocks. The entire school would know what had happened to her. "Go away and leave me alone."

Aloha ignored her. "There are some charms that are effective in reducing the pain," she said, a faint hint of sympathy in her voice. "Or you can learn to make a numbing potion in Alchemy. There are some students who make a fair profit selling such things to the naughtier kids."

Emily looked up at her with tear-stained eyes.

She patted Emily on the back. "Come on," she added, lightly. "Do you think you're the only one to ever have been punished by the Warden?"

Emily flushed, embarrassed. "Was I the only one who nearly killed someone?"

"Rumor has it," Aloha said, "that you challenged Alassa to a formal duel and put her in the infirmary. The smarter idiots claim that the tutors stopped you before you killed her, as a formal duel always ends with the death of one of the participants. They think the reason you're still here is because the duel was averted, which isn't actually permitted, even to save a princess's life."

Her voice shifted. "Or there's the rumor where Alassa's spell reflected off you and struck her instead. Apparently, your special nature as a Child of Destiny prevents you from being rendered completely helpless, so Alassa put herself in the infirmary. The reason they think you haven't been expelled was that she cast the near-fatal spell.

"Or there's the claim that you were influenced by the necromancers, or Alassa's political enemies, and manipulated into injuring her ..."

Emily coughed, fighting to clear her throat. "It wasn't anything like that," she admitted. "I ... I lost my temper and almost killed the stupid bitch."

Aloha looked at her for a long moment. "What happened?"

There was a long pause as Emily tried to think. How far could she trust Aloha? She might take whatever she heard to Sergeant Harkin and ... no, that was silly. The Sergeant would have heard from the Grandmaster and the rest of the tutors. If he wanted to boot her out of Martial Magic, he would have already decided to expel her. Shaking her head, Emily explained the whole story from beginning to end.

Afterwards, Aloha started to giggle. "And you're meant to be a Child of Destiny," she said tartly. "May the gods help us."

Emily started to point out that she *wasn't* a Child of Destiny—again—but settled for giggling instead. It *had* been a mistake—and she was confident that a trained combat sorcerer, or a necromancer, would have been able to brush aside her botched spells and kill her before she could cast something more workable. Alassa wasn't *that* much more advanced than Emily, even if she'd had tutors teaching her spells by rote ever since Alassa's magic had come to life.

Emily shook her head. "Why do they tolerate her? They told me there are no politics in the school."

Aloha snorted. "They like to say that, don't they?"

She tapped Emily's forehead sharply. "There is no way that they can avoid facing the fact that Alassa is the heir to one of the most powerful of the Allied Lands, or that her death would shift the balance of power." She paused. "We may be supposed to learn to get along with our fellow magicians, even ones from rival countries, but Alassa is an extreme case. If she hadn't been the only child of her parents, I think she wouldn't have been sent here at all. Her younger sibling—if she'd had one—could have become her Court Wizard. Or she might have had a brother who would be automatically first in line to the throne."

"Oh," Emily said. She remembered Shadye and shivered. "And why are they so *disunited* when the necromancers are at the gates?"

"Because they're stupid," Aloha said. "Or at least that's what Professor Locke says, boiled down to its nub. The Allied Lands are afraid that someone might attempt to re-establish the Empire, so they watch their fellows as carefully as they watch the necromancers—and the necromancers are a great deal farther away. Unless you happen to live on the borders ..."

"Idiots," Emily said, flatly. "And they just let Alassa make enemies for herself?"

"Kids have been fighting each other with magic since Whitehall was established," Aloha said. "Alassa knows better, I think, than to pick on someone who might actually be *important*. Apart from you, I suppose. A Child of Destiny might up-end her Kingdom in passing."

Emily thought about the ideas she'd sent to Imaiqah's father and went cold. None of them were particularly complex—some of them would probably need some modification before they actually produced something workable—but they would *definitely* up-end local society even if they never spread any further. A system that required accountants who had trained for years wouldn't be happy when Arabic numerals made counting so much easier. And without patents, or at least any way to enforce them, the changes would spread rapidly.

*But you can't overthrow a kingdom with a bra,* she thought. She'd seen footage of topless protestors burning their bras, but she couldn't remember them actually achieving anything beyond creating an internet sensation that lasted for a few hours. *And you can't use accountancy to count the King into surrendering his Kingdom.*

"And it also helps to build up friendships and gangs," Aloha added, unaware of Emily's thoughts. "By the time you get into second-year, you'll discover that you have to work with your allies against other gangs, or you'll be completely on your own. And outnumbered. You and Imaiqah had better start making other friends fast."

"Joy," Emily said. She found herself touching her rear. She shuddered, angrily. "And did all this happen to you?"

"I learned fast," Aloha said. Her voice hardened. "Now tell me; what were you thinking when you cost us so many room credits?"

Emily blinked. "Room credits?"

"Whatever you do reflects on the room and your roommates," Aloha coldly informed her. "I have no doubt that Madame Razz will deduct points from us based on what you did to Alassa."

"But that isn't *right*," Emily said. "Why are you being punished for *my* failing?"

"Because roommates are supposed to help teach their fellows how to behave," Aloha snapped. "You failed, so I failed, so the next visit to Dragon's Den will be less ... pleasant than I expected. Or do you have enough coin to give me an advance?"

Emily stared at her, confused. "Dragon's Den?"

Aloha gave her a surprised look. "I can understand that they sent you here when your magic blossomed into life, but why didn't they give you even a simple introduction to the school?"

"I..." Emily started to say, then stopped. If she told Aloha the truth about where she came from, what would it do to this world? Was it possible that the necromancers might eventually find out about it and invade Earth, or ... hell, who needed the necromancers? Alassa's parents might just decide on a war of conquest themselves. "They were in a tearing hurry."

Or maybe the necromancers *couldn't* go to Earth. Emily had magic, but her magic hadn't come to life until she'd been transported to this *mana*-rich world. It was quite possible that the necromancers would find that they had no powers on her world, or the spells keeping them alive at such great cost would simply collapse and they'd die instantly.

Unless, of course, there actually *was* a secret magical society back home, one that had never bothered to send her an owl inviting Emily to Hogwarts. But somehow, she doubted it.

"Dragon's Den is a free city ten miles west of Whitehall," Aloha explained. "It used to be a trading hub before the necromancers pushed their borders up to the mountain. Now, it's one of the first lines of defense against future incursions. We get to go there every three weeks to buy snacks, supplies and just get out of Whitehall for a few hours. But if we've lost room points over this, I won't have so much to spend."

"I'm sorry," Emily said, and meant it. Aloha had had nothing to do with the fight between her and Alassa, let alone the mixed spells that had nearly killed the silly brat. "If I can draw on some of my pocket money, I'll try and make it up to you."

Aloha shrugged. "We'll see what Madame Razz says, later." She slapped Emily's rear sharply, causing her to cry out in pain. "Just *don't* do that to me again."

Emily glared at her resentfully, before somehow managing to pull herself to her feet and pick up her pencil. "The Warden also wants me to write an essay," she said, bitterly. "I don't even know where to begin."

"You could have been expelled," Aloha said unsympathetically. "Or you could have been ordered to write out lines. Or ... you got away with nearly murdering a Royal Princess. Stop complaining."

"Thank you, Miss Mature," Emily said, finally. Or maybe she was being unfair to her roommate. This wasn't a world where childhood extended until well into one's teenage years, but one where children had to become useful as quickly as possible. Imaiqah had told her that she'd worked for her father from a very early age. "I don't know how to write an essay."

Aloha snorted. "You've had some formal schooling," she said dryly. "Didn't they teach you how to write essays?"

They had, but they'd been written on computers. If Emily had a thought that would better the first paragraph, it could be rewritten with ease, while spelling and grammar was checked by the word processing program. Her handwriting had never been good, partly because she hadn't been forced to practice time and time again.

Here, even a short essay would be an absolute nightmare. Any mistakes would force her to rewrite the entire thing onto a new sheet of parchment, unless she could find an erasing spell. And she was *certain* that she would be marked down for every little spelling mistake. *And* she would have to write the essay in English and hope that their translation spells understood it properly. Her previous work had been enough to convince her that the spells had problems with certain figures of speech.

"You'd better learn fast," Aloha said, her voice still dry. "This is a punishment essay. Failing to complete it will only get you caned. Again."

Emily winced. Once had been quite bad enough.

Aloha saw Emily's face and took pity on her. "Work out what you want to say first, then draft out the essay on parchment," she suggested. "And then write it down section by section, with spells to clear up any mistakes. With a little work, you can save yourself from having to do it over and over again."

Her face tightened. "And *don't* leave it until the last minute. It will only cause you more trouble."

Emily nodded. "Is there no way to create an automatic pencil around here?" Aloha looked blankly at her. "I mean, a pencil charmed to write down whatever you say ... "

"There was a fourth-year who charmed his pencil into writing out 'I will not cheat in class' one thousand times after he was caught by Professor Thande," Aloha said. "He was given an award for original thinking *after* he was severely punished. But all he wanted the pencil to do was repeat the same line, time and time again. I've never heard of a pencil that wrote what you told it to write."

Aloha's voice lowered. "You want me to ask someone from an advanced class?"

"If you could," Emily said, "I would be grateful."

Her mind raced ahead, thinking hard. What if someone could produce a computer made out of magic—or, more practically, something like those crappy word processors they'd had to use before the school had actually invested in computers? Maybe a key could be charmed to represent a single letter and, when pressed, the letter would be displayed in front of the writer. And then some programming would give her a workable word processor.

But producing something like that might be difficult. Except that ... she had a feeling that it would be easier than producing an automatic pen. Lombardi had explained, time and time again, that the easiest way to produce *anything* magical was to break it down as completely as possible, making sure that every spell component worked perfectly.

"And then I might have another idea for them," she said. She'd have to write it all down on parchment. A twinge of pain from her rear reminded her that she didn't dare start working on *this* project, all the while neglecting the punishment she'd been assigned. "I'll have to write down the basic concept first."

"Do your essay first," Aloha advised. "Go to the library now and start researching."

Emily hesitated, thought, and then nodded. But before she did anything else, she needed to know what showed on her face.

Slowly, she walked into the washroom and glanced at the mirror. No one would ever believe that she hadn't been crying; the entire school would know that she had been punished. She didn't want to walk out of the bedroom, knowing that everyone else would know, and yet ... what else could she do?

Carefully, she washed her face, wishing that they had some proper cosmetics. It was irony indeed that when she'd finally found a use for them, she could no longer buy the overpriced junk in stores. No doubt perfume, if it existed in this world, was hideously expensive.

"Good luck," Aloha said, when Emily walked back into the main room and headed for the door. "Don't tell anyone else what happened. Let them wonder and fear you."

Emily snorted, then left the room. Outside, a handful of girls glanced at her and then looked away, too quickly.

Feeling as if someone were drawing a targeting crosshairs on her back, Emily left the dorms and headed down the corridors towards the library. Everyone seemed to be looking at her, staring at the girl who had come so close to murdering a right royal brat. No one said anything, but she could feel their gazes boring into her from behind. It seemed to take hours to reach the library and pass through the silencing field that kept the room reasonably quiet.

Imaiqah wasn't here to help this time, but Emily was starting to see how the library went together. There was a long section on Charms, including several books that discussed magical accidents caused by sorcerers who didn't cast their spells properly.

After picking one of them up and reading for a while, Emily realized in horror that the Warden had actually *understated* the danger. One idiot girl, having brewed a potion to make herself look like another girl, had made the mistake of using a cat hair as the source of genetic material. She'd turned herself into a cat-girl from a comic book, at least on the surface; inwardly, she'd warped her body so far that recovery was impossible. The poor girl would forever remain one of a kind, a strange hybrid of human and cat. Apparently, the book concluded, her technique had been duplicated, deliberately, by a sorcerer who wanted an army of inhuman soldiers. It hadn't worked as well as the monsters created by the necromancers, but it had been bad enough to require a full regiment of troops and a squad of combat sorcerers to clear up the mess.

The next book included brightly-painted images of just what could go wrong. One immature boy had set out to *improve* his genitals. Emily took one look at the picture and shut the book quickly, fighting the urge to be sick. Another sorceress had used magic on her womb while carrying a child, apparently because she believed that it would make the child the most powerful sorcerer in the world. Instead, the child had been born dead, yet somehow alive. A cautionary note suggested that someone else doing the same experiment might have been responsible for the first zombie plagues to hit the Allied Lands.

Even minor accidents could have lethal consequences. Emily started to make a list: the boy who'd stopped his father's heart, the girl who had tried to help her ugly friend by transfiguring her face into that of an angel, only to somehow poison her by botching the transformation ... the list went on and on. And most of the accidents, she realized, had been caused by only *one* spell. Her mistake had been caused by trying to cast two spells at once.

Sitting on a cushion, wincing at the pain, she started to outline the essay. The Warden wanted her to learn; she swore to herself that she *would* learn. She would not make the same mistake again.

Behind her, she knew that they were still staring. Did they fear her, as Aloha had suggested, or were they laughing at her when they thought she wasn't looking? Emily didn't want to know. It would be so easy to become angry and lash out and...

*Wind up a statue*, she thought, ruefully. *As if I had time for that.*

## Chapter Nineteen

Alassa didn't return to classes for three days, by which time everyone in the school seemed to have not only heard what had happened, but added their own spin to each of the crazy rumors whispered around the building. Apparently, the girl was dying and her ghost had already been seen haunting the Garden of the Stoned Philosophers. Exactly why she had turned into a ghost when her body was still alive was not explained. A second set of rumors had it that her parents, the King and Queen of Zangaria, had declared war on Whitehall and dispatched an army to bring back Emily's head, preferably not attached to her body. *That* rumor had caused ungrounded panic before a helpful fifth-year had caused more *grounded* panic by pointing out that if the King and Queen demanded the head of a student–any student - they would hopelessly compromise Whitehall's neutrality.

Emily had considered pointing out that the school wasn't anything like as neutral as it claimed, but held her tongue. There was no point in pouring fuel on the flames.

She'd been a social outcast before, but this was different. Her peers, the other first-years, seemed terrified of her, apart from Imaiqah. *She* had become worshipful, even though she'd received a stiff letter from her father that suggested that he simply didn't know what his daughter had been doing to the King's daughter. Emily had read the letter with a growing sense of disbelief; if Imaiqah hadn't been her friend, she would have looked elsewhere for a suitable merchant and ally. The older students pointed and stared at Emily, as if they wondered what *else* she might do. One older student had even seemed to be on the verge of throwing a spell at her, before he'd looked into her eyes and backed off hastily. What had he thought she could do to him?

It was almost a relief when she saw Alassa walking into Basic Charms, even though she looked like a whipped puppy. Her head was lowered, as if she didn't want to make eye contact with anyone. A ripple of...*something* ran through the class and Alassa flinched, unable to hide her reaction.

"Your seat has moved," Lombardi said to Alassa. "You will sit next to Emily until you have *both* passed Basic Charms."

Emily inwardly winced, feeling guilt twisting at her soul. Lombardi had given her a sharp lecture on the dangers of mixing spells without carefully checking to make sure that they melded together perfectly, even implying that the only reason Alassa *hadn't* been killed had been because Emily had left both endpoints in the combined spell. Emily wasn't entirely sure what she'd done, but she'd listened to the lecture and promised herself not to make a second mistake on such a scale. It had been tempting to ask if some of the horror stories about magical accidents had been *real*, yet she'd held her tongue. She didn't want to know.

She looked over at Alassa as she sat down beside her, studying her jaw. Alassa had always been pale–skin color didn't seem to matter in this world, but Alassa had almost been albino–yet now, her lower jaw was almost pearly white, as if the skin had been replaced and the replacement hadn't yet become its natural color. She remembered seeing girls sunbathing and how their underwear could shield part of their skin from tanning, leaving outlines on their bodies. Perhaps the basic principle was the same.

Alassa winced slightly as she shifted on the seat, enough to convince Emily that she'd been punished as well, probably for instigating the fight. Or perhaps Alassa had been told that she was being punished for picking on a Child of Destiny. Who knew *what* her parents would have said to the Grandmaster, once they got over their outrage at their daughter almost being killed? It was just possible that someone had pointed out to Alassa that she would have to rule their kingdom one day and picking on people with magic might not help keep her throne stable. Apparently, necromancers weren't the only rebels against the Allied Lands. Some of the rebels actually had a *cause.*

"We will commence by considering a simple unlocking charm," Lombardi informed the class. He spoke quietly, but they heard every word. "Or is the charm really as simple as I suggest?"

Emily frowned. Once she'd been slotted into the class - after the first private session with the professor - she'd discovered that he spent one hour lecturing them on various charms and the other hour forcing them to work at practical problems that could then be tested. And she was far from the only pupil who'd had her palm struck to remind her to concentrate and plot out *all* of the components before actually trying the spell.

"Of course it isn't," Lombardi said, answering his own question. "To unlock a door, what do you need? You need a key–and you need the unlocking charm to duplicate the key's effect. So, what do you do?"

Alassa shifted beside Emily, and then leaned over to mutter in her ear. "You transfigure the lock to dust and then push the door open," she whispered. "Why waste time analyzing the lock when you can destroy it?"

Emily blinked in surprise. She was the *last* person she expected Alassa to whisper to, not when it might get both of them punished–again. Was the royal brat trying to be *friendly*? Or was she simply unable to refrain from chatting in the classroom and Emily was the only person close enough to hear her?

"You start by analyzing the lock and seeing how it works," Lombardi explained. If he'd heard Alassa's comment, he gave no sign of it. "This particular component"–he drew the symbols out in the air for them–"determines how the lock can be unlocked. The second component actually does the unlocking. Should you happen to discover that the lock might be spelled to make it difficult to use an unlocking charm, you can add a dispelling charm to the overall spell in the hopes that it will prevent the spell from holding the lock firmly shut.

"And in answer to your question, Alassa," he added, a moment later, "the smart sorcerers work wards into doors to prevent someone from simply destroying the lock. A prison intended to hold a magician would be spelled to make it impossible for a small amount of magic to allow the prisoner to break free. So would a doorway you might have to open without being detected."

Emily flushed in alarm. He *had* heard the whispered comment. But at least he'd answered it–and who would have thought that Alassa had made a valid point? Or maybe it wasn't so surprising. She had grown up in a place where she was expected to learn all sorts of tricks, studying under her parents ... and what she'd read about their kingdom suggested that they spent half of their time either plotting or warding off outside plots. The Mafia didn't seem to have been half as unpleasant as Alassa's distant relatives.

"But I won't be teaching you how to break out of prison just yet," Lombardi reassured the class. There were some titters. "Instead, we will start practicing on the locks in your desks. Get them out and start trying to unlock them. Now."

Emily opened her desk and found a lock that seemed too big to be real. It took her a moment to realize that the locks she'd known from back home were the product of modern metals and production methods, while the locks here could probably be picked by someone with a hairpin and enough patience. And, she guessed, enough magic to sense a spell standing guard over the lock. No doubt the locking spells were programmed to give anyone who tried to pick them a nasty shock. Experimentally, she picked up the key and placed it into the lock, turning it backwards and forwards. There might be nothing particularly complex about the inner workings at all, but there was no way to be sure. Lombardi had been careful to provide locks that were solid enough to prevent them from simply opening them up and taking a look inside.

"Waste of time," Alassa muttered. "I could blast through that lock in seconds."

Emily shook her head. "You have to walk before you can run," she said. What had the Roman Dictator Sulla said to the son of one of his worst enemies? "Learn to row before you take the helm."

Alassa gave her an odd look. "What?"

"Never mind," Emily said. She set the lock on the table and placed the key next to it. "Let's see what happens when we cast the spell."

The first time she tried, nothing happened at all. A quick check revealed that nothing seemed to be wrong, so she tried again. Alassa smirked as the second experiment also failed, before she tried to cast the charm herself, both with and without the wand. Emily didn't bother to smirk back at her for her failure. Instead, she started trying to see what was going wrong. The spell seemed to be drawing on *mana*; it just didn't seem to be doing *anything* else.

*Mana fades into the background once spells are cast,* she recalled. Sorcerers had worked hard to measure just how magic and *mana* were interlinked over the years. They seemed to agree on the basic details and then started arguing over the specifics. One section of the library was full of magical journals, written on parchment, with articles by esteemed sorcerers who seemed more interested in winning the debate than actually advancing the frontiers of knowledge.

Shaking her head, she started to take a more careful look at the charm itself. A startpoint, an analysis component, an action component and an endpoint. But a piece-by-piece look revealed that there was no actual link between the analysis and action components; the first time she'd cast the spell, the action component had simply been bypassed and the spell had gone directly to the endpoint.

Giving Lombardi a sharp look, Emily altered two of the variables and recast the spell. The lock screeched loudly enough to force her to cover her ears as it slowly opened.

The class chuckled as the sound faded away. "Not a very ... *subtle* way to unlock a door," Lombardi observed, mildly. "Perhaps you could do something about that?"

Alassa jabbed her elbow into Emily's arm, hard. "How did you do *that*?"

Emily was tempted not to explain, but her grade was dependent upon Alassa passing Basic Charms. "I looked at the spell," she said, and pointed to the missing link. "The spell he gave us was incomplete."

She shook her head. "And unless you understand what a spell is," she added, "you won't ever be able to *know* what you're doing."

Back home, children had played with building blocks; she'd once owned a space shuttle built out of Legos that had provided hours of enjoyment. She still remembered the day when she'd realized that interlocking the tiny plastic bricks would make the final structure *much* stronger than simply piling the bricks up in straight columns. Reaching for the parchment she was using for notes, she added Lego bricks to the list. They might not be able to produce plastic in this world–she couldn't recall how to even *begin* making plastic–but they could presumably carve bricks out of wood. If they hadn't thought of it already...

"Show me," Alassa said.

Emily tapped the charm and pointed out what was missing. Without the two components linked together, the spell would simply refuse to work. While Alassa worked on producing her own spell, Emily started working on making the unlocking process quieter. If she ever wanted to unlock a door to break into a house, she would have to avoid alerting the owner or anyone else in the neighborhood. But even though she studied the charm carefully, she honestly couldn't see *what* was producing the noise, or how to stop it.

The lock screeched again as Alassa finally managed to open it. "Not bad," she said, once she took her hands away from her ears. "I made it!"

Emily swallowed the urge to point out that Alassa wouldn't have done anything without Emily's help and tapped the charm in some frustration. "I cannot see what is causing the noise," she said. She took a careful look at the lock and blinked in surprise as she realized that the answer had been right in front of her nose all the time. The lock had never been cleaned, let alone oiled. She explained what she'd deduced and then looked over at Alyssa, puzzled. "What do we do to stop that?"

Alassa smirked, rather like a cat that had swallowed the canary. "It's simple," she said. "We just stick a silencing charm on the lock first."

She moved her wand, casting the charm, and then repeated the unlocking spell. The lock clicked open in absolute silence. After a moment, Emily looked down at the original spell and added a third component, muffling sound as the charm did its work. When she finally cast it, it worked perfectly.

"Good work, both of you," Lombardi said. The rest of the class seemed to have finally figured out the missing link as well. "You may go to a study room and tackle your next assignment."

Emily would have liked to have had the study rooms in her old school. They were small, but comfortable; equipped with parchment, pencils and a jug of something that tasted rather like fresh orange juice. If Alassa hadn't been there ... her back twitched, almost as if she expected Alassa to slam a spell into her while she was looking away, but nothing happened. Instead, Emily picked up the assignment and studied it. They had been ordered to compose a spell that would create an image of herself that floated in midair. The instructions didn't use the word hologram—absently, she wondered how many other words were missing from their lexicon—but she couldn't think of it as anything else.

"You could have killed me," Alassa said as she knelt on the chair rather than sitting properly. There were no cushions in the room. "I ... "

Emily felt her temper rise and fought it down savagely. "Listen to me," she said, as calmly as she could. "You are a Royal Princess who will be Queen, one day, of a very powerful country. That country will not survive your reign unless you start realizing that there are limits to your power and you learn how to handle people properly!"

Alassa flushed, one hand twitching towards her wand before she caught herself. "Who are you to lecture me on *anything*?"

"I'm a Child of Destiny," Emily said, before she could think better of it. "What might happen to you if you pick a fight with someone like me? What might happen to your *Kingdom*?"

The whole concept still seemed a little absurd to her, but Alassa rocked back as if she had been slapped. If someone like George Washington was a Child of Destiny, did that mean that he simply *couldn't* fail? But Washington had lost battles and come alarmingly close to losing the entire Revolutionary War on more than one occasion. Could one *really* claim that a higher power had been guiding and protecting him, or was he merely that rare combination of vision and practicality? And if there *was* a higher power, what did that say about General Howe, or Gentleman Johnny Burgoyne ... or Benedict Arnold? Arnold hadn't been a traitor to the newborn United States at first, and might never have become a traitor if Congress hadn't kept unjustly attacking him. Had a higher power pushed him into treason to boost Washington's stature?

But if that were true, she asked herself, what happened to free will?

"You make enemies," she said out loud, "and some of them are going to become *real* sorcerers. Others might become necromancers if you treat them so badly they forget the dangers and reach for whatever source of power they can find. Or maybe one day, all of your population will rise up and hang you in the streets."

"They *can't*," Alassa said, genuinely shocked. "They *love* their princess ... "

"Caesar talked about himself in third person too," Emily muttered. "But Caesar had a hell of a lot more reason to be pleased with himself."

She took a breath. The life of Julius Caesar wouldn't mean anything to Alassa. "There once was an Emperor"–the word Tsar meant Emperor–"who shared the same delusion. But he was an incompetent man trying to govern a country by himself, unwilling to either let his subordinates have enough authority to solve problems themselves or to grant his people the freedoms they desperately needed. Eventually, his land collapsed into civil war and the Emperor and his entire family were executed by the rebels. The rebels were so hardened by their experience that they effectively created their own Emperor to rule their country. And it kept falling apart around them until it was too late.

"You want to rule? Learn *how* to rule first," Emily snapped. "Not just how to give orders, but how to give the *right* orders–and when to step back and *not* issue orders. Because you have enemies and the next one might deliberately set out to kill you!"

She found herself wondering just what Alassa's more distant relatives would do when they realized how close the princess had come to death. Would they see advantage in pushing her into tempting fate again? Or would they suggest–snidely–that Alassa return home, crippling her magical studies? Or ... there were just too many possibilities, few of them good.

Emily shook her head. "We're going to pass Basic Charms. And you are *going* to work with me, parsing spells out piece by piece. And once you master it, you can finally go on to the advanced classes."

Alassa's blue eyes stared into Emily's for a long moment, before Alassa nodded. Up close, she looked alarmingly fragile, as if the healing spells hadn't been quite perfect. Or perhaps the Healers had just wanted to leave her with a mark to remind her of her own foolishness. It would probably fade away sooner or later.

"Good," Emily said. "Now, where should we begin?"

# Chapter Twenty

"TODAY'S LESSON PLAN HAS BEEN ALTERED," SERGEANT HARKIN SAID, GLARING AT HIS students. "It has, in fact, been altered because of one of you."

Emily stood as close to ramrod straight as she could, trying to keep her expression blank. She would be astonished if he were talking about anyone else. The Sergeant knew that Emily had nearly killed Alassa and if Emily had done something so stupid in *his* class she would have been expelled on the spot. And everyone else should know it too. The rumors that she'd killed Alassa had faded away when the girl had returned to classes, but it didn't stop *all* the whispers.

"Emily, step forward," Harkin ordered.

Reluctantly, Emily obeyed.

"In the military, it is vitally important to learn from your mistakes—and you will make mistakes. It is also important"—his gaze swept the remaining students—"to learn from someone else's mistakes. And cheaper than learning from your own."

Emily braced herself, knowing that this wasn't going to be pleasant.

"Emily did not seek out conflict with Princess Alassa," Harkin informed them. "But when challenged, she was too slow to strike at her enemy before she was already affected by Alassa's spell. She managed to break it—a not-inconsiderable feat—and then allowed rage and panic to blind her. By putting two spells together, she nearly killed the Princess."

His voice tightened. "Neither spell on its own was meant to be lethal. Put together, the results could have been disastrous." He tapped his baton against his leg as he paused to allow the message to sink in. "You will all be casting spells intended for battle in this class—and, should you graduate, you will have the opportunity to serve the Allied Lands in combat. You cannot allow panic, or rage, or fear, to govern your response to a threat. If you did, the results can be dangerously unpredictable."

He looked at Emily, his scarred face impassive. "To add to that, Emily did nothing to knock down Alassa's cronies. If they had decided to kill her there and then, they could have done so. Emily allowed the horror of her own mistake to paralyze her. The ultimate objective of warfare is victory; Emily could have won one battle and lost the overall war. She took her eyes off the prize out of horror at what she had done.

"We will be teaching you how to react calmly and appropriately to threats, whatever the provocation," he concluded. "And I will be expecting you all to learn to keep your minds focused, even when your bodies are hurting and enemies are pressing in from all sides. Using poorly-cast spells in combat can be more dangerous to your own side than to the enemy."

Emily felt the students staring at her, even though she didn't dare take her eyes off the Sergeant. "Step back," he ordered, finally. "And *don't* be so careless in my class."

There was a long pause as the class digested the unexpected lesson. "Now," the Sergeant said, "can anyone tell me how many *official* spying spells there are at the moment?"

"Five hundred, or thereabouts," Jade said. He seemed to have everything memorized, Emily thought; her own reading had been nowhere near as complete. But then, he'd had five years at the school to memorize everything he could. "I think there are some that are not recommended."

"Five hundred and sixty-four, as of the last publication of *Peeking Toms*," Harkin said. Some of the students giggled and he glared at them. "The sorcerer who edits it has a warped sense of humor. How many *unofficial* spells are there?"

Jade hesitated and one of the girls jumped in. "I read that there were thousands of makeshift spells to spy on someone. There were so many variants that most of them were related to others in some way."

"Indeed," Harkin agreed. "Spying spells are fairly easy to design, so the same spells have been created by several different magicians at the same time. Some magicians tried to keep their own personal spells to themselves, only to read with horror that someone had independently duplicated their work and published it for everyone to see."

He smiled, unpleasantly. "So tell me ... how effective are those spells?"

"They're not," Emily said, quickly.

Harkin turned his gaze on her. "All those spells are not effective? And are all those sorcerers wasting their time inventing them?"

Emily refused to allow him to intimidate her any further. She'd seen spells for spying on friends, enemies and love interests in the book of practical jokes, only to see that someone had scrawled, just past the front cover, a droll note that most of the spying spells wouldn't work inside Whitehall's protective wards. It was, apparently, a quick way to get a very unpleasant encounter with the Warden.

"Spying spells can be countered," she said. Professor Lombardi had pointed out that there was no such thing as an invincible charm, even if it was produced by a necromancer and powered by mass murder. "If you were a sorcerer who wanted to work in privacy, you'd put up wards to prevent someone from peeking in on you. They might come up with something new, but it would quickly be analyzed and countered by the other sorcerers. Any advantage someone gained by inventing a new spell wouldn't last very long."

"Quite right," Harkin said. He turned his gaze back to the rest of the class. "And what, from a military perspective, does this mean?"

"It means you can't spy on your enemies," a burly boy said. He seemed to be from the same year as Jade and the look he tossed at Emily was far from friendly. His gaze made her want to cringe back and hide. "You'd never know *what* they were doing."

Emily frowned, considering the possibilities. Yes, you could move an army under cover of magic, creating a giant blank spot where spying spells couldn't work properly. But if you did so, the watching defenders would surely spot the zone where their magic didn't work and conclude that the enemy army was hiding in the void. She had a sudden vision of enemy sorcerers creating dozens of blank spots to confuse the defenders, with only one blank spot hiding the real army. Or they might not conceal the army at all, gambling that the defenders would spend so much time trying to penetrate the blank spots that they wouldn't realize that the advancing army was in plain sight.

"True enough," Harkin said. "Although unless they establish a base camp and stand still, their passage is going to be noted. You cannot move upwards of a thousand men without leaving a trail–and that trail will be very visible once the concealment spells fade away."

He smiled, rather darkly. "One sorcerer had the bright idea of trying to create a single spell that would blanket an entire country," he added. "What do you think went wrong?"

Aloha spoke up before anyone else could say a word. "The defenders were affected by the spell directly and they were able to dispel it. That was the Battle of Thornton's Reach."

"A classic example of a sorcerer coming up with a brilliant idea and then being so impressed with his own brilliance that it blinded him to the spell's shortcomings," Harkin agreed. "The idea was tried again the following year, with some slight modifications. It didn't work because the defenders were still able to analyze the spell and, instead of breaking it, simply altered their own spying spells to look through the loopholes. That particularly brilliant and stupid sorcerer died in the second battle, thankfully. Who knows *what* he might have thought of next if he had survived?"

He rubbed his hands together. "So ... how many loopholes are there?"

The boy standing next to Jade started to list them on his fingers. "You can try to alter your own spying spells to match the enemy's spells, in the hopes that they will work perfectly through the enemy's concealing spell. You can take a piece of hair from an enemy commander and use it to gain a sense of him; that's hard to block without specific charms and plenty of people don't bother ... "

"I recall a hustler who tried to sell Captain Hawke a pair of skulls that, he claimed, belonged to General Yeller at two different parts of the General's life," Harkin commented. There were some chuckles, although Emily couldn't see how *anyone* could expect a half-way intelligent officer to fall for such a stupid con. "It isn't actually *that* easy to lay your hands on a piece of hair from an enemy commander's head, let alone flesh, or blood, or bones."

"... Or you could try to slip into the enemy camp," the boy concluded, looking a little nervous. "Maybe you could pose as an enemy commander and ... "

Harkin snorted. "Do you think you could pretend to be me well enough to fool Sergeant Miles?"

The boy shook his head, embarrassed.

"Yet another clever idea that never works out quite right in practice," the Sergeant commented. "Although it *has* been tried."

"As it happens, one final loophole is to actually spy on the enemy camp with your own eyes," he continued. "It is possible to evade or fool most detection spells–and you can use a twinned mirror to get the message out as quickly as possible. If you got caught, of course, you might well be tortured, or hanged as a spy. Is anyone brave enough to volunteer?"

His voice sharpened. "There's an enemy army marching on your city. Your King needs to know where it is to place his own army to intercept it. And he needs to know how strong it is, so he can prepare his battle plans. Will you volunteer to go to take a look at the enemy army, knowing that it could cost you your life?"

"Yes," Jade said flatly.

There was a dull rumble of agreement. "Glad to see that we have so many brave soldiers in our midst," Harkin said. He pointed towards the forest. "A rebellious sorceress, the Lady Ravenna, has determined to wage war on your Kingdom. Having raised a dark army, she now makes her camp in the forest while awaiting the return of her brother and his raiding party. Your mission is to get through the forest, get into a position where you can spy on the army, and report back to your King using the twinned mirrors. Should you be caught, I need not add, you will regret it."

He looked at them. "I'm going to send you in, one by one. You know what you have to do, but remember—any sorcerer or sorceress can be a tricky opponent. Remember what happened the first time you walked through the forest and watch where you put your feet. Jade, since you were the first to volunteer, you can go first." He tossed Jade a small mirror, wrapped in paper. "Oh, and keep your head down."

Emily watched as Jade walked up to the edge of the forest and was swallowed by the blackness. One by one, the other students followed him, until it was her turn. Shivering slightly, she stepped under the canopy and grimaced as darkness fell over the forest. The darkness seemed almost alive, leaving her glancing around nervously before she started picking a path through the trees. There was no sign of any other students.

The sense of being watched grew stronger as she slipped onwards, picking a course at random. She had the feeling that the forest, like everything else in Whitehall, was far larger than it seemed on the outside, perhaps being specially designed to serve as a training area for military students.

A moment later, she jumped backwards as her boot threatened to sink into a hidden bog. She hadn't even realized that it *was* a bog until it had been almost too late. It seemed nearly impossible to separate the dangerous place from the mud ...

She picked up a stick and used it to test the ground. The bog was everywhere, even *behind* her. Cursing the Sergeants under her breath, Emily realized that magic ran through the ground, trying to trap her. If she sank in the mire, could they save her before she drowned? Or what if ...

Desperately, she cast a freeze charm ahead of her. The mud froze, creating an icy path running through the forest. She picked her way along it, slipping and sliding, until she reached the end of the bog and returned to solid ground.

In the distance, the sound of horses neighing broke the eerie silence. Carefully, Emily walked closer to the sound, trying to use the trees to give her some additional cover from prying eyes. A moving shape caught her attention and she stared at an animated suit of armor. Its eyes, if it had eyes, were sweeping the forest. Instinctively, she dropped to the ground, feeling *something* pass over her back. If it had caught her in the open ... she didn't know *what* it would do, but she doubted it would be pleasant.

The ground was muddy, and smelly, but she forced herself to crawl forwards, noting that the armor wasn't looking *behind* itself, just ahead. She slipped past it and towards a light in the distance, where she could see something moving. It was difficult to slip much closer because there didn't seem to be much that she could use as cover. Then she saw a large bush. She was careful to check the bush for hidden surprises before she moved. Apparently, according to one of the books she'd read, some plants were animate and snatched anything—or anyone—who came too close. She wouldn't have put it past the sergeants to hide one of those plants in the forest, just to teach the trainees a lesson about not taking anything for granted.

As she inched forward, the army came into view. Half of it seemed to be composed of other animate suits of armor, although they were walking freely and might have been nothing more remarkable than men clad in armor. The remainder...looked like men, but as they came into view she saw chillingly inhuman faces. They were crossbreeds between humans and something else, something very different. Everything she knew about genetics said that interracial hybrids, such as *Star Trek's* Mr. Spock, were impossible. But in a world of magic, who knew *what* was possible? Maybe orcs and goblins had started out human and had been transfigured by powerful magic, the changes passed down to their descendants. Or maybe...

*Ninety-seven suits of armor*, she thought, counting silently in her head. *And seventy inhuman creatures* ...

A hand grasped her leg and yanked her backwards with terrifying force. Emily cried out in shock as she was flipped over and found herself staring up into a face that looked to be a nasty cross between human and snake. A moment later, the face shifted and she saw tiny snakes emerging from its head ...

*A medusa*, her mind screamed at her. *Mirror. You need a mirror!*

There was a blinding flash of light. Her body locked solid. The ... *creature*, whatever it really was, looked down at her for a long moment before it walked away into the forest, leaving her petrified and utterly immobile.

Emily fought down panic and tried to cast a dispelling charm, but whatever the creature had done to her was far stronger than anything she'd yet seen. She tried to run through all of the cancelling charms she could recall, yet nothing worked and her mind started to blur into nothingness and ...

... And then she lay on the ground, outside the forest. Her entire body felt stiff, but at least she was flesh again. And she hadn't been the only one to be caught. Of twenty-four students, only three of them had completed their mission. She cursed her own mistake as she tried to sit upright, before climbing to her feet. Of course there would have been more guards that just a single suit of charmed armor.

"Not a good display, I feel," Harkin said. "Three of you were caught by Snake Face and turned into stone. Five of you got caught in the bog, which would have killed you if you made a mistake like that in combat. Two of you made the mistake of trying to fight the charmed armor and were knocked on the head. Seven of you got too close to Ravenna and were turned into her puppets. And two more of you talked too loudly and brought the goblin hybrids down on your heads. Those massive ears they have aren't just for show. Didn't anyone tell you that they can hear a cat farting from the opposite side of town?"

Emily hoped that was an exaggeration. She'd made enough noise moving through the forest to alert the goblins if they were *really* that capable. Perhaps Harkin was teasing them, while making a point. They'd all taken too much for granted.

Aloha had a different question. "You keep a pet medusa? I ... I thought that those were illegal?"

"Oh, they are," Harkin said. "And if Snake Face hadn't been properly gelded ... why, who knows *what* might have happened to you?" He gave her a sharp look that seemed to put her firmly in her place. "Tell me something. Was there something I said, at any point, to suggest that Martial Magic was actually *safe*?"

Aloha shook her head, miserably.

"I'm glad to hear it," the Sergeant said. "I would have been losing my touch."

He looked back at the entire class. "Go shower," he said.

Emily was suddenly aware that her uniform was sodden with mud and she stank badly. No one bothered to comment on it. They *all* stank.

"And for the next lesson, I suggest you work out exactly what you did wrong and how you could have done a better job. Because we're going to do it again and again until you know what you're doing.

"Next lesson, we will form into squads and start some *real* fun. I'm sure you will enjoy it as much as we did when I started here."

## Chapter Twenty-One

THE REST OF THE WEEK WENT QUICKLY. TOO QUICKLY. EMILY FOUND HERSELF WORKING IN the library every evening, trying to research and write her punishment essay. It was tricky enough to keep track of the basic concept when there were thousands of examples of what could go wrong, each one more gruesome than the last. In between writing–when her hand ached from using the crude pencil–she sketched out a plan for a magical word processor, or even a simple fountain pen.

All too soon, it was Sunday, and she found herself in the Hall of Shame again, waiting to see what would happen.

This time, the Prefect on duty was not even remotely friendly, let alone sympathetic. She pointed Emily to a space in the corridor without saying a word, apart from growling at one of the other pupils to be quiet as he waited for punishment. Emily felt shame and humiliation as she waited, knowing that she wasn't alone this time, until the Warden finally called her into his office. It took all the courage and determination she had to lower her arms and step through the door. The shame didn't stop when she entered the room.

"Stand," the Warden growled. He was still wearing the cloak that concealed his features behind dark shadow. His voice was as atonal as before. "Professor Lombardi has marked your essay."

Emily shivered, trying to keep her face expressionless. She'd had to hand the essay in to the Professor on Saturday, knowing that it was far from perfect. Maybe presentation wasn't so important in this world–several of the students hadn't known how to read and write until they came to Whitehall, where they had to attend classes–but the essay had been meant as a punishment. Professor Lombardi seemed like a nice guy, but he might jump on every problem in the essay. And then ... her hands twitched, protectively covering her bottom. She didn't want to be caned again.

The Warden seemed to be looking at her, although it was hard to tell. "Did you learn anything from the essay?"

"Yes, sir," Emily said tightly. With the exception of Professor Thande, every tutor had taken the opportunity to point out just how stupid she'd been–and just how close she had come to killing Alassa. So had some of the older students, those that weren't scared of her. The rumors running through the school were becoming absurd. "I learned not to do it again."

"A very good idea," the Warden agreed dryly. He looked down at the small sheaf of parchments. "Professor Lombardi gave you excellent marks for your writing. His only real quibble was with your assertion that damage could be repaired through further transfiguration, which isn't always true. One transfiguration alone would charge the victim with *mana*, which would throw off a second transfiguration spell. It certainly isn't something a Healer would want to do unless there was no other choice."

There was a long pause. "But the use of transfiguration in Healing is an advanced class and you have barely been here for two weeks. Professor Lombardi states that you have done an excellent job. So we do not need to punish you further."

Emily relaxed, very slightly. The marks on her rear hadn't faded away for several days and she *still* felt twinges when she sat down on a hard wooden chair.

"However, you need to understand just how close you came to absolute disaster," the Warden reminded her. "You are unlikely to survive—to *survive*—a second mistake on the same scale. Do you understand me?"

"Yes, sir," Emily said.

"Good," the Warden said. "And how are you and Alassa coping while working as a team?"

Emily flushed. They'd worked together three times so far and while Alassa seemed somewhat insecure, perhaps depressed, they had argued very quietly. Alassa *did* have some skills—Emily had wasted an hour trying to alter one spell component, until Alassa had pointed out that all they really needed to do was leave the original component alone and add a third component—yet Alassa didn't really understand what she was doing. But she was getting there.

"We're coping," she said, finally. Maybe the Warden would laugh at her. Or maybe he wasn't even human enough to laugh. She'd asked Aloha and the older girl had told her that the rumors stated that the Warden was actually a golem who had somehow gained self-awareness, if not actual intelligence. Or that he was human, but under some very strict compulsion spells. No one seemed to know for sure. "We may even pass Basic Charms."

"That is always good to hear," the Warden said. "But you will be working with her for a long time to come."

Emily sighed inwardly, but said nothing. Maybe working with Alassa was intended as extra punishment—although she wasn't sure just which of them was meant to be punished—but she was honest enough to admit that they *had* helped each other. Or maybe it was intended to force them to look past mutual dislike and come to an understanding. Whitehall probably felt they needed to learn such a lesson before they faced the wider world.

"I have been ordered to tell you, if your essay passed, that you are to call upon Mistress Irene after this interview," the Warden said. He passed her the sheets of parchment and Emily took them automatically. "You may leave. I strongly suggest that you don't let me see you again for a while."

"Yes, sir," Emily said.

She took one last look into the darkness inside his hood, wondering if she could just make out a hint of a human head, and then turned to leave the room. No doubt the punishments grew worse until the unlucky student was finally threatened with expulsion, or simply got thrown out of school without a final chance. She glanced at the notes Professor Lombardi had left on the parchments, but then moved along as the Prefect cleared her throat and motioned for Emily to leave the Hall of Shame. Emily was only too quick to comply, since there was no longer any reason for her to be there. She was grateful to have escaped unscathed.

Outside, she read the notes more carefully before stuffing the parchments into her robes and walking towards Mistress Irene's office. The corridors were more deserted than usual; the upper classes had been allowed to take a day's leave and visit Dragon's Den before classes resumed on Monday. She saw a pair of boys who couldn't have been more than fifteen tossing a ball around as they ran through the corridor, bouncing the ball off a stone chest and into one of the suits of armor. The suit of armor came to life, grabbing both boys by the scruff of each neck, then raising them until they both dangled above the ground. Emily fled before the suit of armor could come after her too.

Mistress Irene didn't answer when Emily pressed her hand against her door, leaving Emily uncertain of what to do. The Warden hadn't specified a time for her to visit–and he presumably hadn't known if he would allow Emily to leave, or cane her for a second time, at least until the essay had been marked. Maybe Mistress Irene was somewhere else ...

There was a flicker of magic, then Mistress Irene appeared at the foot of a flight of stairs Emily was sure hadn't been there a moment ago. The interior of Whitehall seemed to be completely mutable.

"Emily," Mistress Irene said coolly. "I assume that you are in a suitable state to learn?"

Emily flushed. "Yes, Mistress. Do you want to see my essay?"

Mistress Irene opened her door and led Emily inside. "I trust Professor Lombardi's opinion. And I don't have time to lecture you on just how stupid you were, understand?"

She nodded for Emily to take a seat as she picked up a wand from the table. "You have mastered a number of spells already," she said, "although you have yet to completely master the art of charging them with *mana*. Alassa's near-death experience occurred, at least in part, because you overcharged both spells. However, I have been ordered to teach you spells that are normally only studied in second year."

Her voice hardened. "These spells are not harmful, at least not in the conventional sense, but they *can* cause problems with your spellcasting. They are not usually taught to first years because your peers are expected to learn to channel *mana* properly before they start experimenting with spells that can teach you bad habits. However, Sergeant Harkin has requested that you learn the spells, or you will be unable to take part in Martial Magic. Suffice it to say that you will be required to spend at least one day a week for the next few months casting these spells over and over again. You'll understand why in a moment."

Emily frowned. "Why didn't the Sergeant teach me himself?"

Mistress Irene threw her a sharp look. "The Sergeant prefers not to teach spells to his students," she said, finally. Emily realized, dimly, that she'd accidentally questioned Mistress Irene's competence. "There is an art to spellcasting that is largely separate from the disciplines of Martial Magic."

She passed Emily the wand and she felt it, carefully. Three new spells were already placed within the device, waiting for her to charge them with *mana*. They felt surprisingly complex, but fragile, as if they were made out of thin air. Emily studied them, trying to pick them apart, but they seemed too complex for easy analysis. She would have to watch them being cast and then use the analysis spell for herself.

"The first spell is a modified shielding charm," Mistress Irene said. "Unlike a normal shielding charm, all it really does is change color when it is struck by a particular spell—and absolutely nothing else. You could cast a dozen of these charms on your person and a single jinx would go right through them and strike your body."

Emily blinked. "It doesn't provide any protection at all?"

"No," Mistress Irene agreed. "The spell's sole purpose is to ensure that you know whenever you get hit by a particular spell."

It made no sense, not for a long moment—and then Emily remembered paintball. She'd never played—that required friends and enthusiasm—but she knew the basic concept. Any disputes over who had actually been hit would be settled by checking to see if the target had a paint stain on her body. If they were training to fight, why *not* use magic for their drills, instead of throwing lethal spells at each other? She was sure that the regular army back home used something comparable, rather than firing live ammunition at their trainees.

The spell was simple to cast—but not so simple to dispel. Emily had to try four times before it finally faded away, but Mistress Irene managed to dispel it with a single snap of her fingers. She noticed Emily's shock and explained, patiently, that the spell was deliberately designed to be difficult for the target to remove to prevent someone from cheating. Or at least cheating very easily. An outsider could work a simple dispelling charm and dissolve the spell.

"Good," Mistress Irene said, finally. "And why can this spell be dangerous?"

"Because it provides no real protection," Emily said. She hesitated, and then asked the obvious question. "Why don't we use real shielding charms?"

"Because real shielding charms don't change color when hit," Mistress Irene said. "And because shielding charms are not always usable in combat. Better to assume that a single strike can mean death than to assume that your charms will always protect you."

She lifted her hand and tossed a spell at Emily. The air around Emily started to sparkle, as if she were a fairy from a Disney film. She waved her hand through the air and left a trail of sparks behind. It was pretty, and yet—no matter how hard she tried—she couldn't dispel it. Every time she cast the dispelling charm, the sparkles actually grew brighter.

"It isn't designed to allow you to simply remove the charm," Mistress Irene said. "Now ... "

Emily felt a faint itching where the charm had struck her body. It grew steadily worse, eventually forcing her to start scratching her abdomen. Unsurprisingly, the itch didn't go away, but only grew stronger, just like the sparkles. Emily started to cast yet another dispelling charm, only to find that the itching made it impossible to concentrate. She'd learned an itching charm from the book of practical jokes, yet this was worse ...

"Get down on the ground," Mistress Irene said. Emily obeyed, feeling the itching fading away as soon as she was on the stone floor. "And why do you think that happens?"

Emily hesitated, and then realized the answer. "Because the spells are meant to simulate lethal spells and if we were hit, we would be dead. It makes sure that we can't get hit and keep fighting."

"Correct," Mistress Irene said. She cast a dispelling charm and the sparkles vanished into thin air. "Actually, the altered shielding charm and itching charm are configured to work together. There are variables that the Sergeant will explain to you later in Martial Magic, but suffice it to say that they are not strong enough for mundane use. You *will* be required to keep practicing with your regular spells. Take a casting chamber and, with one of your friends, work on casting all the spells you know."

She showed Emily how the spell worked, and then instructed her to start casting it. The first few times it simply didn't work, often producing flashes of *mana* rather than anything useful. It took Emily several moments to realize that she was pushing too *much* power into the spell. She had learn how to throttle back and charge the spell with *just* enough for it to work properly. Eventually, she was casting it with some confidence, in the office. She didn't know how well it would work when she was in the fields.

"The third spell is ... somewhat dangerous," Mistress Irene said, after Emily was confident with both charms. She stared grimly into Emily's eyes. "I actually protested when the Sergeant said that you should learn it, because it can kill–and because it *cannot* be blunted, even by an experienced sorcerer. Have you encountered any Mentalism spells yet?"

Emily hesitated. The practical joke book had outlined a number of spells for hitting someone with a suggestion–rather like a post-hypnotic suggestion–but she'd found the entire concept more than a little creepy. Who knew what someone like Alassa could do with a mind control spell if she had been able to cast it? Maybe she would turn her entire Kingdom into an army of devoted slaves. Or a male magician, lost in the flood of teenage hormones, would start influencing his female classmates.

And Void had female servants under powerful charms ...

"The army calls this charm the *Berserker* spell," Mistress Irene said, calling her thoughts back to the present day. "You don't *ever* cast it on anyone, apart from yourself. While under the spell's influence, you will be stronger, faster and far more courageous than you would be normally. However, you will also lose any sense of self-restraint, common sense–and the spell taps directly into your *mana*. It will fall apart as soon as you are drained, leaving you *completely* drained. Maintaining the spell too long could easily kill you."

She looked down at Emily, sharply. "Do *not* meddle with this charm, or fiddle the variables, or anything else while you're at this school. *Always* make sure there is a time limit on the spell and *never* try to push it past ten minutes. In fact, given your youth and inexperience, I'd suggest that you limited it to five minutes only. I've seen people age themselves to death through tampering with spells like *Berserker*."

Emily winced at the thought. Some of her tutors had suggested that, in extremity, a magician could call upon her life force to power her magic. But, unlike *mana*, life force was not so easy to replenish, as the necromancers demonstrated rather convincingly. She would literally trade a year of her life for each spell.

"You will *not* use this charm outside of Martial Magic," Mistress Irene warned. "You will *not* teach it to anyone, anyone at all, whatever the provocation. Do not even *discuss* it with anyone who isn't part of the Martial Magic class. If you break that rule, or endanger your own life through meddling with the variables, I swear to you that the caning you received last week will be nothing compared to the thrashing you will receive from me. Do you understand what I am saying?"

"Yes, Mistress," Emily said, in a very small voice. Mistress Irene didn't sound like she was bluffing—and, if what she'd said about *Berserker* was true, she was right. "How do I cast the spell?"

Mistress Irene eyed her for a long moment, and then demonstrated how to trigger the final spell in the wand. Emily cast it and felt nothing until Mistress Irene told her to stand up, whereupon she stood up with so much force that she banged her head on the stone ceiling. But it didn't hurt at all; it felt rather more like her head was made of wood. She picked up the chair with one hand effortlessly, and then picked up the desk itself and then ...

...The feeling of overwhelming confidence faded away.

Emily found herself struggling to hold the desk upright. Mistress Irene silently cast a moving charm and lowered the desk to the ground as Emily sagged and settled on the floor. She suddenly felt very tired. She had been unable to even question what she was doing under the *Berserker* spell; it hadn't occurred to her that something was wrong. If she used that spell in combat, she might march right at the enemy convinced that they could do nothing to harm her.

For a long moment, she hovered on the edge of fainting. She could barely hear the tutor's next words.

"Yes," Mistress Irene said. "You see now. It is too dangerous to use without desperate need."

## Chapter Twenty-Two

Emily didn't feel right for several hours after casting the *Berserker* spell on herself. Mistress Irene had tried to warn her, but the warning was pitifully inadequate compared to how she felt after leaving her mentor's office. Emily was exhausted, completely drained, and yet ... part of her wanted to recast the spell.

To feel that inhuman confidence all the time... Cold logic told her that she had hurt herself just from a few short minutes of being under the spell; in some ways, she'd gotten off lightly. Emily could easily have damaged the tutor's office—or worse. But cold logic seemed almost unreasonable compared to the thought of using the spell again.

No wonder, she told herself, that the *Berserker* spell was so dangerous. A magician could easily become addicted to the sensation.

The thought of addiction was chilling. As a little girl, she'd tried to smoke ... and quickly discovered that cigarettes made her cough. Unpleasantly. But if she'd continued to smoke, she suspected, eventually she would have become addicted to the sensation and smoked a dozen a day, like some of the older girls she'd known back home. And there were people who drank all day and drug addicts who would steal from their grandmothers for one more hit and ... she shuddered as she realized the only person she would be stealing from would be *herself*.

Yes, the spell offered a chilling temptation. It was one that she had to resist. Because it would be too easy to become an addict and lose all control.

She stumbled back to her bedroom and collapsed on her bed, sleeping for several hours before she woke up, very early at five bells, the following morning. Neither Aloha nor Imaiqah seemed to have tried to wake her, which was probably fortunate. She'd been so drained that their efforts would only have given her a headache. Leaving them to sleep —she had no idea when either of them had gone to bed—she stumbled into the washroom. She inspected her face in the mirror and shuddered. She looked like an addict who had been forced to go cold turkey.

After washing her face, she stumbled back outside and noticed a small box someone had placed beside her bed. She'd been warned that it was a good idea to check for magical surprises before touching anything that looked out of place, but she was too drained to focus enough magic to cast even the testing charm. There didn't *seem* to be any *mana* surrounding the box. Shaking her head, she pulled it open and saw what looked like several slabs of milk chocolate and a handwritten note suggesting that she eat all of the chocolate as soon as she woke up. There was no signature.

Sniffing the chocolate suddenly made her aware of just how ravenous she was, so she took a bite and chewed it thoughtfully. It tasted odd to her, sharper than the chocolate she'd enjoyed back home, although that could be nothing more than differences in production. As a kid, she'd been forced to do a project on making chocolate, which she'd thought would be interesting until she'd discovered that they weren't going to actually *make* chocolate for themselves. Early chocolate, if she recalled correctly, had been sharper than modern hyper-processed chocolates. She couldn't remember why.

The chocolate made her feel better very quickly, replenishing much of the energy she'd lost in casting the spell. Indeed, she felt as if she could recast the charm ...

Furiously, she shook that thought out of her head, cursing herself under her breath. That charm, she knew, would be a temptation until the end of her life. Worse, it was one that she would *have* to use from time to time, for perfectly legitimate reasons. It wasn't as if she could thrust the knowledge out of her head and never find it again.

No *wonder* Mistress Irene had banned her from discussing it with the other students. Emily, at least, knew the dangers of addiction. The other students wouldn't know *anything* about the dangers of drugs, alcohol or smoking. Coming to think of it, did they even have tobacco?

*If they don't, Shadye will probably try to import it,* she thought as she dressed. It was funny how quickly she'd become used to wearing the robes, as well as the undershirt and the slightly itchy knickers. She found her essay in the pockets and glanced at it quickly, wincing at the handful of spelling mistakes. Back home, misspelling a word could lead to embarrassment; here, the consequences could be worse. *Who knows what kind of damage that could do?*

Leaving the other two to sleep, she walked out of the bedroom and down to the massive dining hall. It was almost deserted, apart from a pair of older girls and a handful of boys from the *Ken* teams, bulking themselves up before morning practice. A couple of them shot sharp glances at Emily, but the remainder ignored her completely, too busy arguing over tactics for the next game with one of the other schools. Emily had the impression that there was no such thing as tactics in *Ken*; the game seemed to go to the team that was better at reacting, improvising and cheating. Apparently, cheating was legal if the team got away with it.

Her own table was completely empty, unsurprisingly, but the chefs had food ready to go. Emily took a plate of bacon, eggs, sausages and bread, as well as a sauce that tasted like a strange combination of tomato and chili, and walked back to the table to eat in peace. She couldn't deny that she was eating more at Whitehall than she'd ever done back home, but maybe it wasn't too surprising. Magic cost energy and energy could be replenished by eating; indeed, she hadn't seen any real fatties among the students at all. Even the least sporting of them still had to cast magic. She hadn't put on any extra weight at all.

"But I'm telling you that Jolie has a weak spot," one of the sporting boys said, loudly enough for her to hear him without straining. "I've watched every game and I'm telling you that he can't tell the difference between a real ball and an illusion cast by another player. All we have to do is throw a real ball and a few illusions at him and he'll be in the sin bin for *hours*!"

Emily rolled her eyes as she ate, listening to the argument without paying particular attention. Some things never changed, it seemed, and one of them was school sports. The jocks who were top of the social scale just for kicking a ball around considered themselves the best of the best, and were in for a nasty surprise when they graduated and discovered that playing football wasn't considered a marketable skill. And they'd considered themselves God's gift to girls ... she shuddered at the memory of her stepfather's boasting, then pushed it aside. If he'd had as many conquests as he claimed, on or off the field, he would never have married Emily's mother.

It might be different in a magical world, she told herself. *Ken* taught skills that might be desperately needed in wartime.

The dining hall was slowly filling up as she finished her meal and carried the plate to the collection hatch. Too many of the students were glancing at her and then trying to make it look as if they'd been looking at something else, enough to make her feel horribly exposed. How could they believe *all* the nonsense rumors about her that were spreading through the school? Half of them contradicted the other half, or were demonstrably incorrect. They thought that she was a Child of Destiny, or they were scared to death of her ... Emily shook her head as she walked out of the door and headed up to the library to get some reading done before first period.

Surprisingly, the day went quickly until the final two periods. Basic Charms was simple–this time, Lombardi had given them a complex spell that could be knocked down easily to a pair of components–and she actually managed to brew a working potion in Alchemy. She took the opportunity to ask Thande if they could create transfigured ingredients for alchemical research, ones that actually *relied* on having been touched by magic. Once she'd managed to explain herself, Thande had pointed out that it would still be an unreliable process. If a transfigured ingredient was different from a natural ingredient, and it was, trying to take advantage of it could be dangerous.

"And here we are again," Harkin announced, when they reached Martial Magic. He stood in front of them, one hand tapping his baton against his leg. "I trust that you all managed to have a proper lunch before coming to the field?"

Emily nodded. A couple of students from the first class hadn't eaten properly and regretted it very quickly. After that, they'd all learned their lesson; they should eat and sleep whenever they could, because they never knew when they might be in combat. Harkin often offered words of advice, wisdom passed down from soldier to soldier, that often turned out to be practical surprisingly quickly. He wasn't just telling them stuff, but *showing* them as well. It was a far superior way to learn than anything she'd seen back home.

"Excellent," Harkin said, once they had all nodded. "Now, the squads. There are twenty-four of you, so four teams of six. Let's see, shall we?"

Emily winced as Miles stepped forward, lifting one hand to cast a spell. She'd always hated team selections back home, largely because the team captains always picked her last, along with the fat boys that everyone knew were useless in games. It had been a relief when they'd stopped picking her altogether, if only because she couldn't bring herself to care who won and who lost. There was no way that could be important to her, not back home. But it would be important in Martial Magic.

Miles cast a row of lights into the air; red, green, blue and yellow. There was a moment where the lights stayed stationary in the air, then the lights flashed towards the students, splitting up so that there was one light floating over each head. Emily looked up and saw a red light hanging over her head, just like the one over Jade and four other students. She winced inwardly as she realized that she would be sharing a team with five older boys, all of whom would presumably know more magic than her. At least Aloha wouldn't be dragged down by being on the same team as Emily.

"Divide into your teams," Harkin ordered. Oddly, there was one girl per team. Emily couldn't decide if that was a good or bad thing. "You have ten minutes to learn about each other. I suggest you hurry."

Jade waved to her as the line broke up and Emily walked over to him, slightly puzzled. *She* hadn't known *anyone* until she'd come to Whitehall, but surely the others would know each other ... or perhaps not. Jade was sixth year: two of the others were fifth year and the remaining two were fourth year. They might not be aware of each other unless they happened to have a reputation, like Emily. She winced again, and then shook her head. At least it wasn't a reputation for being a slut or a tease.

"My name is Jade," Jade said. He sounded so serious that Emily found herself smiling helplessly. "My father was a Knight of the Allied Lands; my mother is a seamstress in Farfel City. I had hoped to become a Knight myself, but when I developed magic I was sent directly to Whitehall. And I am a Prefect."

"Yes, I *know*," one of the fourth year boys said. "Does that make you the leader?"

"I think we rotate the position of leader," the other fourth year boy said. "That makes *much* more sense."

Jade tapped his palm impatiently. "You can introduce yourself next. Who are you and where do you come from?"

Emily listened as Cat, Bran, Pillion and Rupert introduced themselves. Cat and Pillion, like Jade, were the children of soldiers, although Cat's father was apparently a high-ranking General while Pillion's father was a mystery. Bran and Rupert came from trading families and neither of them had expected to join the military until they'd been tested and told that they would do well in Martial Magic. Finally, Emily's turn came and she hesitated. At least she now had a workable cover story.

"My guardian is an eccentric magician," she said. It was true enough. She didn't understand the relationship between Void and Whitehall—partly because no one seemed willing to talk about it to her—but Void *was* her guardian, standing in place of her parents. "He discovered that I had a talent for magic and sent me here."

Which was true enough, she knew, in the same sense that one could call a werewolf a fur rug by leaving out most of the important details. Apparently, it wasn't *that* uncommon for independent sorcerers to have servants, and Emily *could* have been the daughter of one of those servants, picking up magic from her mother's master. Unspoken, it seemed, was the possibility that the sorcerer might have *been* her father. And it gave her a good excuse to be reluctant to talk about her origins, or being unsure of the correct etiquette, or simply being unaware of the fragile balance of power in the Allied Lands.

"Excellent," Jade said. He sounded frighteningly like Sergeant Harkin. "This is a team and we are meant to work together. Anyone who doesn't cooperate will regret it. We play together, study together and win together."

Emily scowled inwardly. She liked her time alone, mostly.

"Now all we need is a name," Jade continued. "What should we call ourselves?"

*Slytherin*, Emily thought. She didn't say it out loud. Jade would probably want to know where it came from and what it meant, and she had no idea how to explain *Harry Potter* to them. Besides, if she told him about games played on broomsticks he'd probably want to set one up immediately and expect her to play.

"Stalker's Stalkers," Cat suggested. "My father's old unit was named after his Major."

"Maybe not," Bran countered. "I don't think the Sergeant would approve."

"Red Team," Emily suggested. "Or maybe Redshirts?"

It struck her, a moment later, that that would be a bad omen. But Jade seemed to be taking it seriously.

"Deep in thought, I see," Sergeant Harkin said. Emily jumped as she realized that he was right behind her. "And have you come up with a proper name for your team yet?"

"Ah ... Redshirts, Sergeant," Jade said quickly. "It could be Redcoats, but some of our parents would object."

"Yes," Harkin agreed, flatly.

Emily was puzzled until she remembered that the British Army's officers had used to wear red uniforms to ensure that the blood wouldn't show and discourage their troops. There was no reason why this army wouldn't have followed the same logic, although *she* wasn't sure that it was truly that logical. Identifying the officers for watching snipers struck her as a bad idea.

"Redshirts ... " He looked directly at Emily. "And have you mastered the skirmishing spells?"

"Yes, Sergeant," Emily said, trying to project confidence into her voice. She had learned them from Madame Irene, but she wasn't sure that she could cast them at will. "I think so."

"There is no room for *'I think so'* in war," Harkin informed her. He raised his voice. "Cast the shielding charm now, if you please."

Emily tried to cast it and succeeded on the second try.

"It works," Jade muttered to her. "Well done."

"Now," Harkin said, somehow projecting his voice across the field. "When I blow the whistle, start casting the skirmishing spells at enemy teams. The team with the last player standing wins. Go!"

He blew the whistle. There was a moment of stunned silence, broken by Jade hurling a spell at the nearest player from a different team. His body started to sparkle, just as everyone started hurling spells at very close range. Emily managed to fire a bolt at Sissy, a girl who had shown no interest in her one way or the other, before four different enemy players struck her with their own spells. She hit the deck as sparkles started to form around her body, silently grateful that she hadn't been turned into stone this time. Looking up, it was evident that the only survivor from all four teams was Aloha. Her roommate looked muddy; it took Emily a moment to realize that she'd dropped to the ground as soon as spells started to fly and then picked off the remaining survivors before they realized that she wasn't sparkling.

"Good thinking, Aloha," Harkin said. Emily saw Aloha looking embarrassed–praise from Harkin was rare, it seemed–as she stood upright. "So, what went wrong there?"

His face twisted into an amused scowl. "Only one person had the wit to seek cover, what little cover there was. Everyone else was an easy target–although quite a few spells missed outright. And the person who took a shot at me wasted his chance to win the match." There was a glitter of humor in his eye for a brief second. "Fighting in a crowded room is something that you have to learn to avoid, if possible. The nastier military spells will do as much harm to you and yours as they will to the enemy."

Miles clicked his fingers and the sparkles vanished. "We're going to start altering the positions now," Harkin continued. "And then we'll see if we can't bash some proper tactics into your heads."

Emily found herself enjoying the exercises, much to her surprise, as they played two more rounds in the forest. The trees provided additional cover; the bogs and other nasty surprises made it harder to concentrate on just the opposing team. Harkin watched them, shouting advice when one of the teams made an obvious mistake, once directing a new team into the forest to engage the victors of the first match. Emily managed to take out three other players before being taken out in turn. By the time class came to an end, she was tired, muddy and happy.

"I expect you to spend some time practicing in teams," Harkin said. "Leaders: make sure you take the right safety precautions, or there will be beatings. Next period, we will be discussing proper tactics for magic spells. Why not see what you can find out for yourselves first?"

Emily walked back to the building, unable to resist smiling at the expression on Aloha's face.

Her roommate looked delighted with herself. And she deserved to.

## Chapter Twenty-Three

"YOU'RE NOT THINKING," IMAIQAH SAID REPROVINGLY. "I JUST TOOK YOUR KING."

Emily nodded sourly. She'd played chess as a younger girl–she'd been very good at it, she considered–but Imaiqah was unquestionably a skilful player of kingmaker. The game was close enough to chess to confuse Emily, because–as far as she could tell–the real key piece was the wizard, rather than the king or queen. Worse, the king was a mighty piece and the Queen was almost helpless, an inversion that puzzled her. Most confusingly of all, servants–pawns, by any other name–couldn't always be promoted to replace the queen, if she happened to be lost. The servant she had designated as crown prince became king if–and only if–the original king happened to be lost. If both the king and crown prince were taken, or if the king was 'checkmated', the game ended.

She'd actually drawn out a plan for a chess board–eight by eight, instead of the nine by nine squares used by kingmaker–and listed the rules for Imaiqah, who had pointed out that they weren't very realistic. Real life noted that queens were always weaker than kings, even when the Queen ruled in her own right. And if one king happened to die, there was always another king waiting in the wings, unless he'd died first. Emily had countered by pointing out that in chess the rules didn't seem to change depending on the exact position of the pieces at any one time. And two pieces couldn't occupy the same space.

"Blast," she said, ruefully. The servant she'd designated as her crown prince was too close to Imaiqah's lines for comfort. But she couldn't conceal him any longer. Shaking her head, she removed the servant piece from the board and replaced it with the taken king. "I think you're going to win, again."

Imaiqah moved her castle and checked the new king. "Maybe not," she said, seriously. "Your sergeant can cover him."

Emily snorted. A king in chess, only able to move one square per turn, couldn't easily escape a trap without support from other pieces. In kingmaker, a king could go anywhere as long as he didn't cross a threatened line or took another piece, unless it was on the square next to him. The game was supposed to be more realistic, but it lacked the beautiful simplicity of chess.

She moved the sergeant, hoping that it wouldn't expose her queen too badly. "I think we should go back to the spellcasting chamber. You need to work on your charms."

Imaiqah nodded. They'd spent at least an hour a day for the last week practicing casting spells, both offensive practical jokes–in both senses of the word–and shielding charms. Alassa wasn't the only bully out there, it seemed, and they had to be ready for trouble. Imaiqah seemed to be gaining confidence as she mastered new spells, thankfully.

But Emily still needed Imaiqah's help and advice. Her potions rarely seemed to work properly, even potions Thande called easy and straightforward.

"There," Imaiqah said, moving her own sergeant. "Your King is Mine."

Emily looked at the board and swallowed a curse. She'd moved one piece, only to expose her king to another angle of attack. And this one not only threatened the king, but made it impossible to retreat. She looked for options–one game of chess she'd played had been lost because she hadn't thought to check when her opponent declared checkmate–but saw nothing. There was no way to shield her king or take the attacking piece.

"Congratulations," she said, lifting her king and tapping his head against the board. "Maybe you should teach this game to Alassa."

"I think she already knows it," Imaiqah said seriously. "It is a *very* good representation of her life."

They shared a chuckle, then Imaiqah reached into her bag and produced a small chest, barely larger than one of the magical tomes they'd been studying in the library. "My father sent you this," she said, as she pressed her finger against the latch. There was a brief flash of *mana* and the chest unlocked. "It came through the Portal this morning and I didn't want to open it in front of everyone."

Emily nodded. Student mail was handed out in the dining hall, but most of the students seemed to put mail aside to open up later. Apparently, some of the mail was charmed to prevent strangers from forcing their way inside and reading it before the intended recipient and some of those charms were owned by specific families. But she would have been surprised to learn that Imaiqah's family had a charm of their own. As far as Emily knew, Imaiqah was the first magician in her bloodline.

"Here," Imaiqah said. "The warlock my father hired didn't know your karmic signature, so he used mine."

The chest was surprisingly heavy, but the lid opened easily. Inside ... Emily felt her eyes widen in shock. There was a small pile of glittering gold and silver coins, as well as a letter addressed to Imaiqah. Emily passed her friend the letter and touched the coins, unable to believe that they were quite real. If they were real gold and silver, she was holding more money in her hand than her family had ever enjoyed back home.

"He's been selling the idea of your new numbers and double-entry bookkeeping to everyone in the city," Imaiqah said, reading the letter. "Apparently, he swore them to silence about the exact details, but they were allowed to tell everyone else just how great an idea the new numbers were. And that's your share of the profits."

Emily couldn't believe her eyes. "And how much is the gold actually worth?"

Imaiqah looked puzzled. "It's worth its weight, of course," she said. "What do you mean?"

Not for the first time, Emily found herself wishing that she knew more about economics. She had a faint idea that gold backed modern currencies, and at one time those currencies had been pegged to the gold standard, but she wasn't sure what the gold standard actually *was*. Gold had once been useless, at least in a practical sense; it couldn't actually be destroyed. Or so she thought. Golden jewelry could be melted down to pay for goods and services, if necessary.

But gold might not buy everything. What good was a sack of gold on a desert island? Gold could only be used to buy items and services if those items were available. In one sense, it acted as a middleman between buyer and seller, rather than forcing them to bargain.

But ... she shook her head, confused. Like most subjects, economics seemed very simple until you tried to actually work out what it *meant*, let alone how to apply the lessons in real life. And half of what she knew about economics was just guesswork.

She picked up two of the coins and looked at them. They were stamped with a head that, she suspected, represented Alassa's father, but they were clearly not the same size and weight. She poked through the chest in puzzlement, looking at different coins. Whoever had stamped them out hadn't even bothered to *try* to get them to match. One was large enough to cover her palm, another was barely larger than a fingernail.

"That's why they weigh gold in the shops," Imaiqah said, taking pity on her. Emily was still trying to come to grips with the concept of two gold coins being worth vastly different values. Back home, money had been standardized by the government. "If the coin was too much, they'd either give you silver or clip off what they wanted from the original coin."

"It doesn't sound very precise," Emily said, doubtfully.

"It isn't," Imaiqah agreed. "And you won't believe what banks charge to reshape gold clippings into new coins. Or what punishments are handed out to people who try to make new coins out of tiny clips."

Imaiqah smiled suddenly as she kept reading the letter. "Father has managed to convince a pair of tailors to make your *bras*," she said, stumbling over the unfamiliar word. "He intends to see how well they sell before trying to sell the idea itself; he wonders if I can ask the Princess for Royal Patronage, something that would make it harder for others to copy the idea ... "

Emily stared at her, and then started to laugh. "Alassa! He expects *you* to ask *her* for Patronage?"

"It's the way the world works," Imaiqah said. "Banks won't loan money to father to help him expand without a powerful supporter in the background. And who better than the King's daughter?"

"Right," Emily said, doubtfully. She'd *met* Alassa. Emily had the private suspicion that Alassa wouldn't be able to hand out patronage on a whim, even if there were few other restraints on her behavior. If gold was the only metal of value, there would only be a certain amount of gold available to back investments. "Why don't the banks see his past success and gamble on him producing more money in the future?"

A thought struck Emily and she scowled. "Unless you have to be rich to actually put money in the bank, right?"

Imaiqah nodded.

Emily rolled her eyes. "Why am I not surprised?"

Smart banks, back home, knew better than to try to charge their customers to use their services. Their customers weren't just placing money in the bank; they were effectively *loaning* it to the bank, allowing the bank to use it to make other loans. A bank that charged customers for every little service—even something as simple as withdrawing money from an automated cash dispenser–would rapidly lose business. Here, she suspected, customers were charged for putting money in the bank, let alone everything else.

Suppose your total weekly earnings were ten silver coins, she considered. You should put it in the bank, behind solid doors and powerful wards, but the bank charged you one silver coin for each deposit and another silver coin for withdrawals. A smart merchant wouldn't give away money like that; he'd keep it under the bed, protected by whatever spells he could convince a wizard to make for him. As a result, there would be nothing fuelling economic growth.

"What a mess," she muttered. Coming to think of it, surely *someone* must have thought of opening up an investment bank. But didn't that require impartial laws? "What are you going to tell him?"

"Father always taught me never to promise something I couldn't provide," Imaiqah admitted. "I can try, but ... Alassa isn't going to do something for me, so I'll just have to suggest that he either approaches the King directly or abandons the idea of Royal Patronage. But approaching the King will be expensive."

Emily frowned. "You have to pay to see the King?"

Imaiqah shook her head. "You need an audience with His Majesty, so you approach the Royal Chamberlain or one of his flunkies. The King is supposed to see all comers, but the Royal Chamberlain is the one who determines who gets to go in before the King gets bored. So you have to cover his palm with silver to get him to let you in early, yet"–she shook her head again–"if someone with more money or higher status arrives after you, you might not be allowed to see the King at all."

"Typical corrupt politician," Emily said dryly. "He doesn't even stay bribed."

"And then the King's advisors might have something to say about your plea," Imaiqah added. "They might want a bribe themselves, or a share in the profits. Your competitors might have bribed them to try to prevent you from gaining patronage, or the guilds might think that you're trespassing on their territory, or ..."

"I see," Emily said. It was a wonder that *anything* got done, even in a relatively small Kingdom in the Allied Lands, though the rulers had absolute power. Maybe she should introduce the idea of democracy instead ... except it would probably lead to civil war, after which the necromancers would happily march in once the Allied Lands had finished tearing themselves apart. "Maybe he should just start selling them, knowing that they will be copied. At least the Royal Court won't be making a profit."

"Taxes," Imaiqah reminded her. "Another good reason not to put money in the bank. And if they think you're profitable enough to be interesting, they might try to muscle their way into your shop."

Emily closed the chest, thinking hard. She had a chunk of money now, and Void had given her some more, and there were other ways to make profits in the future. Once she had enough money, she could open a bank herself, maybe somewhere where the aristocrats would have difficulty seizing the money. Or maybe ...

She'd left her purse with Void, because it was useless. Her debit card wouldn't be anything more than a curiosity to the locals, but what if she could duplicate the basic idea behind the card? It was simple, apparently, to link two mirrors together in an unbreakable manner and use them as ... well, cell phones. One could be linked to a bank, which would verify that the carrier had fifty gold coins in their account and issue a promissory note to pay the seller when they or a designated representative visited the bank. She'd have to set up a helpdesk for her customers, maybe staffed at all hours. Who knew when someone would call? Maybe the mirrors could be keyed to only work for one person. She scribbled that idea down so she wouldn't forget it, reminding herself to look into how the city-states operated. They might be more tolerant of an investment bank than any of the monarchies.

"And now I am rich," she said, looking at the money. "What should I do with it?"

"Father says that if anyone asks, I should tell her to go purchase something at his store," Imaiqah said. They shared a laugh. "More seriously, you either need to place it in storage here or purchase your own treasure chest. That one is keyed to me, not to you. Storage is safer, but if you place it there Madame Razz will be able to monitor what you do with it."

Emily scowled. Madame Razz seemed to strike her as exactly the wrong sort of person to know what Emily was doing at any given time. They'd barely talked since Emily had entered the school, but Emily could sense Madame Razz's looming presence—and disapproval—every time she walked into the dorm. Emily had even heard her giving an angry lecture to a first-year girl who had apparently forgotten items she was meant to bring from home, a lecture that had reduced the younger girl to tears.

"Another good reason to create a proper bank," Emily said to herself. Parents and teachers never seemed to learn that kids kept things to themselves if the school refused to keep their secrets. A bank that didn't ask questions might earn vast profits through silence. "But if I lose the money, I don't get it back."

"Of course not," Imaiqah said. "You'd only get it repaid if it went into storage and you lost it anyway."

Imaiqah frowned. "Ask Aloha to put in her chest until after the visit to Dragon's Den," she suggested. "She'll probably try to charge you a gold coin for the service, but she won't try to steal any of the money. Or we can seal that chest before you give it to her. When you're in the city, buy a proper chest from a reputable Enchanter and have it delivered to the school. It can be a good thing to have a chest that no one, not even a tutor, can open without destroying the contents."

Emily blinked. "You mean they look inside our cupboards?"

"I wouldn't be too surprised if they did," Imaiqah said darkly. "Do you know how many dangerous alchemical ingredients we're not supposed to bring into the school?"

"No," Emily admitted.

"Dragon's Blood is the prime example; it's so hugely magical that you can break through almost any ward by applying it properly," Imaiqah said. "You barely need to prepare it at all, according to Professor Thande. Or there's venom from a Basilisk, eyes from a Cockatrice ... apparently, there's a function for Centaur's blood that Thande told us we weren't supposed to know until we graduated. Anyone who is caught with any of those ingredients can be expelled. They're *that* dangerous."

"Oh," Emily said. There was a pause. "They can't force you to open your chest?"

Imaiqah looked shocked. "Of course not. You *can't* open a magician's chest without their permission. Outside Whitehall, only an idiot or someone tired of life would try to break into a magician's house. The magician could do *anything* to them and no one would dare complain. It's one of the fundamental rules of magic!"

Emily looked down at the board and suspected that she knew why. "No one's told me when we're going to Dragon's Den," she said, changing the subject. "When *are* we going?"

"Two weeks, I think," Imaiqah said. "It's not a *right*, so if you manage to get in trouble—again—you probably won't be allowed to go. I've heard that some students have begged to be caned rather than denied the chance to get out of the school for a few hours."

"Oh," Emily said. "And what does the Warden say?"

"Tells them not to waste his time," Imaiqah said. She chuckled. "Perhaps they should pretend that they don't care about going."

Emily wasn't sure if *she* cared. She wouldn't have cared back home, but here ... she'd seen almost nothing of life, apart from Void's tower, Whitehall and ruined cities. It would be nice to see how ordinary people lived. Perhaps it would give her more ideas for things that could be introduced from her world.

"Ask your father about stirrups," Emily said, finally. She'd confirmed that they didn't exist in this world, which wasn't too surprising. The Persians who had fought the Roman Empire had relied on their horsemen, but they had never invented stirrups either. "Maybe he can offer them to the Kingdom's army. *That* should earn him some patronage."

## Chapter Twenty-Four

The air near Dragon's Den smelled...*odd*.

Emily stuck her head out of the carriage window and peered out as they drove down the slope towards the city. Dragon's Den was situated in the middle of a large valley, surrounded by a handful of farms concealed and protected by the vast mountains that also protected Whitehall from the necromancers. The farms didn't seem large enough to feed an entire city, but if they had portals, she reasoned, they could bring in food from anywhere else if necessary. She sniffed the air and winced as she realized that the city–more like a large town, by her world's standards–didn't have anything reassembling proper sanitation, not like Whitehall. The population must be living in squalor.

The horse-drawn carriages shuddered as they crossed a bridge and headed towards a giant stone dragon placed in front of the town, looking north. It was remarkably lifelike, so lifelike that she couldn't help wondering if it was a real dragon that had been turned to stone by a medusa like Snake Face. Up close, the dragon was ugly as sin, but there was a certain nobility about it that held her gaze. She wanted to see if she could cast a spell to release it from petrification, if it was a real dragon, yet what sort of spell would work on it?

The carriages rumbled past the statue and towards the walls surrounding the city. Ahead of them, the gates were slowly starting to open.

Emily's eyes opened wide as the carriages advanced through the gate–through a section that was obviously intended to trap anyone trying to storm the city–and into the city itself. It was small, but intensely populated, with massive buildings piled on top of other buildings which provided enough living space for thousands of people. The buildings looked vaguely Roman, reminding her of artwork she'd seen in comics about an indomitable Gaul. Many of them had a statue placed in front of the entrances - all human. They couldn't *all* be petrified humans, could they?

"They're local gods," Imaiqah said when Emily asked. "They're raised up to protect the people who live inside the buildings."

The carriages rumbled to a halt inside a large courtyard. Mistress Irene shouted for them to climb out.

Emily found herself gagging as she stumbled down to the ground, breathing in something she didn't even *want* to identify. The ground was covered in cobblestones that *looked* clean–probably wiped by servants or slaves - but the smell of horse poop was ever-present. She suddenly remembered reading about the problems New York had with the horse-drawn carriages back in the 1800s and shuddered. Dragon's Den would likely have the same problems, without even the hope of automobiles to make the problem go away.

"Some of you have been here before," Mistress Irene said, after the students had gathered around her. "For those of you who haven't, Dragon's Den is a free city. Try not to irritate the City Guard too much as the Grandmaster will be very annoyed if he has to smooth out ruffled feathers."

Her voice hardened. "Keep one hand on your money pouches at all times and don't ever drop your locking spells. If you do happen to run into trouble, cast a summoning spell and call me at once. Don't let any shopkeeper push you into buying anything, unless you break it. Bargain at will.

"I'll expect you all back here by sixteen bells. Anyone who returns too late will not be coming here next month."

Imaiqah grabbed Emily's arm as the students started to disperse out of the courtyard, and into the city. "We have plenty of time to explore," she said. "Where would you like to go first?"

Emily hesitated. The only kind of shopping she really enjoyed was book shopping, but books were hideously expensive in this world. It was remarkable just how many books Whitehall had been able to amass over the years if every book had to be handmade. Maybe the accountants from the Accounting Guilds would become bookmakers once they were put completely out of business, making books a little cheaper. And maybe the ability to read would spread further, enough to widen the market a little. Only a relative handful of people in this world knew how to read.

"Anywhere," she said finally. She *did* have gold coins in her money pouch, after all. "I need to buy a chest, don't I?"

Imaiqah nodded. "So we go find a reputable Enchanter. Let's go visit the market."

The smell grew stronger as they walked through the streets, passing blank apartment blocks and shops that sold a mix of fruit and vegetables. Emily saw apples and oranges, as well as several fruits–at least she thought they were fruits–that she didn't recognize. One stall, well apart from the others, sold something that looked like pineapples, but they stank so terribly that she couldn't understand why anyone would want to buy them. The trader still seemed to be doing a roaring trade. She paused outside a shop selling musical instruments and had to smile when she recognized a pair of bagpipes. There were violins, trumpets and a harp, but no guitars.

"My father wants my sister to become a player," Imaiqah said. "A decent harpist can make plenty of money, and the shop can't support all of us."

Emily felt cold as the implications sank in. Historically, male children were more *useful* than female children; they could work harder and didn't have to leave the household when they got married. And girls needed a dowry that could wreck a poor family's finances. Having too many children meant that the parents might have to sell their kids or worse just to stay alive. It was a point about the medieval world that her teachers had glossed over when she'd studied it in school.

She opened her mouth, but found herself speechless. What could she say?

They turned a corner onto a crowded street and stopped to allow a black-painted carriage to drive past, the driver whipping the horse to make it walk straight at the crowds blocking its way. Imaiqah identified the carriage as belonging to one of the Great Houses of Dragon's Den, the families that between them owned much of the city and effectively ran it to suit themselves. They paid the City Guard to keep order and, just incidentally, keep their competitors under control.

"They're not as bad as some aristocrats," Imaiqah explained as the carriage vanished into the distance. "They do sometimes listen to the population. And they're cheaper to bribe."

"Oh," Emily said. "What happens when someone makes money independently of the Great Houses?"

"They invite the newcomer to join them," Imaiqah said, with a quick grin. "My father wants that status for ourselves, even if we have to move into the nearest city-state. The Great Houses respect ability far more than anyone outside the cities."

Emily nodded, thoughtfully. A revolution in a city-state—even a brief rebellion that was put down quickly—would wreak more havoc than one in a monarchy, where there was a powerful army and a more beaten-down population. The Great Houses might be more inclined to listen to their population than they were prepared to admit, as well as rewarding those who did well by allowing them to join the local power structure. Perhaps, if they believed that wealth—or rather the ability to create wealth—was inheritable, they were strengthening their own bloodlines by bringing newcomers into the family.

She looked over at Imaiqah. "Is it likely that Alassa will ever marry a commoner?"

Imaiqah laughed out loud. "Of course not! Her marriage will be arranged by her parents, probably to a fop who won't ever threaten their Kingdom. Or to someone they want to keep close to their family."

*Or perhaps to someone who can rule properly,* Emily thought, and shivered.

They turned into another street and stopped. Emily stared at a man who was tossing fireballs in the air and swallowing them one by one. Behind him, another man struck poses like a demented martial arts poser, but magic crackled over him every time he snapped his fingers or pointed at the ground. It took Emily a moment to realize that they were looking at street performers, magicians with just enough power to entertain pedestrians. The lead magician caught her eye and waved his hand through the air. A shimmering image of Emily's face formed from fire and drifted in front of her, just before it dispelled itself into nothingness.

"Show off," Imaiqah said as they walked past. "This street houses most of the magicians in town."

Emily nodded as she took in the shops. There were four different stores selling magical ingredients, two that sold various tools for young magicians and a single bookstore, crammed with scrolls and handmade books. A Healer's shop sat beyond them, the writing on the wall promising a cure for everything from cold to deadly poison. It was followed by a large pet store.

At first, Emily couldn't understand why a pet store would count as magic, before she remembered what she'd read about familiars. An animal with enough magic would be able to help its owner cast spells, in exchange for food, drink and a mental link. The books she'd read had warned that there was always a price for such magic, with the owners often taking on the characteristics of their pet. It wasn't practiced at Whitehall until Second Year.

"Some magic students never really develop the potential to study at Whitehall," Imaiqah said softly. "Most apprentice themselves to local magicians and study under them, brewing basic potions or enchanting artifacts for their customers. They're skilled, in their own way, but I think they don't really understand what they're doing. My father wanted to apprentice me to one before Whitehall's journeyman convinced him that it would be dangerous for both me and him."

Emily nodded. Imaiqah's father seemed like a practical man. He hadn't asked any questions about where Emily's ideas came from, although he *had* to be bursting with curiosity. Emily would have asked long ago, if she'd been in his place, but he was a merchant who wouldn't want to kill the goose that laid the golden eggs. It wasn't as if she was selling him something that had a nasty sting in the tail.

"Very dangerous," a voice said, from behind them. "It would have crippled the poor girl."

Emily spun around as the world blurred around her, raising her hands to cast a defensive spell. A man was right behind her, wearing a hood that concealed his features ... how had he come so close without her being aware of his presence? Imaiqah seemed to be frozen, along with the rest of the street, her form slightly blurred ... Then the figure pulled back his hood to reveal his face. Emily relaxed in relief as she recognized Void.

"We don't have too long to talk," Void said. Now that she knew much more about magic, she could sense the vast reserves of power surrounding the sorcerer. "The spell that isolates us from the world can't be maintained for very long."

Emily glanced at Imaiqah. Her friend was frozen solid, as if time itself had been stopped ...

"You've stopped *time*," she gasped, in absolute disbelief. She'd once watched a movie based on that premise, but it had been silly and probably unrealistic. "What ... how have you done it?"

"Only in a very small area," Void said. He was uncomfortably close to her, but as Emily looked around she realized that the spell was barely a meter in radius. "And we can't actually move outside the bubble without collapsing it. Time doesn't seem to like people who attempt to defy her rules."

Emily nodded, gathering herself. "What are you doing here?"

"I merely wanted to see how you were coping with Whitehall," Void said. "You've created quite a stir, you know? There's an Accounting Guild that wants your head on a platter, preferably not attached to your body."

Emily swallowed. "I didn't mean to ruin their lives ..."

"Oh, don't worry about it," Void said. He waved his hand through the air dismissively. "And don't worry about what you did to that silly brat of a princess either. It's good to remind the nobility that sorcerers have power from time to time. Keeps them properly respectful."

"I nearly killed her," Emily pointed out. "Would *you* have killed her when you were my age?"

"My magic surfaced a bit earlier than yours," Void said absently. His eyes sharpened, suddenly. "And I would probably have transformed her into something awful and left her that way long enough to teach her a lesson."

Emily *looked* at him. "What's the story between you and the Grandmaster, anyway?"

Void shrugged. "Why do you want to know?"

"Because the Grandmaster seems to be willing to give me classes that I shouldn't be able to take for years. Because I practically got away with almost murdering a Royal Princess. Because ... because they seem willing to do exactly what you suggest."

"Let's just say," Void said, after a long moment, "that the Grandmaster and I have many differences of opinion, but we are on the same side."

"Yes, but you seem to live an independent existence," Emily pointed out. "How many sorcerers are there like you?"

"That's a result of power," Void said. "You may end up in a Tower of your own one day."

Emily sensed that she wasn't going to get a straighter answer, so she changed the subject. "Why are they all so stupid?"

Void smiled. "I beg your pardon?"

"The Allied Lands," Emily said. "They should unite against the necromancers, but they spend half of their time fighting each other."

"Just like the necromancers," Void said. He looked down at his pale hands. "Many of the aristocrats who are in power at the moment are descended from those who ruled the First Empire. They made themselves Kings when the Empire was destroyed. Do you think that they want to accept subordination again?"

He snorted. "There are rumors that there once was a missing heir to the Empire's throne. They killed him, just to make sure the Empire could never rise again."

"I see," Emily said. "And there are no blood descendants anywhere?"

"Not as far as anyone knows," Void admitted. He shook his head. "But you're right. They are crippling the war effort."

He looked over at Imaiqah's frozen form. "Wouldn't it work so much better if this one was in charge of the war?"

"Probably," Emily said. "Why don't you take over the world?"

Void gave her a long, searching look. "There have been magicians who sought vast power over the world. Care to guess what happened to them?"

Emily winced as the realization struck her. "They became necromancers. Why ... why did they become so corrupt?"

"They wanted *power* and power tends to corrupt," Void observed. He paused, as if he was trying to decide if he should tell her something. "There are ... *accidents*, sometimes, when a magician gains vastly boosted powers. They are *always* terrifying to the rest of the world because the magician might be driven mad, or plunge headlong into necromancy. And then there are the idiots who think they can handle necromancy and use its power for good."

He shook his head. "There was a King who believed he could keep control of himself if he asked for volunteers to be sacrificed. It seemed to work fine, at first, until his mind became so twisted that he deluded himself that his entire Kingdom had volunteered to be sacrificed. He would have killed them all if his son hadn't stuck a knife in his back."

Emily nodded, thoughtfully. If *Berserker* was addictive, necromancy had to be even more dangerous. Void seemed to be suggesting that *no one* managed to avoid addiction, which inevitably led to disaster.

"But never mind that for the moment," Void said. He looked down into her eyes. "You are aware that you have been noticed, aren't you?"

"You sent me to Whitehall on a Dragon," Emily pointed out. "And you told everyone that I was a Child of Destiny."

"You *are* a Child of Destiny," Void said. "I never told them a lie."

"Yes, but ..." Emily found herself groping for words and failing. "I'm not a Child of Destiny in the sense that they mean."

"What does that have to do with anything?" Void asked, honestly puzzled. "The world may not revolve around you, but you became very important the moment our friend from the dark side plucked you out of your world and brought you here. And you have already crippled a Guild that was known for being corrupt, greedy, bloated and stupid. And you have given a royal brat a lesson she needs for the future. And your stirrups may change the way we fight wars."

He grinned, mischievously. "Child of Destiny or not, you are changing the world," he reminded her. "I'd suggest you never tell them the truth. If they think that you *are* a Child of Destiny, they're likely to be careful about tangling with you. Your very nature might cause their plots to fail spectacularly."

"But they *won't*," Emily insisted, feeling as if she'd been thrown to the lions. "I'm not what they think I am!"

"But perhaps you're what they *need*," Void said seriously. He shrugged. "If nothing else, remember that the necromancers are still out there. Anything you can do to help the Allied Lands defeat them for good would be very much appreciated."

He lifted one hand and frowned. "The spell is about to collapse. I suggest that you don't mention this discussion to anyone."

"Wait," Emily said. "Is there a reliable Enchanter in this city?"

Void smiled. "Try Yodel," he advised. "He can produce almost anything if you give him enough time. I've known sorcerers who weren't too proud to go to him and ask for help."

He pulled his invisibility spell around himself and vanished, just as time started to return to normal.

## Chapter Twenty-Five

IMAIQAH DIDN'T SEEM TO HAVE NOTICED THAT ANYTHING HAD HAPPENED, WHICH WAS SOMEthing of a relief. Emily's thoughts were churning as they walked onwards, and Imaiqah's chatter helped distract her from her worries. Just what had she started by introducing a concept as simple as Arabic numerals, or even bras? Or stirrups?

"This is an Enchanter's store," Imaiqah said, as they paused outside a stone building marked *YODEL*. She hesitated. "They normally allow only one person to enter the shop at a time, so I'll go visit the clothes store while you purchase a chest."

Emily nodded. "Very well. I'll see you after I'm done."

Imaiqah had been rewarded by her father for discovering Emily; he'd sent her enough money to buy a formal dress for the next public event in Whitehall. Alassa had made fun of Imaiqah's clothes, among other things, and Emily could understand why Imaiqah would want a change.

The door opened as she approached, allowing her to step into a darkened room smelling faintly of wood. It was crammed with dozens of artifacts, some apparently recognizable and others completely beyond her understanding. One table held a human hand with the fingers removed and replaced by candles; another held a skull with glowing rubies in place of eyes. Emily studied the hand for a long moment, sensing powerful magic flickering around it, but she couldn't even begin to determine its purpose. Instead, she looked at a candlestick and frowned. It seemed perfectly normal, one she could have bought back home. As far as she could tell, it didn't seem to have any magic at all.

"You'd discover that it only works when lit," a voice said, from behind her. She spun around to see a little old man, wearing a workshop robe and dark glasses. "Should you light it, you will be the only one able to see the light. It is a simple charm, but very effective."

"Clever," Emily said.

"Yep," Yodel agreed. He pointed to the skull. "Long ago, there was a great magician who copied his mind into his friend's skull so that future generations would have access to his wisdom. The spell was duplicated and there are now countless copies of long-gone mages floating throughout the world. Do you wish advice from a past master of the art?"

Emily hesitated, and then shook her head.

"A wise decision," Yodel said. "I find that their screaming tends to outweigh the prospect of learning advanced magical knowledge from them. Besides, the *real* masters never try to duplicate their smarts."

He turned and led her further into the store, pointing at various objects. "I could give you a crystal spelled to alert you when your enemies are near. Or you could have a glass that always provides fresh water. Or even a metal wand for charging ward-spells."

Emily nodded towards a tiny carving of a bird. "What's that?"

"Touch it," Yodel said. He smiled at her expression. "It's quite harmless, I assure you. I do good work."

Up close, the wooden bird was *very* detailed. Emily allowed her fingers to touch it lightly and ...

... She was flying through the air, her wings beating as she soared over the land far below ...

... And then she was back in her own body, staggering back.

"Not many people manage to cope for long, their first time," Yodel said kindly. "I charmed a bird's memories into it, and then allowed people to feel them for themselves. They miss out on so much when all they can do is transfigure themselves and others into birds."

Emily stared at him. "I found it ... disconcerting," she said, after a long beat. She could feel her heart thudding in her chest. "Do people actually buy things like that?"

"You'd be surprised," Yodel said. He tapped a kingmaker board. "Perhaps I can sell you one charmed to actually play by itself? Or one designed to enhance your own playing skills?"

"Cheating, you mean," Emily said. She'd once played a boy who'd used an Ipad to cheat before she'd caught on to what he was doing. "I wouldn't learn anything from that, would I?"

"Matter of opinion," Yodel said. He stopped and looked directly at her. "And what, really, do you want?"

"I need a storage chest," Emily said. "I was told that you were the best enchanter in town."

"The best for half the continent," Yodel informed her. He led Emily into one of his backrooms and summoned a ball of light. "As you can see, I have seven different chests in stock at the moment, all charmed to hold almost anything and sealed to one user. Or I can make you another chest to your specifications, but that will cost more."

Emily looked at one of the chests and fell in love. It was a mahogany treasure chest right out of a pirate movie, with a single large golden lock on the front. She touched it, very lightly, and felt spells crackling around the wood, waiting for the wrong person to try to open it.

Yodel tapped the lock and it opened, revealing an interior that seemed to stretch to infinity and beyond. He picked up a wand and dropped it into the darkness, then held his hand over the chest.

"Wand," he said. The wand popped up into his hand. "Should you forget what you put into the chest, you can order it to show you everything, or merely empty itself out onto the floor."

"Clever," Emily said much more sincerely this time. "How secure is it?"

"The charms are guaranteed to stand up against anyone but a first-rank cursebreaker," Yodel informed her. "But if someone breaks the charms without the correct spells, it will collapse the pocket dimension and everything inside will be lost. I can produce a chest that connects to a permanent pocket dimension, allowing you to recover your property later, but that will be rather more expensive. This one costs approximately twenty gold coins."

Emily looked at the chest and couldn't resist asking the obvious question. "What if *I* wanted to sleep inside the box?"

"The preservation spells—which are of my own design—wouldn't let you," Yodel said. "I have known sorcerers who have tried to design chests with sleeping accommodations, but the spells are far from simple and easily frayed. It is not recommended."

"Pity," Emily said. She'd been having visions of something rather like the TARDIS. "Can you have it shipped to Whitehall?"

"Once you purchase it, I can have it transported to the building," Yodel said. "You'll have to bond yourself to the chest here and now, but there would be no problem with shipping it to you. It would be useless to anyone else, including me."

He straightened up and closed the lid. "Do you want to buy it?"

Emily looked at the other chests, and then back at the original. "Yes," she said, reaching into her money pouch. "Twenty gold coins, right?"

Yodel took the money and ordered her to press her hand against the chest's lock, while muttering a spell under his breath. Emily felt a slight tingle and nothing more, but when she tried to open the lock it opened easily, almost as if the heavy wood weighed nothing at all. She put it down and watched as Yodel weighed the gold, before nodding and passing her a parchment scroll. It was written in a spidery hand that she found difficult to read.

"Instructions," Yodel grunted. "And is there anything else you can buy while you're here?"

"I don't think so," Emily said as he escorted her back to the door. "What is that ... hand and candle thing *for*?"

"It's a Hand of Glory," Yodel said. "You can use it to open doors, or gateways; you could go *anywhere* with it. Very few people know how to make them and the price is staggering."

Emily looked at the hand and made a mental note to consider the possible implications later, then paused in the doorway. "When will the chest arrive at the school?"

"Tomorrow, probably," Yodel said. "I'll have to see what else is purchased today, and then send it all up in one carriage."

Outside, Emily gathered herself as the noise of the city returned to her ears, before glancing into the nearby clothes store. Imaiqah was still inside, trying on dresses; Emily rolled her eyes and looked around for another store, one that might be more interesting.

There was an Apothecary on the other side of the street and, remembering what Professor Thande had said about buying ingredients from Apothecaries, Emily walked over and opened the door. Inside, there was a large room crammed with shelves, each one containing bottles and jars of ingredients. There was a faint smell hanging in the air that reminded her of spices from Earth. She had to fight down the urge to sneeze.

"Welcome to my store," a voice said. She looked up and saw a fat woman with a big smile that didn't quite touch her eyes. "I hope that you're not planning to leave without paying for what you take?"

Emily blinked in surprise, and then anger. "I am just browsing," she said, annoyed. How *dare* a shopkeeper accuse her of planning to steal from her store? "Do you treat all your customers like this?"

The woman drew back. "I can see that you have too much pride to steal. And are you looking for something special? I have crushed dandelions that can be used to charm an unwary heart into love or care. Or I can sell you seeds that grow into sweet-flavored leaves. Very good for those who want to relax."

"I'm just looking," Emily said, picking up a jar marked Bat Urine. She couldn't imagine what it could do, but she'd seen Professor Thande produce all kinds of potions with weird ingredients. "Do you have anything ... *interesting*?"

"I have a very small bottle of Dragon's Blood, but it was promised to another customer," the woman said. Her smiled grew wider. "It is going for the low price of five *hundred* gold coins, but it can be yours for *six* hundred ..."

Emily started to laugh. Dragon's Blood was rare, very rare. Very few books agreed on the subject of dragons, but they all said that dragons were very hard to kill, let alone bleed for their magically-charged blood. And they were powerful, shielded from almost all charms by scaly armor and the raw magic field that allowed them to fly. There were legends of entire countries destroyed in the past by angry dragons. None of them made pleasant reading.

It *had* to be fake. One might as well buy a luxury yacht for ten dollars.

"Ah, I can see that you're a *real* magician," the woman said. "I can sell you something *really* interesting, if you'll come with me ..."

She walked through a curtain into a rear compartment. Emily followed her and readied a shielding charm just in case it was a trap. She stepped into what looked like a strange pet shop. One cage was filled with spiders, each one larger than her hand, endlessly scuttling around behind the glass walls. Emily felt her skin crawl as the spiders turned to look at her, before returning to their dance. She looked away and saw another tank filled with sparkly fish, reminding her of the charms they'd used in Martial Magic. A third cage held a pair of white mice and a dozen rats; apart from twitching, they seemed to be doing almost nothing.

"They were produced by an animalist magician with plenty of magic and a willingness to do *anything* just to see what would happen," the woman informed her. "They can actually *think* for themselves, would you believe? I shudder to think of what would happen if they got loose among the rats in the town."

Emily shook her head in disbelief, a little overwhelmed by the sight.

The shopkeeper misunderstood. "You think that that isn't fascinating? Come and look at *this*!"

She tapped a birdcage angrily. Something stirred in the far corner.

Emily frowned. At first, she thought that she was looking at a tiny bird, complete with wings, and then she saw the body between the wings. It was impossible ... and yet, she'd seen enough over the past weeks to know that nothing was truly impossible when it came to magic.

"Ah," the woman said. "I've impressed you at last, have I?"

Emily said nothing as she stared at the fairy. She was tiny, barely larger than Emily's middle finger, but chillingly human. Her naked body suggested a teenage girl, with blonde hair and perfectly-shaped breasts, yet she had black wings growing out of her bare back. Emily couldn't believe what she saw.

Slowly, the fairy settled back in the cage, as if she were trying to cover herself in a desperate search for modesty–or merely hide from their gaze. Very briefly, she met the fairy's dark eyes. It was impossible to escape the sense that the fairy was an intelligent creature in her own right.

Emily felt guilty–and dirty - for even *looking* at the poor creature.

"What ... ?" She swallowed hard, and then started again. "What do you intend to do with her?"

"It, dear," the woman said. "Not *her.* I intend to cut off her wings and use them to produce a very specific potion, and then sell her to one of the city's selectmen with rather curious tastes in ..."

"You can't," Emily interrupted her. "That isn't something you can just *kill.*"

"She isn't human," the woman said. Emily felt sick, fighting down the urge to cast the botched spells she'd tried to use on Alassa again. Only the danger of challenging a magician of unknown power convinced her to stay her hand. "I bought her fair and square." Her voice became calculating. "Unless, of course, you wish to buy her for yourself?"

Emily stared at her, not bothering to disguise her loathing. "How much?"

"Interesting," the woman mused. "You want the entire creature, I presume? That could cost you ten gold coins."

"Ten gold coins," Emily repeated. The price for fake Dragon's Blood made that look like nothing, but ten gold coins was a major chunk of her savings. "How much would you make if you sold her and her wings?"

The fairy howled as she heard the words, a thin sound that almost made Emily's heart break.

"Maybe seven gold coins," the woman mused. "But you could easily make your money back if you ground her up and mixed the remains with ..."

"I'll give you eight gold coins," Emily said. It might not be a smart thing to do–she had no idea how many fairies there were–but she felt as if she had no choice. She wasn't going to leave the fairy to be mutilated and then used for whatever horrifying purpose the town's selectman had in mind. "And that's the best offer you will get."

The woman reached into the cage, picked up the fairy by her gossamer wings and pulled her out of the cage. Emily winced when she saw the dark wings, shimmering like a soap bubble on the verge of bursting, just before the fairy was dumped into her hand. She resisted the urge to stroke the creature as she put her down on the table and reached into her coin pouch for the money. Maybe she *had* been cheated, but she couldn't do anything else. The fairy's plight had affected her on a very basic level.

"Here," she snarled, and gave the shopkeeper the money. "Thank you!"

She picked up the fairy and stalked out of the store, into the open air. The fairy's wings came to life at once, beating against her palm until she opened her hand and let the fairy drift up into the air like a giant bee. Her dark wings were moving so rapidly that the fairy seemed surrounded by inky darkness.

Feeling like a pervert, Emily looked away, embarrassed. When she looked back, the fairy was gone.

Imaiqah was *still* trying on clothes, utterly unaware of what Emily had just done. Some of the clothes looked like silk, which came–if Emily recalled correctly–from living creatures. Were they animals in this world, or were they as intelligent as the fairy she'd liberated? The thought sickened her. Professor Locke had claimed that human mistreatment of other intelligent creatures had helped lead to the wars that had almost destroyed humanity. How many other crimes, beside slaughtered fairies and bled dragons, were committed in the name of magic?

Shaking her head, Emily walked onwards until she happened to glance into a courtyard and saw Alassa sitting in front of a table, a glass of red liquid sitting in front of her. The Princess didn't look happy at all, Emily realized; in fact, it almost looked as if she had been crying. Emily hesitated, unsure of what she should do, before stepping into the courtyard and realizing that it was an upscale drinking establishment, almost completely deserted. Alassa looked up, saw her, and made a face.

Emily almost walked away, but something told her to stay. She'd worked with Alassa on Basic Charms long enough to know that there *was* a human being buried under the royal arrogance and carelessness that seemed to make up her public persona. Besides, she *had* hurt Alassa very badly, even if it had been thoroughly deserved. No one could experience something like that without being badly scarred, even if nothing was visible.

"Hi," Emily said, as lightly as she could. "Do you want to talk about it?"

Alassa's hand twitched, as if she were on the verge of reaching for her wand. "Do you *think* I want to talk about it?"

Emily almost walked away a second time, and then forced herself to sit down. "I think you *need* to talk about it," she said seriously. Alassa's face reminded her of her own, back when she'd seen no way out of her life, apart from death. "You seem depressed."

Alassa began to laugh, bitterly. "Depressed," she repeated. "I have a problem and I don't know how to cope with it. I'd say I'm depressed!"

Emily studied her for a long moment. "And what is your problem?"

Alassa's laugh became a cruel, sardonic giggle. "My problem?" She repeated, between giggles. "My problem is you!"

## Chapter Twenty-Six

"ME?"

Alassa nodded, looking down at her glass. "You. You've ruined my life."

Emily stared at her, puzzled. How, exactly, had she ruined Alassa's life?

True, the Royal Brat had needed a lesson in the dangers of picking on people, and she was actually making progress on Basic Charms - with Emily's help.

But then, Emily thought, it was possible that Alassa, unlike many of the other students, had never had to grow up. Instead, she'd been a Royal Princess, coddled from the moment she drew her first breath.

One of Emily's older teachers from back home had told his class that there was a difference between urban children and those from the countryside. Urban children were rarely taught anything useful, at least in a *practical* sense, while the children from the countryside started helping their parents from a very early age. Emily hadn't believed him at the time–she knew kids who'd had paper routes to earn money–but right now she understood what he meant. A child like Imaiqah, born to a hard-working merchant, needed to help her father as soon as she could walk, just to repay the resources he'd invested in her. Imaiqah had needed to grow up very quickly; indeed, Emily suspected that Imaiqah's natural mathematical talents were far greater than anyone Emily had known back home, perhaps because Imaiqah had been figuring sums for her father as soon as she could grasp the concept of two plus two.

Alassa, on the other hand, had never really had to learn anything, let alone work for a living or train for war. A Crown Prince was taken to the field as soon as he could walk in order to be schooled in the arts of fighting, but no one would dream of exposing a Crown Princess to such treatment. Those delicate little girls were the mothers of the next generation of royalty. They were to be cosseted and protected and...

...Whatever else could be said about Alassa's upbringing, she had not been properly prepared for the real world. Alassa was a Mary of Scotland, Emily decided, rather than Elizabeth of England. And Mary had ended up having her head cut off by her cousin, the first Queen Elizabeth.

"I didn't mean to ruin your life," Emily said after a long pause. It was hard to pick and choose the right words. Her school had once sent her to a psychologist and she'd found the entire process maddening. The moron had asked silly questions and then not even bothered to listen to the answers. Now, she felt a twinge of sympathy for him. "And I didn't mean to get you paddled either."

Alassa glared at her. "Did you mean to almost kill me?"

"No, but you *did* start it," Emily said. She wasn't about to prostrate herself in front of a spoiled brat, even if Alassa *had* started to grow up. "You turned me into ... *something* and you tormented my friend. Didn't anyone tell you not to do someone a *small* injury?"

Alassa picked up her glass and took a swig. "My parents told me that I would be Queen one day," she said, absently. "I tried to act like a Princess."

"I'd say you succeeded," Emily said, unable to resist the chance to be snide. Of course, Alassa didn't understand the joke. She turned back to the original topic of conversation. "What happened?"

"I don't understand," Alassa said. "Where did I go wrong?"

Emily felt her eyes narrow. "What did your parents say to you?"

Alassa looked up at her, meeting her eyes. "Where do you come from, really?"

"Somewhere else," Emily said, discarding the thought of lying outright. "Why does it matter?"

"My parents sent me a letter," Alassa said. She took another sip of her drink. "Their Man-At-Arms has told them that a merchant in their city has introduced his horsemen to something called *stirrups*. This same merchant has also introduced a new system for counting numbers that has pushed the Accounting Guild into demanding action. And all of these innovations already have names. Duncan tells me that the accounting system is *mature*."

She didn't take her eyes off Emily's face. "Even *I* know that a new spell, one created from scratch, needs time and effort before it is workable. Your accounting system seems perfect, too perfect to be true."

Emily blinked. "*My* accounting system?"

"The merchant who introduced it is Imaiqah's father," Alassa said tartly. "How many different ideas can one man have?"

*Benjamin Franklin had thousands of ideas*, Emily thought. But Franklin—or even his son—wouldn't have been considered a suitable influence in this world. And he, too, had stood on the shoulders of giants.

"You gave your friend these ideas and she gave them to her father," Alassa said. Her voice held no doubt at all. "And now they're already upsetting the world."

She tapped the table. "And my parents have told me, they *ordered* me, to get close to the Child of Destiny. They said that I was to encourage you to help us without causing further disruptions in the Kingdom ... They said I was to help *you*, to learn from *you* ... I told them that you were tutoring me and they were *proud*! My father said that I could even invite you home for the holidays!"

Emily stared at her in absolute disbelief, and then found her voice. "You have to be kidding. Me? Visit a King and Queen?"

"You're a Child of Destiny," Alassa said. "Anointed by a dragon. What am I to you?"

"I - I don't know," Emily admitted. She *wasn't* a Child of Destiny. And yet she'd already upset the world. Did Alassa's parents believe that Emily could be used to secure their Kingdom, if they made nice with her, or did they think they could use her to keep control as the ripples of change grew stronger? If they had known—or suspected—some of the other concepts that Emily had suggested to Imaiqah's father, they would have fainted. "I didn't ask for this."

"I looked in a book," Alassa said. "No Child of Destiny has ever *wanted* to be a Child of Destiny. That doesn't stop them from changing the world."

Emily suspected they'd read the same book. *Children of Destiny* was thin, barely passing for genuine scholarship. It was really nothing more than a list of Children and their exploits, some rather extraordinary. The one factor that almost all of them had had in common was that they had been declared Children of Destiny *after* they had already changed the world. Hindsight, it seemed, allowed them to be identified easily.

Curious, Emily had tried to determine if magic could be used to see the future. The books had been quite vague on the subject, which suggested to her that it wasn't really possible, at least not in any useful way. That fitted in with what Emily knew of the many-worlds theory, along with simple common sense. If she were told that doing something would kill her, she'd do something else, which would invalidate the prophecy.

But Shadye had clearly believed that he *could* identify a Child of Destiny—and failed spectacularly.

Yet Emily *was* changing the world.

*And if you believe that you're infallible,* a little voice whispered at the back of her mind, *you'll fall down hard for sure.*

"I didn't mean to do that either," Emily admitted. "And I am sorry for whatever I have done to you."

"You're sorry?" Alassa demanded. She swept the glass off the table and watched as it crashed to the ground. "You're *sorry?*"

Her voice hardened, as if she was trying hard not to cry. "I'm the laughing stock of the school. I can't even cast a simple spell properly. A girl with barely a week's experience in magic almost kills me. The Warden whips me and then leaves me to stand, in the corridor, as I cry. My friends snigger at me behind my back. No one takes me seriously any longer."

Emily saw real tears in Alassa's eyes as she raged on. "And now my parents tell me that I should cuddle up to you, the girl who shattered everything I ever had, and convince you to be my friend. I'd rather die! Do you know what it's like to have everyone laughing at you behind your back?"

"Yes," Emily said flatly. She knew what it was like to be alone, and friendless ... and Alassa hadn't had any real friends. Maybe no one would dare touch her, or pick on her, but being alone was enough of a torment for a growing teenage girl. Or maybe, now that Emily had escaped serious punishment for almost killing her, others would be emboldened to strike back at their former tormentor. "I used to be very alone."

She hesitated, looking for the right words. "You're still the Crown Princess, aren't you?"

Alassa looked up, through tears. "Yes, but what does that matter?"

"So you haven't lost everything at all," Emily pointed out, in a calm and reasonable voice. "You will pass Basic Charms and start mastering more complex spells. Over time, you will mature and become a Queen your subjects can respect and follow. All that you have really lost is the delusion that your cronies were actually your friends."

She hesitated, then gambled. "Maybe my task as a Child of Destiny is to steer you into becoming the best Queen of all time. You would have needed that lesson to grow up."

Alassa coughed, Emily could tell that Alassa was trying not to cry outright. "And you are so wise because you're a Child of Destiny?"

"No," Emily admitted. "I just went through something similar myself."

The thought made Emily scowl. Back home, the rich kids had definitely seemed to have an easier time of life. People said that money couldn't buy happiness, but it *could* buy a pretty good approximation of it. And yet ... how many friends had been effectively purchased with money, or presents, or merely the hint of rewards to come? Alassa's family could reward those who took care of their daughter with gifts beyond their wildest dreams.

But Alassa would never have been given true friendship.

Emily looked at the Princess, then produced a handkerchief from her robes. "Here," she said. "Dry your eyes. Then we can talk properly."

She looked over into the building and saw ... nothing. "What *is* this place?"

"A bar," Alassa said, as she wiped her eyes dry. "A place for students to come and drink when they have finished their shopping."

Emily frowned, looking at the remains of the bright red liquid on the ground. "What–exactly–were you drinking?"

"Red Rose," Alassa said. The name meant nothing to Emily. "I just wanted to forget the world and make it go away."

Something alcoholic, Emily guessed. Of course; this world probably wouldn't have any compunctions about selling alcohol to minors. They didn't even have a definition for *minor child*, let alone child labor laws. Imaiqah had told her that some neighborhood kids had gone to work for merchants for a copper or two per week. Emily suspected that the kids were being badly underpaid.

She looked back into the building and waved at a moving shape. "Bring us some hot Kava," she ordered as soon as the young girl appeared in the doorway. "And some bread as well."

Alassa stared at her. "What are you doing?"

"We're going to talk," Emily said. "You know–we're going to talk like friends."

She waited until the serving girl had brought them two steaming mugs of Kava and a plate of hot bread, then passed the girl a silver coin. From her stare–and Alassa's chuckle–it was clear that she had massively overpaid, but the girl took the coin and vanished before Emily could take it back. Emily didn't mind too much; she just hoped that the girl's mother or father or whoever else she worked for wouldn't take it for themselves.

"So," Alassa said, after a long moment. "Where *do* you come from?"

Emily thought quickly. If she told Alassa the truth ... what would happen? Emily couldn't see any danger to her own world by letting the secret slip, but there would be danger for Emily herself. The easiest way to prevent a Child of Destiny from actually doing whatever Destiny wanted her to do was to kill her first.

What would Alassa tell her parents and what would they do to keep themselves on top?

"Long story," she said, after a long pause. "Can you keep a secret from everyone else?"

Alassa hesitated, and then made a visible decision to be honest. "I can't keep secrets from my parents," she admitted. "It's part of the Royal Bloodline."

Part of Emily's mind wondered just how literally accurate that statement was. Kings and Queens had justified their behavior throughout the centuries by claiming to rule by Divine Right, but that struck her as little more than the same justification that retrospectively anointed Children of Destiny. If God had given the monarchs the right to rule, why hadn't He made them *good* rulers?

"What do you mean?" Emily asked. "The Royal Bloodline?"

Alassa flushed bright red. "The nobles of Zangaria swear loyalty to my father's bloodline. Those oaths are blurred with ancient magic handed down from monarch to monarch. My father has many strange abilities running through his bloodline; I *cannot* lie to him. Nor can my mother, or anyone who swore themselves to him permanently."

Emily considered it. "You mean he always knows when you are lying?"

"I mean I *can't* lie," Alassa said. "If he asks a question, I have to answer truthfully and completely. It's written into the Royal Bloodline."

"That doesn't make sense," Emily protested. "Your mother isn't a blood relative, is she?"

"She swore to him when they married," Alassa said. "And when I have children, they won't be able to lie to me either."

Emily winced. *She* wouldn't have wanted to grow up in a household where she had to answer every question truthfully, although she could see the logic behind the charm. When Queen Elizabeth the First had been a Princess, she'd been caught in a compromising situation that could have easily led to her execution, if only because a Royal Princess had to be above suspicion. If she'd been under a spell that made her speak truthfully, she would have been proclaimed innocent quickly enough ... or condemned, if she had been guilty. It made sense, all right, but it sickened her. There was such a thing as too much truth.

"I'll tell you when you become Queen," Emily said, finally.

Alassa looked at her for a long moment, and then nodded reluctantly.

Emily smiled in relief, then asked a question that had been nagging at her for a while. "How were you treated as you grew up?"

Alassa started to talk, sipping her Kava as she spoke. As Emily had expected, Alassa had been treated very well from birth, with a governess who had escorted her everywhere. It had been a dream life, but not one that had prepared her to rule. Emily wondered if her parents had still been trying for a boy, or if they'd thought Alassa would learn how to rule through watching how her father ruled his Kingdom. Unsurprisingly, all of the flattery and praise had gone to her head; it had been a shock to discover that Whitehall didn't want to treat her with the deference to which she was accustomed.

Emily took a bite of the bread and smiled in enjoyment. Bread wasn't something she had really appreciated back home, but even the simplest bread at Whitehall was a marvelous taste sensation. It almost made up for all the modern conveniences that Whitehall lacked, things like computers and televisions and air conditioning. Alassa ate with less delight, but at least she was eating. Somewhere under the brat, Emily decided, was a worthwhile human being.

"They hired a tutor to teach me magic," Alassa explained as they finished the snack. "I never realized that he was crippling me from learning on my own."

"You might want to ask your father why he was chosen," Emily said. The intrigues that had swarmed through Royal Courts in her world would be nastier in a world with magic. "Perhaps someone intended to cripple you when you assumed the Throne."

Alassa blanched. "I never considered it," she said. "Do you think that's possible?"

"It could be," Emily said. It was also possible that the tutor had tried to teach Alassa Basic Charms and found it impossible, so he'd simply helped her to memorize a number of spells. But she kept that opinion to herself. "What would happen if you couldn't understand spells on your own?"

"I'd have to hire a Court Wizard," Alassa said. Her voice went flat, as if she were remembering something her parents had told her in one of their few parental moments. "They tend to have bad attitudes."

Emily remembered kingmaker and shivered. "I can imagine," she said, as she stood up. No doubt the Court Wizards considered themselves the powers behind the thrones. "I have to find Imaiqah. Why don't you come shopping with us?"

She almost laughed as Alassa gaped at her. "You might try to make proper friends instead of merely summoning cronies," Emily said. She had to fight down the urge to suggest that it was part of her destiny. That would have been cruel. "Imaiqah is a decent person and she might make a proper friend if you approached her right. And you owe her a few apologies."

"I ..." Alassa stopped and looked confused. She *was* growing up, after all. Maybe she could master the concept of respecting people even if they weren't well-born. "You might be right."

Emily nodded, then allowed Alassa to proceed her out of the courtyard, into an alleyway.

A figure stood at one end of it, his face hidden by a mask. Emily felt a thrill of alarm; she started to cast a spell, only to see it deflected off a wand the figure carried in one hand.

Seconds later, something stuck both girls and sent them crashing to the ground. There was a flickering burst of pain, and then ... darkness.

## Chapter Twenty-Seven

"SHE'S WAKING UP," A SCRATCHY VOICE SAID. "I CAN KEEP HER UNDER, IF YOU WOULD PREfer."

"No need to worry," a deeper voice said. "Besides, we should see what they can offer."

Emily slowly fought her way to wakefulness. Her head felt as if she'd been hit several times–or, part of her mind offered, as if she'd drunk something she really shouldn't have considered drinking. There was a foul taste in her mouth, the remnants of something she'd drunk–or someone had forced down her throat. She coughed and felt the remains of herbs and spices and something unidentifiable tickling down her throat.

Something was *definitely* wrong.

Her arms hurt badly. In her confused state, it took her several moments to realize that the reason she couldn't move was not paralysis, but restraints binding her to an uncomfortable wooden chair. Her hands were tied behind her back and her feet felt as if they had been lashed to the chair. Movement was almost impossible, no matter how hard she struggled.

Oddly, she found that reassuring. Shadye would have used a spell to paralyze her; *he* wouldn't have needed common ropes and knots.

*Magic*, she thought, and remembered the wand that had been used to stun her. Whoever had captured her–and Alassa, she assumed–wasn't a very powerful magician, if he was a magician at all. Sergeant Harkin's endless textbooks on magical warfare had told her that magicians could enchant wands, daggers and other weapons for non-magicians to use, if they were willing to spare the power.

Or she could just have had the ill luck to run into a mage who had never learned to cast spells without his wand. There were just too many possibilities for her to draw any firm conclusions.

A finger touched her cheek; she drew back, reflexively. "You may as well open your eyes," the deep voice said. "We know you're awake."

Emily opened her eyes and found herself staring into a pair of surprisingly warm brown eyes. The speaker stepped backwards, allowing her to see him properly. It took her a moment to realize that he was actually *posing* for her. He was a tall man, with more muscles on his arms than anyone else she'd seen apart from the Sergeants, wearing a strange set of armor that covered little more than the average female bathing suit. His chest was covered, as was his neck, but his legs were as naked as they'd been the day he was born. Long dark hair, so black and shiny that she was convinced that he took very good care of it, framed a face that would have been handsome if it hadn't been so battered. And if he had lacked a moustache that reminded her of Adolf Hitler's trademark appearance.

"Who ... ?" She swallowed, and tried again. "Who are you?"

The man snorted. "My name is ..."

"That will do," a third voice said sharply. "I thought even you would know better than to speak your name to a magician."

"Do not fret," the scratchy voice said. "I fed her a potion derived from the Durian. She has as little spark and tar as you do, Ambrose."

Emily looked at the magician and shivered. He was inhumanly tall and thin, so thin that the only thing seeming to keep him upright was magic. A long white beard dangled towards the floor. His eyes, half-hidden within shadow, sparkled with malevolent light. He looked too ... poor to be a necromancer, , but if he'd fed her a potion she doubted that he was a very good wizard. Carefully, she tried to cast a spell and discovered he was right. Her *mana* seemed drained, almost gone.

The loss shocked her. She'd only known that magic was possible for six weeks and now it was gone.

Or was it? Thande had said nothing about magic-dampening potions, but he had implied that most potions had a very limited lifespan and–eventually–stopped working altogether. If she could hold on until the potion left her bloodstream, her magic should return and she could use it ... and she hadn't depended on magic before Shadye had accidentally snatched her up. She knew how to live without it.

"Pretty bird," the third speaker said. "It is almost a shame that we have ... contractors waiting for you, and for the Princess."

Emily heard a groan from beside her and turned her head, as best as she could. Alassa was tied to another chair, her once-fine white robe stained with a greenish liquid that had dribbled from her chin. The Royal Princess's eyes were unfocused, but she was slowly recovering from being stunned.

Emily looked back at the third speaker, noting that he was an older version of the first bandit, and scowled. They had to be insane to kidnap, of all people, a Royal Princess. Whitehall would *never* stop searching for Alassa.

*Contractors*, the third speaker had said. But who were they? And who were they working for? Emily worked the problem out in her head as the three kidnappers chatted quietly amongst themselves, trying to understand what had happened–and why. If Alassa had been the target, why hadn't they slit Emily's throat as soon as they'd had both girls helpless? And if they'd wanted Emily, for whatever reason that might make sense to their minds, why hadn't they killed Alassa?

Actually, that wasn't a hard puzzle to solve. Alassa's family would want bloody revenge if their only daughter–their only *Heir*–met her end in Dragon's Den.

Or ... what if the Accountants Guild wanted *Emily* dead? But they were far away, and even if they had sent kidnappers all the way to Dragon's Den to kidnap her, if they'd even worked out that Emily had supplied the advanced numbers, why would they kidnap their own Royal Princess? They'd have to be completely insane.

But the only people Emily knew who were insane enough that it wouldn't matter to them were the necromancers.

She snorted, which drew the attention of all three men for a long moment, before they returned to their huddle. For all she knew, the kidnappers had picked them completely at random and they didn't know they'd kidnapped a Royal Princess. But surely someone couldn't just *walk* into a cliché like that...

"Whitehall will be looking for them," the third man pointed out. "How do we get them out of the city?"

"They will be safe here until dark, as long as you can keep your fool yaps shut," the sorcerer growled. He looked down at Emily, and then ruffled her hair like a proud father. "This one will fetch us plenty of gold, and that one"–he nodded at Alassa–"is worth a King's ransom."

Emily cleared her throat. "So which of us is the target and which of us is the innocent bystander?"

The sorcerer drew back his hand and slapped her across the cheek.

Emily yelped, tasting blood. She desperately tried to cast one of the painkilling spells she'd learned from books. The spell refused to work properly, but the mental disciplines helped push the pain to one side.

The sorcerer cackled and turned back to his allies.

"You can see that this one is a Child of Destiny," he said flatly. "She shows as little fear as she can, for she knows that Destiny will not let her die."

"I could kill her now," the first bandit said. He produced a small knife from his belt and held it up in front of Emily's face. "One slash and Destiny will find himself cheated ..."

The sorcerer moved his hand in a simple pattern and the bandit was hurled across the room, right into a solid stone wall. "You're a fool," he growled. "She's worth nothing to us dead."

"Wait," Alassa said. Her voice sounded fearful but determined. "You must know that you won't get away with this."

"One of the terms of your ransom will be a mighty oath from your father that he will not seek revenge on his daughter's kidnappers," the sorcerer informed her. His face, twisted more by old age and malice than magic, leered at her. "And if he refuses to deal, we can always offer our services to the rest of your family."

He smirked as Alassa choked back a sob. "You won't have any magic until you are released," he said, nastily. "But just to keep you from talking ..."

The sorcerer picked up a lump of cloth from a table and stuffed it into Alassa's mouth, ignoring her protests. A moment later, he did the same to Emily, who found herself forced to leave the makeshift gag in her mouth. He could have cast a spell to silence them both, she thought frantically, trying to keep down the fear hidden at the back of her mind. There had to be a reason why he wasn't relying on magic to keep them prisoner. Maybe he just wasn't a very strong magician?

"Get some rest," he advised as he headed for the locked door. "You have a long trip ahead of you tonight."

Emily could hear his laughter for several minutes as he and his allies walked through the door and banged it closed behind them.

She promptly glanced at Alassa, saw the fear in her eyes, and then looked down at the chair. The knots remained firmly tied no matter how hard she struggled against them, even leaning back in the chair ... *wait a minute!*

Leaning *was* the answer. The realization hit her like a physical blow. She put it into action before she could think better of it. Emily pushed the chair back, hoping and praying that she could put enough pressure on the weak wooden structure to break the legs and smash the chair.

At first, all the chair would do was creak. And then it made a much louder noise ... and then, to Emily's delight, the chair shattered with a terrifying crash. She looked up, listening for sounds of the sorcerer coming to see what had made the noise, but heard nothing.

*Good*, she thought, as she started to pull her hands free. The sorcerer had tied them to the chair, rather than tying them separately. Several seconds of wiggling freed her hands, allowing her to push the rest of the ropes aside. She was *free*!

Emily reached into her mouth and pulled out the gag, throwing it into a far corner. Alassa looked up gratefully and then nodded in understanding as Emily tapped her lips before starting to untie the Princess. Once she was free, Alassa picked up a chunk of wood and prepared to fight, although Emily was less sure that it would be a useful weapon. The chairs had been so decayed that it was a minor miracle they hadn't broken before Emily had forced the issue.

"Thank you," Alassa said, rubbing her wrists.

Emily glanced down at her own wrists and saw evil red marks where the ropes had cut into the flesh.

Alassa blinked at her. "But how are we going to get out of here without magic?"

Emily looked around, cursing her own stupidity. She should have checked out the room *before* she started her ill-planned escape. It was almost completely empty, just like a storm cellar, apart from a stone table in one corner and a glowing magic crystal to provide lighting. The door was wooden, but solid. Irritatingly, a single unlocking charm would have sufficed to break the lock if they'd had a spark of magic between them.

"I can't feel any hexes waiting for us," Alassa whispered. "Is ... is that normal?"

"I don't know," Emily admitted. It had never even occurred to her that there *was* a way to dampen magic, at least for a short while. The necromancers wouldn't have been so dangerous if they could easily be rendered powerless. She pushed her palm against the wood and tried to sense any magical booby traps waiting for her, but felt nothing. Did that mean that there were none, which seemed unlikely in a sorcerer's house, or that she could no longer sense their presence?

"They left the key in the lock," Alassa muttered. "The wrong side, naturally."

"Of course," Emily agreed. It *would* have been pretty silly if they'd put the key on their side of the lock. That only happened in stories about evil wizards who were stupid as well as evil, twirling their moustaches while they obligingly told their captive everything because he was locked up and therefore somehow no longer dangerous. "Do you have anything we could use to pick the lock?"

"Just a few dozen hairpins," Alassa said, removing one of them from her head. "I don't think its strong enough to move the lock."

Emily nodded. Practical lock-picking hadn't been taught in Whitehall, or in any other school she'd attended. Or, for that matter, how to make gunpowder or modern medicine or anything else she had to reinvent on her own. Whoever had come up with the list of subjects for modern kids needed her head slapped, several times. Before coming to this world, Emily didn't seem to have been taught anything useful at all...

She looked at the lock, then she looked at where the door met the floor, then she looked at the lock again. If someone was behind the door, they'd be caught instantly, but there was no choice. Pulling off her undershirt–and ignoring Alassa's gasp of shock - Emily carefully pushed the fabric under the door. It would have been easier with a newspaper or a sheet of parchment, but she had to make do with what she had. A moment later, she took the hairpin and started to push at the key's head, trying to maneuver it out of the lock. There was a clinking sound as it hit the fabric. Grinning, Emily pulled her shirt back into the cell along with the key.

"Clever," Alassa said, her face lighting up like the sun. "How did you think of it?"

"I was desperate," Emily muttered back, as she picked up the key. It appeared to be made from solid iron rather than anything more exotic. She half-expected a hex to explode in her face the moment she inserted the key in the lock, but it clicked open normally. They stepped into the hallway. "Keep very quiet..."

The sorcerer's home–if it *was* the sorcerer's home–was eerily silent, almost deserted. No matter how much she listened, she could hear nothing. The sorcerer might be gone, or he might have used silencing charms to keep unwanted guests from hearing his footsteps. There was barely any lighting at all.

Emily crept along the hallway towards a hint of light in the distance. Alassa followed, still carrying the chunk of wood. She looked like a warrior princess, complete with a determined expression that surprised Emily. But Alassa *had* been raised to be a Princess.

They turned a corner–

- and walked right into the young bandit. He let out a yelp of surprise, grabbing Emily and shoving her back against the stone wall.

Emily tried to bring her knee up to strike him in the groin, but his armor absorbed the blow. The Sergeant would have given her a sharp rebuke if he'd been there, part of her mind noted ...

... just before Alassa brought her wooden club down on the bandit's head. He folded and hit the ground with brutal force, groaning in pain. Emily knelt down beside his body and stripped the bandit of sword and dagger.

"Kill him," Alassa ordered.

Emily stared at her in horror. She couldn't kill someone in cold blood, not yet–and perhaps not ever. But Alassa was right; if the bandit raised the alarm, they might be unable to escape. Emily gripped the sword tightly, ready to bring it down and slice through his head, and then lowered it again.

"No," she said, and hoped that she wasn't making a mistake. "Hit him again and then we can run."

Alassa gave her a sharp unreadable look, then struck the bandit a second time. Once he'd stopped moving, she and Emily moved quickly down the corridor.

"The sorcerer must be watching for us," Alassa gasped. "Most sorcerers know everything that happens in their house."

Emily nodded, holding the bandit's sword in front of her like a talisman against evil. It wouldn't be enough, she knew, if they *did* encounter the sorcerer. There were books about what happened to swordsmen who fought sorcerers on even terms, all written in the same mocking style as the Darwin Awards back home. The rare times that a swordsman overcame a sorcerer helped to winnow out weak and useless sorcerers from the gene pool, not that they'd put it quite like that.

But no magic reached out to snare them - or to kill them - as they reached the main door. It might have been hexed, so Emily used the sword to lever it open. Nothing happened, so they stumbled out into the bright sunlight. They didn't seem to have moved too far in the city at all, although it was difficult to tell. Alassa grabbed her arm and pulled her onto the streets, ignoring her tattered clothing and distinctly unpleasant appearance. She, at least, seemed to know where they were.

"You," a voice snapped. Emily turned to see a man wearing chainmail armor, escorted by three other armsmen. "You're the missing Princess?"

Alassa pulled herself up to her full height. "I am Princess Alassa of Zangaria," she informed him, in a tone that left no doubt that she was telling the truth. "And we have escaped from the kidnappers who took us from your city. My father will hear of this."

"I must escort you to City Hall," the guard said. Emily found herself wondering if he'd actually meant to say City Hall, or if it was the closest adaption the translation spell could do. "The City Fathers have been very concerned."

"I suggest you have the bandits in that building arrested," Emily said before they could be led away. No doubt the City Fathers would be relieved to find Alassa safe and sound, but the kidnappers were still alive and free. "They might take the time to escape."

"More guardsmen are on their way," the guardsman informed her. His voice was insufferably confident, mixed with a fear that Emily didn't quite understand. But then, *someone* would have had to pay for the lapse in security. "The bandits will not escape."

## Chapter Twenty-Eight

As it happened, the City Fathers weren't the only ones who wanted to see them. Mistress Irene had been staying at City Hall and, by the looks of things had been wearing out the carpet by pacing back and forth while waiting for news of her missing charges. Judging from the comments Emily had overheard as they were escorted into the building, Mistress Irene been an unwelcome guest, probably because she took her responsibilities seriously. God help anyone who got in Mistress Irene's way.

City Hall itself was a massive building that reminded Emily of the Roman Senate. Dozens of young men ran around the building, carrying letters and packets from one room to another, while a cluster of older men supervised their every move. There were no women at all, apart from Mistress Irene—and, given the looks that the two girls received as they entered the building, Emily suspected that women were generally barred from entering City Hall. Like so much else about the strange new world she'd discovered, it seemed surprisingly primitive—and barbaric.

"May all the Gods be praised," Mistress Irene said when Emily and Alassa were escorted into the small antechamber. "I feared that the worst had happened when your friend told me that you were gone."

Emily and Alassa exchanged glances.

"I had to send the others back to Whitehall under escort," Mistress Irene said. "Now tell me, what happened to you?" Her eyes darkened. "And if this was some kind of practical joke ..."

"No," Alassa said in a very small voice. She sounded as if she were going into shock, now that the immediate danger was over. "Mistress, we were abducted."

Mistress Irene looked towards the open door and glared at one of the young men. "Fetch some Kava and be quick about it, or I will turn you into the pig you are," she snarled. She turned back to Alassa as the boy fled for his life. "Start at the beginning and tell me what happened."

Emily took a moment to gather herself as Alassa ran through the entire story, from the moment they'd been stunned to when they'd run into the City Guard. In hindsight, she couldn't understand why they hadn't been guarded more carefully, or simply left drugged until the time came to move them to a more permanent prison. Alassa was worth her weight in gold, literally, and Emily ... Who *wouldn't* want to get their hands on a Child of Destiny?

Void had told her that the status might come in handy. He *hadn't* told her that it might also be a magnet for thugs, kidnappers and murderers.

Her lips twitched. Void had probably felt it went without saying.

"I see," Mistress Irene said, after Alassa had finished speaking. "Emily, do you have something you want to add?"

The young man returned with a jug of Kava and three golden goblets. Slowly, he started to pour out the Kava, obviously hoping to hear more of the story before anyone else. Mistress Irene growled at him as soon as he had finished filling the goblets and waved him out of the room impatiently. He retreated with as much dignity as he could muster.

"Not really," Emily said. The Kava tasted strange, oddly fouled by the bad taste in her mouth. "Alassa knocked out a bandit with a club of wood."

"Good for you," Mistress Irene said to Alassa. The Royal Princess had glossed over that part of the story. "Now, I'm afraid that the City Fathers wish to see you -"

Alassa caught her arm. "My parents? Do they know - ?"

"I'm afraid the City Fathers sent them an urgent message," Mistress Irene said. Her brown eyes held a hint of sympathy. "They were quick to try to duck blame for whatever had happened to you."

"And so they should," Alassa said, her eyes flaring. "I was told that Dragon's Den was *safe*!"

"The kidnappers should have known that Whitehall would never have let you simply vanish," Mistress Irene said. "We could have put a hundred combat sorcerers into the city and searched it from end to end. I can't imagine how they intended to get you out without being noticed."

Emily frowned. "A portal? Or teleportation?"

"Perhaps, but the city's wards would have made that difficult," Mistress Irene said. "Setting up an unregistered portal is a crime almost everywhere - and it could hardly have gone undetected. The simplest way would be to take you out on a cart, but the City Guard sealed the gates and have been searching everything."

The tutor shook her head. "Perhaps they were just very stupid bandits. But stupid magicians don't tend to live very long."

Mistress Irene headed for the door, giving another young man a brief message as she walked outside.

Emily thought hard. They'd *definitely* escaped too easily, which meant ... what? That their kidnappers had thought stripping them of magic would be enough to prevent them from escaping? Or that they'd somehow been *meant* to escape? Perhaps the whole episode had been intended as a warning to Alassa's parents that their daughter was vulnerable, that she could be threatened. But all it would do would cause them to raise their guard.

Her head spun again as she tried to figure out all the angles. If what Alassa had told her was true, there were times in the Royal Court where you didn't dare scratch your nose for fear that someone would take it as a sign to start something violent.

"Follow me," Mistress Irene said. "And keep your hands to yourselves. It was hard enough to convince them to let you enter the building."

They walked up a long flight of stone stairs and into a corridor that led towards a pair of marble doors, guarded by men wearing shining silver armor and carrying short swords. One of them insisted on taking the sword Emily had been carrying ever since she took it off the bandit, the other took the dagger and ran a wand over the two girls.

A detector of some kind, Emily guessed, as the guard nodded to his comrade to open the door. They'd been classed and rated as harmless.

Inside, the nine City Fathers of Dragon's Den looked down upon them with varying levels of disapproval. Unsurprisingly, they were all men, all old enough to be Emily's grandfather. Appearances could be deceptive in this world, she reminded herself; hard-working people could look seventy when they were actually thirty, and someone wealthy enough to buy rejuvenation spells could easily be over a hundred. They wore black shirts and trousers, along with golden medallions hanging from their necks. It was impossible to escape the sense that they were well aware of their own importance.

On the far side of the room, she saw the guardsman who had met them as soon as they escaped the sorcerer's house. She studied him, trying to decide if it had been a coincidence that he'd been right outside, or if someone had set up the whole encounter. But none of her theories as to why anyone would bother to waste time with such an absurd plot made sense.

Maybe someone had just wanted to embarrass the City Fathers. It seemed as good a theory as any.

"Make your report," one of the City Fathers said to the guardsman. "We must know what happened."

"We searched the building where the Princess was held," the guardsman said. He didn't mention Emily, for which she was both grateful and a little insulted. Didn't she count in a world that included aristocrats and monarchies? "We found the bodies of Bruno and Ambrose, a father and son team of conmen, thugs, kidnappers and cutthroats. They were both killed by magic."

Mistress Irene stepped forward. "How do you know they were killed by magic?"

"You have no right to ask questions in this chamber," one of the City Fathers said quickly. "You may submit your questions through us and ..."

"Don't be silly," another City Father interrupted. "She speaks for Whitehall."

"And the Heir of Zangaria was kidnapped in our city," an elderly City Father quavered. "We do not wish to seem obstructive."

"We do not kiss the buttocks of royals," the objecting City Father said. "We value our independence."

"Which may not last if this leads to war," Mistress Irene said, her cold voice cutting through the chatter. "Guardsman, how do you know the bandits were killed by magic?"

"Their hearts had exploded inside their chests," the guardsman said. "We were fortunate enough to get a forensic sorcerer to the building before the vibrations had faded away and he confirmed that it was the work of a Dark Wizard. The only one whose current location cannot be confirmed is the Sorcerer Malefic."

The City Fathers exchanged glances. "He would not stoop so low," one of them said. "I believe him to be a true son of the city."

"Begging your pardon, sir," the guardsman said, "but it is my observation that Malefic would do anything for gold."

Emily nudged Mistress Irene. "Who is Malefic?"

"A practicing magician who claims to be a full-fledged sorcerer whenever he can get away with it," Mistress Irene said. "I've seen his work before; husbands hexed by their wives, wives spelled to be obedient, workers convinced to work for nothing ... Like the guardsman said, he would do anything for a gold coin. But he should have had more sense than to challenge the Grandmaster, let alone *your* patron."

"And my family," Alassa added. "They will send men after Malefic."

"They'd do better to send combat sorcerers," Mistress Irene said tightly. "Even a low-level magic user has to be taken seriously. You make sure they know that before they send a small army to be slaughtered."

"We are continuing to hunt for Malefic," the guardsman continued, ignoring the interruption. "However, we have no idea where he might be hiding."

"He may have left the city," one of the City Fathers said. He looked around the table, finally looking directly at Mistress Irene. "I think we can declare the matter closed, can't we?"

"No," Mistress Irene said. "Two of my students were kidnapped—however briefly—while in your city. One of them is a Royal Princess that could have started a war between Dragon's Den and Zangaria—and Zangaria would have the support of Whitehall. We expect your *thorough* cooperation in tracking down the miscreants and handing them over for punishment."

"The citizens of a free city cannot be handed over to anyone," a City Father objected. "It goes against our most basic principles."

"Then I suggest you decide if your principles mean more to you than fighting a hopeless war," Mistress Irene said sharply. "Do you *really* wish to push this any further?"

There was a long uncomfortable silence. "We will try them when we catch them," one of the City Fathers said after several minutes. "And if they are proved to be guilty, we will hand them over to you. However, we cannot surrender anyone until their guilt has been confirmed. We have no proof that it was *really* Malefic who provided the magic and potion for their capture and confinement."

"There *was* someone behind the two thugs," the guardsman said. "Neither Bruno nor Ambrose were known for high intelligence. Someone—either Malefic or another sorcerer—was pulling their strings."

He hesitated. "There is a limit to how far we can pressure the sorcerers in this city," he added. "Perhaps Whitehall could offer to provide support if necessary."

Emily hesitated, then spoke out into the chamber. "You said you have magicians working for you. Can't you ... can't you do something like summoning their ghosts and interrogating them?"

There was immediate uproar. Mistress Irene's face darkened, one hand lifted as if she were about to slap Emily across the face before thinking better of it. The City Fathers were all talking rapidly, as if she'd just suggested something horrifying, perhaps even on the verge of necromancy itself ... Even Alassa looked shocked, although she also looked amused.

Emily's mistake had been so basic that she hadn't even realized it *was* a mistake until it was too late.

"You *dare* bring someone like *her* into this chamber?" One of the City Fathers said. "Take her out; take her for punishment and..."

"That will do," Mistress Irene overrode him, in a tone that brooked no dissent. "The young sorceress is from a faraway country and knows not of what she speaks. It will be dealt with when we return to Whitehall."

Her gaze swept the room. "We will expect to receive regular reports on your progress," she said, addressing the senior City Father. "Should you require any support from us, you only have to ask. I will see that you receive it directly."

She nodded, once. "Emily, Alassa; come. We have to return to Whitehall."

They recovered their weapons, then descended the steps and headed for the main door. The young men outside stared at them again as they passed. Oddly, Emily found that their attention no longer bothered her.

Mistress Irene sniffed as she took a look at Emily's sword, before suggesting that she show it to the Sergeants and ask for their opinion on carrying it. The sword's former owner was dead and there was no point in leaving it in the city, where just *anyone* could use it. She said nothing else until they were in the carriage and rattling out of the gates, back onto the road to Whitehall.

"You should have kept your mouth shut," Mistress Irene said without heat.

Emily flushed.

"Those who traffic with the dead come to bad ends," Mistress Irene went on. "Even the most insane of necromancers would think twice before attempting to penetrate the veil between the mortal world and the land of the dead. Your suggestion ... you could have questioned their legitimacy and the status of their mothers and received a less unpleasant response."

"You could desecrate a temple and receive less of a whipping," Alassa said. The Princess grinned at her, although there was no real malice in her voice. It seemed that the experience might have changed Alassa for the better. "I'm surprised they didn't push the demand that you be immediately punished for your carelessness. You could hardly have suggested anything worse."

Emily looked down, feeling ashamed. She *should* have thought, and the fact that she was tired, hurting and stripped of magic wasn't a very good excuse. None of the books she'd read had discussed any form of magic that could traffic with the dead in detail, but they *had* warned her that such spells were considered taboo. And then she hadn't taken the taboo *seriously*.

"They're always careful about dealing with students from Whitehall," Mistress Irene said absently, but with an odd cold anger behind her voice. "We have been sending students to Dragon's Den for years and this is the first kidnapping we've *ever* had. The normal problems are students playing jokes on the citizens or discovering that they don't have enough money to pay for their food after eating themselves silly."

"It wasn't your fault," Emily said.

"I can tell my parents that it wasn't your fault," Alassa added. She gulped, as if she had just realized something unpleasant. "They're going to want to discuss it with me, aren't they?"

"Of course," Mistress Irene said. Her voice was soft, but somehow *wrong*. "And you can tell them whatever you like. I don't think that it would make much difference."

Emily nodded sadly as she looked out of the hatch, towards the darkening sky. It looked as though it was going to rain. As the dark clouds advanced towards the city, strange flickers of multicolored light danced high overhead as *mana* discharged into the lightning. She was sure that the peasants in the fields were already taking their animals into their barns, preparing for the coming downpour. Emily wondered if the coach would be safe as they headed further up the mountains, before realizing that Mistress Irene would have other problems.

Mistress Irene could be fired over this.

Back home, there always had to be someone to blame. Accidents happened, but it was human nature to search for a scapegoat–and there were lawyers ready to make money off someone's misfortune. Teachers, drivers, farmers...someone would be singled out, cast as the villain and chased until they lost everything. The fact that Whitehall had done everything they could to ensure safety would be lost in the general witch-hunting atmosphere created by the lawyers. Emily still remembered all the petty little rules and regulations created by people desperate to avoid a lawsuit, rules that had never made much sense. And no other school she'd ever visited had included royalty.

She looked away as thunder crackled in the dark sky, followed by a sudden shower of raindrops that grew rapidly into a deluge. Brilliant flashes of lightning illuminated the distant mountain peaks as the rain grew heavier and the carriage started to slip and slide on the muddy road. Emily braced herself and glanced back outside, seeing a small stream of water rushing down from the higher mountains and running under the carriage's wheels. Small animals were running down with the water, tiny rodents that reassembled mutated hamsters. She couldn't tell what–if anything–they truly were. A faint squeaking followed them for long moments after the animals had faded away into the growing darkness and mist.

The trip seemed to last for hours before the carriage finally rattled to a stop, outside Whitehall. "You'll need to go to the Infirmary," Mistress Irene said, before she opened the door and stepped out into the rain. No charm deflected rainfall as they started to follow her towards the school. "The building will take you there."

Emily *looked* at her, despite the water soaking her hair and robes. "Are you going to be all right?"

"I do not know," Mistress Irene said. There was a bitter hopelessness in her voice that stung Emily's heart. Emily hadn't *planned* to be kidnapped, but what would that matter? "The Grandmaster will decide my fate."

# Chapter Twenty-Nine

"I HOPED NOT TO HAVE TO SEE YOU AGAIN," A MIDDLE-AGED WOMAN WITH PREMATURELY grey hair said, to Alassa. "And who exactly is this?"

"Emily," Emily said tightly. She was too busy worrying about Mistress Irene to be polite. "And who exactly are you?"

The woman smiled. "I am Kyla, Healer of Whitehall." She pointed one long finger towards a pair of doors. "Each of you, pick a door and go inside. When the door is closed, remove all your clothes and lie down on the bed. Whatever that half-baked potions brewer fed you stinks badly enough to poison the entire ward."

Emily hesitated, then did as she was told. The small room was barely large enough for a bed, a handful of magical tools of unknown purpose, and a single light blazing down from high overhead. She had never been comfortable removing her clothes for a doctor back home, but with her robes drenched in an unfamiliar potion she realized she had no choice. Stripping naked, she lay down on the bed and stared up at the ceiling. She hadn't recognized it earlier, yet there was something almost comforting about the pearly white light.

The door opened and she flinched, hands racing to cover herself. Kyla snorted at her as she closed the door, opened the bag she was carrying and took out a metal wand. She waved it over Emily's body. Strange lights flickered into existence for long seconds, before fading back into nothingness.

The lights meant nothing to Emily, but they clearly meant something to the healer.

"Someone *definitely* slipped you a faulty potion," she said. "The fool's pretty lucky that it worked as well as it did. A few more drops of Extract of Ebon and it would have killed the pair of you."

Emily winced. "Can - can you remove it?"

"Most of it has already spent its *mana* and is on the way to passing out of your body," Kyla said. "I think a simple cleansing potion should speed up the effect, but I'd prefer to have Professor Thande analyze the stains from your robe before we try to feed you anything. A potion that wasn't properly prepared could react oddly with any standard cure."

She shrugged as she held her wand over Emily's head for a long moment. "You know you have a cut here, on your cheek?"

"No," Emily said, reaching up to touch her face. The sorcerer–Malefic - had slapped her, hard. "Is it infected?"

Kyla shot her a sharp look. "It should be fine," she said after a moment. "The same goes for the bumps and scratches on your hands and wrists. Whatever you did to break free wounded you. I'd suggest a day or two of rest before you return to your studies."

Emily looked down at her hands and winced. She'd been so relieved at escaping her bonds that she hadn't noticed the pain, or the marks on her arms. Kyla passed her a small gourd of lotion and instructed her to rub it on her arm, making most of the damage simply fade away into nothingness. She hoped that the other signs of trauma would fade just as quickly.

"I'll do my best," Emily promised. She had to speak to the Grandmaster, and perhaps to Void. "I –"

"You'll stay right here until I let you go," Kyla interrupted. "I've known plenty of young magicians get themselves badly hurt because they thought they were healed when the hard work had only just begun. Your magic may make you feel better, but it is nothing more than an illusion."

Emily opened her mouth to protest as Kyla started waving the wand over her again. "You're definitely not from around here," Kyla said after another moment. "There are some interesting traces in your bloodstream ... one day, I must study your blood and determine if it could be harnessed. And someone has given you a spell to boost your system against disease and perhaps even bodily harm. A very good precaution, I'd say."

"Oh," Emily said. She was really too tired to care, even though she knew it was important. "What else can I expect as the potion wears off?"

"Stay near a toilet," Kyla advised. "And when your magic starts to flicker back to life, resist the impulse to use it until I give permission. You are in a very delicate state."

She passed Emily a loose shift–Emily couldn't help thinking of it as a hospital gown - and watched as she donned it automatically. "I'm going to assign you a bed in the sleeping ward. You will be next to your friend and you can have books sent up to you from the library, but you are *not* to try to leave the room without my permission. I am allowed to use charms to keep you in bed, if necessary."

Emily stood up, feeling the room starting to spin around her. "I won't leave," she said, as the Healer took her arm and guided her through another door into a much larger chamber. The bed was small and simple, but right then it was just what she needed. "I just need something to eat."

"Lie down," Kyla said. "I will have something sent up as soon as I have seen to your friend."

Emily closed her eyes.

When she opened them again, light streamed in through a side window and The Grandmaster sat next to her, leafing through an old parchment-bound book that he had to have taken from the library. She felt oddly flattered that the master of the school had taken such an interest in her, even though he was probably more interested in Alassa.

The Grandmaster looked up. His eyes met hers, then he placed the book on the table and leaned forward.

"I have heard from Dragon's Den," he said. "They have been unable to locate the Sorcerer Malefic."

"I see," Emily rasped. Her mouth tasted better than it had yesterday, but it was far from normal. The Grandmaster picked up a glass of water and passed it to her. She sipped it gratefully. "What happened to Mistress Irene?"

The Grandmaster gave her a sharp look. "The Princess took pains to make it clear to her parents that Mistress Irene was not responsible for what happened." He nodded towards the next bed, where Alassa's blonde tresses dangled down the side of the bed. "Not that I would have held her completely responsible in any case. We had no reason to assume that anyone would be stupid enough to kidnap one of our children."

Emily finished her water and looked around, hoping to see a jug.

The Grandmaster snapped his fingers and the glass refilled, automatically.

"She has been given a stern warning, but I feel that there is no need to continue," the Grandmaster added. "I am the Master of Whitehall. My opinion is paramount."

He looked at her thoughtfully. "The real question is simple. Which of you—Alassa or yourself—was the real target?"

"I don't know," Emily said. She hesitated, then asked the question that had been nagging at her since the kidnapping. "Is Malefic a necromancer?"

"Unlikely," the Grandmaster said. "The sheer level of power within a necromancer's wards should have alerted any other sorcerer nearby. And then he had to take commissions from stupid people and a necromancer would probably have lost control once or twice while dealing with them. But he is, very definitely, a Dark Wizard."

His eyes narrowed. "And stupid magicians don't tend to live very long, but what he did to you was stupid. Unless there was something else involved that we're not seeing."

Emily listened as he spoke. He seemed astonishingly verbose, but as he continued it dawned on her that he was trying to reassure her. A Dark Wizard was bad; a necromancer would be far worse.

"Malefic simply had too much at risk for too little gain," the Grandmaster said. "He had to know that Whitehall would hunt for you, and that he was no match for a combat sorcerer. And then Alassa's parents would tear the city apart looking for her. The insane plot involved kidnapping the two children who would be sure to provoke a very powerful response, so why even try? What made him think that he could kidnap you and survive?"

"It was too easy to escape," Emily said, after a moment. "Maybe we weren't intended to remain kidnapped for long."

"But that raises other issues," the Grandmaster pointed out. "Did he want to embarrass the City Fathers, or alarm Alassa's parents, or even provoke a response from your patron? Or is there something here that we're not seeing?"

Emily frowned. "Maybe we were a diversion," she said, carefully. "Did something *else* happen while we were kidnapped?"

"Interesting thought," the Grandmaster said. "Nothing happened that we know about, but with necromancers involved we can never know for sure."

"My head is spinning," Emily complained. "What's going to happen now?"

The Grandmaster shrugged. "We're going to have to take another look at the security precautions for trips outside the wards. I'm afraid that we will have to do something to make it safer, or else restrict the number of children who can go on them."

He shook his head. "The best thing you can do is learn more magic as quickly as possible. You do have enemies out there, some of whom are insane enough to believe that they can breach these walls—or desperate enough to ignore the odds. People you have never met are arguing for your assassination. I suggest that you study harder. Politics is casting a long shadow over this whole affair."

The Grandmaster picked up his book, turned to go, and then hesitated. "I have granted you permission to read certain books from the Black Archive," he said. "It would be most preferable if you never mentioned that to *anyone* else. The Librarian has the list and will prepare them for you upon request."

Emily stared after him in puzzlement. What was all *that* about?

She closed her eyes again and fell into a deep, dreamless sleep, only to be awoken by Kyla. The Healer was carrying a pair of potion gourds. She passed one to Alassa and the other one to Emily. Feeling faintly absurd, Emily placed the gourd to her lips and drank the clear liquid inside. She felt it as it washed through her body, flushing out the remains of the magic-draining potion.

Emily felt alive with power. Magic crackled through her body, reminding her of how helpless she'd felt without it. But who knew who might try to kidnap her and force her to drink a potion again?

"You should not use magic just yet," Kyla reminded them. "It will be a day or two before you can go back to classes properly."

Alassa stared at Emily, who nodded back. "Thank you," Alassa said. "What can we do here?"

"I suggest that you stay in bed, read books and eat sweets," Kyla said. She dropped a box of boiled sweets on Emily's bed. "You're both very low on energy right now, so suck these every time you feel hungry or thirsty. If you want to give the librarian a list of books, I'm sure he will send them up for you. I can also give you board games if you feel the urge for something a little more active."

Emily scowled. The library at Whitehall was far more interesting than any she'd seen back home, but it was also primitive. There was no computer catalogue of books, no automated system that could recommend books on similar subjects, only a librarian who was down in the library, unwilling or unable to come to the infirmary. It struck her, suddenly, that there were books in her bedroom that wouldn't be returned on time. She had no idea what the penalty was for not returning books before their due date, but she doubted that it would be pleasant. Perhaps she could ask her roommates to return them ... No, that wouldn't be possible. She'd taken the precaution of hiding them in her cupboard, which had been sealed with a locking charm she'd pulled out of one of the books.

"Stay in bed," Kyla said, as she left. "I'll have a proper meal sent up in an hour or so. By then, you should be ready to eat."

The two girls were now alone in the ward "You saved my life," Alassa said flatly. Even though she'd obviously also slept, Alassa still seemed too stunned to really think about everything that had happened. "My parents wish to thank you personally."

Emily flushed. "I saved my own life too. I don't know *which* of us was the target."

"Maybe it was a necromantic plot to capture both of us," Alassa said. "I don't know of anyone else who would come up with a plan that required both targets to be together and then expect it to succeed."

"Maybe," Emily said. She tried to sit up, felt dizzy and laid back down again. "But if you hadn't clubbed that bandit halfway to death, we would both still be prisoners."

"That's true," Alassa agreed. Her face twitched into a brilliant smile. "I guess I saved your life too."

Emily laughed, although she was still wondering just what had really happened. If the attack had been aimed at her ... Was it possible that Void had organized it all? Maybe he'd thought that it would serve as a test, or a harsh lesson for her in life outside Whitehall's walls. The City Guard could have been primed to rescue them once they'd already completed their escape. And Void might simply have dismissed the sorcerer once he'd done his part of the task...

... Or Shadye might have expected Malefic to do better and not bothered to supervise him too closely ...

She shook her head angrily. "I guess you did," she agreed, pushing her thoughts aside. "I think you'd better start learning as fast as you can."

"My father said that to me," Alassa admitted. Her face fell. "He was not happy to hear about my progress before you came to this school."

Emily studied her, wondering what *that* meant. Had her father, the King, wanted his daughter to become a better magician, or a better *person*? But was a nice person able to keep a firm grip on a throne?

"He said that I should keep studying with you," Alassa added after a moment. "And he expects me to pass my next Basic Charms exam."

"I think I'm expected to pass too," Emily said. She managed to sit up and started poking through the cabinet beside the bed. It held a kingmaker board and something that looked like a Snakes and Ladders game, although it ran in circles rather than squares. "When exactly are we going to be *taking* the exam?"

"When Professor Lombardi feels that we are ready for it," Alassa said. Her voice lowered. "I had to confess to my father that I cheated on the previous tests. He was not happy."

"A king cannot afford to fool himself, or he will be unable to rule," Emily said. Her parents probably wouldn't have cared if she had cheated or not; she'd keep moving through the school system anyway. But here ... here, she wanted to *succeed*. "What did he say about it?"

"He said that if I didn't pass the next exam with a Child of Destiny helping me, he'd have to start looking for other options," Alassa said. "What if...what if he puts my mother aside and finds another wife? One who can still give him children?"

Emily blinked in surprise. Every time she thought she was used to how different her new world was to Earth, something else appeared to shock her. "I think you can best preserve yourself against that by working hard and learning as much as you can," she said. But Mary hadn't been saved when Henry VIII had wanted a boy-child. And the boy hadn't lived long enough to make a proper mark on history. "And I will teach you."

Emily hesitated. "And you had better teach me more about this world," she added. "I won't know what to do if I were introduced to your parents."

"I hate those lessons on courtly etiquette," Alassa said. She grimaced. "Do you know that the difference between social acceptance and social disgrace can be measured by what pair of knives and forks you use, or where you put your glass after taking a sip of wine? And don't even *think* about the princes from other countries–all second sons–who keep bringing you wild animals because they've heard you love hunting ..."

She grinned, suddenly. "But you're a Child of Destiny. They'll *expect* you to be a little strange. And then they will hang on your every word like it will change the world."

Emily rolled her eyes. "I see what you mean," she said, as the curtain rattled. A moment later, Imaiqah poked her head through and smiled at Emily. "Hey!"

"I was so worried," Imaiqah said, as she let the curtain fall down behind her. "I thought ... I thought that the worst had happened."

"I told my parents you helped save my life," Alassa said, seriously. Both of the other girls stared at her. "I think that they'll agree that you deserve some reward."

"Just be friendly," Emily said. She motioned for Imaiqah to push over a small table, allowing her to start setting up the game board. "You could learn a great deal from each other."

"Sergeant Harkin said he was going to send you some books," Imaiqah said as she found a seat. "Something about you not wasting your time in bed."

"That's ... good of him," Emily said. Most of the books on the reading list for Martial Magic assumed that the reader knew something about military affairs. Emily had to confess that some of the information made absolutely no sense to her at all. "What happened when you got back to Whitehall?"

"They said nothing until you got back," Imaiqah said. She looked over at Alassa. "There were all kinds of rumors."

"There always are," Alassa said. She picked up the dice and rolled a three. "Just ignore them. That's what I do."

# Chapter Thirty

KYLA DIDN'T LET THEM LEAVE THE INFIRMARY FOR THREE DAYS, BY WHICH TIME IMAIQAH and Alassa had become friends, of a sort. Emily could see the social barriers between them, barriers that magic alone would never be able to break down completely, but at least they were trying. It helped that they both wanted to remain on good terms with Emily, although for different reasons, and that none of Alassa's cronies had come to visit her. They couldn't have made their feelings clearer if they'd taken out advertisements in newspapers.

Emily privately considered it a relief that none of the cronies had come to visit, although she kept her thoughts to herself since Alassa was obviously upset. Without them, Alassa would have a chance to be a better person—and besides, *Emily* didn't want a gaggle of inbred idiots giggling at them while they tried to recover from their experience. One day, maybe Alassa would want to talk about it, but for the moment she said nothing. At least she'd drawn the right lesson from the experience.

It felt odd to relax after spending so long studying, but she had no choice. Emily spent the time playing games, reading the Sergeant's collection of books and jotting down ideas for Imaiqah's father. Lying in bed had given her time to try to work out the basic details for a printing press, ideas that she hoped a skilled craftsman could take and turn into something practical. If it had been possible to produce one back in Earth's distant past, it should be possible to produce one here. The real trick would be doing it without magic. Emily wasn't entirely sure how magic interacted with society, but she suspected that it was one of the factors preventing modern technology from developing.

There was also a list of other ideas that might—or might not—prove workable, once she outlined them for anyone interested. She had seriously considered sending a message to Void to ask if they could steal some textbooks from her old world, or perhaps a single copy of *The Way Things Work*. There were so many things she knew would be useful, but she couldn't even begin to work out how they went together. Emily suspected that she wouldn't think of others until Imaiqah's father—or someone else—gave her a problem to solve, whereupon she would try to see how her old society coped with it. She'd picked up more than she'd thought over the years.

*But there are limits*, she thought as they walked down the stairs to the dining hall. *I couldn't design them a working computer without using magic.*

She was used to people staring at her by now, but as they entered the dining hall almost everyone turned to look at them. God alone knew what rumors they'd heard about the kidnap attempt, or what might have happened if the kidnappers had succeeded in transporting them out of the city. Emily hadn't seen anything to contradict her suspicion that the kidnappers had captured them and then deliberately allowed them to escape, apart from the fact that the younger bandit had been surprised to see them when he'd tried to stop them leaving. But he might not have expected them to leave so quickly. Or it might have been the sorcerer who'd deliberately dangled a way to escape under their eyes, before he'd killed his companions.

Eyes still followed them as they picked up plates of food and took them to their table to eat. It was a relief to eat something delicious after the infirmary's food, which was bland and almost completely tasteless, even though they had been warned to be careful on the first day. They would only have two classes, followed by three free periods they could use to study. Alassa had already asked Emily to do more work on Basic Charms, but she had told Alassa that she needed to check books in the library first. The Grandmaster had told her that specific books had been put aside for her to read. At least Kyla had written her an excuse note for the overdue books.

The day passed surprisingly quickly, once she'd dropped back into the flow of regular classes and caught up on what she'd missed. Basic Charms hadn't seemed to move too far ahead, but Professor Thande informed her that she would have to do some additional work on the weekend. There were potions that she was meant to master that she'd missed while she'd been in the infirmary. Emily bit down the temptation to point out that it hadn't been *her* idea to be kidnapped, or to spend three days in bed, knowing that it would do no good. Whitehall seemed to prefer practical work to theory.

It was almost seventeen bells when she finally managed to visit the library.

There was a different librarian on duty when she walked through the door, a tall elegant woman with long brown hair that dangled almost to the floor. "The Grandmaster has authorized you to have access to select books from the Black Archive," she said, before Emily could say a word. She'd clearly recognized Emily from the dining hall. "Are you familiar with the reading rooms?"

Emily shook her head.

The new librarian led her to a concealed door within the wards and opened it, revealing a small room with a desk, a chair and nothing else. "The books will be brought to you," she explained. "You are forbidden to take them out of the room, to copy anything down or invite anyone to join you in the reading room. If you break those rules, the security charms will hold you until the librarians investigate. Do you understand me?"

"Yes," Emily said.

The librarian tapped the wall and it opened to reveal a small pile of books. "Here you are," she said, and placed the books on the table. "Put the books back in the alcove before you leave the room for any reason. Once you're finished, let me know and I'll return them to the Black Archive."

Emily watched the librarian go, closing the door behind her, then turned her attention to the first book in the pile. Whoever had named it had a sense of humor; they'd called it *The Little Black Book*. It was small, made from a material that Emily didn't recognize, but smelled rather like an inkpad from back home. The material used to make the inner pages wasn't parchment, but something else. Even touching it made Emily feel queasy.

She glanced at the next few books in the pile and frowned. *A Compendium of Curses*, followed by *Dark Magic and Malice*, *The Naming of Things* and *The Story of Russell the Bold*. The last one seemed out of place until Emily glanced through it, eventually realizing that she was looking at a story–fictional or not–that also seemed to be an instructional manual. And then the final book–*Necromantic Nightmares*–caught her eye and she shivered. It claimed to be nothing less than a primer on how to become a necromancer.

The book felt *evil* in her hand as she picked it up, staring down at the neat golden letters on the front cover. Perhaps she was imagining it, but it was very hard to open the book to the first page, almost as if her fingers refused to move properly. Someone–either the original writer or the librarian who had catalogued it–might have charmed the book to make it hard to read. She opened the first page and recoiled as she saw the brownish letters drawn–almost painted–on the strange leathery material. The unknown writer had written the book in blood!

"Blood is very magically significant," Professor Thande had said, when lecturing a girl who had cut herself while slicing up vegetables for an energy-boosting potion. "Your life is represented in your blood. To use it in magical rites is to tap into your life and soul itself."

Emily shuddered and started to read the book. Her first impression was that the author hadn't had a very ordered mind. The text seemed to veer alarmingly from a dispassionate, cold-blooded analysis of necromancy to outright raving, some of which simply didn't make any sense to her at all. At one point, the author wrote two whole pages on the life and health of his pet cat, before the writing degenerated into scribbling that the translation spell couldn't, or wouldn't, adapt properly. Maybe there just wasn't any meaning to it at all.

Slowly, part of the story began to emerge, a story that didn't fully agree with Professor Locke's version of history. There had been a great war and humanity had been pushed to the brink of extinction before someone had accidentally discovered that murder could be used as a source of magical power. They'd tried to keep that power in the ancient magical bloodlines at first, but then the technique had leaked and necromancy had spread rapidly. It had beaten the Faerie, or at least pushed them back long enough to give humanity time to recover, yet the cure might have been worse than the disease. The necromancers went rogue soon afterwards.

There were a hundred cautionary tales about men–and a handful of women–who had tried to use necromancy. Some of them had merely wanted power; oddly, they'd lasted longer than the ones who had tried to use necromancy out of good intentions. Emily couldn't understand why until it occurred to her that well-intentioned people might have ideals that could be twisted easier than a simple, if selfish, desire for power. The latter kind of person would know himself better than the idealist. Or so she told herself.

Professor Locke had mentioned a King who had tried to bargain with the necromancers and eventually lost his Kingdom, but that merely scratched the surface. There were Kings and Princess–and one Princess–who had experimented with necromancy, only to be either killed by their followers or overwhelmed by their new power. She couldn't see if there was any better explanation than Professor Locke's for why the power drove everyone insane, but it didn't seem to matter. No matter who took up necromancy, for whatever reason, they invariably went mad. It was not a very reassuring thought.

She stared down at the pages instructing the reader in the art of necromancy, unable to understand why the Grandmaster had instructed her to read the book. Surely Whitehall would have a vested interest in *preventing* people from learning how to use necromancy; there had certainly been no hint of a class teaching the students how to use the dark arts. But as she read through the ritual, she realized—to her horror—that it was really very simple. A magician with enough theoretical background could easily reinvent it if Whitehall were to prevent him from learning from the Black Archive. No *wonder* they were reminded, time and time again, of every necromantic failure. It was the only way to prevent thousands of necromancers springing up everywhere.

*But maybe they do,* she thought, as she read through the rest of the book. Necromancers weren't sane. They tended to harm themselves, or to run out of power, or to make simple mistakes that allowed their enemies to kill them before it was too late. Several dozen, according to the book, had been poisoned. The smart ones enslaved everyone around them just to make sure that they couldn't stick a knife in their backs. Later, as the power slowly transfigured them, they became much harder to kill - if they lasted so long. Emily remembered looking into Shadye's eyes and shivered. He might have been human at one time, but he wasn't now.

Drain the *mana*, then drain the soul. It was so *easy*.

Carefully, she closed the book and stared down at the inky cover, before placing it back in the alcove and picking up *Dark Magic and Malice*. Malefic had been a Dark Wizard, apparently, but he'd been allowed to practice his trade in Dragon's Den without anyone trying to stop him. The City Guard had known what he'd been doing for anyone with enough money to pay him and they hadn't given a damn. There was no way to know if that was because they were nervous about confronting a magician or because they were bribed into condoning his offences.

*Dark Magic and Malice* had been written by someone with an unholy fascination with the dark arts, she decided after reading the first few pages. The writer had listed thousands of charms, curses and magical rites that were terrifyingly evil, ranging from compulsion and enslavement spells to hexes and jinxes that would be sure to have a lethal effect. Emily found herself remembering Thande's warnings about blood when she read the outline of one of the enslavement spells, shuddering at the mere possibility of being turned into a slave. An even more disgusting spell used blood to kill its target from thousands of miles away, unless the target had proper protections woven into his flesh. Emily made a mental note to get those protections immediately. There was no excuse for being vulnerable.

The writer took an even darker glee in listing stories of dark magicians. Some were familiar enough that Emily wondered if they were truly historical—a witch turning a prince into a frog, for whatever reason—and others were so cruel that she felt sick even reading through the precise details. How could *anyone* tolerate such evil magicians living close to them? Or didn't it matter as long as the dark wizards didn't go after *important* people?

There was a dark wizard who had taken over a small town in the mountains and turned it into his personal fiefdom, declaring himself the lord and master of all he surveyed. The King who ruled the land had chosen to leave the dark wizard there, rather than risk a fight he might not win, and the dark wizard had tormented his subjects for years until a travelling sorcerer defeated him in a magical duel. But there was no happy ending for his former subjects; apparently, it had been less than a week before *another* dark wizard moved in to fill the power vacuum. And *this* one had eventually been defeated by a necromancer and the remaining subjects had been killed to feed his lust for power.

The next chapter discussed a witch who had apparently rebelled against the right and lawful place of women, according to the author. For once, his sickening admiration of dark wizards was replaced by sexist claptrap that would have impressed even John Knox or the Taliban. It wasn't much of an improvement, Emily decided; the witch had taken over the village, killed most of the men and eventually started trying to save herself from death by draining the life forces of the remaining village girls. Her story had been turned into a cautionary tale about what happened when witches were allowed to gain too much power, although Emily suspected the truth was rather different. If nothing else, draining life forces sounded alarmingly like necromancy.

She closed the book in disgust and picked up the next one. *The Story of Russell the Bold* was written, at least, by a author who actually knew how to write. If he hadn't paused the story every few pages to explain how this or that worked, it might have been a great deal more entertaining. As it was, Emily found herself skipping entire paragraphs as she left the instructions and concentrated on the story itself. Russell the Bold, it seemed, had been a travelling sorcerer who had gone from Kingdom to Kingdom fighting dark magicians, defusing hidden traps created by sorcerers and generally serving the Allied Lands. Eventually, he'd even beaten a necromancer in single combat, mainly through trickery. A necromancer might be vastly more powerful than a magician smart enough not to use necromancy, but he or she could still lose. Emily found that something of a relief.

Rubbing her eyes, she put the book down and looked at her watch. It was late; she'd spent too long reading and missed dinner. Shaking her head, she returned all of the books to the alcove and left the private room, stepping back into the library. There were more students than ever before crammed into the massive chamber, hunting for books in the certain knowledge that exams were coming up. Emily caught sight of Jade and winked at him, but the older boy pretended not to see her. He *was* with three of his peers, after all.

The librarian nodded to her as she stepped through the silencing wards and up to the desk. "Do you want the books held for you, or should I return them to storage?"

Emily hesitated. "Hold them for a few more days," she said. She had no idea if the Grandmaster would allow them to be brought out of the archive for a second time. "I didn't quite finish reading them."

"There are students who would study overnight to read them," the librarian said. Her elegant face twisted in a manner that reminded Emily of Alassa. "I will put them on hold for three days. After that, they will be returned to storage."

She paused, significantly. "And you have books out to you that are overdue. The Healer's note doesn't extend past the time you leave her care."

Emily cursed her own mistake. She hadn't had time to go back to her bedroom, so the fact that she had books still out to her had slipped her mind. And she couldn't claim to be drugged *this* time.

"Luckily, no one has requested them," the librarian said. "Make sure you return them tomorrow, or you'll be serving a detention in the library. We need people to help us sort out books and return them to the shelves and there's a shortage of volunteers."

"Right," Emily said, relieved. She'd been expecting a return visit to the Hall of Shame, or perhaps an hour spent as a statue. "I'll get them back to you tomorrow."

She walked out of the library and headed towards the dining hall. There should just be time to get something to eat before she had to be in her bedroom at twenty bells. And then she could finish reading the books and return them to the library before time ran out. A detention would be embarrassing, to say the least.

*Or maybe I should just volunteer to work in the library,* she thought, after a moment. *I would certainly see more books of interest if I saw what everyone else took out to read.*

## Chapter Thirty-One

"Emily," Harkin said. "It's your turn to serve as team leader."

Emily winced inwardly. Jade had been the first, but three of the other boys had taken their own turn to take command in a set of different training exercises where they tried to apply their theoretical knowledge to reality. One of them had succeeded outright; the others had lost through making mistakes. Harkin had bawled them out, even though one of the mistakes had been caused by false intelligence provided by the Sergeants. He'd told them to check and recheck *everything*, but none of them had realized that also included the mission briefing itself.

"Across yonder field lies a fortress of the dreaded Snakes," Harkin continued, pointing towards a thicket of trees and, beyond it, a barricade that looked depressingly solid. "You have to get through the fortress before their leaders realize that they're under attack and send reinforcements to stop you from breaking through. Go."

Emily stared at the fortress, willing herself to think. Harkin had explained, at great length, that they were expected to *lead*–and that meant they weren't allowed to ask for suggestions from their subordinates. The Sergeant had explained that it was meant to give them all a chance to take command, but Emily suspected that it was also intended to weed out those who couldn't think for themselves or learn from their failures. All of their previous failures had been worked over, extensively, with the Sergeant pointing out every little mistake and explaining why it had led to disaster.

The problem was simple enough - too simple. An opposing team, the Snakes, held the fortress. To win, all the Snakes had to do was hold it long enough for reinforcements to arrive. And they had solid walls that would block magical attacks, giving them a protection that her team would lack, badly. If they marched right up to the fortress, they would be mowed down before they could actually do anything. A frontal assault would lead to bloody disaster.

Some of the boys had been skeptical of having a girl in their midst, no matter how hard they tried to hide it. They didn't think she could handle Martial Magic; some had been condescending, while some had been outright rude. One of them had actually offered to carry her pack on one of the five-mile marches Sergeant Harkin had led them on, even knowing that it would get them both in trouble. Her cheeks stung at the memory as she turned to face her team. She was *not* going to let this opportunity to prove herself slip away.

"Jade, I want you and Rupert to pretend to launch a frontal assault," she said. They *could* use the trees for cover, as long as they didn't get too close. "Don't actually press it, but force them to keep their heads down."

"Understood," Jade said. He might have doubted her, yet she knew that he would follow orders. She would have been surprised if he didn't resent taking orders from a mere first-year, but at least one of their failures had occurred because someone hadn't obeyed orders quickly enough to save the day. "We'll engage them at long range and just keep firing."

Emily smiled. "Cat and Bran go left, sneak around and take them from that side. Pillion and I will go right. Hopefully, they'll be looking at Jade and not to either side."

It *sounded* workable, but she was coming to learn that there was a difference between a plan outlined on paper, or in words, and actually putting it into operation. None of them questioned her openly, thankfully. She wasn't sure *what* she would have done, even though she did have the right to chew them out for questioning her. They couldn't escape the fact that she was nothing more than a first-year, although she had escaped a would-be kidnapper.

Jade and Rupert headed off towards the enemy fort. A moment later, she heard the sound of charms flying through the air. She hesitated, then cast an anti-surveillance spell into the air, putting as much power into it as she could. Bran copied her, hopefully blanketing enough of the battlefield to confuse any enemy troopers trying to spy on them. In their place, Emily would certainly have tried to spy on the attackers before she got into firing range.

"All right," she said to Bran. "Go."

Staying low, she started to run around the thicket before dropping to the muddy ground. It was never a pleasant sensation at the best of times–the mud clung to her body every time she moved–but it was better than being stunned by a charm. Or running into a concealed hex and being frozen in place. She glanced at Pillion, who had hit the ground beside her, then started to crawl forward, keeping her senses primed for magical booby traps. If she'd been charged with holding a small position with only a handful of men, she would have scattered landmines around liberally.

The sound of spells being exchanged grew louder as Jade and Rupert pressed their attack. She saw flickers of light from where they were hiding, pounding away at the makeshift fort as they slowly crawled forward. The defenders were firing back through murder holes they'd placed within their structure, trying to see the attackers as they came into view. It didn't seem to have occurred to them that the main attack might be just a diversion.

*Every time you think a plan is going perfectly,* one of the books had said, *you're just about to lose.* Emily shivered and kept crawling forward, watching for mines as the enemy fort came into view. It wasn't really a fort at all, she told herself, as she spied three of the enemy defenders, including Aloha. There was no sign of the other three at all and that bothered her. Sergeant Harkin had told her that the defenders intended to defend, but he *hadn't* said that they were bound to stay in the fort. The books also claimed that the best defense was a heavy offense.

She exchanged glances with Pillion, trying to decide what to do. They could attack, now, and be reasonably sure of removing all three of the visible defenders from the exercise, but where were the others? Were they trying to launch a counter-attack, or were they setting an ambush, or ... what? It would be easy to take the fort and lose all of the team in the process. That, the Sergeant had pointed out more than once, was no victory.

Shaking her head, knowing they might be seen at any moment, she used her hand to signal a countdown, before throwing the first charm into the undefended rear of the fort. Hobo, a tough sixth-year who was probably the strongest in the class, was first to fall.

A hail of charms blazed out of the woods as the three visible defenders fell to the ground, pretending to be dead. The other three *had* been trying to counter-attack against Jade and Rupert. Emily hugged the muddy ground as the blasts of light flashed over her head, just before the other assault team engaged the remaining defenders from the rear. And then it was all over.

Sergeant Harkin blew his whistle, signifying the end of the exercise. Emily stood up, looking down at her uniform and rolling her eyes. As always, she'd ended up covered in mud, but no one seemed to care. Apart from the Sergeant, who was always impeccable, everyone else was dripping with mud too. She caught sight of Aloha and looked away, unwilling to make eye contact with her roommate. No matter what else happened, Aloha and her team would be embarrassed by being beaten so easily. But it sure hadn't felt easy at the time.

"Well done," Jade said, clapping her on the shoulder as they walked back to the Sergeant's position. "I hope we were sufficiently diverting?"

"You were very diverting," Emily said. They'd be debriefed, of course, and then lectured on what they'd done wrong. And after that, they could go for a shower. "Although I think they nearly managed to counterattack you."

"Yeah," Jade said. He grinned. "We thought we'd let them get very close before dealing with them."

Sergeant Harkin studied them as they lined up in front of him. They had changed, Emily realized, since they'd first started the class, lining up automatically rather than being hectored into position. And, despite the aching in every muscle, she knew she was fitter than she'd been back home, and probably stronger too. Nothing built muscle like heavy exercise and unsympathetic pushing from a Sergeant. Maybe she'd never be a strong as Jade, or Hobo, but she was coming along. The Sergeant had even promised that they'd be studying unarmed combat soon enough.

"A terrible defeat for the Snakes," Harkin observed, without preamble. "Where, exactly, did you go wrong?"

Aloha's current team leader spoke up, reluctantly. "We didn't watch all of the possible angles of approach. And we allowed ourselves to be forced to remain under cover."

"A good answer," Harkin said. "Where else did you go wrong?"

There was a long pause, before Aloha tried to answer. "We sent three people away to counterattack. We weakened ourselves at the wrong moment."

Harkin smiled. "And was that really a mistake?"

It was a trick question, Emily was sure. The books noted that in war, the simplest things were hard and the easy answers tended to lead to more problems further down the line. And yet they'd also been told that to stand still risked eventual defeat. There didn't seem to be any real answer at all.

"Yes," Aloha's leader said. "It weakened us at the wrong moment."

"As Aloha said," Harkin reminded him, coldly. "But she was right, for the wrong reason. Why was it a mistake? Why would it have been a mistake even if Emily had launched a frontal assault with her entire team?"

*We'd have been slaughtered*, Emily thought. Losing everyone would have been a black mark on her record, even if there were no other repercussions. *Unless* ...

Harkin looked from face to face. "Would anyone like to tell him the answer?"

Emily saw it in a sudden flash of inspiration. "They had reinforcements on the way. All they had to do was hold on until relieved."

"And how do you know," Harkin inquired, in a uncomfortably polite voice, "that they had reinforcements on the way?"

"Because they should have called for them as soon as Jade launched the frontal assault," Emily said, fighting to keep her temper under control. The Sergeant could get under her skin far quicker than any other tutor, even though there was no genuine malice in his words. "They would have had to call, because we might have been the spear-point of an entire army intending to ram itself through the hole."

There were some chuckles, which faded away as the Sergeant glared around him. "You're right," he said finally. "By splitting their numbers, the defenders weakened themselves when all they had to do was wait and hold position. They were aggressive and paid for it by losing their position. The road to the nearest city now lies open."

He looked over at the defenders, and then back at the Redshirts. "I've told you before that the objective is victory. Throwing away your own people for nothing weakens you more than it weakens the enemy. Always keep one eye on your final objective.

"Congratulations, Redshirts," he concluded. "And now that we have all had a chance to discuss the recent exercise, you can follow me on a run. Incidentally, anyone who falls behind Sergeant Miles will be the punching bag in the next exercise."

He turned and sprinted off towards the running track. There was a pause, and then Jade led the students after him. Emily forced herself to keep her speed under control as she ran, having learned that pushing her legs to run as fast as they could go would exhaust her very quickly. Sweat poured down her back as she heard Miles barking encouragement behind her, along with the occasional tap of his baton to the rear of any straggling student. She'd been tapped enough with his baton to know that she didn't want to be tapped again.

"Come on," Harkin bellowed, just like a gym teacher. "You think that the enemy's going to stop chasing you because you're tired?"

Emily winced. One of their exercises had involved trying to hide from enemy huntsmen who knew the forest like the back of their hands. She'd been caught quickly, tied up and left helpless until the exercise had terminated. The huntsmen had known more about tying knots than the Sorcerer Malefic, she'd decided later. Escape had been completely impossible. Harkin had promised them that they'd do the exercise again, later. Emily wasn't looking forward to it.

Her heart was pounding and she was breathing heavily when Harkin finally called a halt, just outside the school. Before, she wouldn't have been able to complete such a run, not without staggering to a halt and begging for mercy. Now, she knew that she would recover very quickly, if only because of a mixture of good food and solid exercise. Harkin cast an eye over them as they lined up in front of him, studying their muddy uniforms. At least he didn't seem to expect them to keep their clothes *clean*.

"Good," he said, finally. "We may be graduating to more advanced running next week."

Emily groaned, inwardly. More *advanced* running? She could see ways to toughen up the other exercises, or the climbing frame device that he'd used to teach them how to scramble up and down trees, cliffs and even house walls, but how could they run harder? Maybe he intended to force them to run faster, or get walloped with the baton. It seemed clear to her that both of the Sergeants were deliberately holding back as they ran.

"Each team will also be expected to join us on a ramble through the countryside," the Sergeant added, after a moment. Emily suspected that it was going to be more of a hellish cross-country march. "There will be five days spent away from Whitehall in the mountains, where we will live off the land as we visit some places of historical interest. We will sleep under the stars, just as fully-trained soldiers do when on campaign."

He smiled, rather dryly. "You are responsible for ensuring that your other tutors know that you will be gone, once we post the rota," he warned them. "There shouldn't be any real disruption to your studies, but if your tutors kick up a fuss, inform us and we'll see what we can do. If worst comes to worst, we can add you to a different team for the trip. I suggest that you do your reading and make sure you know what you want to bring."

Emily winced at the droll amusement in his voice. He'd let them make mistakes because they hadn't read the material properly, and then pointed them out after it was too late to easily fix the mistakes. It wasn't a mistake she intended to repeat, particularly if they had to carry everything on a five-day route march. The five-mile marches were bad enough.

"Now, you may go shower," he concluded. "Emily, stay behind for a moment."

Emily watched as the rest of the class headed for the showers, wondering nervously what Harkin intended to say to her. It could be anything from congratulations to a private rebuke, one so unpleasant that even the Sergeant would hesitate to issue it in front of the entire team.

"You did well," Harkin said. "But you do realize that you capitalized on an enemy mistake?"

"Yes," Emily said tightly. But if all six of the defenders had remained in place, they would still have been caught between two fires. Three, perhaps, if Jade ran forward to join the attack. "I understand."

"Make sure that you read the list of camping supplies carefully," Harkin added. "I won't be assigning a team leader to *this* trip."

*So we can make our own mistakes*, Emily thought, sourly. But it did make a certain kind of sense.

"And draw some potions from Mistress Kyla," Harkin said. If Emily hadn't known better, she would have thought that he was embarrassed. "There are specific potions for these camping trips. Make sure you bring them with you, or it won't be so pleasant."

He pointed her towards the showers and Emily nodded, walking through the door and into the changing room. Thankfully, Aloha had finished washing and gone to eat, leaving Emily alone as she stripped off and dumped the muddy uniform in the cleaning basket. The water was hot and clean, much to her relief. There had been times when they had been forced to shower with cold water. Incentive, Aloha had pointed out later, to learn how to cast heating spells for pails of water.

Her body ached as she finished washing and used a towel to dry before donning her robes and wrapping up her hair. Outside, she was surprised to walk right into Jade and the rest of the Redshirts, all standing to attention.

"Well done, Captain," Jade said. The praise didn't seem forced at all. "Come join us for dinner."

Emily flushed, and then allowed them to lead her to the dining hall. Harkin had held her back. Had he *known* this would happen? They hadn't escorted Jade anywhere when *he'd* led the team to victory, but Emily had pulled off the first bloodless victory the Redshirts had enjoyed. It seemed to be something to celebrate.

"You won," Bran said. He winked at her. "Next time, I'll win."

## Chapter Thirty-Two

Emily stopped dead. There was a shambling monstrosity in the middle of the ceremonial garden. At first, she'd thought that it was a thoroughly weird scarecrow, but then the creature had started to move. It looked like a towering column of jelly, wearing what the remains of an oversized set of robes, topped with a single eye that looked permanently malevolent. Slimy tentacles emerged from within its bulging robes, each tentacle carrying a different kind of gardening tool.

She found it hard to speak as the creature's eye fixed on her. "What is *that*?"

"No one's quite sure," Imaiqah admitted. "Apparently, Professor Thande once threw a thousand different potion components into a caldron and boiled them up just to see what would happen. When it had finished bubbling, that ... *thing* crawled out and pronounced itself to be a thinking being. Naturally, they put it in the gardens."

Alassa looked equally stunned. "It's *alive*?"

A long tentacle reached out towards her and tapped her on the forehead. "I think I am alive, so I *am* alive," the monster said, in a burbling voice. "Is it really such a surprise to discover that intelligence takes on many different forms?"

"Don't scare the children, CT," a feminine voice said. Emily turned, and saw a young woman who wore a green robe and carried a small knife in one hand. "This is their first lesson in Magical Creatures. We want them to come back next week."

The creature seemed to nod—it was hard to be sure, as it was difficult to tell where its head actually began—and shambled away down a long row of flower beds.

Alassa rubbed at her forehead where CT had touched her and sent Emily an appalled look. Emily silently agreed with Alassa's assessment, although Emily *had* encountered other intelligent creatures in this world. But CT was definitely something different. Had Thande really produced it in a fit of absent-mindedness, or was that a cover story hiding something far worse?

"Welcome to Magical Creatures," the woman said. She seemed almost insultingly healthy, with bronzed skin and a smile that lit up her face like the sun. "I am Mistress Kirdáne, charged with ensuring that you know enough about magical creatures to survive, should you encounter any of the really *dangerous* animals. If any of you prove to have a genuine talent for handling magical animals, I will make arrangements for you to study the subject in your second-year onwards, perhaps with an eye towards becoming an animal mage. It isn't a common talent, though, so I will not be disappointed if none of you decide to stay in the course in second-year."

Her smile grew even brighter. "Some of these animals are very dangerous, while others are intelligent. If you don't know how to handle them, stay back and let me show you what to do. Follow me."

The zoo—or so Emily came to think of it—stretched out for miles. There were a small set of blockhouses that housed some of the animals, but most of the rest lived in their natural habitats, or as close to them as Whitehall could produce. Strange mists shimmered in the air, which prevented the students from looking deeply into the fields.

Then they reached a small doorway in the middle of nowhere that stood upright without any visible means of support. Mistress Kirdáne winked at her class, stepped through the door and vanished.

After a moment, the students, led by Imaiqah, followed her through the doorway and the world changed around them.

They appeared to be standing on a hillside, far away from any human habitation.

In the distance, Emily could see what looked like a herd of horses, but as they walked closer Emily could make out horns sprouting from their foreheads. Each of them was a different color, ranging from house-brown to bright pink. Emily had never enjoyed playing with toy ponies as a child, yet there was something about the unicorns that called to her, inviting her to play with them. Up close, they smelled of a strange, almost seductive perfume. Their eyes were soft, warm and infinitively caring.

"Boys, remain where you are and don't try to approach the herd," Mistress Kirdáne said. The class halted. "Unicorns don't like men approaching them at any time; if you go too close, you may be gored or hexed by their magic. They're creatures of wild magic, so undoing whatever they do to you may be impossible."

Her voice softened as she looked back at the unicorns. "Girls, you may approach the herd carefully, but if they move away don't follow them. Their tolerance for women is limited, even though they do have a certain affinity for unmarried girls."

The unicorns were so strange that they were almost surreal. Emily had grown used to magic, to charms and potions and even the rigorous training the Sergeants offered, but the unicorns left her feeling numb, as if they couldn't be real. She walked towards a unicorn–one roughly the size of a small pony, with bright red fur–feeling her senses starting to swim. The creature eyed her, winked–she was sure that she had winked–and then walked away, as if she were daring Emily to follow her.

Emily took two steps after her before she remembered the warning and stopped. She backed away and walked towards a different unicorn, one with green fur and over-large brown eyes. This one seemed willing to allow Emily to stroke her fur, but not to touch its horn. She felt a strange tingle as she reached for it, warning her not to press any further. Emily tried to send the creature an apologetic look; the unicorn merely shook her mane in response. She was definitely a creature of wild magic.

It was impossible for her to imagine that the creatures might be dangerous, she realized. They were ... well, *innocent* in a way that few humans could equal, and yet they had wild magic running through them. Professor Thande had said, in passing, that the horn of a unicorn had any number of alchemical uses. Emily found herself wondering just how many unicorns had been killed by men for them to develop a refusal to even *tolerate* human males. Or was there a deeper significance to their actions?

She looked down at the unicorn, then forced herself to look away. Mistress Kirdáne was looking at her, one eyebrow raised.

Emily looked around at the rest of the class. Imaiqah and Alassa were playing with a unicorn infant, which rubbed her head against their legs. Most of the other girls had found a unicorn willing to play with them; one of the girls was actually trying to *mount* a unicorn with white fur. It seemed to think that it was just a big game and kept moving at precisely the wrong moment. The boys watched resentfully, but they were apparently unwilling to risk coming too close.

Then again, anyone who grew up in this world would understand the dangers of wild magic.

Emily gave the unicorn one final stroke, then walked over to the tutor. "How do you tell which of them is male and which is female?"

Mistress Kirdáne laughed. "They're *all* female. And to answer what I believe will be your *next* question, we don't know *how* they reproduce. No one has ever managed to convince them to tell us."

Emily stared at her. "But there must be males, right?"

"We assume so," Mistress Kirdáne said. "We just don't know for sure. If anyone has ever encountered a unicorn herd of males, they have never returned to tell the tale."

She clapped her hands and led the class back down towards the doorway back to Whitehall. Once they were through the gate, she led them into one of the blockhouses and cast a spell in the air, allowing them to see in the dark.

At first, Emily could see nothing, but then she realized that the darkness itself was alive. It loomed towards her with deadly menace. She caught a glimpse of wings–or at least she thought they were wings–in the darkness, before the creature butted right into an invisible field and stopped dead.

Several of the girls gasped in shock.

*The wards*, Emily realized. They were safe.

"Nightshades are very rare, thankfully," Mistress Kirdáne informed them. "They are only active at night. The creatures hunt large animals so they can drag them back to their lairs and consume them over the space of a few days."

Emily swallowed. She wasn't the only one who looked nervous–or shocked.

Mistress Kirdáne continued, giving them no time to digest what she'd said. "You can't see their claws without proper lighting, but suffice it to say they carry a deadly poison that paralyses the victim and holds them in suspension as the Nightshade devours them. There was no cure until Professor Thande invented a potion that counteracts the worst of the damage. Even so, the victim is permanently scarred by his experience."

Emily had no trouble believing it as she took one last look at the Nightshade. There was *nothing* like it on Earth, any more than there were unicorns, fairies and ... whatever CT was. What *else* didn't she know about her new home? Her tutors seemed to assume that she knew everything a normal pupil would know, without taking her origins into account.

She was still mulling it over as Mistress Kirdáne led them to the next blockhouse. This one was situated next to a field containing a dozen sheep, bleating pathetically at the students as they passed. Emily felt strong wards surrounding the blockhouse as Mistress Kirdáne opened the door–which was made of solid iron, apparently–and beckoned for them to follow her inside. The light was dim, but there was no need to use a spell to see.

Emily's thought the blockhouse was empty at first—and then she saw the mist. It hung in the absolute centre of the pen, a sparkling mass that glowed, pulsing with malevolent intent. Emily looked at it and shuddered, having the uneasy sense that the mist was looking right back at her. The more she looked at it, the more she *knew* it was alive and intelligent, a predator in a world of prey. She wanted to run; only pride kept her in her place.

Whatever it was, it was behind the wards. They were perfectly safe.

"By the Goddess," Alassa breathed. "Is that ... is that a *Mimic*?"

"Quite right," Mistress Kirdáne said, surprised. "That *is* a Mimic. Again, they are very rare, but as no one is quite sure how to kill them, they can cause great suffering wherever they go."

She clicked her fingers. A door opened in the far wall, revealing a sheep that was slowly dragged into the room by an unseen force. The animal was *terrified*, Emily realized. As soon as the magic snapped out of existence it tried to flee back through the door it had used to enter. But that door was now closed.

As the sheep started to try to find another way out of the room, the mist's glow grew brighter. A moment later, the sheep staggered to the ground, collapsing into dust. Emily felt cold horror, but the worst was yet to come. The mist, chillingly, began to take on a sheep-like form. The mimicry was so perfect that if Emily hadn't seen it, she wouldn't have believed it.

"The Mimic becomes a copy of its prey," Mistress Kirdáne explained, as they stepped back out into the light. "Though a magic we don't fully understand, the creature even takes on the *memories* of its prey, which allows it to pass for human when it devours a human life force. It does it so well that it doesn't *know* that it isn't human until the human form starts to break down, which can take several years. Once it returns to its normal form, it starts to hunt for other prey."

Emily nodded in understanding. The Sheep-Mimic didn't know that it *was* a Mimic, so it wasn't scared ... but the sheep had been scared. Maybe sheep were too stupid to react to a threat unless it was immediate. She glanced at her classmates and shivered. One of them could be a Mimic and never know it.

Mistress Kirdáne's voice tightened. "The only known defense against a Mimic is to run away as fast as possible," she continued. "If you find yourself within eyeshot of a Mimic, *run*. There are some reports that whatever it does to drain life force takes several minutes for a human, so if you get out of range in time you should be safe."

Emily gulped. "How do you *capture* a Mimic?"

"Very carefully," Mistress Kirdáne said. "Luckily, they can't drain wards or other magical constructs, so it is possible to trap one and hold it prisoner. We have tried to starve Mimics in captivity, but the creatures have been known to live for years without feeding. There's a great deal about them we don't know."

Alassa held up a hand. "How do you tell if someone is a Mimic?"

"You can't," Mistress Kirdáne said flatly. The students exchanged shocked glances. "Think about it. The Mimic has all the memories of its prey. It may not even know it's true nature itself. You could put it under a truth spell and it will say what it believes to be the truth; as far as it knows, it is a human being, without any knowledge of what it *really* is. No spell has been found that will detect a Mimic until it finally starts to shed its acquired form."

Emily looked back at the closed door and shivered again.

"And you can't kill someone on suspicion of being a Mimic, either," Mistress Kirdáne added. "Almost every Kingdom in the Allied Lands has laws against this practice. No matter why you suspect that someone might be a Mimic, it isn't considered an acceptable excuse to kill until you catch the human being discovering back into its natural form."

*Good thing too*, Emily thought. She could imagine the witch-hunts if people *were* allowed to kill their fellows on suspicion of mimicry.

"Besides," Mistress Kirdáne said, "do you really *want* to be right?"

Emily scowled at the thought. If Mimics were impossible to kill, the newly-revealed Mimic might just turn on its would-be slayer and consume them next.

Leaving the Mimic behind, they left the blockhouse and headed towards another doorway. "We're going to see a herd of Centaurs," Mistress Kirdáne said, as they paused outside the door. "Girls, you are *not* to attempt to go near the Centaurs. If any of you try, now or ever, you'll regret it for the rest of your days. Believe me, the consequences can be worse for you here than they are for boys who go too close to unicorns."

She stepped through the doorway before Emily could ask her what she meant. Instead, a boy she barely knew followed their teacher right into a forest that reminded Emily of the Martial Magic training ground. This one seemed more alive, somehow, with a scent in the air that made her heartbeat pound in her ears. She looked around and saw that the other girls had also started to pick up on the scent. But what was it?

"Stay here," Mistress Kirdáne said, sharply.

Emily looked down and discovered that she'd started to walk towards the Centaurs. Flushing, she walked back to the doorway and waited with the girls as the boys headed towards the creatures. The Centaurs looked like human torsos and heads grafted onto horse-like bodies, but there was something about the way they moved suggested that they were very far from human. One of them turned to look at Emily and she felt her head swim, as if she had been drugged again. Part of her mind insisted that the Centaur was the most beautiful creature she'd ever seen; the rest of her screamed that she should run for her life. The boys didn't seem to be in any danger, thankfully. Mistress Kirdáne kept a sharp eye on them from a distance.

"Why ... ?" Emily swallowed and tried again. "Why are they so dangerous?"

"You really don't want to know," Alassa said, from right beside her–how had she come so close without Emily noticing her friend? The Royal Princess sounded stressed, dangerously so. "My father told me, once, that I was never to deal directly with any Centaurs. They have strange powers over womankind."

Emily would have dismissed that as more sexist claptrap, except for the fact that she *did* feel an odd, almost hypnotic pull towards the creatures.

It was a relief when Mistress Kirdáne called the boys back and led them through the doorway, back to Whitehall. The class was very quiet as they headed back towards the ceremonial gardens and the colossal beehive set up in the midst of all kinds of flowers. Emily had been taught that some flowers that had been touched by *mana* were very dangerous, but she couldn't see any of them in the gardens. Indeed, the massive creature Professor Thande had created seemed utterly unbothered as it worked on one of the beehives, ignoring the creatures swarming around its giant eye.

"These bees were the subject of a sorcerer's experiments in increasing honey production in his farms," Mistress Kirdáne explained. "He believed that if he managed to improve them through exposure to *mana*, they would become more powerful and capable; instead, they developed a hive mind and started to bargain with him. Terrified, he sent them to Whitehall and retired from beekeeping."

One of the girls found her voice. "Are they dangerous?"

"They can think and act as one," Mistress Kirdáne said. "One sting wouldn't kill you, but a few hundred would easily end your life. Unlike mundane bees, they can sting you time and time again without dying. CT is the only one who can actually reach into their hives without dying."

"They know better than to sting me," CT said in its bubbly voice. "Bees in a beehive must beehive."

Emily groaned at the pun.

"What you will learn, over the coming weeks, is how to defend yourself against various magical creatures," Mistress Kirdáne continued. "I expect you to read about the subject—a reading list will be provided—and familiarize yourselves with the other creatures in the gardens. After that, we will take field trips to visit creatures that cannot be penned for long, if at all: dragons, werewolves, orcs and goblins. Those of you who do not satisfy me that you know how to cope with them will not be going on the field trips."

She smiled at the students warmly. "Some of you may find yourselves living close to areas rich in *mana*," she reminded them. "You will need such training to keep yourself alive, as well as keeping your people safe. Or, for that matter"—she threw a glance at Alassa—"if you ever have to negotiate with those creatures. Even knowing the possible dangers can make it easier to cope when the time comes."

Mistress Kirdáne clapped her hands together. "Class dismissed. See you all next week."

Emily hung behind as the rest of the class headed back towards the castle. "Mistress," she said, "are you going to introduce us to the fairies?"

Mistress Kirdáne blinked in surprise. "Maybe, but they can be very dangerous," she said slowly. "Why do you ask?"

Emily hesitated. "If someone wanted to buy a live fairy in a shop, how much would it cost?"

"They're rare," Mistress Kirdáne said. "Catching one is dangerous even if they go docile after they have been captured. Maybe two or three gold coins."

Her eyes narrowed. "Is there a point to this question?"

"I was cheated," Emily said, remembering the fairy she'd saved. She explained, briefly, what had happened. "And then the fairy just vanished."

Mistress Kirdáne laughed at her. "Serves you right for not bargaining properly," she said mockingly. "Didn't Mistress Irene tell you that you were supposed to bargain?"

Emily flushed. They hadn't been taught *how* to bargain. It wasn't a skill she had developed on Earth.

"It's your money," the tutor reminded her. "But at least you can know that you freed the fairy. The rules that govern them say they can leave when they're freed."

Emily thanked her and left, walking back towards where Alassa and Imaiqah waited for her. She'd found herself wondering if she'd been cheated while lying in the infirmary, but she hadn't been sure who she could ask to find out. At least the fairy was free ... Who knew, maybe they'd see each other again. Fairies were something she could look up when they were next in the library.

Alassa smiled as they entered the school. "I always thought that would be boring," she confessed. "But do you think they'd bring us a dragon to ride?"

Emily opened her mouth, but before she could say a word there was a brilliant flash of light. Her entire body locked solid. She couldn't move a muscle.

"You," a voice said, from out of nowhere. "You are going to pay."

## Chapter Thirty-Three

*An invisibility spell*, part of Emily's mind yammered. *They were waiting in ambush for you!*

She couldn't move a single voluntary muscle; she didn't even know how she was breathing. If someone could be turned into stone for an hour, perhaps there was a spell to hold the body in stasis while the mind thought desperately, looking for a way out of the trap. Beside her, she heard Alassa yelp in shock as three figures appeared out of nowhere, advancing towards her with their hands raised. She couldn't see or hear Imaiqah at all.

"Well, well, well," the lead figure said. She was a girl with long, red hair and a face that would have been stunningly pretty if it hadn't been twisted into a sneer. "Did you think, *Princess*, that you were safe without your gaggle of cronies?"

Emily saw Alassa move out of the corner of her eye as the princess lifted her wand. There was a sudden sense of magic and the wand was yanked right out of the Princess's hand.

It flew through the air to be caught by the newcomer, who glanced at it and stuck it in her robe. Her two companions—a dark-skinned girl and a girl who looked vaguely Oriental—grinned as they spread out, both of them staring at Alassa. Emily struggled mentally, but her entire body was as stiff and unmoving as a rock. Unlike Alassa's spells, the newcomer's spells were too strong to easily overcome.

"Melissa," Alassa said. She sounded confident, but Emily could hear the fear in her voice—and knew Melissa could probably hear it too. "You don't have to hurt my friends ..."

"You didn't have to hurt my friends either," Melissa snapped. "What were you thinking when you turned Hast into a frog? Or when your cronies cast five different spells on me and walked away, leaving me trying desperately to get them off?"

Emily would have rolled her eyes if she had been able to move. Of course she wouldn't have been the only person Alassa had tried to pick on, before she'd been almost killed and then kidnapped. Melissa sounded as if she wanted revenge; naturally, Alassa's old cronies would have been very good at protecting their leader's back, even if Alassa couldn't do spells for herself. But Emily hadn't seen any of them since Alassa's near-death experience.

"It was pointed out to me that I acted poorly," Alassa said stiffly. Emily could just imagine the lectures she would have had from Mistress Kyla, let alone the Warden and the Grandmaster. A Royal Princess had no business risking her life by bullying students who weren't properly respectful. "And I am sorry for what I did to you."

"You're sorry?" Melissa asked. She lifted one hand, shaping it into a claw. "You don't know the meaning of the word."

She was posturing, Emily realized, believing it to be perfectly safe. Sergeant Harkin had made it clear that those who took time to show off on the battlefield ended up dead very quickly, as their enemy snapped off killing spells while they were showing off. But Alassa had been working with Emily ever since they'd been jammed together in Basic Charms and she knew more about casting spells without a wand than Melissa would believe. Maybe she could take out all three of the girls before it was too late ...

Alassa raised a hand and snapped off a charm towards Melissa.

Melissa looked bored as the charm slammed into her protections and was harmlessly deflected towards the ceiling. A moment later, she tossed a spell back at Alassa, striking the Princess directly in the chest.

Alassa shrank rapidly. Her robe fell to the ground and covered her as she vanished from Emily's sight. Emily heard something scratching, just before an oversized rat came into view. That *had* to be Alassa ...

"Have fun countering that spell," Melissa said. "I put some real teeth into its structure."

She looked at Emily as if she were thinking about casting a second spell on her, but instead walked away. Her two friends followed.

Emily helplessly watched her go as cold anger burned through her mind. She *hated* being helpless at the best of times; being frozen reminded her far too much of being Shadye's captive. The magic which bound her, and held her firmly in place, seemed solid. She struggled to cast a dispelling charm and escape, but the magic seemed disinclined to work properly.

The rat squeaked, reminding Emily that it could have been worse. It honestly hadn't occurred to her that Alassa could be ambushed at any moment, an oversight that had left all three of them thoroughly humiliated. She made a mental note to see if there were spells that could give her a magical spider-sense, or at least some early warning when someone was creeping up on her or lying in ambush. Sergeant Harkin would probably disapprove—he'd been tested their natural abilities, not their magically-enhanced powers—but she had a feeling she was going to need it. That was the *second* time she'd been caught by surprise.

Time seemed to slow down until she felt the spell slowly begin to unlock. Her entire body went wobbly, just before she crashed to the stone floor like a sack of potatoes. A second later, she heard a gasp of pain as Imaiqah hit the deck behind her.

But Alassa, it seemed, was still a rat. Emily somehow managed to roll over and look at Imaiqah, who looked on the verge of tears. She wanted to comfort her friend—both of her friends—but it was so hard to move. Her body felt completely drained.

*Chocolate*, she thought, as she reached into her pouch. She'd made a habit of carrying a bar ever since experimenting with the *Berserker* spell. Slowly, she managed to swallow a couple of chunks, then she passed the rest to Imaiqah. The chocolate gave her enough energy to stagger to her feet and look down at Alassa, who was *still* a rat. Melissa probably hadn't intended the spell to be removed easily, if at all.

Alassa looked up, her nose twitching in a manner that would have been comical if it hadn't been so serious, and waved her paws in the air. It was easy to understand what she wanted.

"I'll try," Emily said. "I just don't have much energy."

She cast a single dispelling charm in the air and watched, unsurprised, as it failed to return Alassa to human form. It figured that Melissa had thought of that simple countermeasure and ensured her spell was designed to resist it.

Next, Emily cast the analysis spell and watched as Melissa's transfiguration spell appeared in front of her face. It looked to be a simple copy of a spell she'd seen in the book of practical jokes–again, it struck Emily that no one sane could regard a forced transformation as a practical joke–but Melissa had added a nasty component to make it harder to remove.

"We'll have to cast the charm together," Imaiqah said. Her other friend looked completely exhausted, but her eyes were bright. "That particular twist can be beaten because it can only react to one charm at a time. On three. One, two, three ..."

The dispelling charm worked perfectly the second time around. Alassa's form twisted uncomfortably, then returned to human, leaving her crawling on the floor. Emily looked away as Alassa grabbed her robe and pulled it over her head, muttering words in a language that her translation spell declined to adapt properly. Or maybe it was a perfect translation. Most insulting remarks from foreign countries and mindsets didn't seem so insulting when translated into plain English.

"I'm sorry," Alassa said, after another minute. Her voice was muffled as she tried to pull her undershirt on after donning the robe, rather than the other way round. "I didn't think."

Emily wasn't too surprised. Before she'd arrived at Whitehall, Alassa had her reputation, her family and a gang of cronies who did her bidding, even though she wasn't a strong magician in her own right. No doubt the cronies had the magic skills to keep Alassa from having a knife shoved in her back by one of her victims. But now...what had happened to the cronies anyway? Had they been sent home in disgrace?

"They don't want to be with me anymore," Alassa admitted when Emily asked. "Their parents said I was *dangerous*."

Emily leaned against the wall and took a long breath. "What did you do to Melissa?"

Alassa didn't answer for a long moment. "She was irritating me. I cast a jinx on her that ensured that she would say the wrong thing at the wrong time. She called a tutor a nasty name and ended up being sent to the Hall of Shame."

"Oh," Emily said. It was hard to blame Melissa for wanting to strike back, and yet Emily was still very angry. How in all the universe had Melissa blamed *Emily* for what Alassa had done before she'd even arrived in this world? It struck her a moment later: Emily had shocked Alassa, befriended her and then started to teach her how to cast spells properly. Melissa probably suspected that Alassa would become even *more* of a terror once she knew what she was actually *doing*. "What were you thinking?"

"I was a fool," Alassa said bleakly. She looked up, her bright eyes blazing with anger. "We have to strike back."

Emily hesitated. The mature and responsible part of her mind pointed out that Melissa had a good reason to be angry with Alassa, and perhaps, now that she'd had her fun, it wouldn't happen again. But the part of her mind that had been a target of bullying knew that it wouldn't end so easily. Children who were bullied often became bullies themselves because it was the only way they knew how to take care of themselves. Melissa and her two friends might start casting charms and hexes on Emily and *her* friends at every opportunity.

And she'd been rendered helpless, forced to watch as Alassa was transfigured, then wait for what felt like hours before the spell had finally worn off. She was *angry* at Melissa, just as she'd been angry at Alassa when *she'd* hexed Emily. And poor Imaiqah hadn't done anything to deserve being frozen in place either.

And Emily was unused to having friends. What would happen if she said no?

Imaiqah spoke into the silence. "But Melissa's a skilled spell-caster," she said, weakly. "We can't just walk up to her and start casting spells..."

"No," Alassa agreed. She bitterly looked down at her hands. "Maybe we should play a joke on her."

Emily winced at her tone. The Royal Princess had never had to face an equal - much less a superior - opponent before, unless one counted the kidnappers. And Alassa had beaten one of them halfway to death. She might be a stubborn girl, unwilling to use her intelligence when her status would do, but she didn't give up.

"I think we should go back to my bedroom and sort ourselves out," Emily said. They'd missed tea while frozen, but the kitchens produced late meals for some of the students, as well as emergency food for those who overstrained themselves. "And then we can decide what to do."

There was no sign of Aloha when they entered her bedroom, so Emily picked up the books on practical jokes while Alassa first undressed and in private, then dressed again, properly. There were thousands of different charms they could use for amusement, but most of them would be easy for someone like Melissa to detect and remove before it was too late. Emily hadn't seen Melissa at all before now, which meant that she had definitely tested out of the basic classes and gone on to prepare herself for her second year. She was certainly more competent with charms and hexes than Emily.

"We could just turn her into something unpleasant," Alassa said as she finished dressing. "A spider perhaps, or a crab, or ..."

Emily shuddered. The people of this world might regard forced transformations as a harmless prank, but it wasn't an attitude she shared. Maybe she would have felt differently if she'd grown up in a world where magic existed. Besides, she'd come alarmingly close to killing Alassa through merging a transfiguration spell with another charm. The results could have been disastrous.

"Or we could hit her with the Idiot Ball," Imaiqah offered. "*That* would give her a nasty fright."

"I don't know how to cast it," Alassa admitted. The distance between her and Imaiqah seemed to have faded away through shared adversity. "Do you?"

Emily frowned. "The Idiot Ball?"

"It's a spell that dampens the target's intelligence," Alassa explained. She smirked.

"I admit that it is sometimes easy to believe that the boys here have been struck by the Idiot Ball ..."

"You can't just cast it on someone, because all of their basic protections will ward them against it," Imaiqah added. "You have to stick it on something and then slip it into their presence, perhaps by dropping it into their robes. And then it starts affecting them at once. A simple sum like two plus two becomes impossible."

Emily hesitated. All of the practical jokes she'd seen involving mind manipulation had been very limited, because even *this* world admitted that mind manipulation wasn't funny. A post-hypnotic suggestion could cause some amusement, but it could also cause disaster; the Idiot Ball might even cause worse problems.

"Or there's the Gender Key," Alassa suggested. "Do you think she'd enjoy waking up to discover that she's a boy?"

"That would get us all in very hot water," Imaiqah reminded her. Emily stared at them both blankly. "Someone introduced a gender-swapping spell into Whitehall two years ago, or so I was told. The results were absolute chaos. Eventually, the spell was banned and we were warned that if we used it, we would be sent to face the Warden."

Emily shook her head in disbelief. She had grown accustomed to her new world, a process made easier by the fact that there was nothing and no one back in her old world who she wanted to see again. And yet there were times when the sheer *strangeness* of the new world came up and slapped her right across the face. A spell to turn someone into an idiot, a spell to turn a girl into a boy or vice versa ... or, for that matter, a school that allowed its children to carry lethal weapons everywhere. Because that was what magic was, a lethal weapon. If Alassa had been dangerous with only a few spells, how dangerous would a combat sorcerer be to his enemies?

"A good thing too," Emily said, remembering the boys from her old school. They'd been jerks, every single one of them, particularly after they'd discovered that girls weren't just oddly-shaped men. The mere flash of a smile from one of the popular girls turned them into drooling zombies. Boys were dirty and smelly and gross and there was no way that she would want to be one.

But then, some of the girls hadn't been so clever, either. There was more to life than counting the number of guys who would do something stupid if you batted your eyelashes at them. Or trying to make yourself popular by dating the most popular guy in the school.

A thought struck her as she looked over at Alassa. "If your parents wanted a boy," she said, "why didn't they just use magic to alter your sex?"

Alassa gaped at her, and then swallowed. "Wherever you come from has to be a very long way away. Don't you know that such magic doesn't always work properly?"

"It doesn't always alter the mind," Imaiqah added. "You could end up with a boy in a girl's body if you weren't careful."

"And if you messed around with their mind," Alassa said, "you might make a bad situation much worse."

Emily nodded in understanding. Most transfiguration spells were configured to avoid causing mental damage, because the long-term effects of mind manipulation could be dangerously unpredictable. In this case, if a girl became a boy, she'd still think of herself as a girl on the inside, presumably also being attracted to other boys. Her lips twitched; it was quite possible that she—he—would become homosexual, at least by the strict definition of the term. And vice versa for a boy who became a girl. Actually, if the boys back home could have been put into female bodies for a few days, it might teach them a valuable lesson. They'd picked on weaker boys they'd accused of being homosexual, even though Emily had known that those weaker boys lusted after girls too. They'd picked on everyone who had seemed weaker than them.

She had no idea what this world thought of homosexuality, but it would likely be disastrous for a monarchy. She had no idea how Alassa's Kingdom in particular would react to a homosexual monarch—particularly if they didn't know that he'd originally been female—but at the very least it would call his/her ability to continue the succession into question. And what if he literally *couldn't* have children, even with a woman who had been *born* a woman? The line of succession would be destroyed. Or if...

Her imagination produced too many possibilities, none of them good.

"If we hit her with the Idiot Ball," Alassa said finally, "how do we get it into her possession? She is a little paranoid about locking her door."

"With reason," Emily pointed out. She wasn't sure if she wanted to go ahead with it, but Melissa *did* need a lesson in picking on the wrong person. "Maybe we should just throw a hex at her when her back is turned."

Imaiqah giggled. "I know how we can hex her," she said. Emily and Alassa both stared at her in surprise. "Her clothes will be drying off in the laundry after being washed. All we have to do is hex her undershirt, then wait for her to put it on."

"Very good," Alassa said. She rubbed her hands together with glee. "Tomorrow... we strike!"

# Chapter Thirty-Four

*I MUST BE OUT OF MY MIND*, EMILY THOUGHT AS SHE OPENED HER EYES. A GLANCE AT HER watch revealed that it was five bells, precisely when she'd timed the sleep spell to lift. *I must be completely out of my mind.*

She rolled over and pushed the blanket aside, climbing out of bed. Imaiqah was waking up too, but Aloha still slept soundly after coming in late the previous evening. Emily had heard that Aloha had been practicing with her Martial Magic team, something that Emily intended to suggest to Jade the next time she saw him. There had to be some way to practice the dangerous spells outside class without getting into trouble. Perhaps Sergeant Harkin expected them to figure it out for themselves.

It was Saturday morning, a day that was used more for revision and private study than actual classes. Emily knew most students wouldn't bother to get up until later, allowing those who did to have unimpeded access to the library and the spellcasting chambers. Tapping her lips at Imaiqah—they didn't want to wake Aloha, who might ask questions if she saw them leaving so early—she pulled on her robe, then splashed water on her face. As soon as they were both dressed, they slipped out of the room and into the deserted hallway.

"The laundry is at the end of the corridor," Imaiqah murmured, as they walked down the hallway. It was charmed to prevent people from disturbing students who were trying to sleep, but Madame Razz had been known to reprimand students for making too much noise anyway. "The only problem will be getting inside."

A door opened ahead of them to reveal Alassa, wearing a midnight black nightgown, studded with jewels that had to be worth a small fortune. "I meant to ask," she hissed, as she closed her bedroom door behind her. "How did you know about the laundry anyway?"

Imaiqah grinned. It transformed her face from cute to beautiful. "I made a terrible mess in the hallway when I accidentally dropped a bag on the floor," she admitted. "Madame Strictly"—Madame Razz, Emily guessed—"gave me detention and sent me to help the maids do the laundry. It was not a pleasant task."

"They must have needed help that day," Alassa whispered. "They don't normally allow the servants to interact with us at all."

Emily frowned, wondering just what—if anything—that meant. She hadn't seen many of the school's domestic servants, apart from the cooks—and the cooks seemed to enjoy a higher status than one might have guessed. They *were* very good cooks. But for all she knew, the laundry and cleaning might as well have been done by House Elves.

Her lips twitched. What little they'd learned about Elves in class—and through reading history books—had made it clear that trying to enslave them was asking for trouble. Some places had humans hiring Brownies and suchlike to do the cleaning, in exchange for milk and alcohol, but Whitehall preferred to keep most magical creatures firmly on the outside of the walls. It wasn't too surprising; the Mimics were enough to give *anyone* nightmares and the thought of introducing one of them into the school ...

She shuddered as a disquieting thought struck her. *How would anyone know if they had?*

She pushed that thought aside as they reached a solid stone door at the end of the hallway. "I think the charm on the door doesn't change," Imaiqah said as she pressed her hand against the knob. "It should be easy to open."

Emily exchanged glances with Alassa. Booby-trapping a door was all too easy for students, which meant the staff could easily do it themselves. Maybe it would just refuse to open for them, or perhaps it would be keyed to throw a freeze spell at the person trying to open it–and anyone else standing nearby. But why would anyone want to lock a laundry room?

She laughed at herself a moment later. Their plan was an *excellent* example of why someone *would* want to lock a laundry room.

"It might be time to come up with an explanation," Emily said quickly. "Something we can tell Madame Razz if this goes wrong ..."

There was a click. The door opened, releasing a wave of hot air and steam. Emily stepped inside, shaking her head in disbelief. The laundry room was vast, with newly-cleaned robes and undershirts hanging from railings or placed in hampers for later attention. It was difficult to see very far because of the steam, but in the distance she thought she saw someone move.

Alassa stepped forward and snapped off a spell Emily didn't recognize, just before the steam parted enough for her to see a young girl dressed in black at the end of the room. The girl had been frozen solid by Alassa's spell.

"Don't worry," Alassa said reassuringly, as Emily stared at her in horror. "That isn't your basic freeze spell. Time will just have stopped for her; she won't realize that she was spelled at all, ever. We'll do what we came to do and then release her just before we leave."

"But ..." Emily found it hard to speak. "But what did she do to deserve it?"

"Think about it," Alassa said, as if she didn't understand why Emily was alarmed. "She would have told Madame Strictly if I hadn't frozen her. And then we *would* have been caught and punished and I don't want to be punished again!"

Emily shook her head, angrily. It was too much to expect Alassa to have reformed completely; she had been brought up to consider servants as objects, rather than people. And Alassa was right. If the maid did report them, Madame Razz would take a dim view of it–and then they wouldn't be able to hit Melissa with the Idiot Ball. But it was still wrong to treat people like objects, Emily reminded herself, and swore to make her feelings clear later.

Imaiqah moved from hamper to hamper. "All of the clothes belonging to the first year girls are washed together," she said. "And they should be marked with a nametag just to make sure that we don't accidentally swap undershirts or knickers. If this hamper here belongs to me, this one here should be for you and this other one for Melissa."

She paused, holding up an undershirt. "Got her," she said. "This is Melissa's shirt."

Alassa walked forward to take it from her. "Are you sure?"

"That's her name right there," Imaiqah pointed out dryly. "There's only one Melissa, period. If there were two people with her name in first year, one of them would have been urged to take a different name to keep from any possible confusion."

"Very good," Alassa said. She produced a sheet of parchment from her pocket and passed it to Emily. "I added a second hex to the charm; can you check it?"

Emily scanned it quickly. Alassa had noticed a flaw in their plan, one that hadn't occurred to Emily when they'd worked out the original charm. There was no guarantee that Melissa would wear the charmed shirt at once, which meant that it might be several days before their charm took effect. Alassa had added a simple glamour to the spell that would urge Melissa to wear the charmed shirt at once, a glamour so subtle that even an experienced magician would have problems detecting it. Or so Emily hoped.

"It should work," Emily said, after a moment. The last thing they needed was the spell unraveling before it could take effect. "And it should be unnoticeable."

"Cast it quickly, then," Imaiqah urged. "The longer the maid remains frozen, the more likely it is that she will notice something odd when the spell wears off."

Alassa had no lack of raw power, Emily noted as she felt Alassa cast the spell. There was a long moment of nothingness, and then she felt the charm briefly settle on the undershirt before it faded away into the background. Emily hoped it was firmly attached to the shirt, but there was no way to tell without running a complete set of detection spells - which would probably overwhelm and destroy the charm before it could be activated.

Shaking her head in disbelief at what they were doing–and her own collaboration - Emily put the shirt back on the railing and then looked over at Alassa meaningfully. The Royal Princess nodded, walked over to the maid and altered the charm on her slightly, before heading to the door.

"It will wear off in two minutes," Alassa murmured as they closed the door behind them. "She won't notice a thing."

Emily scowled as they walked down the corridor. The paralysis spell was bad enough, but at least the victim *knew* that she had been paralyzed. Alassa's stasis spell would leave the victim completely unaware of what had happened, at least unless the person had some precautionary spells set up to alert them afterwards. One of the books she'd read had talked about the charms and tricks wizards used to counter the effect of memory charms, ranging from keywords to memory dumps into the nearest receptacle. She doubted the maid had any magic at all–she would have been studying at Whitehall herself if she did–but that didn't make mistreating her acceptable. At least Melissa had started the fight.

*But the maid was to us what I was to Melissa,* she thought, feeling a twinge of guilt. *Someone in the way.*

They were all far too keyed up to go back to sleep, so they ended up in one of the private study rooms attached to the library. Imaiqah picked up a book on magical herbs and started to read it, leaving Emily trying to think of a way to explain to Alassa that what she'd done to the maid was wrong. But Alassa had been raised in a world where the upper classes were allowed to do whatever they liked to the lower classes, and where magic was often the dividing line between control and servitude. How did one explain to someone like that the error of their ways?

"If I hadn't frozen her," Alassa pointed out, after Emily had made a halting attempt at such an explanation, "we would be explaining ourselves to Madame Strictly right now. And I doubt she would be happy with us."

Emily scowled. She was right, of course, which didn't make her morally correct. Imaiqah might have objected more—she was from the lower classes, after all—but she said nothing. Emily couldn't tell if her friend didn't want to pick a fight with Alassa, or if she *agreed* with the Princess. People on the wrong side of the social divide, but still not right at the bottom, might take it more seriously than those right at the top. It validated their position, or so Emily had read. But it seemed absurd.

"People are not objects," Emily snapped. An idea occurred to her and she smiled. "Do you know what...what a very ancient civilization used to call their slaves?"

Alassa blinked. "Slaves?"

Emily snorted. "They used to call them Tools That Thought," she said. The Romans had been smarter than the slave-owners of Dixie, or the Ottoman Empire. They'd known that slaves could become productive citizens and had worked hard to integrate them into Roman society once they were manumitted. "They knew that slaves could be dangerous."

"They didn't know any charms for keeping them in their place?" Alassa asked. Emily remembered Void's servants and shuddered, inwardly. "Or didn't they know better than to let them take liberties?"

Emily pushed her thoughts aside and glared at her friend. "Melissa was weak while you were supported by your friends," she snapped. The nagging guilt pushed her onwards. "And when *you* were weak, she attacked and humiliated you. How much more humiliated are the slaves? Be careful which toes you tread on today, because you might be kissing those feet tomorrow!"

Alassa started to speak, but Emily spoke over her. "People *think*, they have feelings; if you hurt those feelings, they're going to want revenge. What do you expect will happen if you create a mass of angry people under your throne? You might not live long enough to pass it down to your daughter!"

"A maid can't hurt me," Alassa protested.

Emily laughed humorlessly. "And you don't think that what we just did shows exactly how she *can* hurt you? You don't need magic to make someone's life a misery."

And then she shook her head. "Learn that lesson before it's too late. Your kingdom might depend on it."

She watched Alassa furrow her brow in thought, considering. It was too much to hope that Alassa would change at once, but at least *thinking* about it was a step in the right direction. She hadn't *planned* to be born a Royal Princess, after all. Unless that was possible in this world ... Emily considered it for a long moment, and then dismissed the thought. Everyone would be doing it if it were possible.

Changing the subject, she opened up a Basic Charms textbook and started to read and work through the sample exam questions at the rear of the book. Alassa joined her a moment later. They'd been told that they would be tested in a week, and Emily suspected that she wouldn't be allowed to progress until Alassa passed the test, too. Some of the Basic questions were surprisingly easy, while others were treacherously complicated. Unlike the exams she remembered from back home, she–they–were being tested on what they'd learned and how they could apply it, not just regurgitating memorized facts and figures.

*It might work differently here,* she thought, as she answered one question and then glanced at the answer page. *I'll be using these skills for the rest of my life.*

One particular charm seemed impossible to dismantle until Alassa pointed out that it was actually a set of hexes, all of which had to be cancelled in the right order. Looking at it, Emily suspected that the writer had deliberately created one to make students think on their feet, because when it was cast in real life the results of an unsuccessful attempt to dismantle it were likely to be unpleasant. He'd included a great many spell components that didn't seem to do anything at all; it took Emily several minutes to realize that they *didn't* do anything, apart from confusing the unwary student. But she would have to check each component carefully, just in case. Some of them seemed to be woven into the active spell components.

Feeling hungry after an hour of study, they left the library and headed down to the dining hall. A small number of students were already there, eating their way through large plates of food before going to their weekend classes. Emily had been warned that she would have to learn courtly etiquette from a tutor before they risked sending her to any Royal Court, except perhaps for Alassa's own Court. The Grandmaster had told Emily that the King and Queen were relieved she'd helped save their daughter from kidnapping, or worse.

A crash made them all jump. Melissa and her friends had entered the dining hall to pick up plates of food for themselves, but there was definitely something wrong with Melissa. She'd just dropped a plateful of food on the ground and was giggling, rather like a dumb bimbo. Her friends were gathered around her, trying to either clean up the mess or figure out what was wrong; judging from their comments, Melissa had been out of sorts all morning. She *had* to be wearing the charmed shirt under her robes.

Emily caught sight of Melissa's eyes and shuddered, wishing that she'd never heard of the Idiot Ball curse. Melissa looked ... vapid, almost completely stupid. Her expression seemed to change at terrifying speed, as if her mood was swinging madly from sheer delight to outright fear. The giggling was becoming increasingly hysterical as she tried, and failed, to clean up the mess she'd created. What had they *done* to her?

"A stronger curse than I intended," Alassa muttered. "Now someone will discover it before she goes into classes."

Emily swallowed the response that came to mind, picked up her plate and dumped it–and the remaining food–through the hatch. She didn't feel like eating any longer. If she could have removed the hex without revealing what they'd done, she would have done so without a second thought. As it was ... she took one last look at Melissa, who was starting to drool like a kid who thought it was funny to pretend to be dumb, and left the hall. The urge to be violently sick was almost overpowering.

And they'd considered it a prank!

"We are *not* going to do that again," Emily snapped. She'd been humiliated when Melissa had frozen her, but their response had been utterly over the top. "We went too far."

Alassa gave her an odd look, but didn't argue. It was almost a relief when they entered the hallway and almost walked right into Madame Razz, who practically dragged them into her office. It was a barren room with a sofa, a desk and a small crystal ball standing in one corner.

"You have some explaining to do," Madame Razz said sharply. "Why did you enter the laundry room?"

Emily hesitated. Alassa spoke first, quickly. "I wanted to recover some of my clothes for today. I thought that that was permitted."

"It *might* be permitted," Madame Razz said. Her eyes narrowed. "But why did you freeze the maid?"

Alassa gulped. "Because I panicked," she said. Emily found herself wondering how Madame Razz had known what they'd done. She clearly didn't know about the Idiot Ball, or ... what *would* she do, if she knew? Whitehall seemed to turn a blind eye to pranks as long as they weren't likely to cause serious injury or death. "I reacted instinctively."

"I don't think I believe you," Madame Razz said. Her voice hardened. "It is quite hard to convince anyone to work at a school for young magicians. I have to make all kinds of promises to prospective maids, *including a promise that they won't be charmed by every magician who thinks she has a sense of humor.* I am going to have to offer them a raise just to prevent them from walking out."

She opened a drawer in the desk and produced something that looked like a shoe - no, a slipper. "And I also have to deal with you," she added. She tapped the slipper against her palm meaningfully. "All three of you, bend over the sofa. Now."

Afterwards, when they were commiserating with each other, Emily felt a moment of relief despite the pain. The maids weren't slaves after all. They were paid, treated reasonably decently and allowed to leave if they wanted to go.

But how had Madame Razz known what they'd done?

"Stop complaining," she said to Alassa. "We both know that we all deserved that."

## Chapter Thirty-Five

"I BELIEVE THAT, FOR *SOME* OF YOU, THIS IS YOUR FIRST EXAM," PROFESSOR LOMBARDI SAID. "The procedure is quite simple."

He looked around the room, his bright eyes glinting with suppressed amusement. "Once you are finished preparing–and I hope you brought everything you were told to bring–I will escort you into a small exam room. You will be given a sheaf of parchments with the first set of exam questions; the exam starts the moment you open the first piece of parchment. For the theory questions, write down your answers on the parchment below the question, fold it up again and seal it with your karmic signature. Bear in mind that you *cannot* reopen the parchment after it has been sealed.

"You have two hours to answer as many questions as possible. I suggest that you spend the last ten minutes rechecking your answers and then sealing the parchments, as an unsealed parchment is considered invalid. Should you leave the exam room, you will be considered to have completed the exam and you will not be allowed to re-enter the chamber. Do *not* leave the room unless you are *certain* that you have finished, or in case of desperate need.

"Once the exam is completed, you may return to this classroom to wait for the tutor who will give you the practical part of the exam. Do *not* attempt to enter any other exam room for whatever reason. It may mean automatic failure for both students involved, as well as a certain caning for the student who tried to open the door. So don't do it. You may leave this classroom to find food and drink while you're waiting, but being late for the second part of the exam will count against you. Are there any questions?"

There were none.

"Good," Lombardi said. "There are a pair of reference books in the exam rooms, if you need them, along with quills and parchment. You are *not* allowed to take anything but drink and a snack into the chamber. I suggest that you empty out your robes here and leave everything in the classroom. It won't be touched while you're busy."

Emily and Alassa exchanged glances as they slowly emptied their pockets of everything they'd been carrying. The Professor hadn't mentioned anything about how that rule was enforced, but after they'd been caught in the laundry room Emily had realized that they were under far tighter scrutiny than she'd assumed. Chances were there were wards around the exam chamber to catch anyone who tried to smuggle something in with them. Not that she intended to try. Passing this exam on the first attempt had become an obsession after she'd started tutoring Alassa.

"Drink and food," Lombardi repeated as they stood up. "Follow me."

There was yet another corridor behind the charms classroom, one leading to an endless series of solid doors. The students waited nervously as, one by one, Lombardi took them into a chamber, explained how to use it and then left, closing the door behind him. Emily's room was a barren chamber, little different from the study rooms in the library. The only real difference was a small toilet compartment and a set of folded parchments on the table.

*I should have finished devising the word processor,* she thought, as Lombardi motioned for her to sit down. The exam chamber was infused with wards, each one keyed to preventing someone from slipping information into the room. She was surprised that they weren't keyed to keep unwanted intruders out, or perhaps they were and Lombardi had merely issued his warning to keep their minds focused on avoiding even the *appearance* of cheating.

Lombardi jabbed his finger into one corner. A glowing countdown appeared in midair. "The timer will start as soon as you open the first parchment," he said again. Emily nodded impatiently, feeling the butterflies in her stomach that she'd always felt before an important exam. "Remember, leaving the room for any reason counts as ending the exam. If you need help—and it had better be important—dispel the timer. It will summon a tutor to attend to you at once."

*And if it isn't important,* Emily thought sourly, *you'll be trying to finish the exam standing up.*

"Good luck," Lombardi said.

He walked to the door, stepped through it and was gone. A moment later, Emily felt the remaining locking wards shiver into place. Shaking her head, she put her bottle of juice down on the table and checked the two textbooks on the shelf. They were nothing more than pointers, rather than something that would give her the answer. She would still have to know what she was doing—to comprehend it—to pass.

Placing both books within arm's reach, she picked up the first piece of parchment and opened it slowly. A chime rang through the room as soon as she looked down at the question. She frowned as she read it twice to be sure that she understood. She had to write down a complex set of components for a spell, several of them only to be activated when—if—certain preconditions were met. Annoyingly, it would have been easy to do the whole thing with several separate spells, but that wouldn't answer the question.

Carefully, she wrote out what she wanted to do, outlined the various spell components, and then wrote it all up into one spell. At the front, she added—as she had been taught—SP. She had a feeling that adding a *real* startpoint would have cost her the exam.

Opening up the next sheet of parchment, she was surprised to discover a very different question. It was difficult to use a charm to counteract poison, but it *was* easy to detect the presence of poison, either through a sample of someone's blood or through scanning their entire body. The second question wanted to know precisely *how* the charm worked, and what to do if it produced a negative response.

Emily silently thanked God that she'd read around the topic and encouraged Alassa to do the same. Lombardi had never told them directly that poison could be detected if one keyed the spell to look for something alien in a human body. He'd expected them to learn on their own.

There were ten pieces of parchment in all. Emily worked through them, trying not to sweat as the questions grew harder. One of them discussed how to detect subtle charms and hexes, a reminder of what they'd done to Melissa. Her mind started to wander Someone *had* to have discovered the Idiot Ball by now, surely. Melissa wasn't stupid and she'd been acting in a manner that practically *screamed* that she'd been hexed in some way ...

Emily pushed the thought out of her head and wrote down the answer to the question; a sufficiently careful scan of a person's body would reveal the presence of a hex, if the caster hadn't managed to hide it behind a stealth charm. But doing that tended to weaken the hex to the point where it was nearly useless. Emily had once tried to ask if that had something to do with the observer effect and had been greeted by blank looks from her tutors.

Ninety minutes passed before she finished writing out the answers, then she went back to reread what she'd written. She wasn't very happy with one of the questions, but there just seemed to be too many variables for any charm to cover. Absently, she wrote that after her attempt at an answer and suggested using three separate spells as a potential solution. Perhaps it was a trick question. The tutors seemed willing to force them to think, whatever it took.

Shaking her head, she glanced at the timer, then started to seal up the parchments. Her head felt too thick to continue, even after she took a long swig of water and a bite of chocolate. Once all the parchments were sealed, she stood and walked to the door, unsure what to do with her answers. Eventually, she left them on the desk.

She walked out of the room and headed back to the classroom. She wasn't surprised to discover four other students sitting at their desks, one of them very upset. But there was no sign of Alassa at all.

The Royal Princess didn't arrive until the final seconds had ticked away. She looked tired and worn and not at all confident, just like Emily felt. They exchanged brief comments as they rested, before the first of the tutors—a very thin man Emily had never seen before—arrived to take one of the students to the practical exam. She'd never really realized how many tutors there were until the exam. Whitehall seemed to have hundreds of them.

"My brain feels weak," Alassa muttered. "I *hate* exams."

"Me too," Emily agreed. She didn't have a clue how many answers she'd managed to get right. Or even if she had got *any* of them right. "Do you want to get something to eat?"

"Yeah," Alassa said. "We'd better hurry."

They left the classroom and ran to the kitchen, where they discovered the kitchen staff had prepared loaves of bread, ham and cheese. Emily had suggested sandwiches to the staff, only to discover that they *had* heard of the concept, they just didn't think it was particularly appropriate for the students. Apparently, only *commoners* ate sandwiches. Given the story behind the invention of the sandwich in Emily's world—which might or might not be true—she couldn't help snorting at the irony. But making her own sandwiches could be fun.

"I hear you're doing the exam again today," a voice called. Emily's blood ran cold as she recognized Melissa's voice. "Try to fail it again, *Princess*. It will only spare you the humiliation of advanced class!"

Alassa glared after Melissa as she ran down the corridor, one hand grasping for her wand. "I could ..."

"Don't," Emily advised. She was more relieved than she wanted to admit that Melissa was all right. Who knew what prolonged exposure to the Idiot Ball would have done? "We have to finish the exam, remember?"

Back at the classroom, they munched their way through the makeshift sandwiches while waiting for the next tutor. Emily couldn't understand why they weren't just told to come back at a specific time, when the tutors would be ready for them, but perhaps that was part of the exam. They couldn't count on knowing exactly when they would have to use their magic in the real world, either.

It took nearly twenty minutes before a woman who looked like a cross between Indian and Chinese, complete with slanted eyes and dark skin, appeared and nodded to Emily. It was time to begin the second part of the exam.

Someone had taken the parchments and the desk from the exam chamber, Emily noted as soon as they returned to the room. Instead, there were three chairs, one holding an oversized doll in a roughly humanoid form. The other two were empty. Emily took one of them at the tutor's nod and waited, bracing herself as best she could. There had been very little detail on what to expect in the second part of the exam. Apparently, the exam changed every time.

"This is the practical part of Basic Charms," the tutor said. "I am Mistress Sun."

She tapped the doll with one long finger. "This is Nod. He has *volunteered* to assist us in testing your grasp of Basic Charms."

Emily blinked in surprise. Was Nod intelligent, or was it a joke? There was no way to tell.

"You should have no problem completing all of the tests," Mistress Sun informed her. "In the event of you feeling unable to proceed, inform me at once and we will move on to the next test. However, failing to complete at least six tests will mean certain failure; depending on your score in the theory exam, you may fail even if you complete seven or eight. There is no overall time limit on these tests, but certain of them must be completed very quickly once you begin. Do you understand me?"

"Yes," Emily said.

"Good," Mistress Sun said. She reached into her pocket and produced a small box, little larger than Emily's hand. "Open that box."

Emily reached for the box, then caught herself. There was no trace of emotion on the tutor's face as Emily paused and ran through the detection spell before deciding the box surface was actually harmless. Taking the box, she examined it carefully and discovered a single, tiny charm worked into the latch. The standard dispelling spell worked fine, it seemed, but some basic caution made her run the detection spell again before opening the lid. This time, she detected a second hex that needed a more complex spell to remove it. Finally, she opened the box and removed a single pearl.

"This is the second test," Mistress Sun said. "That pearl is actually hexed to twist a person's magic when they swallow it. Your objective is to swallow the pearl and then neutralize it *before* it can have a significant effect on you."

Emily hesitated. She couldn't believe the effects would be *that* serious, but it was quite possible that if she tried and failed to defeat it, she wouldn't be able to complete the rest of the exam. And yet if she refused to try, who knew *what* would happen then?

"I'd like to put this aside for the moment," she said. "Can I do it at the end?"

Mistress Sun showed no sign of approval or disapproval. "As you wish," she said, as she stood up. "Put it on the table."

She stood behind Nod and smiled thinly. "Nod has been cursed by a powerful witch. You will notice that a single, very complex curse has been wrapped around his soul. It does not merely push him into compliance with her demands, but works to reshape his mind until he is what she wishes him to be. The curse punishes unwanted thoughts and feelings, slowly wearing him down to nothing. He will become a puppet unless you save him."

"Brainwashing," Emily muttered. It certainly sounded like the concept she'd heard of back home. Punish someone for thinking a certain thought often enough and they'd stop thinking of it, sooner or later. "You want me to remove the curse?"

"It is a task often performed by independent sorcerers," Mistress Sun agreed. "The witch is either unaware of the long-term effects of such curses, or she simply doesn't care. Poor Nod will end up with his brain mashed to a pulp unless you save him."

Emily swallowed. "I understand," she said. They'd been taught something about removing charms and hexes, but a full-fledged curse? "How long do I have?"

Mistress Sun smiled. "You'll see." She waved a languid hand at Nod. "Off you go, girl. Good luck."

Emily nodded and cast the analysis spell on Nod. The curse appeared in front of her, a glittering mass of deadly spell components, each one tuned to a separate thought. It was so deeply embedded in his mind that she honestly couldn't see how it could be removed without tearing his mind apart. Half of the curse seemed capable of scanning his thoughts and recognizing what he was thinking; the other half seemed designed to cause pain by manipulating parts of his brain. Merely looking at it made Emily feel dirty, and soiled.

Every time she thought she'd found a place to begin, she realized that there was another part in front of it. It was a tangled mass of spells far more complex than anything else she'd ever seen.

*But independent sorcerers deal with this all the time,* she told herself. *There has to be a solution.*

Carefully, she placed her magic in contact with the curse and plunged her mind into its tangled web. Deadly spell components, primed to strike at anyone foolish enough to attempt to remove the spell, came to life, blasting streams of pain towards her. Emily gritted her teeth and ignored them, finally understanding why the spell was so difficult to remove ...

...And then she grasped its only weakness. The witch had tangled the spell together like bad knitting, but half of the curse simply wasn't important. All that really mattered was removing the parts that would cause Nod pain or kill him if someone tried to remove the curse.

Working at a frantic speed Emily hadn't known she could muster, she cancelled the torturing parts of the spell before withdrawing from the remains of the curse. The mind-reading sections could be removed at leisure. A final flicker of deadly energy almost killed Nod, before she deflected it away and absorbed it within her own protections.

And then she burst out of the curse, suddenly aware of just how badly she was sweating.

Mistress Sun let her drink some water and nibble chocolate before continuing. Nothing seemed to faze her. Emily wondered, suddenly, if Advanced Charms students had to remove curses all the time. Or if they were more prone to playing jokes than the younger students.

"The fifth part of the test is as follows," Mistress Sun said. "You will carry out the following instructions ..."

The practical exam lasted for nearly four hours. By the end of the day, Emily was tired and just wanted to go to her bedroom and collapse into bed. She'd completed nine of the assigned tests, but failed the last one through exhaustion, something that she suspected would be counted against her. And, no matter how well she did, she wouldn't pass unless Alassa passed as well. She would almost rather have visited the Warden again.

"You are excused for the rest of the day," Mistress Sun informed her. "Drink sugar water, eat a proper meal and get some sleep. You will be told how well you performed once the parchments are marked."

Emily nodded and headed to the kitchens. She could get some food and drink, then go to her bedroom. All she wanted to do was sleep.

## Chapter Thirty-Six

TWO DAYS PASSED BEFORE EMILY WAS SUMMONED TO FACE PROFESSOR LOMBARDI, TWO DAYS that she spent fretting about failure and wondering what–if anything–she should have done differently. The promise of a Basic Alchemy exam coming up soon–and tests for Martial Magic–helped keep her awake at night, despite using sleeping spells in the hopes they would make her sleep. Talking to Alassa didn't help. When they compared notes, it was clear they had been given different exams. There was no way to tell if everyone had been given different questions or if Emily had been given a harder test than the others. Being called to the Charms classroom was almost a relief.

Professor Lombardi nodded politely to her as she entered the room and closed the door behind her. "Take a seat," he said kindly. "We're just waiting for Mistress Irene."

Emily blinked in surprise. She'd asked Aloha what had happened when she'd passed Basic Charms and Aloha had told her that she'd only faced Professor Lombardi.

Uncertain of what was going on, she took a seat and waited, trying to keep her heartbeat under control. Mistress Irene arrived two minutes later, carrying a parchment scroll and a strange, dagger-like device that she passed to Lombardi before taking a seat.

"You may have realized that you were given a harder practical test than the other students," Professor Lombardi said without preamble. "Your progress has been monitored and it has become clear that you have a definite talent for charms. You passed the practical test with flying colors."

"Thank you," Emily said. "But why ...?"

"All students need to be poked and prodded to force them to develop their talents," Mistress Irene said seriously. "We pushed you harder in Charms because it was clear that your talents lay in that direction. A normal first-year student would not be able to dismantle the curse surrounding Nod. It requires genuine talent to handle such a curse without killing either the victim or yourself."

Emily shivered, remembering the nightmares she'd had afterwards. She'd thought that practical jokes, even the Idiot Ball, were bad enough, but curses like that were terrifying. It was easy to see why the victim couldn't free himself, no matter how powerful he was. The curse just twisted and tore at his mind. Mistress Sun had pointed out that independent magicians often found themselves dismantling unpleasant curses. Emily had wondered if it was a future career for her. And then she'd wondered if she should be trying to avoid it.

"You did make some mistakes, but you passed the exam," Lombardi continued. He took the parchment from Mistress Irene and opened it, holding it out to Emily. "Congratulations."

Emily took the parchment and stared down at it numbly. It certified that she had passed Basic Charms and a Level Three Practical Exam. There was a glowing magic seal on the sheet of parchment that would be impossible to fake, no matter what anyone did. She touched it lightly with her finger and felt a shock as it shouted the identity of the examiner into her mind.

"Thank you," she said after a long pause. She hesitated again, then asked the question that had been haunting her nightmares since the exam. "Was Nod ... was Nod a real human under a curse?"

Lombardi looked at her in some surprise. "Of course not," he said finally. "He's nothing more than a doll, gifted with an impression of humanity that allows him to carry a curse designed to latch onto a person's mind. If you had failed, the curses wouldn't have done any real damage to him."

*But they would have done damage to me,* Emily thought. There were too many horrific examples of what could go wrong while curse-breaking in her books. A single mistake could have destroyed her mind, her magic, or—worst of all—transferred the curse to her. In hindsight, she couldn't believe that she'd tamely accepted the practical exam as Basic Charms. She should have known it wasn't intended to be so brutal.

"Your success leaves us with the question of what to do with you next," Lombardi continued after a long moment. "You will be attending Advanced Charms, of course, as you will need the groundwork to understand what you're doing, but you will also be tutored privately by Mistress Sun, who will be pushing you as fast as possible. We expect that you will be working at a fourth-year level by the end of second-year."

Emily gulped. "You're moving me up a year *now*?"

Mistress Irene chuckled rather dryly. "I'm afraid we couldn't justify it unless you proved to be a prodigy in *every* class. Professor Thande informs me that you are still burning your caldron every second lesson."

Emily nodded in embarrassment. There were times when she thought that she would never get the hang of Alchemy. It seemed to depend on her mastering a precision too much for anyone to master quickly. Her rational mind kept arguing that surely it didn't matter if a certain potion was stirred ten times instead of eleven, no matter what the instructions said. Thande had pointed out that she might master the basics, but it was unlikely that she would ever become a full-fledged Alchemist.

"There are two weeks until the next Advanced Charms class opens," Lombardi said into the silence. "You will be provided with a reading list; I suggest that you spend the time reading as much as you can around the subject, because you will *not* be told everything in class. I will arrange the timetable for your private sessions as well."

"She has Martial Magic too," Mistress Irene reminded him. "Make sure that you don't clash the two together."

Emily nodded. She would have read everything she could anyway, but the reading list was a good place to start, even though the Basic Charms reading list had included several books that didn't seem to have much—if anything—to do with Charms. Maybe they made sense later, or maybe Lombardi was testing them to see who would have the common sense to question the reading list before wasting their time reading the books.

"I'll see to it," Lombardi assured her. He looked over at Emily. "You seem to lead an exciting life. I'm afraid it may be about to become more exciting."

Emily snorted. She'd been kidnapped from her own universe and almost sacrificed by a necromancer, rescued and sent to a school for magic children, almost killed a Princess, kidnapped by bandits and forced to escape ... and then she'd been caught up in a prank war between schoolchildren armed with magic. How *could* her life become more exciting?

"Take the parchment and store it carefully," Mistress Irene said. "If it should happen to be lost, there is a fine of ten gold coins for a replacement."

"Thank you," Emily said as she pocketed the parchment. "Is there anything I should know about how well I performed in the exam?"

"You passed?" Lombardi replied, dryly.

Emily flushed bright red.

"Mistress Sun will go over what you did right–and what you did wrong - later. Until then, enjoy a few days without studying Charms. Advanced Charms will push you a great deal harder."

Emily stood up, then paused. "Can I ask a question?" She asked, then plunged ahead anyway. "Did *Alassa* pass?"

The tutors exchanged glances. They'd told Emily that *her* grade would depend upon *Alassa's* grade–and even though they'd decided that she deserved to move ahead in classes, the original punishment might still hold. What would she do if Alassa failed again? Would she have to retake Basic Charms again and again?

"She passed," Lombardi said, after a long beat.

Emily relaxed in relief.

"We have asked her to visit the office after you so we can discuss her results, and her entry into Advanced Charms. Your assistance might have made the difference between success and failure for her."

*Except that everyone is supposed to be able to pass Basic Charms on their first try,* Emily thought sourly. If you couldn't progress without grasping the basics, it stood to reason that you would try to grasp them as quickly as possible. Alassa hadn't seemed to recognize that they were even *there* before Emily had walked her through them, as carefully as possible. But then, Alassa had definitely had a very poor tutor before attending Whitehall.

"Do not speak to anyone as you leave the room," Mistress Irene added. "You can talk to your friends after they have all been told their results."

Emily nodded, thanked them again and left the room. Three other students, including Alassa, were outside, waiting impatiently to hear the results of their exam. Emily winked at Alassa before she left the room and headed up towards her bedroom, where she opened her chest, stowed away her parchment and retrieved the list of supplies Sergeant Harkin had ordered her to prepare for the camping trip. It was surprisingly long and, in truth, she wasn't sure *how* she could hope to carry all of them in a single rucksack. She'd looked into various spells that should have made it easier before the Sergeant had informed the team that they weren't allowed to use magic to make their rucksacks weightless. They were intended to carry everything under their own power.

The door opened, revealing Aloha. "Hey," she said. "I wanted to show you this."

Aloha produced a wooden box and placed it on the bed, opening it up to reveal a makeshift keyboard attached to a metal wand. When she pressed one of the keys, a glowing letter appeared above the box, causing Emily to giggle out loud. It was a very primitive word processor, powered by magic. Maybe she couldn't remember—if she'd ever known—anything about producing a computer, but she had been able to give them the general idea behind word processors.

"Watch," Aloha said in some delight. She pushed several keys at once, writing out a whole word. "See? It works!"

Emily felt an odd pang of something that she eventually recognized as homesickness. She had never really regretted leaving Earth for this magical world, even though this world had poor plumbing, a decidedly sexist attitude, medieval systems of government and a necromancer who wanted her dead because he'd bungled the spell that had summoned her in the first place. But now, looking at the weird word processor, she remembered the hours of fun she'd had on the computer back home. She'd had Facebook and Twitter and YouTube and all the other internet games that simply couldn't exist in the magical world.

*Yet*, she told herself, firmly. There didn't seem to be any fundamental reason why high technology would not work in her new universe. The technology had simply never been developed. Given enough time, they would probably come up with computers that didn't need *mana* to function, maybe sooner if Emily could give them enough pointers to start them down the right track. If ... she'd written down everything she could remember about the concept of printing presses, but she hadn't heard back from Imaiqah's father regarding them. The craftsman he'd hired might not be able to duplicate the printing press from Emily's instructions.

"So it does," Emily said, finally. She reached over and pushed a key, watching the letter flare into existence in front of her. "How do you transfer what you've written to parchment?"

"It gets burned into the parchment when you're ready to copy it," Aloha explained. "My friend, the one who made it work, says he doesn't know how useful it will be in the long run."

"What use is a newborn baby?" Emily asked seriously. The first computers in her world had seemed useless, right up to the point where brilliant scientists had predicted, in all honesty, that the world would never need more than a handful of computers. But when she'd been taken, there had been more computers in the world than people. "This is just the start of something brilliant."

She looked down at the machine and wondered, inwardly, where *this* innovation would lead. Everyone knew that necromancers went insane because they tried to channel vast amounts of magic through their brains. Even if they didn't kill themselves outright, their minds were warped—and they had no way of knowing just how badly they'd been damaged before it was too late. But what if someone could eventually channel such vast streams of power through a magical computer? Computers had made so many things easier back home. Here, those things might eventually include mass murder and genocide.

Alassa's parents had worried about the impact of something as tiny as Arabic numbers on their Kingdom. God alone knew what they would think of a magical computer, or the printing press, or ...

"I'll take your word for it," Aloha said, breaking into Emily's train of thought. "He actually wants to talk to you and see what else you can suggest for his device. The idea of producing a counting spell for the device..."

Something *clicked* in Emily's mind. She'd heard of abacuses, even seen one ... but it hadn't occurred to her that they might be missing from her new world. The concept was so simple that it was hard to understand how it had been missed, *if* it had been missed. She scribbled down a reminder to herself—she would have to ask Imaiqah, *before* spending hours reinventing the wheel—and then looked down at the makeshift computer. The designer was already thinking about magical calculators. Where else would his mind take him?

She shook her head. What use was a newborn baby, indeed?

"Later," Emily said, feeling unsure of what to do. "I have to sort out the gear for our camping trip."

"You're going before us," Aloha said. She grinned mischievously. "Be sure and tell me all about it, all right?"

Emily snorted as she skimmed down the list of supplies. "I thought we weren't allowed to share notes," she said as she stood up. "Or do you want to spend the next few hours doing push-ups while the Sergeant questions your ancestry?"

"I want to succeed," Aloha said. She stood up and headed over to her cabinet. "I'll come with you. We may as well get our supplies together."

The commissary was situated on the ground floor, open only to students who were studying Martial Magic. They had been warned in no uncertain terms that students who were *not* part of the class were forbidden to enter, whatever the excuse. It was easy to see why as soon as Emily stepped inside; there were mountains of supplies, weapons and tools, all seemingly unguarded. Emily suspected the vast chamber was actually protected by wards that only allowed them to pass because they were both in Martial Magic. It was hard to be sure. Whitehall's strange interior made it difficult to sense additional magic near the commissary.

"Make sure you account for everything you take," Aloha reminded her. The Sergeant had told them that too, when he'd been lecturing them on logistics. Everything had to be accounted for, even if it was just the simplest little thing. "And don't forget your special supplies."

Emily flushed as she started working through the list. The first section covered clothing suitable for a field trip, including a heavy, quilted leather shirt and thick trousers. This world had clearly never heard of shorts, or miniskirts. The thought made her smile. She wouldn't want to wear anything of the sort on a field trip with five teenage boys and a pair of male Sergeants.

The next section covered camping supplies and weapons. She was expected to carry a knife, a dagger, a short sword, a bow and ten arrows, a set of tools ... the list seemed endless. Emily looked down at the pile of supplies and blanched. How could *anyone* carry so much without help? The Sergeants had told her that infantrymen regularly carried their own weight in supplies, but Emily found it hard to believe. How could anyone be that strong?

"At least you know how to use the sword," Aloha said lightly. "The bow and arrows might be more dangerous to the Redshirts than anyone else."

Emily flushed. For a class that claimed to be about Martial Magic, they spent a surprising amount of time practicing with conventional weapons. Basic swordplay had been tricky, to say the least; there had been so much to unlearn before she could start using a sword properly. She'd expected archery to be easier, but it had been even harder. A single slip while drawing back the string and the arrow would go flying off in the wrong direction. The Sergeants had pointed out that advancing armies had been slaughtered by archers, describing battles that reminded Emily of the Battle of Agincourt. It wasn't a reassuring thought.

The final section of the list included a tent, a set of blankets and several potions that Emily didn't recognize. One glance at the tent told her that it was large enough to take all eight of them comfortably. There seemed to be no such thing as a private tent, nor would there be on campaign, she realized. All the books she'd read about female warriors had glossed over *that* part.

Shuddering at the thought, she piled up the tent and the rest of the supplies, then stared at them in disbelief. She'd thought it was bad, but now ...? How could she hope to carry even *half* of the supplies?

"Maybe it's a test of some kind," Aloha said. "How would you do it if you had a choice?"

*A camper van,* Emily thought. Useless, of course; there were no vehicles here. Maybe they'd be allowed to take horses ... no, the Sergeant had specifically stated that they would be walking. They had to carry everything with them at all times...

"I'm an idiot," she said out loud. The answer had been right in front of her face and she hadn't seen it. "It's definitely another test."

She laughed at herself in some irritation. "We don't need *six* tents, do we? And that's what we'll get if we all do this separately."

## Chapter Thirty-Seven

Sergeant Harkin stared at the Redshirts. He didn't look happy.

"I presume," he said finally, "that you have an explanation for this?"

Jade, as spokesman, stepped forward. "Yes, Sergeant. Your list gave us plenty of duplicates. We discussed the matter and decided to trim it down."

The Sergeant eyed him nastily. "And exactly when did I give you the authority to decide what you could and could not carry?"

Jade held up the briefing note they'd been given on the camping trip. "It says here that the team may be required to reinterpret orders to produce something practical," he said. "That is exactly what we have done."

There was a long pause, just long enough for Emily to wonder if she'd ruined *all* of their chances of passing. "Very good," Harkin said, finally. "And what, exactly, have you decided?"

Jade didn't relax at all. "One tent for the eight of us. Only one set of cooking tools, because we don't need more than one. Rucksacks repacked with the supplies and then passed around in a rota so we all have a chance to carry the heavy bags ..."

He went on until he reached the end of his list.

"Not too bad," Harkin sneered. "And do you think that you are *ready* for the walk?"

"Yes," Jade said. "We're ready."

Emily shifted uncomfortably as Harkin's gaze passed over her. Like the boys, she was dressed in shirt and trousers, rather than the loose and comfortable robes she'd worn ever since coming to Whitehall. The clothes itched and she had the unpleasant thought that she was going to sweat like a pig while wearing them.

One thing they hadn't been able to reduce had been the canteens of water. They'd been warned to drink whenever they felt thirsty.

"We shall see," Harkin said. He raised his voice. "We will be travelling through the desolation towards the ruins of the Dark City. There may be dangerous creatures on the hunt for anyone foolish enough to enter their territory. Keep a watchful eye on your surroundings and be careful where you lay your head. Are there any questions?"

Bran raised a hand. "Are we going into"–he suddenly looked very nervous–"into necromantic territory?"

"We will remain on our side of the mountains," Harkin said. "You're not ready to travel into the Blighted Lands just yet."

He glanced from face to face. "This march will be hard," he promised, "so just keep this in mind. You won't be marching anything like as hard as infantry soldiers trying to lift a siege before it is too late."

Emily gulped as she hefted the rucksack and pulled it on. It seemingly weighed a ton and she staggered under the weight. The guys had offered to give her one of the lighter bags, but she'd refused, knowing that the Sergeant would mark her down for it. She could take one of the lighter bags later, after she'd completed the first part of the march.

Jade winked at her as Harkin led them to the door and out into the field.

"I think we should have asked them if they wanted to spread the weight," he murmured to her. He motioned to the Sergeants, who didn't seem to have any trouble carrying their rucksacks. "Who knows what *they* are carrying?"

Emily looked at the muscles rippling along Harkin's arms and shrugged. "I think they know what they're doing," she said, hoping that she was right. "They would have asked us if they wanted us to carry some of their weight."

Jade nodded, thoughtfully. "Let's move," he said. "They won't want us to be late."

The trail led out of Whitehall's grounds and up into the mountains, the opposite direction from Dragon's Den. In a very brief amount of time, Emily found herself sweating as she felt the sun beating down on her back; she staggered slightly under the rucksack's weight. But no one else seemed to be having any problems, so she swallowed any complaints and forced her legs to walk onwards.

The longer she walked, the more she felt as if she were walking through a swamp, no matter how hard she forced herself to move. The weight on her back seemed to double, then triple. She wanted to stop and catch her breath, but her team was forging ahead and she didn't want to be last. Who knew *what* Sergeant Miles would do if she started to lag behind?

It seemed to grow hotter as they stumbled further up the trail. Glancing to the left, Emily realized that they were already higher than Whitehall, and bare meters from a long drop to the stony valley floor below. In the distance, she could see the towns in the Allied Lands, all illuminated by the bright sunlight. The landscape looked strange without cars and other vehicles, and so quiet. There were no planes flying through the air ...

Bracing herself, she walked onwards as the trail grew harder to follow. Rocks were scattered everywhere and she had to catch herself before she tripped over one, grimly aware that if she fell with such a heavy weight on her back she might not be able to get up again. The pressure grew stronger and she didn't know what she could do to force herself to take another step ...

...and then she felt herself relax. She'd heard that if she forced herself to keep going, eventually she'd push through her body's resistance, but she hadn't experienced it until now. And to think she'd doubted the Sergeant's word.

The trail reached the highest point it could, then started to descend. Soon, it led into a hidden valley, which concealed a forest from human eyes. Emily heard the sound of running water before they actually saw it. Crystal-clear water came down from high overhead, where the mountain peaks vanished into the clouds.

On Sergeant Harkin's barked orders, they stumbled gratefully to a halt. They unbuckled their rucksacks and placed them on the stony ground. Cat managed to break one of the bottles of potion and had to endure a long lecture from Harkin on taking care of his equipment, all the while trying to salvage what he could. Most of it, judging by the smell, had gone off the moment it had been exposed to the open air.

"Break out your bread and eat," Harkin ordered. "We move on in twenty minutes."

Emily was surprised to discover that she was hungry and thirsty—and that she'd somehow drunk more than half of her water without being aware of it. How badly had she zoned out during the walk?

The bread and cheese was dry, treated by the chefs to ensure that it would remain edible for months, if necessary. It tasted like manna from heaven, even though the water from her canteen was warm and tasted faintly brackish. After finishing all of her water, she stood up, used a spell to test the water in the stream, and then refilled her canteen.

"Swap bags," Jade ordered as they started to prepare to leave. "Emily, take this bag. No arguing this time."

"What a *Captain*," Harkin observed dryly.

Jade flushed. None of them had been appointed team leader, although Emily couldn't decide if they were meant to appoint their own or if they should be solving problems together.

Harkin's next comment surprised both of them. "And are you ready to take on life and death decisions?"

"No, sir," Jade said.

"You'd better get ready," Harkin said. He pulled on his own rucksack and glanced at the students. "Follow me."

The path grew more treacherous as they stumbled down into the hidden valley. Bran almost tripped and fell, catching himself at the very last moment. The walk would have been tricky without the rucksacks; as it was, Emily's second pack wasn't light enough to make the walk easy. If the others hadn't been taking it so calmly, she might have turned and scrambled down backwards as the path grew worse.

It was a relief to finally walk into the forest and relax for five minutes under a rocky ledge that provided shelter. When she looked up at the path, she couldn't believe they'd walked down it.

"A pool," Bran called. He put his rucksack on the ground and started to undo his leather trousers. "We can go for a swim!"

"No you bloody can't," Harkin snarled. "Have I taught you nothing?"

He picked up a stone and tossed it into the pool. The moment it hit the water, the pool exploded into life. Claws snapped at thin air, clacking away horribly before withdrawing back under the liquid.

Emily almost fell over backwards in shock; Jade let out a swearword ... *everyone* had been badly shocked. She didn't know what the rest of the creature looked like and she didn't want to find out. Those claws had looked sharp enough to cut through her body like a knife through butter.

"I'm sure I have told you," Harkin said into the appalled silence, "that still water is always suspicious. *Always.* And it's doubly suspicious when it's in a place where there are no animal droppings lying around the pond. Anything that sticks its neck in there isn't going to come out again."

Emily found her voice. "What ... what *is* that thing?"

"I have absolutely no idea," Harkin said. "It could be some necromancer's idea of a joke. Or it could be a creature that has been mutated by exposure to *mana*. Or it could be something the Faerie left behind to discourage visitors to their city."

Emily stared at the still waters and shivered.

Harkin allowed them a few moments to relax - and contemplate their near-disaster - before leading them on a dog-leg around the forest's edge. Cat asked why they didn't simply walk *through* the forest and Harkin, in a tone that suggested he was running out of patience with idiotic questions, pointed out that the forest *wasn't* uninhabited. Even with that warning, it took Emily several minutes to spot the spiders lurking in the darkness, following the team as they walked. It was impossible to escape the sense that the spiders were part of one vast hive mind, just waiting for unwary victims to enter the forest.

"We need to get CT out here," she muttered to Jade as they avoided a suspicious-looking patch of shadow under an isolated tree. "Or maybe burn the entire forest to the ground."

Jade nodded. "My father used to tell me stories about hunting," he said. "There was a ... creature that had escaped the mountains and started to hunt near a town. We never knew if it had been sent to terrorize us or if it were merely trying to survive, but father told me that killing it was difficult. Eventually, they had to burn down a house after trapping the monster inside. And even then he had his doubts. They never found a body."

"Consider it a lesson in what lurks where human life is scarce," Sergeant Miles put in suddenly. Emily would have jumped if she hadn't been carrying the rucksack; she hadn't known that he was listening to their conversation. "If you go on to be combat sorcerers, you will be expected to fight such creatures as well as dark wizards, necromancers and other unpleasant problems. You cannot afford to relax for an instant."

The opposite side of the valley was a sheer cliff wall, utterly impossible to climb even without the rucksacks. Emily thought they might be trapped before Harkin silently led them around a rock and pointed out a hidden tunnel that was concealed by a very strange form of magic. Every time she looked at it, she felt her attention being subtly diverted elsewhere, so slyly that she would have missed it and never noticed the tunnel if the Sergeant hadn't pointed it out. The others had similar reactions.

Inside the tunnel, all she could see was darkness. After what she'd seen in the zoo, it was unnerving.

Rupert seemed equally nervous. "Are there more spiders in there?"

"Of course not," Sergeant Harkin said with a nasty grin. "The scorpions ate them all."

Emily blanched. "Scorpions?"

"Giant mutated creatures with lethal stings and bad attitudes," Harkin informed them. His grin twisted into a smirk. "But don't worry about them. They're actually quite friendly as long as you leave them alone."

His smile melted away. "Cast an illumination spell that only works for you," he ordered, his tone darkening. "When we're in the tunnels, walk up the exact centre; do *not* try to enter *any* of the side tunnels. The scorpions will *not* like you wandering into any of their nests. If you *see* one of them, which is unlikely, keep your distance. They're very territorial and they might mistake you for a rival."

Jade coughed. "What if they mistake us for prey?"

"Use a fire spell if there is no other choice, and be prepared to kill," Sergeant Miles said. "If you do have to fight one, you can't force it to back away. Kill it and then leave the carcass strictly alone."

Emily was still trembling at the thought as Sergeant Miles cast a light spell, then stepped into the tunnel. Jade followed him; Harkin pushed Emily to go immediately afterwards. Darkness dropped on her like a physical blow, reminding her to cast her own spell to light her way. Slowly, she followed Jade up the tunnel, feeling an uncomfortable itching sensation pressing down on her mind. It was impossible to escape the sense that they were being watched.

The passage was far more than just a tunnel, she realized, as she glanced around. It looked as though someone had carved out an entire town which had then been buried under the mountain. But she couldn't tell if it had been an accident or if someone had started to carve into the rock deliberately. Strange writing was scattered everywhere, all completely indecipherable. In the distance, she thought she heard something scuttling in the darkness. A scorpion, perhaps, or maybe it was something else. What little she'd read about *mana*-touched creatures suggested they evolved very rapidly.

Sergeant Miles led them onwards, passing a set of dark doorways that led further into the mountain. As instructed, Emily kept her distance from them, although she couldn't resist peeking as they passed. She saw nothing, apart from vague hints of something lying there, watching them. The tunnel narrowed as they left the doors behind, forcing them to walk in single-file. It wasn't very reassuring.

Before Emily knew it, the tunnel widened to reveal a river running right *through* the mountain. If they hadn't been casting charms to light their way, they would have walked right into the water and been swept away to their deaths. It was hard to tell in the strange light, but the river looked to be the color of blood ...

...And it was completely silent. The running water made no noise. Which was impossible, wasn't it?

"The bridge is there," Miles whispered. It sounded deafeningly loud in the confined space. "I will cross it first; follow me one person at a time. Do *not* clown around while you're on the bridge."

Emily shivered as she saw the bridge for the first time. It seemed solid enough, but it was barely forty centimeters wide, seemingly too thin for safety. Jade followed Miles as he crossed the river, but Emily hesitated for a long moment before she stepped onto the bridge. It felt fragile as she advanced; she kept her eyes off the drop and on her destination, and hoped that the bridge would hold up. Somehow, when she reached the far end, it felt as if she had been crossing the bridge for an eternity.

"We don't know where the river comes from," Miles commented. "A team of explorers set out to map these caves some years ago. We never heard anything from them after they left."

"The scorpions got them," Jade suggested.

"Or something else, something that preys on scorpions, got them," Harkin added. "There are hundreds of places like this, left behind after the war with the Faerie. Very few of them have ever been charted and rendered *safe*."

The tunnel banked upwards after the bridge. They saw light streaming in from the far end.

As they stepped out of the tunnel, into another valley filled with trees and running water, Emily sighed in relief. She caught sight of another pond and stared at it suspiciously, before making a mental note not to go anywhere near it. And then she turned and looked upwards.

A giant statue stood in front of the mountains, towering high overhead. She remembered that she'd seen it when the dragon had flown her from Void's tower to Whitehall. Behind the statue, she saw the rest of the city–and shivered as she realized, for the first time, just how eerily alien it was. She'd understood the buildings in Dragon's Den even if they were primitive, but *these* didn't seem designed for human occupation at all.

"Well, here we are," Sergeant Harkin said. He nodded towards the setting sun. "We can camp here, and hunt for food. And tomorrow the real fun begins."

Emily blinked in surprise. "Near that pool of water?"

Harkin tossed a stone into it. Nothing happened. "This place is safer than the hidden valley," he said. "Even so, you did well to question. You have to be very careful in these places."

The team started to unpack, setting up the tent and preparing to sleep, while Sergeant Miles hunted for an animal. He came back with a deer he'd killed with an arrow, allowing him to give Emily her first lesson in cutting up an animal for the cook-pot. Emily could barely stand to watch as he sliced the meat away from its bones and passed it to Jade, who put it in the cook-pot. She was suddenly *very* aware of just where all of her food came from.

But then, that had been true of farms back home too. No one could really believe that raw meat came out of nowhere.

"I'd prefer to roast it on a spit," Miles said as he stirred the stew. "But that takes too long."

He took Jade's bowl, ladled him out a decent helping and motioned for him to sit near the tent. Emily passed him her bowl, watched as he spooned meat and liquid out for her, and then took it to sit next to Jade. The stew was hot, but surprisingly good. After they'd all been served, Miles prepared the pot to simmer overnight. The remainder of the meat would be taken with them, apparently.

"Sleep tight," Harkin ordered. He would be taking the first watch. "Tomorrow is going to be a very busy day."

She felt dirty and smelly as they settled down to sleep, too tired to care that she was sleeping next to seven older men. Her entire body ached, but sleep came easily. There weren't even any nightmares to trouble her dreams. After everything they'd seen on the hike the absence of nightmares would have surprised her, if she hadn't been too tired to care.

For this one evening, she was just too tired to dream.

# Chapter Thirty-Eight

THE FOLLOWING MORNING, HER ENTIRE BODY *HURT.*

She stumbled out of the tent and tried to run through the basic exercises she'd been taught. Her body felt as if she had been brutally beaten by a small army of thugs. She didn't want to undress and look at herself for fear of seeing her entire body turned black and blue.

Sergeant Harkin gave her a sharp look as he prepared the cook-pot. "I take it you never marched like that before?"

Emily nodded, then tried to do a push-up. Her arms failed her after two single movements and she collapsed on the grass. She needed a hot bath and a massage, but she wasn't going to get either. No wonder few of the infantrymen in pictures had looked happy ... and *they* were experienced soldiers. She had never walked so hard, or carried so much in her entire life.

"Keep moving," Harkin suggested as Jade and Bran stumbled out of the tent. Emily was relieved to see that both of them looked as though they were aching too. "And drink some of the potion. You'll find that it helps with the pain."

He grinned nastily. "In fact, why don't the three of you run over to the tunnel and back? It will get your blood flowing again."

Emily obeyed and discovered, rather to her surprise, that he was right. If something had been chasing her, she wasn't sure she could have escaped, but her attempt at running did make her feel better. Once drunk, the potion sent a warm glow throughout her entire body and eased away some of the pain. It might be hours before she could walk properly, but at least she could move.

Breakfast consisted of more of the deer, some bread from their rucksacks and a stew made from various plants the Sergeants had found. Emily watched as they cooked it, reminding the students—again—that they had to be very careful when picking certain plants because it could be difficult to tell which ones were safe to eat. There *were* spells for checking, but apparently they weren't always completely reliable. Mushrooms, it seemed, could fool the spells and poison anyone stupid enough to eat the wrong one. They'd been taught how to tell if something was safe to eat, but only in theory. Emily had never had to try in real life.

"The Dark City was once the home of the Faerie," Sergeant Harkin said as he spooned out the stew to his students. He nodded towards the giant statue, which had sharply pointed ears and a face too narrow to be human. "From here, they ruled most of the world, until a necromantic storm drove the Great Lords of the Fair Folk away from humanity. Their city was left behind to rot into nothingness."

His eyes narrowed. "We bring you here to show you what you may be fighting and to introduce you to some of the stranger natural magic out there. Remember everything we taught you about avoiding magical traps, because there *are* dangers in what remains of the city and some of them can be fatal."

"Most of them can be fatal," Miles added. "Or they'll make you wish you were dead."

Emily nodded. She'd read books on just what the Fair Folk had done to humans who had fallen into their clutches and most of them had made the necromancers look sane and reasonable. There had been a young boy who'd been given a tongue that always rhymed, forcing him to become a poet; a young girl who had been frozen at nine years old, no matter how old she became; a married couple who had literally been bound together ... and, unlike other curses, Faerie "gifts" were impossible to remove. It hadn't been clear if the Faerie thought they were actually giving gifts or if they were just tormenting people, but the end result was always the same.

Those who were given gifts by the Faerie came to regret it.

The stew tasted surprisingly good in the crisp morning air. They checked the pond again before taking water from it to wash their plates, piling them up in the tent along with most of the supplies. Sergeant Miles cast a simple ward to keep away bandits, thieves and wild animals, ensuring that they didn't have to carry the rucksacks up to the Dark City. Emily was relieved as they started on the trail up to the giant statue. The path was hard enough without carrying a massive rucksack with them.

Up close, the statue was inhumanly perfect as well as alien, leaving her to wonder if there had been a giant Faerie who had been petrified by some long-forgotten magic. Strange wisps of wild magic danced around the statue's feet, suggesting that it might be dangerous to go too close.

Emily was grateful when Sergeant Miles led them around the statue and into the city proper. She felt her eyes go wide as she stared, unable to fully comprehend the alien majesty of the city. It was a maze of giant ziggurats, pyramids and statues of strange creatures that couldn't possibly exist in real life. A chill ran down the back of her neck as she realized that parts of the city seemed to change every time she looked away, pathways twisting in and out of existence, probably leading to places beyond her comprehension.

The sense of being inside something completely alien grew stronger as she realized what was missing. There was no sound at all within the city, not even the chirping of flying birds. She couldn't see any living thing at all, apart from the team.

One of the buildings, a giant pyramid, was covered in strange pictures, none of them very pleasant. One showed an elf tormenting a group of humans, the second showed a strange hybrid between human and animal and the third showed an elf being strangled to death by a hangman's cord. She looked away for a heartbeat, then looked back; she realized in horror that the elf in the third picture had moved slightly.

Could that picture be real? Or was it just a twisted form of artwork? There was no way for her to know.

A second building seemed to be built from mirrors. Emily looked into it and saw her reflection looking back at her, just before her reflection twisted and started to change. She saw herself wearing a ballroom gown and smirking, rather like Alassa before she'd been shocked into changing her ways, before the gown became rags and she found herself on her knees. The image blinked out of existence a moment later, only to be replaced by a black-suited Emily carrying a gun in one hand and a small computer in the other. And then there was a version of her with vampire fangs, wearing a gothic outfit that she wouldn't have touched in a million years...

Emily stumbled back in shock.

"We don't know *what* that building does," Miles offered. The Sergeant didn't seem surprised by her reaction. "One of the Professors from Whitehall believes the Faerie could see into alternate worlds and show us what we might have been, if we'd grown up in a different world. Another believes that it merely shows us nightmares from our own minds. There's no way to tell the difference."

"Yeah," Emily said, glancing back at the mirror. She saw a tall sorceress carrying a wand, her face twisted in a permanent sneer. It took her a moment to realize that it *was* her, just with different hair and wearing a dress that made the gothic outfit look reasonable. Maybe if she'd allowed Alassa to corrupt her instead of trying to change the Princess ... or was it her future, if she kept playing pranks and abusing her powers? "Can ... can just anyone use it?"

"Anyone who comes here can use it," Miles said. "But very few people come to the city."

Emily could see why as they walked through the remainder of the complex. It was eerie, so eerie that she would have run away long ago if she'd been alone. It was deserted, yet she sensed she was being watched at all times. Some of the doorways gaped invitingly, suggesting that she could follow the Faerie to wherever they'd gone after being defeated by humanity. And yet she had the feeling that following them would be the worst thing she could do.

The next part of the city was a strange pool of shimmering liquid. It felt dangerous, even though she couldn't put a finger on why; it was a relief when Harkin ordered them to stay away from it. Perhaps there was something lurking in the liquid, or perhaps it was something far more dangerous than any human could comprehend. She was reluctant to turn her back on it and, as they all headed back towards the open square in the centre of the city, she saw that the others had the same reaction.

The city was a place of nightmares.

She could have asked if the Sergeants knew what the pool was, but she didn't want to know.

"The Faerie used to bring humans here for their amusement," Harkin said. Somehow, even *his* voice sounded tinny and weak in the Dark City. "They would play with their captives, controlling their every movement–or throw them to the monsters they developed in their secret laboratories. Each death made the Faerie laugh. They sucked up souls and stored them for later use. And when the Faerie were finally defeated, the souls were completely destroyed, just out of spite. They were not allowed to pass on to the next world."

Emily shivered. She'd never been very religious, but even *she* had problems accepting the thought that something could destroy a soul.

Or could it? Perhaps the Faerie had been wrong and they'd held nothing more than an impression of each person they'd killed, their souls going onwards to the next world. But if ghosts existed in this world, did that mean there was no afterlife?

The thought bothered her as they explored the remainder of the city. No human was comfortable with the thought of their existence being completely terminated. Even the idiots who blew themselves up for political reasons believed in an afterlife where they would be rewarded by God for their suicides. But if their lives–and all that they were - just *stopped* when they died ... the thought was awful.

What if there *was* no afterlife?

Maybe it was fear of discovering that death was truly the end that drove necromancers to suck out life and *mana* from their victims. They knew that they would vanish when they died.

And if there was no afterlife, no judgment, why *not* indulge yourself as much as possible?

Emily had been horrified when Alassa had frozen the maid, believing it to be an abuse of power as well as an unprovoked attack on an innocent. Alassa hadn't really understood Emily's point, because *her* culture said that the lower classes were there for the use of the upper classes. But if there was no final judgment, then who was to say *which* system of morality was right?

Perhaps there was no such thing as morality in the first place. All they had was the delusion that they had a working system.

She was still mulling over this question when they started to clamber down out of the Dark City and back towards where they had left their tents. As before, the Sergeants gave the forest a wide berth, even though they had told their students that it was safe. Emily allowed herself to wonder if they had their own reasons for avoiding it, or if they were just trying to keep the students aware of possible dangers. It was a more productive thing to wonder about than the existence–or non-existence–of souls.

"There are creepier places to visit," Miles said, in answer to a question from Jade. "You may be lucky enough to visit Ashfall one day. A necromancer died there, fifty years ago, and the land is still screaming."

"No one wants to go there," Harkin added dryly. "What about the Desert of Death?"

Emily looked at him. "The Desert of Death?"

"Rumor has it that an immensely powerful witch was beaten to death there for daring to fall in love with the wrong man," Harkin informed her. "Which does, of course, raise the question of how she was killed in the first place, if she was so powerful."

Harkin snorted. "When she died, she cursed the entire land to wither and die. The land became barren within a year, and the entire population had to flee. I think many of them became slaves in the nearby countryside because there was nowhere else to go."

"That's one story," Miles said, with a shrug. "Another one is that the local lord was experimenting with necromancy and it all went horribly wrong, or more horribly wrong than normal, seeing that no experiments with limited necromancy ever end well. Somehow, and no one knows how, he drew the life out of a hundred square miles around his castle, wiping out his subjects, their livestock and every plant in the area. The entire country became a desert afterwards."

Emily shivered, wondering which of the two stories was actually true. This world didn't have television and reporters to bring people the news directly into their homes; it didn't even have newspapers, just broadsheet readers and heralds. A rumor could grow completely out of proportion by the time it crossed from one end of the Allied Lands to the other, creating a myth that bore no resemblance to reality. No wonder that the Allied Lands didn't seem to take necromancy and the necromancers quite seriously. There was always an air of detachment in the news she heard rather than the immediacy she remembered from back home.

Jade frowned thoughtfully. "No one has ever tried to replant the area?"

"They've tried," Miles said. "It's never worked. I think that some of the nearby countries believe the desert is actually expanding, very slowly. Given time, it may swallow up the entire continent."

"I hope that's not true," Emily said, shaking her head in disbelief. Back home, they'd managed to stop deserts from advancing, but here there was magic involved. Wild magic tainted with necromancy, if the second story was the true one. "What are they going to do if the desert reaches their Kingdoms?"

"Pray," Harkin said. He chuckled darkly. "What else can they do?"

"Sergeant," a voice shouted. Bran and Cat had gone ahead of the rest of the team. "The tent!"

Harkin sprang forward, running ahead of Emily and Jade. They followed him, running around the edge of the forest, only to see a pile of ashes where their tent–and supplies–had been. Emily stared in numb horror as the Sergeant slowed to a halt, looking down at the ashes. Their rucksacks, their food, their blankets ... they had all been destroyed. And there was a strange, almost *oily* scent in the air.

"Hellfire," Sergeant Harkin muttered. He glanced from side to side, sniffing the air. "Draw your swords, all of you. And ready your defensive spells."

Emily obeyed automatically. The short sword she'd been given hadn't been charmed to be unstoppable–apparently, there was no such thing as an unstoppable weapon–but she knew how to use it, she reminded herself. She was tempted to also draw her dagger as the team looked around, searching for possible threats. The strange stink in the air was growing stronger.

"We're sitting targets here," Harkin said after a moment. "When I give the word, move back towards the tunnel at speed, but keep your swords at the ready. If something appears that isn't one of us, hit first and ask questions later. And keep your voices down."

Emily glanced at Jade, but he looked as puzzled as she was. If their tents had been burned, someone or something was hunting them, probably something *intelligent.* Was this a test of some kind, Emily asked herself silently as she braced herself to move, or was it *real?* She couldn't believe that the Sergeants would throw away everything in the rucksacks, including the potions, just for a test. But they'd surprised her before.

"That stink is almost certainly goblins," Miles muttered. He was making passes through the air, casting spying spells in the hopes of catching sight of their enemy. "And probably backed up by Orcs. I think there's definitely some Orc in the air."

"Or maybe they're just trying to confuse us," Harkin muttered back. He raised his voice. "Jade, Emily, Cat: follow Miles back to the tunnel. The rest of you, stay here at the ready."

Emily felt her heart pounding in her chest as she started to move, eyes darting around desperately for unseen threats. Goblins, according to the books she'd read, could be clever and dangerous; Orcs were rarely clever, but those that were tended to be smarter than the average human. And both semi-human races infested lands held by the necromancers. She kept looking around, seeing nothing, until they reached the tunnel. Miles jumped back as blades lashed out at him, trying to drive them back from the tunnel mouth.

"Damn it," Jade said. He raised his sword as blades kept slashing out of the tunnel's mouth. "We're being *hunted*!"

Emily looked back at the forest and saw a small wave of inhuman figures appearing out of the darkness. "Use your magic," Harkin ordered sharply. Unlike the Redshirts, he didn't sound as though he were on the verge of panic. "Take down as many of them as you can, now!"

"Use *Berserker*," Jade said as the goblins advanced. The largest barely came up to Emily's abdomen, but there was nothing weak about them. They were carrying swords that were bigger than they were. "You *cannot* fight them without it."

Emily took a deep breath, concentrated and triggered the spell.

## Chapter Thirty-Nine

THE SPELL TOOK EFFECT AT ONCE. TIME SEEMED TO SLOW DOWN AS EMILY LIFTED HER sword, seeing the goblins inching towards them in terrifying slow motion. Part of her mind noted that they were ugly creatures, humanoid with big eyes, bigger ears and very sharp teeth; the rest of her focused on fighting them. She sprang forward as the goblins lifted their weapons and sliced through the lead goblin's neck. The goblin collapsed, greenish blood leaking from its neck, but Emily barely noticed–or cared. *Berserker* hummed through her system as she threw herself at the goblins, moving far faster than the tiny savages could hope to match. It was easy to avoid their stabbing blows and slice them apart.

A goblin lashed out at her, but he moved slowly and Emily found it easy to dodge. Her confidence was building rapidly, along with her strength; she slammed her sword into the goblin's makeshift armor and sent the little creature stumbling backwards. Another goblin leapt in and cut her with a knife, but Emily felt nothing. *Berserker* countered pain while the spell was operating, leaving her unheeding of the blood trickling down her arm. She knew that she would pay for that afterwards–the sense of invulnerability was an illusion–but she found it hard to care. The spell held her firmly in its grasp.

Magic flared beside her as Jade and the rest of the team fought with their various powers. Goblins died in flame or froze solid before toppling over and dying. The Sergeants fought with a cold precision and power that was all the more terrifying for having no *Berserker* aiding them. Emily felt her blood pound in her ears as she lashed out at the final goblin and cut it apart, just before the world started to spin around her ...

The world faded to black.

The next thing she noticed was that the sun was starting to set. She was lying on the ground, dazed. Her head was spinning and she felt incredibly weak, while her body ached with pain. It took her several minutes to remember the goblins and the blurred memories of the fight, where she'd killed at least a dozen creatures while lost in the battle-trance of *Berserker.* The memories rose up in front of her and she swallowed hard, unable to repress the feeling of sickness at what she'd done. She'd killed intelligent creatures, creatures that might be cousins to humanity ... and she'd done so without even *caring.* Even the knowledge that the goblins would have killed them all if they hadn't been killed first didn't make her feel any better.

Jade knelt down beside her and tapped her shoulder. "Are you all right?"

"Dizzy," Emily said after a moment. *Berserker* took a lot out of her; in hindsight, it might not have been the best choice of spell for the battle. But without it ... would she have been able to fight so effectively? "What ... what happened?"

"You killed a dozen goblins, then collapsed," Jade said. "I think you won the battle single-handedly. We killed the remainder and then fled away from the tunnels, carrying you with us."

"Keep your voice down," a gruff voice added. Emily twisted her neck–it was suddenly difficult to move–and saw Sergeant Harkin standing there. "We're still being hunted."

Emily tried to stumble to her feet, only to be held down gently by Jade. "You need to drink another potion," Jade said, passing her a gourd. He must have carried it with him through the city, rather than leaving it in the tent. "*Berserker* nearly killed you."

"I know," Emily admitted. Mistress Irene had warned her that the sensation of power, of being utterly fearless and invulnerable, was addictive. But the spell drained magic and then it went onwards to drain life force. If she'd been alone...eventually, the spell would have failed, leaving her in the midst of angry enemies and drained of all her power. "Why...why didn't you use it?"

"*You* didn't have enough experience to fight without it," Harkin said. There was something in his tone that bothered Emily, before she realized that she'd turned into a liability. She would barely be able to walk for hours after using the spell. "Can you walk now?"

Emily finished drinking the potion–it tasted foul, unsurprisingly–and managed to stumble to her feet with Jade's help. Her legs felt like useless sacks of potatoes, no matter how hard she tried to force them to move. Only the sense that she was slowing down the rest of the team kept her upright as she leaned against Jade, eyes darting from side to side. They were hidden within a small forest of trees, with no sign of any more goblins, but she couldn't escape the sense that they were being watched.

Harkin was right; they *were* being hunted.

"We had to carry you as we fled the Dark City," Jade said, filling her in as the Sergeant walked back to the watchers. "They said that going into the tunnels would be too dangerous; we'd either be caught by the goblins or attract attention from other creatures as we fought our way through them. But we've heard sounds from other goblin hunting parties..."

Cat looked up as Emily staggered back into the group. "I've never heard of goblins operating in unison," he said, grimly. There was a fresh nasty-looking scar running down his cheek, far worse than the scar they'd inflicted on Emily in the fight. Someone had bound the wound, bandaging it with a shirt. "They're not known for being friendly souls."

"Maybe someone has been encouraging them," Jade offered. He picked up a fruit and passed it to Emily, who was too tired to care what it was. She nibbled it gratefully and dropped the remains in the hole they'd dug to bury all traces of their passing. "We're not *that* far from the necromancers."

Emily shivered. Had the goblins set out to capture *her*? The thought was a terrifying one, yet she couldn't see how the goblins had known in advance that she would be coming, let alone get organized in time to try to snatch her. And they *had* tried to kill her when she'd been fighting them...the memories welled up in front of her eyes and she felt sick. She'd killed–slaughtered–intelligent creatures and felt nothing, not until afterwards. Had they deserved to die?

"It could be a great deal worse," Harkin said, keeping his voice low. "We all assumed that the mountains blocked the necromancers from advancing forward, unless they went through the pass. But if they've managed to find a tunnel, or cut one, that allows them to outflank Whitehall - we could be in some considerable trouble."

He looked around, his dark face furrowed in thought. "We're going to have to move out in two minutes. Your orders are simple: you are to head back to Whitehall and inform the Grandmaster, whatever happens. Someone *has* to report that there may be a tunnel allowing the necromancers access to the Allied Lands."

Jade frowned. "Don't you have a mirror?"

"One isn't working and the others were lost in the fire," Harkin admitted. "We have to assume the worst."

And the worst, Emily knew, was that the goblins were being led by a powerful magician, one powerful enough to cow the inhuman creatures *and* jam the mirror Harkin would otherwise use to summon help. A necromancer wasn't needed specifically to disrupt communications spells–any Dark Wizard could do that - but the Sergeant was right; they had to assume the worst. A full-fledged necromancer might be following them, intent on killing them to add their life energies to his power.

She scowled as they hid the remaining traces of their presence and prepared to move out. If they were lucky, if there *was* a necromancer chasing them, they would be able to outsmart him and escape. All the sources agreed that necromancers were prone to arrogance, overconfidence and self-delusion. But they'd also been very *unclear* on how to actually defeat a necromancer in open combat.

*Don't be silly,* she told herself as they started to slip up the pathway around the nearest mountain. *None of you are ready to fight a necromancer. Even Void only gave Shadye a bloody nose and ran.*

The march rapidly became a nightmare. Emily felt tired, so tired that she knew if she closed her eyes she would fall asleep and never get up again. But she had to keep going, somehow. Twilight had fallen, leaving the shadows to spill across the ground and creating brief suggestions that something was watching them.

Emily clutched her sword tightly, looking into the darkness as if she could catch something and skewer it before whatever it was could react. The sensation of being hunted kept growing stronger, even though they saw and heard nothing, not even birds in the sky, or small animals on the ground. After experiencing the life running through the lands surrounding Whitehall, Emily found that ominous.

Harkin dropped back to walk beside her for a long moment, his twisted face concerned, even worried. Emily wanted to tell him to leave her, knowing she was slowing down the entire team, but she held her tongue. She was really too tired to speak.

"It never gets any easier," Harkin said softly.

Emily blinked in surprise. Compassionate words from the Sergeant–either of the Sergeants–were few and far between.

"Killing goblins isn't too far from killing humans," he said.

Emily nodded. Back home, the only person she had ever seriously considered killing was herself. She wasn't one of those people who took a gun into school and sought bloody revenge for real or imagined slights—and she'd certainly never thought about joining the army. Perhaps that was why *Berserker* had consumed her. That spell made it impossible to care at the time that she was slaughtering the goblins, which might have been why Jade had ordered her to use it.

She'd had no time for reflection, let alone self-doubt. If she had, it might have killed her.

"They would have killed us, if we had been lucky," Harkin added a moment later. "And if we had been unlucky, they would have done far worse."

Emily nodded. She'd read about goblins—and other monsters that infested the mountains—before she'd gone on the field trip. But they rarely bothered humans, unless their victims were completely alone; they knew that the nearby human cities would mount punitive operations. It was quite possible that *someone* had stirred them up and sent them against the Redshirts, or that the team had simply been very unlucky. There was no way to know for sure.

"Just hold it together until we reach home," Harkin said. "After that, if you want to talk about it ..."

Emily shook her head and concentrated on putting one foot in front of the other. In truth, she didn't know *how* she felt about killing the goblins. Part of her felt guilty, even though she knew they had intended to kill her; part of her took a secret delight in slicing through the creatures as if they had been made of paper. And all of her training had paid off, even if she *had* needed to use *Berserker*. The time she'd spent exercising and practicing swordplay with the Redshirts had not been wasted.

They plunged into darkness as the last remaining flickers of sunlight vanished below the mountains. Jade and Sergeant Miles both cast spells intended to illuminate their path, which shaded the entire world in an eerie grey light that made Emily's head ache.

She kept going, somehow, keeping a watchful eye out for traps. But she was so tired that she suspected she would just walk into a trap even if she saw it. The semi-darkness outside the range of the illumination spell was playing tricks on her mind. She thought she could see all kinds of creatures lurking beyond the pool of grey light, just waiting for their chance to strike.

All around them, the forest slowly came to life. Emily heard birds and animals calling to one another in the distance, a series of chirps and birdcalls that eventually gave way to hisses and a single terrifying roar. She hadn't ever been interested in mundane creatures, so she couldn't remember if there were lions in this world or not, but it certainly *sounded* like a lion. The roar faded away and was replaced by howls, each one more terrifying than the last.

But Sergeant Harkin didn't seem bothered. In fact, she heard him chuckle quietly under his breath.

"Ah, the children of the night," he said. "Hear how they sing!"

Emily gave him a sharp glance. Whatever was making those howls didn't sound like something she wanted to meet, certainly not when she was too tired to use magic or even lift a sword. On the other hand, the sound was certainly encouragement to keep going, rather than slowing down to take a breather. Who knew what else, apart from goblins, might be chasing them in the darkness?

"Get down," Jade snapped. "*Now*!"

Emily dropped to the muddy path automatically as *something* hissed through the air above their heads. Arrows crashed into the trees and fell around them; she realized in horror that they had blundered into another goblin ambush. Harkin had kept them moving hard, hoping they could stay ahead of the goblins, but they'd failed.

The goblins were displaying a degree of cooperation that, according to the books, they *never* showed. How could they when no goblin could trust his rivals not to betray him? It suggested that they'd definitely acquired a strong leader.

"Crawl forward," Harkin ordered. He was holding his bow in his hand, searching for targets. "Extend the lighting spell towards them, now!"

The goblins didn't have lighting spells, Emily realized as she crawled through the slimy dirt; they didn't *need* magic to see in the dark. And they apparently couldn't see the spell that the team had been using to light their way.

Harkin, Miles and Cat shot back as soon as the goblins came into view—the goblins hadn't bothered to take cover, because they'd *known* they couldn't be seen—and three goblins toppled backwards, arrows driven through their skulls. Emily crawled faster at the Sergeant's command, silently grateful that they'd lost their baggage when the goblins had burned down the tent. It would only have slowed them down, as well as making them a bigger target.

"Keep crawling," Harkin hissed, looking back towards where the goblins had been. The remaining goblins had dropped for cover as soon as they had realized they could be seen, effectively concealing them from human eyes. "Don't slow down for *anything*."

Emily was too tired to care that they were crawling through mud, mud which seemed to be covering the remains of a fallen building. Behind her, she heard horns as the goblins called for reinforcements, perhaps using them to direct other teams of goblins into position in order to intercept the human fugitives. She found herself wondering just how well the goblins knew the forest, before realizing that they, unlike humanity, probably spent most of their time within the *mana*-rich environment. They probably knew it as well as they knew themselves.

A second volley of arrows shot through the air, out of the darkness. Emily heard someone grunt in pain and cursed inwardly. They'd been hit.

"Bran," Jade hissed. "Sergeant, he's been *hit*!"

"I'll deal with him," Harkin snapped back. "Keep moving. Crawl south and pray that they don't come after you."

Emily hesitated beside Bran's groaning form, before Harkin growled at her to keep moving south. Bran had been pinned to the ground by the arrow; Emily winced in sympathy as Harkin reached under Bran's chest and snapped the arrowhead away from the wooden shaft, before pushing Bran forward. Everything she knew about first aid screamed at her, insisting that Bran shouldn't be moved at all, but there was no choice. The goblins would catch him if they left him behind and they'd do much worse to any captives than merely ramming an arrow through his chest.

The sound of goblin horns grew louder as they kept moving, Harkin half-crawling on his knees as he carried Bran. More arrows hissed at them out of the darkness, as if the goblins were trying to wear them down before closing in for the kill. Their tactics made no sense to Emily until she realized that the goblins had good reason to fear magic. They couldn't be certain that the magicians were completely drained. If she'd had enough magic left to start a fire ...

"We couldn't outrun it, even if we *could* set the forest on fire," Harkin said when she suggested it. "Forest fires can spread very quickly."

Emily could feel the goblins closing in on them as they pushed their way through the remains of another city, now half-buried in the mud. Bran was groaning as if he'd become delirious, which was a very real possibility. Emily couldn't remember enough about medicine to be helpful, but she did know that he needed a Healer; Hell, they should have put him in stasis right at the start. Alassa's time-freeze spell might make the difference between Bran living or dying, if Emily could recall how to cast it. And if she'd had enough magic to use it.

"Good thinking," Jade said. Oddly, his approval sent a flush of warmth running through Emily's tired body. He stumbled back to where Harkin was still holding Bran. "Sergeant, we can freeze him and then ..."

"And then carrying him will be impossible," Harkin snapped, tiredly. He sounded utterly exhausted, his composure finally breaking. "We have to get him to a Healer."

"We need somewhere defensible," Miles called back. There didn't seem to be any point in stealth any longer. The goblins certainly knew where they were. "You want to head for the Temple of Tat?"

"We don't have the manpower to hold it," Harkin countered. There was a pause. "But there's nowhere else to go."

It was already too late, Emily realized, as the goblins came swarming out of the darkness. Somehow, she found the energy to lift her sword and parry a thrust that would have skewered her, just before a goblin shoved her into a stone wall. The world spun around her as the wall collapsed; she fell into darkness. She heard a final howl from the goblin and then ...

Silence.

# Chapter Forty

DARKNESS HUNG AROUND HER LIKE A LIVING THING.

Emily looked around, but saw nothing. She seemed to be lying on a bed of grass, from what she could feel, yet the darkness made it impossible to be certain of anything. The air held an eerie silence, the world was just waiting for someone to clear her throat and introduce herself. It was a feeling of pregnant possibility on the verge of flowering into life. She reached for her magic and started to cast a lighting spell, but something muffled the magic and absorbed it into nothingness.

Where *was* she?

She had to have blacked out again; the goblin had hit her, the wall had collapsed and then ... darkness. Her magic felt as if it had recovered, as if she could cast spells if she poured enough *mana* into them, and yet some sense told her that casting more spells would not be a good idea. She held a hand in front of her face, but couldn't see anything apart from the darkness.

And then she heard the humming.

It seemed to come from all around her at first, a sound vibrating on the air and pressing down on her, almost as if it too were a living thing. Emily covered her ears as the sound grew louder, but it echoed through her hands and went deep into her soul. She had to bite her lip to keep herself from screaming.

And then the sound dropped away into a single deep note that hung on the air, coming from right in front of her.

Emily opened her eyes, unaware that she'd even closed them, and saw a handful of multicolored lights drifting towards her. They spread out as they came closer, taking on shape and form; despite herself, she smiled in delight. The lights were winged fairies, just like the one she'd liberated at Dragon's Den. One by one, they came to a halt facing her, just before the darkness was banished by a brilliant flash of light.

"Human," a voice said, or was it voices? It sounded as if dozens of smaller voices were speaking in harmony. "Why do you trespass on our land?"

Emily glanced around. She didn't seem to be anywhere near the forest, or the old buildings where the Redshirts had made their final stand. The fairies occupied a giant cavern, which stretched away into the distance; ahead of her, she saw a massive underground lake, surrounded by strange trees and growths. There was no clear source of light; it seemed to diffuse from high overhead. And the lake was surrounded by statues of humankind ...

"I fell down from above," Emily said finally. Like the statues she'd seen in Whitehall's library, the statues by the lake were alarmingly lifelike. Too lifelike. "I didn't mean to trespass."

"Your kind has driven us from the world above," the voice said. It struck Emily suddenly that the fairies had a hive mentality rather than being individuals. Maybe it made sense. Magic or no magic, she couldn't see how a tiny fairy brain could support independent thought. "This is our last refuge from your kind. Your presence is not welcome."

"Then I will leave," Emily said, feeling wild magic crackling through the air. The entire chamber might be protected, or expanded, by wild magic. Like Whitehall, the fairy complex might be far larger on the inside than on the outside. "Please show me the way to return to the world above."

"You may speak of us to others of your kind," the voice said. It grew harder, colder, as the waves of wild magic grew stronger. "They will come to find us, to cut off our wings and grind up our bodies for magic to fuel your race's perverted desires. We cannot allow you to return to the world above."

Emily hesitated, thinking frantically. None of the books she'd glanced at had mentioned anything like *this*! They'd all implied that the fairies were animals at best, probably to justify using their bodies as components for spells. Like dragons, they were heavily magical; unlike dragons, a lone fairy couldn't really defend itself. But as a swarm they would be lethal to anyone unlucky enough to encounter them without powerful magic at their disposal.

Another swarm of fairies swooped across the lake and joined the swarm facing her. They seemed to dance together, sharing thoughts and feelings as the two hive minds merged into one, leaving Emily to think desperately. Each of the fairies *looked* human, almost perfectly human apart from the slightly elf-like faces, yet they clearly didn't *think* like humans. Or maybe they were more human than they wanted to admit. If Emily had been Anne Frank, with a German accidentally stumbling into the Secret Annex, *she* would have seriously considered cutting the German's throat too.

"You freed one of our kind," the new voice said. It sounded different, somehow, as if the second swarm had been more inclined to be tolerant than the first. "You are not from this world."

"No," Emily said, wondering how they'd known *that*. Perhaps they could smell it on her, or perhaps her attitudes were simply too different from the local humans. "I come from a very different world."

"We are not ungrateful for what you did," the voice said. "And yet we dare not risk returning you to the world above. You may lead your people to our final resting place."

Emily shivered. "I will not speak of you to anyone," she said, realizing that she was pleading for her life. The fairies were powerful, and very dangerous. "You have my word -"

The voice cut her off. "And yet you may be a Child of Destiny," it added. The fairies shifted around in the swarm, their wings beating so fast that they were nothing more than a blur. "To hold you here until the end of time would risk upsetting forces that have an interest in appeasing Destiny. We are divided on what to do."

There was a long pause. Emily thought hard, trying to think of something she could say. But there was nothing.

And then the massed voice spoke again. "We will return you to the surface and provide you with assistance in rescuing your comrades, in exchange for two promises from you. First, we will require you to swear a solemn oath, upon your power, that you will never speak of us to another human. Second, we may need your help one day. Should we call, you will answer and help us to the best of your ability."

Emily hesitated. Oaths were sacred in her new world, partly because they were backed by magic. Swearing and then breaking an oath would have unpleasant consequences, consequences that would be much worse if she made a cold-blooded decision to break the agreement. The books had been divided on what would happen if she was forced into breaking the oath, but she had a feeling that the fairies would take a very dim view of any oath-breaking, even under torture. And she had no idea what they might want her to do, one day.

But she knew she couldn't stay with them forever. Even if they didn't add her to their collection of statues, she couldn't leave the Redshirts in goblin hands. And if the necromancers *were* behind the attack on the Redshirts, they would search for Emily and they might find their way to the fairy stronghold. It was too much to hope that the mere act of breaching its walls would kill them. The raw power at their disposal might be enough to crush the fairies like bugs.

"I will swear," she said. "Where are my comrades now?"

"They are being held, under guard, near the Temple of Tat," the voice said. "The goblins have handed them over to Orcs. Swear your oath and we will give you the best assistance we can provide."

Emily worked out the oath in her mind and swore it out loud. The voice hummed in pleasure, just as the fairies started to drift back over to the lake.

"Drink from our water," the voice said. "It will give you all that you need."

Emily looked at the humming swarm, and then knelt down to scoop up the water with her hands. If they'd wanted to poison her–or worse–they didn't need to trick her to do it. The water tasted sweet as she swallowed it ...

And then her entire body glowed with light. Her magic had been replenished; the tiredness that had been gripping her body was blown away almost effortlessly. She felt as if she could arm-wrestle a bear and win. But it wasn't *Berserker*. She was still herself.

The world shimmered around her. Her head spun, forcing her to close her eyes for a moment. When she opened them, she was standing in the forest, looking down at the muddy ground. There was no sign of the fairies.

Emily shook her head, feeling the reserves of magic inside her, and started to walk towards the temple. A moment later, she cast a concealing spell Sergeant Miles had taught them. It should ensure that even the best tracker couldn't find the caster effectively.

She gritted her teeth as she smelled the Orcs, minutes before she actually saw them. They were loud, too ,as they crashed their way through the forest around the Temple of Tat. Unlike goblins, they were huge, easily two meters tall; like the Goblins, their faces were mocking parodies of humanity. Their bodies seemed to be nothing but muscle; they casually carried swords that Emily couldn't have hoped to lift, making it look easy. They wore nothing, apart from loincloths and belts. Looking at their brown-blue skin, Emily could see why they didn't bother with armor. Their skin looked tough enough to turn a blade on its own.

The Sergeants had trained her to watch for guards, but it didn't look as if the Orcs had posted *any* guards. Given the way they were stamping about, they probably thought they didn't need to bother. The concealment spell seemed to be holding, for now, but it wouldn't hold forever. She had to move quickly.

Covering her nose, she slipped through the ruins until she reached a point where she could look into the courtyard. The Redshirts were sitting in the exact centre of the yard, their hands and legs chained to massive pillars of wood. It took Emily a moment to work out that even the strongest human would have trouble moving while carrying such a weight, if they could stand up while wearing the chains. Five Orcs marched around them constantly, grunting unpleasantly as they stood guard, their eyes flickering from prisoner to prisoner like a snake hunting its next meal. All of the prisoners were injured.

*They said they'd provide assistance,* Emily thought sourly. But where were they? Were they even coming?

No matter how long she stared at them, she that she couldn't beat the Orcs on her own. *Berserker* would grant her speed and strength for as long as her magic lasted, but if she couldn't kill them all by then, she would die when they tore her apart. She picked up ideas and tossed them around in her mind, before discarding them one after the other. Her magic was just too limited to kill them all before it was too late. Unless ...

The books had said that Orcs were violent and very quick to anger. Before she could think better of it, she shaped a spell in her mind and cast it towards a pile of rubble behind one of the Orcs. A piece of stone flew through the air past one of the Orcs, and slammed into the back of a different Orc. The Orc spun around, snarling in pain, clearly believing that its comrade had thrown the stone. They exchanged angry hisses for a long moment, before slowly turning away, still snarling. Emily repeated the spell and hit the same Orc with another stone. This time, the Orc spun around and charged right at the Orc he'd challenged before. A moment later, they were exchanging blows with terrifying force.

*No swords,* Emily noted as she carefully manipulated another piece of stone to throw at the third Orc. The other three Orcs looked as if they were torn between the impulse to guard the prisoners or join in the fight. Judging from their slack-jawed expressions, they *really* wanted to join the fight. She threw the third piece of stone and, without thinking, the Orcs hurled themselves into the battle. Emily blanched as she realized that she might have miscalculated–the fighters could end up pulverizing the prisoners in the crossfire–but there was no time to worry now. Instead, she started preparing spells to intervene if the fighting grew worse.

The Orcs were built to take a *lot* of punishment, she realized. They fought like boxers, but without any referee or anyone else to tell them when to stop. By the time two of the five Orcs dropped to the ground, they had been battered bloody; the remaining three kept fighting each other, lost in battle lust. A victor finally emerged, staggering away from the stunned Orcs and bleeding from a dozen nasty-looking wounds. Emily picked up the final piece of rock and launched it towards him with as much force as she could muster. It struck his head with a terrifying crack.

There was a long pause - long enough for her to wonder if she'd hit him hard enough, before he finally toppled over and hit the ground.

Emily ran forward, dropping her concealment spell as she reached the prisoners. The Orcs had chained them heavily, using manacles that made it difficult for their wearers to use magic, but they were easy for her to unlock using the standard unlocking charm. Jade stared at her in disbelief as his chains fell away, then caught her up in a bear hug that almost crushed Emily's ribs. Harkin growled at him to put her down as he tended to Bran—who looked on the verge of death—and Cat, who'd taken a nasty stab wound to the leg. Neither of them would be able to walk very far ...

A thought occurred to Emily and she shivered in horror, before speaking up. "We could turn them into something small and carry them out of here," she suggested. "Or we could freeze them now and carry them ...?"

"Transfigure them," Harkin said, after a long moment. There was something in his voice that suggested he hated the whole idea, but she worked the spell anyway. "Good thinking."

"And well done for saving us," Jade added. "What happened to you?"

"Later," Harkin snapped before Emily could think of a plausible lie. She'd given the fairies her oath, even though they hadn't really provided much assistance in freeing the prisoners. Maybe they'd hoped they could reward her for saving one of them and then watch her die, knowing she would take their secret to the next world. "We're not out of the woods just yet."

There was a terrifying roar from outside as the patrolling Orcs finally realized that something was wrong. Emily turned to see the Orcs run towards them, their footsteps shaking the ground as they brandished edged weapons and clubs the size of tree trunks. Whoever had used them as shock troops clearly hadn't anticipated them losing control of themselves, or maybe they just didn't care. Or ...

"Get up onto the roofs," Harkin snapped. Emily saw what he meant at once. The Orcs would have real problems climbing up the remains of the stairs; they'd definitely have to come at the humans one by one. "There's nowhere else to go."

He was right, Emily realized. There *was* nowhere to run. She knew no magic that could deal with *all* of the Orcs before they ran her down and crushed her into a bloody pulp. And the others were badly drained. She could call on *Berserker* again, but ...

Another idea struck her. Working at frantic speed, she cast an illusion into the air, a shimmering multicolored patch of mist that appeared out of nowhere and drifted towards the Orcs. The lead Orcs stopped dead as they saw the Mimic, their comrades from behind them slamming into their backs and sending them tumbling to the ground like ninepins. Then they stumbled to their feet and ran, howling their fear in their strange and unpleasant language. The Mimic-illusion drifted forwards, clearly hunting for prey—and the only known defense against a Mimic was to be somewhere else.

The Orcs ran away very quickly.

"Good thinking," Harkin said. "Can you move the illusion so it covers us?"

He led the way towards where the Orcs had tied up their horses.

Emily nodded and used the illusion to hide them as they reached the horses and scrambled up into the saddle. She'd never ridden a horse before coming to Whitehall, but Alassa had been tutoring her in the finer points of horsemanship ... thankfully, as she'd been nervous the first time she'd mounted a horse. If she'd had to learn on the run ...

... But there was no choice. They needed to put as much distance as they could between them and the Orcs before they overcame their fear of the Mimic and started crawling back.

*But they might not take prisoners the next time,* she thought. *They might think that we're all Mimics.*

Carefully ignoring the smell from the horse's saddlebags, she pushed the unwilling creature into a canter as Harkin led them down a trail that headed northwards from the temple. It occurred to her that the Orcs might have other pickets out there—Whitehall *might* realize that something was wrong and send help—but there was nothing they could do about it, at least until they encountered them. But nothing blocked their path as they emerged from the forest and cantered up a stone road that had to have been built by the Allied Lands. If the Orcs had realized that they'd been tricked, they'd given up on pursuit.

"We'll be back at Whitehall within the hour," Harkin said, pulling his horse up beside hers. "Once we get there, take the wounded directly to the infirmary and brief the Healers *before* you undo the transformation. And then report back to me."

"Understood," Emily said. "What are we going to do about the Orcs?"

Harkin winced. "I have to inform the Grandmaster that the Allied Lands may be in terrible danger," he said. "It will not be a pleasant conversation."

## Chapter Forty-One

KYLA LISTENED CAREFULLY TO EMILY'S EXPLANATION OF WHAT HAD HAPPENED, THEN NODded.

"Place them on separate beds and then prepare to surrender the charm to me," she ordered. "Do you know how to do that?"

Emily mutely shook her head.

"Then listen carefully and follow instructions," Kyla said firmly. She outlined a complicated procedure that Emily followed as best she could. "Good. I can now release the charm once we're ready to deal with them."

Kyla looked over at Emily. "What happened to you? I know something did."

"I used *Berserker* too much," Emily admitted. She felt tired and sore, even though she could still feel the water the fairies had given her pulsing through her system. "And I'm drained."

"I wouldn't know it to look at you with just my eyes," Kyla said. She sounded ... suspicious, as if she thought that Emily had done something stupid. "I'd suggest that you spend some time in the infirmary yourself, if the Sergeant hadn't called you back to him. Go find him, then take this."

She passed Emily a small potion gourd. "It should help you to sleep for at least twelve hours. You weren't due back for another three days, but if any of your tutors give you trouble, refer them to me. I think you need sleep more than lessons."

Emily nodded and walked out of the infirmary, nearly walking right into Alassa.

"There are rumors everywhere," her friend said. There was a funny mark on her face, the remains of a single hex. "And the Grandmaster wants me to escort you to his office."

"Oh," Emily said. Now she was safe, everything she'd done was starting to catch up with her again. The goblins she'd slain, the Orcs who had beaten themselves up because of her trickery ... not to mention the desperate flight from captivity. "What happened to you?"

"Melissa threw a couple of hexes at me," Alassa admitted as they walked up to the Grandmaster's office. "You ready to play another prank on her?"

Emily snorted. "Maybe one that doesn't involve someone else caught in the crossfire," she said. "Or are you that eager to annoy Madame Razz again?"

"She's always been a pain in the bum, according to rumor," Alassa said. "And what, exactly, happened to you?"

Emily outlined most of the story as they reached the Grandmaster's office and knocked on the door. "I have to go sleep after this," she said tiredly. "We can catch up with Melissa later, all right?"

The Grandmaster's office looked cramped with the two Sergeants, Jade and a man Emily didn't recognize, as well as the Grandmaster himself. He looked deeply worried, something that bothered Emily; the Grandmaster was known to be one of the most powerful sorcerers in the world. What could worry him?

The Sergeants glanced over at Emily as she entered. Harkin seemed his normal grim self, but Miles winked at her as she stood beside them. And the man she didn't recognize gave her a sharp look, as if he'd expected her to be different, somehow.

"Orcs are rarely found on this side of the mountains," the Grandmaster said, bluntly. "We must assume they have found a way of getting through–or under–the mountains that shield us from the necromancers."

Emily nodded, deciding not to mention that the Sergeants had already drawn that conclusion. It was easy to see why that bothered him. Whitehall plugged the pass between the Allied Lands and territory held by the necromancers, rendering it impossible for the necromancers to launch a major attack before reinforcements arrived at Whitehall. But if there was another way through the mountains, the school might be bypassed as the necromancers raged down upon the cities and farmland along the border.

The Grandmaster looked directly at Emily. "It is also possible that the Orcs were ordered to capture you. If that is the case, we owe you an apology for sending you into danger, as well as congratulations for rescuing your teammates."

"There was no way to know there were so many Orcs and Goblins in the area," the unnamed man said flatly. "Goblins are not inclined to work together."

"It doesn't matter," Sergeant Harkin said. "We can place the blame later. What matters now is securing the school."

"I have sent an urgent request for reinforcements from the Allied Lands," the Grandmaster said. "However, Dragon's Den, the closest possible source of reinforcements, has announced that it intends to keep its City Guard in the city until reinforced by other cities. The prospect of an Orc army rampaging through the fields and countryside has concentrated a few minds."

"On their own protection," Harkin observed. "I thought that we could draw troops from the garrison at Flodden."

"They're currently involved with rioting in Lane," the unnamed man said. "And if you think that is a coincidence, I have some holdings in Greenfield I would like to sell you."

Jade leaned over and whispered in Emily's ear. "Greenfield was overrun by the necromancers thirty years ago," he explained. "Everyone who was trapped in the country was either enslaved or sacrificed. Land there is worthless."

Emily nodded. The unnamed man was probably right; the necromancers had fomented trouble further to the north to distract reinforcements from reaching Whitehall. She recalled the maps she'd seen in Professor Locke's classroom and tried to imagine where the tunnel had to be, before realizing that it was impossible. The tunnel could be anywhere.

"They only attacked us when we reached the Dark City," Harkin said, "and then they spent considerable effort in hunting us down before we could escape. Logically, their tunnel entrance has to be somewhere nearby, perhaps linked into the scorpion-infested tunnels that we used to reach the city ourselves. They certainly tried to set an ambush when we attempted to use the tunnels to escape."

"Possible," the unnamed man agreed. "But it *could* be intended as a diversion."

Harkin slapped one hand against his leather trousers. "Yes, it *could*," he said, "but the best defense is a good offence. If we were to dispatch a regiment of soldiers to the Dark City and search it thoroughly, we would at least force them to react to us for a change."

"If we *had* a regiment," the unnamed man said. "Grandmaster, do you have no favors you can call in from the rest of the Allied Lands?"

"I have asked for troops to be sent through portals," the Grandmaster said. "However, it may be several days before the northernmost Kingdoms dispatch aid ..."

"Naturally," Harkin said. He shook his head. "With your permission, Grandmaster, I will continue my students' intensive training. We need to prepare for an attack."

The Grandmaster frowned. "Even the most powerful necromancer in existence would find it impossible to break through our wards," he said. "But they might be crazy enough to believe they could succeed."

He thought for a time, then shook his head. "Prepare as best as you can," he ordered. He looked at Emily and seemed to realize that she was dropping asleep on her feet. "And make sure that everyone you brought back gets some rest. They'll need it."

Outside the Grandmaster's office, Harkin caught Emily's hand before she could head back to her bedroom. "You did well, back there," he said, gruffly. "You saved my life and those of the entire team."

"Thank you," Emily said. She swallowed, hard. There was a question she wanted answered. "How ... how do you beat a necromancer?"

Harkin studied her for a long moment. "It isn't easy. There were three nameless sorcerers who believed they had a certain method to defeat a necromancer in magical combat. They all ended up dead, or worse than dead."

*And what were they called*? Emily asked herself. There had to be some reason their names were concealed if they were dead. *Master Wredd Schyrt, Master Kannun Phodda and Master Deddman Warkin*?

He hesitated. "Necromancers *have* died before. But the only way anyone has found that seems likely to work is to force them to use up all of their power before they can kill you, and that isn't easy. Even a raw blast of magic can kill, or warp you into something truly horrible. Sometimes you can trick them, or exploit flaws in their plans, but...the only real advantage the Allied Lands have is that they fight each other as much as they fight us. More, perhaps."

Emily frowned. "What would happen if we were to destroy their slaves?"

"You mean eliminate their source of power?" Harkin asked. He shook his head. "It doesn't work like that, sadly. They'd still have enough power to crash into the Allied Lands and capture more people to slaughter to power their magic."

He stepped back and shrugged. "Go get some rest. You and the rest of the Redshirts can report to me tomorrow, as classes will be cancelled. We need to go over what happened to us so others won't make the same mistake."

Emily nodded and returned to her bedroom, where there was no sign of either of her roommates. Aloha would be joining the rest of the Martial Magic class, of course, and Imaiqah was probably in the library. She'd admitted that she needed to study more for her Alchemy class, a sentiment Emily fully shared, even though she doubted that she'd ever get the hang of Alchemy. It just offended her sense of how the universe worked–and her concept of the scientific method. But no one here seemed to question it.

After undressing, washing herself in the shower and donning a nightshirt, she returned to her bed, lay down and drank the potion. The world seemed to spin around her as she plunged into a dreamless sleep, unbroken until she finally opened her eyes, cast a lighting spell and glanced at the clockwork watch. She had slept for nearly twelve hours as it was midnight. Emily felt her stomach rumble as she looked over at the other beds and saw Imaiqah and Aloha safely there. She felt an odd sense of relief. Having friends, it seemed, took some getting used to, she decided as she pulled herself out of bed. There was a little chocolate stored in her chest, so she retrieved it and nibbled it carefully. It wasn't enough to satisfy her hunger.

*Girls in bad semi-romance novels about schools are always having midnight feasts,* she thought ruefully. Maybe Whitehall *did* have a tradition of midnight feasts; for a moment, she seriously considered waking up her roommates before pushing the thought aside in some irritation. They needed their sleep and to even *think* of waking them up was a selfish act under the circumstances. Instead, she stepped out of the door, into the darkened hallway. She had no idea if the kitchen still served food at midnight, but curfew didn't apply to older students. It was quite possible that they would want food late at night. She was reaching the end of the corridor when she heard a dry cough behind her and jumped.

"I trust that you have a very good explanation for wanting to leave the dorm at midnight," Madame Razz said. Her voice was calm, but there was an undercurrent of irritation. Maybe Emily had woken her when she'd entered the hallway. "Or should I just send you back to bed?"

"I need to eat," Emily said. "The Grandmaster ordered me to get some sleep and I slept through dinner and supper."

Madame Razz studied her before nodding slowly. "First-years are not allowed out of their dorms at night," she said, flatly. "But I will give you something to eat; then, you will go back to bed."

"Thank you," Emily said, relieved. She'd known tutors who would be much less reasonable when they enforced the rules. "I didn't mean to sleep through supper."

"No one ever does," Madame Razz said. She led Emily into her office and rummaged around in a chest, finally producing a set of chewing bars. "Eat these here, then go back to your room. Make sure you eat in the morning."

Emily obeyed. The chewing bars, whatever they were, didn't taste very nice at all, but they filled her grumbling stomach. Once she had eaten, she went back to her bedroom, lay down on the bed and closed her eyes again. She was awoken, seven hours later, by Aloha's alarm gong.

"Welcome home," Aloha said as Emily sat upright. The gong was meant to be audible to its owner–and no one else–but Aloha kept fumbling the spells. "I hear you fought off a million Orcs on your own, and killed a thousand Goblins."

Emily rubbed her hand against her face. "I didn't do anything of the sort," she said crossly. The thought of killing the Goblins still tormented her, no matter how much she told herself that it had been a choice between killing them or being killed herself. "How can anyone believe such nonsense?"

"Rumors always have a grain of truth," Aloha pointed out, as Imaiqah sat up and yawned. "And we've been told that all classes have been cancelled while the tutors see to the defenses. Whatever happened on your field trip?"

Emily found herself flushing as she outlined the basic details of what had happened at the Dark City, leaving out only the fairies and her oath. And *Berserker*, which she had been told never to mention to anyone outside Martial Magic. Aloha and Imaiqah listened in awe as they dressed themselves and then followed her down to breakfast, clearly impressed by everything she'd done. Emily wasn't sure why they were so impressed, or why so many students were throwing her admiring looks. She certainly hadn't fought an Orc and beaten him with her bare hands. Even the Sergeants, she suspected, would have difficulty outfighting an Orc without weapons.

"Melissa was looking very green," Alassa informed her when they met at the breakfast table. "I think you've scared her."

"Oh," Emily said. She shook her head tiredly. There were more rumors surrounding her than there were around Harry Potter, *and* for far less reason. She couldn't have just abandoned the rest of the team, not least because she didn't know the way back to Whitehall. And besides, if the Orcs *had* been after her, their captivity was her fault. "Can't we forget about playing pranks for the moment?"

"I heard from my parents," Alassa said, after an awkward pause. "They want me to go back through the portal to safety."

Emily didn't blame the King and Queen of Zangaria. Alassa *was* the only real Heir they had and if she died, Zangaria would probably be torn apart by civil war. Or, if the necromancers happened to capture her, who knew *what* they could do with such an important hostage? They could start by unlocking the secrets of the Royal Bloodline and then go on from there. Maybe they could find a way to curse everyone touched by the Blood.

"It may be a good idea," Emily said. She didn't want to urge Alassa to run—she had too few friends as it was—but it might be the best possible choice for her to make. "Are you going to go?"

"Everyone back home would say that I ran," Alassa said miserably. "I don't know what to do."

"This place is supposed to be impregnable," Aloha pointed out. "It would take a madman to even *think* they could get through the wards."

*But ... necromancers are mad*, Emily thought. She kept that to herself. And yet...she couldn't see *how* the necromancers intended to break through the wards. Powered as they were from the local ley lines, they were stronger than any magic anyone, even a necromancer, could bring to bear against them. Maybe they just intended to seal off Whitehall while they crushed the rest of the Allied Lands. Or maybe they had something *really* nasty up their sleeves.

A dull gong rang throughout the school, followed by immediate panic. Emily glanced around in alarm as students jumped back from their chairs while tutors stood up and ran from the hall. She looked over at Aloha and saw that her roommate was panicking too as a second gong echoed in the air.

"What ... ?"

"That's the emergency gong," Aloha gasped. "The school is under attack!"

Emily stared at her. No one had told her what to do if the school was attacked. "What do we do?"

"We're in Martial Magic," Aloha reminded her sharply. "We have to get to the Sergeants!"

"Attention, all pupils," the Grandmaster's voice said. It echoed through the school, drowning out the sounds of panic. "The school is surrounded by a hostile army. All first to fourth year students are to return to their bedrooms, unless they are taking either Martial Magic or Healing. Martial Magic students are to report to the Sergeants; Healers are to report to the Infirmary. Fifth and sixth year students are to report to their common rooms where tutors will issue further instructions."

There was a long pause. "The wards remain intact and the enemy does not seem to have the ability to break them," the Grandmaster added. "Do not panic. Whitehall has stood against attacks before and will continue to do so as long as the Allied Lands endure."

Alassa exchanged a long glance with Imaiqah. "Do you mind if I share your room?" She asked. "I don't want to be alone."

Emily hid her smile as she pushed away the remains of her breakfast and headed for the door, following Aloha towards the armory. The Sergeants were passing out weapons, encouragement and the occasional lecture to students who had some training in defending themselves. Neither of them looked very happy.

"Look," Aloha said quietly.

Emily followed her finger and stared at the mirror showing the view outside the castle. Outside the wards, Whitehall's worst nightmare was taking on shape and form. A vast army of monsters were standing there, waiting. But what were they waiting for?

"Take your weapons," the Sergeant ordered. "Right now, this building is under siege!"

## Chapter Forty-Two

"H..." ALOHA SWALLOWED AND STARTED AGAIN. "HOW MANY OF THEM ARE OUT THERE?"

Emily shook her head, unable to answer. The school was surrounded by monsters, each one more horrific than the last. There were Goblins and Orcs, armed to the teeth, backed up by human crossbreeds with all kinds of non-human creatures. Humanoid snakes rubbed shoulders with walking bees, which stood beside crawling octopus-like monsters. She caught sight of a medusa before hastily looking away. Who knew how far their petrification ability could reach?

"Thousands," Sergeant Harkin said quietly. "Perhaps many more."

Aloha looked over at him. "How did they get so close without being detected?"

"Magic, I suspect," Harkin said. "A simple cloaking spell might have hidden much of their army assuming they stayed out of our wards, or the wards around Dragon's Den. Or they might have ..."

He shook his head. "Not that it really matters. The important detail is that they're here."

Emily swallowed hard when she saw a giant snake's head lifting above the colossal army. A single humanoid figure was perched on the creature, one hand holding a long black staff. It had been months since she'd last seen Shadye, but the necromancer was unmistakable. He looked older than he'd looked when they'd first met - when he'd kidnapped her for use as a human sacrifice - yet she could still sense the aura of raw power crackling around him. The necromancer had come to lead the attack on Whitehall in person.

"That's a necromancer," one of Aloha's teammates said. He sounded as if he were going into shock. None of them were trained to the point where they could fight a necromancer and hope to win, if such a thing were possible. "What's *he* doing here?"

Emily remembered how she'd tricked the Orcs into fleeing and wondered if she could do something similar with Shadye. But the Orcs, according to all the books, were not very bright, while Shadye was both brilliant and insane.

On the other hand, necromancers weren't known for being patient. It was possible that Shadye could be convinced to throw himself against the wards rather than wait for the defenders to sally out and try to drive the necromantic army away from the walls.

"Get the archers up to the battlements," Sergeant Harkin ordered. "I don't think we can kill the scumbag, but we can certainly *try*."

*And it might annoy him to the point that he does something stupid*, Emily thought grimly.

Aloha's teammate poked her in the ribs, none too gently. "You're meant to be a Child of Destiny," he sneered. "What do *you* think he's doing here?"

Emily scowled at him, thinking hard. The locals took the safety of their wards for granted, but their confidence seemed fully justified. Whitehall was built on a ley line crossroads and the school's main wards were linked directly into the nexus, a vast source of *mana* that far exceeded anything any magician could hope to produce on his own. Even a necromancer wouldn't be able to knock the wards down by brute force. It was possible, she supposed, that Shadye might intend to crack them one by one, but the Grandmaster and his staff would be monitoring them, ready to counter any such move. And even trying would expose Shadye to the ravages of wild magic.

A thought struck her and she shivered, looking over at the Sergeants. "Can you ... can you shift the ley line nexus somehow? Or excite it to the point that it explodes?"

Surprisingly, it was Sergeant Miles who answered. "Ley line nexuses are woven into the soil," he said. "I have never heard of one being moved, anywhere. It isn't even theoretically possible."

He paused, considering. "You could agitate one to the point where it produces a magical upsurge, but you'd have to be inside the wards to do it. And even a necromancer wouldn't be able to survive the surge of magic. The results would be disastrous for him if he tried."

"Unless he thinks he can survive the upsurge, somehow," Emily said darkly. Shadye had been sacrificing humans for years, both for power and simple survival. "How much power can a necromancer channel?"

"Nothing a necromancer could do would come close to the sheer level of wild magic that would be released, if the nexus were upset," Sergeant Miles assured her. "A foolish boy tried it, back during a civil war between a King and his bastard son. He intended to destroy his father's castle. Instead, he ended up wiping out half the kingdom."

"It went up like a volcano," Sergeant Harkin put in. "Hundreds of thousands of lives were blotted out in a split-second."

Emily nodded slowly, looking back towards the monstrous army—and the dark figure waiting patiently on top of his snake. Shadye had to have something in mind, but what?

"Maybe this is the diversion," she said after a long pause. It was her best guess. "He might be dispatching an army towards Dragon's Den or somewhere else, using his force here to pin us down while he achieves his real objectives."

"It's hard to imagine anywhere else as important as Whitehall," Sergeant Harkin said, "but you might be right. Still, we *are* going to be bringing in troops and combat sorcerers through the portal, once the Allied Lands get off their duffs and start dispatching reinforcements. We're not going to let that army stay there forever."

"Maybe that's what he's counting on," Emily said. "Us leaving the safety of the wards and fighting him in the open."

The sun rose higher in the sky as the defenders watched the necromantic army and waited for the other shoe to drop. Emily found herself moving from defensive position to defensive position, hastily learning what she needed to know to take part in the defense if the necromancer managed to crack his way through the wards. But Shadye seemed to be doing nothing, apart from waiting; he didn't even seem to be trying to hack into the wards and dismantle them. It was strange; every book she'd read had suggested that necromancers wanted instant gratification and used their powers to get what they wanted, without hesitation. And yet Shadye was waiting for something ...

"Maybe he wants to surprise us by attacking at nightfall," she suggested, when the remaining Redshirts assembled to continue their training. A book she'd once read had talked about the "looming volcano" theory of military surprise, suggesting that some defenders had simply grown used to looking at the attackers as they waited on one side of the border. *Then* they had been surprised when the attackers suddenly switched from passively waiting to thrusting into the defender's territory as hard as they could. And the Germans had won the Battle of France, if not the war. "Or maybe he thinks we'll forget they're out there if he waits long enough."

Jade rubbed his nose. "They'd have to be insane," he said, dryly. "Those creatures *stink*!"

Emily had to smile. He was right. Every time the wind changed, it blew the stench towards the castle, which caused the defenders to recoil. Emily had wondered if Shadye had come up with the concept of poison gas, or biological warfare, but when she'd mentioned it to the Sergeants she'd been informed that the wards would keep out anything that was actively dangerous. *That* had left her wondering about the concept of chemical weapons that were really two separate–and individually harmless–compounds mixed together, which could probably pass harmlessly through the wards and combine to do great harm on the other side.

Yet this world knew little of chemistry. It was unlikely that the thought would occur to anyone, apart from her.

Or so she hoped.

Shadye presumably had spies in the Allied Lands. The books she'd read had recorded countless cases of outright treason, either by willing traitors or spell-controlled victims, and he might know that Emily had already started introducing concepts from her old world into this new one. In fact, in some ways, he'd be in the best place to deduce what she'd done; he already believed her to be a Child of Destiny, and he knew where she'd come from. What if he'd managed to bring something *else* from her world? An atomic bomb, perhaps, or maybe a shipload of AK-47s? But would they *work* in this world?

*He'd have to tell his servants what he wanted them to bring,* Emily thought, and prayed that she was right. *How could Shadye know enough about atomic bombs to describe them to his servants? And how could he detonate one if he did manage to bring it to this world?*

Once, years ago, she had read a fantasy novel by an author who had never bothered to think through the implications of her universe. The writer–who had been little more than a glorified romance hack–had actually argued that life in a medieval world was better than life in the modern universe. She'd insisted that progress was death and that introducing new ideas had destroyed the fabric of human society. The whole concept of working to uplift a primitive society towards modern technology had been outrageous to her.

But that author had never had to live in such a society. How could she really understand what it meant to live there unless she'd tried?

As it stood, Emily *did* live in such a society–and as much as she loved her new world, it needed improvement. Technology made the lives of ordinary people so much easier, back home, and it had helped to create a more democratic world. Who knew *what* it would do here? If it had the chance, that is.

The hours dragged on. Classes were cancelled, of course, while the older students worked hard to prepare the castle's defenses. Sergeant Harkin ordered Emily to take a break from training and get something to eat, then to relax. The younger students had been driving each other crazy as they waited for the necromancers to attack. Unsure of what to do or where to go, she ended up picking up bread and cheese rolls in the kitchen and then heading to the library. She needed to do more research.

Besides, reading books would distract her from thoughts of Shadye.

"They won't get their hands on my books," the librarian said as she entered the darkened room. He and his female assistant–or fellow librarian; Emily had never been quite sure of the relationship between them–were frantically preparing additional defensive wards for the library. "I intend to seal them in a pocket dimension in the event of the school being destroyed. The Librarian's Guild will recover them and ensure they don't fall into enemy hands."

Emily nodded. Necromancers had raw power, but they often lacked proper training. If they had access to more information, they'd probably become far more dangerous–which was why the librarians had to be so careful. No librarian could ever countenance destroying books outright–she had a feeling that was why there were so many forbidden texts stored in Whitehall–yet they did have to do whatever it took to keep them out of enemy hands. The risk of losing the key to a pocket dimension was preferable to seeing them used by Shadye and his ilk.

The library itself held a handful of students, but Emily ignored them as she walked to the shelves and started to hunt for anything that touched on magical oaths. One day, she promised herself, she would have to introduce the Dewey Decimal System or something comparable to Whitehall; the system they used made little sense even to the librarians. There were times when she suspected that books were just put back on the shelves at random, either by students or the librarians. The former was understandable, if annoying; the latter should know better. Even the simple Library of Congress system would work better than the one they used at Whitehall.

She had to look carefully for *anything* on the fairies, even though she assumed they were related to the Faerie, who had built the Dark City. There seemed to be a surprising shortage of curiosity about them in the world, which seemed rather odd; *this* world had fought a war with the Faerie that had almost destroyed the human race. Or maybe the books were all stored in the restricted section ... it was quite possible that *someone* would be idiotic enough to try and duplicate the powers that birth had granted to the god-like Faerie, but she was sure that Whitehall would rather they did their experiments a long way from the school.

Finally, she pulled out a book on magical oaths and walked over to one of the tables to read it.

The book–*Magical Oaths and Those Who Swear*–was slim, as if the writer hadn't wanted to list every known example in history. Emily opened it and skimmed through the first few pages, swallowing the urge to swear out loud when she realized that the oath she'd sworn to the fairies had merged with her magic. The writer danced around the subject, almost as if he found himself reluctant to come straight out and say what he meant, but eventually she managed to put it all together. Failure to keep the oath, as she had already deduced, would mean death, or worse. It all depended on just how she acted. If she refused to carry out the oath, she would die; if she deliberately created a situation where she couldn't carry out the oath, she would die.

On the other hand, if she couldn't carry out the oath because of something that *wasn't* her fault, the magic wouldn't kill her. But she couldn't lie to herself, or to the magic. There was no way to avoid the oath deliberately.

Very few of the examples were reassuring. A young witch had sworn to marry her suitor when she returned from Whitehall, only to fall in love with another magician while studying in school. She'd tried to avoid the oath by using a love potion to convince her former lover to marry a girl from the village, but the magic had clearly considered that an attempt to evade the terms of her oath. The poor girl had died, badly. A stepfather had sworn to treat his adopted daughter like his own child. The book didn't know exactly what had happened next–or the writer hadn't dared write it down–but he'd died, seemingly at his own hand.

She had to smile at one of the other examples. An elderly warlock had a small retinue of slaves, all bound to him by magic; he'd made his son swear to free them upon his death. But the son had tried to evade his oath, only to end up bound by the same servitude spell that had gripped his father's servants. That too had ended badly. Shaking her head, Emily finished skimming through the book and nearly swore out loud–again–when she realized what she'd done. She'd effectively written the fairies a blank check, to be called in at any time. They could demand a favor from her and she'd have to give it to them, or die.

Or worse.

The thought made her blood run cold. They could ask for *anything*. Maybe they'd demand that she prevent humans from hunting them and grinding their bones for potion components, or maybe they'd demand that she integrate them into human society. Or ... it could be *anything*, and she would have to comply. Or die. She swallowed, cursing her own mistake, even though she knew there had been little choice. They could demand anything of her ...

*If it is too much, I will allow the oath to kill me*, she thought bitterly.

She pushed the thought aside and looked down at the book, wondering why no one was asked to swear an oath abjuring necromancy. Or could necromancers evade the terms of their oaths without suffering fatal consequences? She glanced through the book again until she guessed the answer from the writer's half-hearted hints; magicians regarded being asked to swear such an oath as insulting, dangerously so.

Even if Whitehall had introduced such an oath as part of the entrance conditions, other magical schools might not agree ... and the more powerful students, or the ones who were offended by the presumption that they might be tempted by necromancy, would go elsewhere. It might even tempt other magicians to mess with necromancy to prove they could handle it ...

... And *that* never ended well.

Emily stood up, mulling over the terms of the other oath, the one not to reveal anything about the fairies to anyone else. So far, no one had asked her how she'd managed to recover enough magic to attack the Orcs and rescue the Redshirts, but she knew the question would be asked soon enough. And she had the feeling that trying to lie to the Sergeants—or the Grandmaster—would be futile. Perhaps she could just write the answer down ... no, that would be dangerous. The oath would know she was cheating because *she* would know she was cheating. She'd have to come up with something better.

The sun was setting as she walked back down to the armory. Outside, the monsters were still waiting—and so was Shadye, still standing on the giant snake. Emily shook her head in disbelief. No one she'd met could be so patient, not when there were plenty of other things to do. The Sergeants took one look at her and ordered her to bed. They'd call her, they promised, if the school came under attack.

Shaking her head, Emily walked back to her bedroom, unsurprised to discover that Alassa had dragged in a set of blankets and lay on the floor, next to Imaiqah's bed. Both girls looked nervous; they'd been reading books on potions and complex spells in a desperate attempt to distract themselves. Emily reassured them as best as she could, even though she knew it would be futile, and crawled into her own bed, closing her eyes. Sleep overcame her and she plunged into darkness ...

And dreamed.

## Chapter Forty-Three

*SHE HAD TO MOVE. SHE KNEW THAT FOR A FACT, SOMETHING SO DEEPLY EMBEDDED IN HER mind that questioning was impossible.*

*She had to move.*

*And yet she could not move. Her legs felt as if they were trapped in concrete. Movement was impossible ...*

*... She was dreaming. She knew she was dreaming, believed it to be true. And yet something was wrong.*

*An alarm bell rang at the back of her mind, screaming an alert, but every time she tried to focus on it her mind slipped away. She knew something was wrong and yet she could do nothing.*

*It was a nightmare and nightmares had to be endured ...*

*... She stood up. In her dream, she saw nothing wrong with this, or with the fact that she still felt as if she couldn't move. Two contradictory things could be true at the same time in a dream, she knew, even if the logical part of her mind suggested otherwise. The alarm bell grew louder, but she could still do nothing. Her legs moved of their own accord as she walked to the doorway and stepped into the long hallway ...*

*... Blood was everywhere. There were nearly a hundred students in the strange stunted classes that made up the first year curriculum at Whitehall–and they were all dead. Her dazed mind believed it, without reservation, even as she tried to understand how she alone had survived to tell the world.*

*She caught sight of Melissa and her two friends, their bodies torn apart by giant monstrous claws, and felt nothing. Their eyes looked at her. Staring. Accusing. Judging. Something about the whole scene bothered her, but she couldn't understand what. A strange mist had fallen over her thoughts ...*

*... She was in shock, she told herself, and it seemed logical. No sane human being could look on a scene of mass slaughter and not feel horror and revulsion. She had to be in shock; later, she would remember what she'd seen and* feel *it. Melissa hadn't deserved to die like that, nor had her friends. How could anyone be blamed for wanting to strike back at Alassa?*

*Emily pushed the thought aside as she crept down the corridor towards the exit. Whitehall had been invaded; the tutors were dead, along with the rest of the students. She was on her own ...*

*... A demon rose up in front of her, snarling its fury. Emily lashed out with her magic, feeling power surge through her as if she were tapping the vast fields stored within the school itself. The demon stumbled backwards, hitting the floor with a mighty crash.*

*Emily stepped through the now demon-less door and out into the school itself. Blood and bodies lay everywhere; the monstrous army had torn through everyone in the school, even the youngest students. Emily pushed herself into the shadows as she heard monsters approaching, knowing that she didn't dare be seen. She was the last defender of Whitehall and she would see to it that the monsters paid for their crimes...*

*... She hadn't known about any secret passageways until she opened one of them, stepping into a darkened tunnel that led downwards - into the bowels of the school. She*

*walked down the stone corridor, glancing through peepholes that allowed her to see into different classrooms; the monsters had torn through the students in front of the tutors, before murdering the tutors and pinning them to the walls. Professor Thande had been beheaded and tipped upside down, his blood flowing to the floor; Professor Lombardi had been cut into a dozen pieces and scattered around his classroom. She was alone in the school, apart from the monsters ...*

*...Something was definitely wrong, but cold resolve pushed her doubts aside. Whitehall, her new home, the home she'd embraced so completely that she had never looked back, was dead. And all she could do was avenge it.*

*The sound of alarm bells grew louder, yet she thought nothing of them. All that mattered was extracting revenge. Even the discovery that one of the peepholes looked out into the changing rooms didn't distract her from her quest...*

*...She stepped out of the passageway, spells charged and primed, ready for the command to unleash themselves. There would be monsters blocking her path, she knew. They'd have to be killed and killed quickly, before they could summon reinforcements. But, instead, there were bodies scattered everywhere. Emily recoiled in horror as she realized that she was staring down at the last stand of the Redshirts. Jade had died from a sword wound to the throat that had almost beheaded him. Cat had been partially transfigured and then left to die of shock. Bran had a long spear rammed through his head. Rupert had been poisoned, judging by the look of agony on his face. And there was no sign of Pillion at all. It took her a long chilling moment to realize that his body had been blown apart and she was walking through the remains of her teammate. They'd fought bravely and they'd lost ...*

*... But something was wrong.*

*Emily stopped, staring at the bodies. Something was nagging at her mind, something so obvious that she should see it at once, and yet it was so hard to think clearly. What was wrong with her? Aside from shock.*

*A monster howled behind her. Startled, she headed towards the doors that led into the castle's deepest secret, the magical core that linked directly to the ley line nexus. The monsters would be sorry that they'd ever invaded Whitehall and slaughtered her friends. They would pay ...*

*... The door opened, revealing five necromancers. Emily reacted on instinct, unleashing the spells that she'd stored inside her body; they tumbled backwards. Waves of magic spun around her as she ran past them, heading towards the nexus, a source of mana so powerful that it took the most complex wards she'd ever seen to tap and use it for the school. Behind her, the necromancers were rallying, putting aside their differences to stop her; she found herself deflecting freeze spells and even a deadly killing curse without difficulty.*

*This had to be a dream ...*

*... She ran right into the wards, feeling something welling up from inside her, and the world went black...*

Emily's eyes snapped open. The Grandmaster was staring down at her, his face twisted with anger ... and fear. What was he doing in her bedroom?

No, she wasn't *in* her bedroom. Instead, she lay on the floor of a chamber she didn't recognize ...

... And something was very wrong. It took her a moment to realize the wards that had been an ever-present background noise since she had come to Whitehall were ... gone.

The Grandmaster hauled her bodily to her feet. "What have you done?"

Emily stared at him, confused and disoriented. She wore her nightgown, part of her mind noted. What had happened to her? The last thing she recalled was going to sleep and dreaming and ...

He shook her, raw magic crackling around his fingertips. "*What have you done?*"

"Sympathetic magic," Professor Thande said. Emily looked at him, feeling her head spinning. Wasn't he dead? She'd seen the body ... hadn't she? "Look at her hands, Grandmaster."

The Grandmaster caught Emily's left hand and wrenched it open, twisting it sharply enough for Emily to cry out in pain. There was a bloody mark on her hand, where she'd squeezed it so tightly that her nails had cut into her skin. She'd done it to herself ... her head, still spinning, couldn't cope with what she saw. If the Grandmaster hadn't held her upright, she would have collapsed and probably fainted on the stone floor.

"There were necromancers," she said, finally. But ... but necromancers *never* worked together for long–and none of them would want their rivals to gain control of Whitehall. "I saw necromancers ..."

"You nearly killed a dozen of my staff," the Grandmaster snarled. Emily stared at him, slowly realizing that her nightmare had been more than just a nightmare. "And the wards are coming down."

"She doesn't know, Grandmaster," Thande said patiently. "Very few top-rank magicians could master a protection against sympathetic magic once the caster had their hooks in them. A first-year student couldn't *hope* to defend herself."

Emily stared at him. "What ... what happened?"

"You were cut when you were kidnapped in Dragon's Den," the Grandmaster said bluntly. He relaxed his grip on her, just enough to allow her to breathe normally. "Malefic cut you and then left you alone, knowing you would escape. Once he'd killed his two allies, he took your blood to the necromancer, who used it to influence your mind. Whatever you thought you were seeing wasn't real. He used you as his puppet."

Emily ... felt soiled. Violated. She'd known that mind control spells existed; she'd seen them on her very first day in the new world. And yet, she had never really grasped the fact that she could be ... *influenced* by someone outside the school's wards. All the little practical jokes she'd learned were nothing compared to the delusion that had been inflicted on her ...

... It struck her, in a moment of horror, that she might have killed some of her friends. Shadye had woven a net around her mind and manipulated her as easily as she might manipulate a character in a computer game. And she hadn't known the difference.

"He used you to bring down the wards," Thande said. "The school is now defenseless."

"But..." Emily swallowed and started again. "But I thought there were spells to cut the link between me and my blood. Weren't they performed at the infirmary?"

"You *can't* sever the link completely," the Grandmaster said flatly. "All you can really do is ... weaken it to the point where it's effectively useless for magic. Kyla performed the spells to weaken the link at my request, but Shadye must have done something to ensure that the link could only be rendered dormant, not destroyed. And then he used it when the time was right."

Emily stared at him, realizing–for the first time–just how patiently Shadye had plotted and schemed ever since Void had snatched her from his clutches. Void had risked his life to save her, which meant that Emily had to be important–and everything she'd done since then only underlined her status as a Child of Destiny. And he had to have been *delighted* when his servants had kidnapped Alassa as well. No one would consider that Emily had been the prime target when the kidnappers had also walked away with a Royal Princess. But it had all been intended to obtain a sample of Emily's blood, then allow her to escape, never knowing that had been the plan all along. And Whitehall had performed the standard checks and *known* that Emily was safe ...

And then he'd forced her to betray Whitehall ...

The Grandmaster frowned. "I am going to have to scan your mind," he said. "Please try to relax. It can be painful if you fight."

Emily had no time to object before he locked eyes with her. She found herself unable to look away. The sense of being violated returned, a thousand times stronger, as she felt the Grandmaster rummage through her thoughts. Oddly, the sense of being isolated from her own mind, as if she were looking down at herself from the outside, allowed her to see the subtle tendrils Shadye had crafted and spun into her mind. And how her own mind, responding to his prompts, had created a scenario powerful enough to keep her enthralled until it was far too late.

"I'm going to have to cut those links," the Grandmaster said - or thought. Their minds were so entangled that Emily honestly couldn't tell the difference. Mr. Spock couldn't have done a better job. "And you really shouldn't have sworn that oath."

Emily winced, expecting immediate death. But she hadn't intended to betray the fairies–she hadn't realized that the Grandmaster intended to scan her mind in time to say anything–and the oath didn't seem to consider it a breach of contract. And yet she had still failed ...

"Don't worry about it," the Grandmaster ordered. "There is little need for fairies to be slaughtered, save for spells that"–there was a hint of hesitation–"you are really too young to know about. I will keep their secret."

Emily smiled, but didn't relax. "Will you swear an oath to that effect?"

"Smart people try to avoid swearing oaths," the Grandmaster said. There was a moment as he peered into the delusions her mind had created. "You were a tool in the hands of a necromancer with power and knowledge."

"I feel bad enough already," Emily snapped. Mind-to-mind, there was no way to conceal anything from him, or to swallow her tongue before she said anything. She flushed hotly, embarrassed; it was a feeling that was only made worse by his shimmer of amusement. "Can you stop him from doing it again?"

"Yes," the Grandmaster said patiently. There was a moment when he seemed to be working directly on her mind. "It is done."

Emily felt her head spin one final time, just as Thande pushed a potion-filled gourd into her hand . He urged her to drink it. It tasted foul—all medical potions tasted foul, for some reason—but as soon as she swallowed the first drops she felt a great deal better.

But she couldn't rest for long. A clanging alarm in the distance brought her to her feet—without any clear memory of how she'd once again been on the floor—and reaching for her sword before remembering that she was in her nightgown. At least she was decent, thankfully. One of the ones she'd considered wearing back home would have shocked local opinion.

"The outer wards are gone," the Grandmaster said, quietly. "The spells that redirected the power of the nexus are collapsing. It won't be long before the inner wards are gone too."

Emily stared down at her bloodstained hands, knowing she had failed. She'd *loved* Whitehall far more than any other school she'd attended, for it had given her a chance at a very different life. The tutors hadn't treated her as an idiot, nor had they been idiots themselves. Even the harsh discipline seemed unimportant compared to what she had learned to do.

But she'd betrayed the school. There was no way they'd let her attend another magic school after this, assuming she survived the next few hours. The scenarios her mind had constructed might come true after all. Shadye would want to capture as many of the students as possible—he could sacrifice them to boost his power—but he wouldn't want to risk capturing the tutors. They knew enough magic to be dangerous.

"I'm sorry," she said, finally. It seemed so inadequate. "I ... I didn't know ..."

"Very few people could have realized what was going on and broken free," Professor Thande assured her. "You are *far* from alone."

The Grandmaster stood up. "Professor Thande, I need you to start evacuating the younger students through the portals. The school's interior dimensions are based on different spells, so they should remain stable until the necromancers reach this room and start trying to fiddle with the wards. I'll have Whitehall open sealed corridors for the students to escape."

"I have war potions brewing in my office," Thande said. He sounded ... reluctant to run. "I can't leave the building ..."

"You can return once the younger students are out of here," the Grandmaster said. There was no give in his voice at all. "The building's interior defenses are still intact–Shadye wouldn't have known about them when he was a student–so we should be able to put up a good fight, but we have to assume the worst."

There was a bleakness in his voice that almost crushed Emily's soul. Whitehall was the linchpin of the southern defenses. If it fell, the necromancers would be able to ravage at least eight countries before they ran into more natural barriers to their expansion. The Allied Lands would be weakened, perhaps crippled, even if they *did* finally put all of their differences aside and unite behind a single monarch.

And it was all her fault.

She looked up suddenly. "Shadye was a student here?"

"There was a ... difference of opinion," the Grandmaster said. "He left the school and vanished. It was a long time before he resurfaced and longer still before we realized that Shadye had once been one of our students."

Emily looked back down at her hands. "So you know his name," she said. "Couldn't you ..."

"Not enough of it to matter," the Grandmaster admitted. "And even if we did, he knows how to ward himself. Using his full name against him is unlikely to work."

He turned and marched to the door. "I can't put you on the front lines. Shadye is crafty and has plenty of raw power, perhaps enough to re-establish a link between his sample of your blood and *you*. We cannot take the risk."

Emily hesitated, then nodded once, bitterly. *She* wouldn't have trusted herself either, because there was no easy way to know if she was acting of her own will, or if Shadye was mentally influencing her until she thought that stabbing the Grandmaster in the back was a good idea. Shadye could twist her mind to the point where she could become convinced that black was white, right was wrong and monarchy was actually a viable governing system.

"I'm going to put you in my office," he said as they left the chamber. There were bloodstains on the floor where she had fought the demons, unaware that she was smashing her way through tutors. Naturally, there were no bodies *outside* the chamber. "You can wait there until the battle is won, or I order you to run. They won't allow you through the portal so you'll have to flee into the countryside and hope that your patron picks you up."

Emily scowled. It was unlikely that Void would want anything to do with her after she'd been so badly compromised.

"We could call him," she suggested instead. "Wouldn't he help?"

"If we cannot use the interior defenses to hold Shadye back until he exhausts himself," the Grandmaster admitted, "we'd just be bringing him more targets."

"But..." Emily changed her mind and returned to the original subject. "But don't you think that he could influence me in your office?"

The Grandmaster smirked. "I never keep anything of importance there," he admitted. At her look of surprise, he snorted. "Do you know how much time sorcerers spend spying on each other? They can ransack my office all they like and all they'll get out of it is a chance to learn a great deal about codes and devious spelling. You can't cause any harm there."

## Chapter Forty-Four

The Grandmaster's office seemed smaller than Emily remembered, but perhaps that was due to her sense of being confined. One glance at the bookshelves revealed nothing of great interest, beyond a transfiguration textbook that looked alarmingly dog-eared. The portraits on the wall would probably have been instantly recognizable to a native of this world, but meant nothing to Emily. On impulse, she checked his desk drawers for security spells, and discovered that they were crawling with particularly unpleasant charms. The Grandmaster clearly intended to make any intruder work for his useless knowledge.

"You can use the crystal ball, if you like," the Grandmaster had said, before leaving her alone. He hadn't exactly locked the door, but he'd made it clear that she wasn't to leave until the situation became desperate. Emily had been tempted to point out that the situation had already gone *beyond* desperate, but had held her tongue. "Keep an eye on the corridor leading up to my office."

The crystal ball included charms and infused spells that took her some time to work out how to activate. It seemed to draw power directly from the user, which—she decided—was one way to ensure that someone didn't waste their time spying on people rather than doing something useful.

*And perhaps if televisions required someone to power them by running on a treadmill,* she thought darkly, *they would be less addictive.*

The Grandmaster hadn't bothered to explain any of it, perhaps believing that figuring it out would keep Emily busy for a while. He was probably right.

She felt the school's remaining protections fall away, one by one. The Grandmaster might have started to work on restoring what she'd destroyed, but she had a feeling that it would take hours—perhaps days—before the wards were back up and running. Building wards was something that she hadn't even touched upon, yet she knew enough from books to understand that wards could be very complex and difficult to erect. Guilt tore at her mind before she finally managed to push some power into the crystal ball.

No matter what happened, she would always bear some of the blame for what had happened to Whitehall. The failing had been hers.

The crystal ball lit up, displaying a dozen different scenes. When she pressed her fingers against it, the ball focused the view on the invading army. A horde of heavily-armed Orcs advanced through the gardens, weapons at the ready, only to run right into a horde of bees from the beehives. The Orcs stumbled backwards in dismay as the tiny creatures stung at them, only to rally and advance again.

*Of course,* Emily realized; *their skins are so tough that the bees could barely hurt them.*

The beehives were rapidly destroyed, leaving the bees buzzing angrily around the Orcs or raging off towards the rest of the army. Perhaps they'd sting Shadye and put an end to it before it went any further.

She shook her head. There was no way it would be that easy.

A moment later, a dozen Orcs stumbled and fell to the ground. CT reared up in front of them, his giant eye ablaze with fury as tentacles grew out of his body and sliced through the Orcs, ripping them to shreds. They cut back with their swords, but they couldn't make any impression on CT - a creature that seemed to be made of jelly. Eventually, they fell back as CT advanced menacingly, growing new weapons out of his body ...

And then a bolt of light from Shadye struck CT and froze him solid. Wary now, the remaining Orcs launched fire arrows into the zoo and then fell back. They'd missed their chance to come face to face with a *real* Mimic.

Shadye's forces advanced against the walls, firing arrows to force the defenders to keep their heads down. Emily couldn't understand why Shadye wasn't using his magic to simply punch a hole through the walls until she realized that there was so much magic running through the stone that destroying it would be difficult–and if he succeeded, he might accidentally cause the school to explode as a vastly larger interior tried to expand into a much smaller exterior. Giant spiders ran past his army, scuttling along the ground, then started to crawl *up* the walls.

Emily stared in horror. As a child, she had been deathly afraid of spiders and had been relieved to discover that they couldn't grow very big without being unable to move. The necromancers, it seemed, had managed to produce spiders which defied whatever law that usually prevented spiders from growing that big ...

Streaks of light blasted down from the battlements, smashing the spiders and sending their bodies falling to the ground. Emily pulled the crystal ball back and saw students, led by Professor Lombardi, propelling items into the enemy army at terrifying speed.

Shadye countered, one by one, but there seemed to be an inexhaustible supply of ammunition. His archers moved their attention to the students, only to see their arrows deflected by a handful of other students who were maintaining a magical barrier. Necromancers never worked together, Emily remembered; cooperation was the only real advantage the good guys had.

Shadye threw back projectiles of his own, including one that slammed into the ward so hard it shattered. Several students were knocked back with blood pouring from their ears and noses. They'd fuelled the ward directly, and the feedback had almost killed them.

While they were distracted, a second set of spiders crawled up the battlements, leaving sticky webs behind them. A small army of Goblins followed, a handful being crushed when a student knocked down a spider which landed on top of them.

But it didn't matter, Emily realized. Shadye seemed to have an inexhaustible supply of cannon fodder.

The giant spiders reached the battlements and slashed into the defenders with teeth and claws, followed by a trio of creatures that looked like a cross between dragons and griffins. A handful of older students met them, lashing out with powerful curses and hexes that sent one of the creatures falling to its doom. The other two breathed green smoke at the defenders, who started to choke and collapse on the ground.

Emily winced in pain. She'd been careful not to introduce the concept of poison gas, knowing that it would suit the necromancers perfectly, but they'd thought of it without her.

Inch by inch, the attackers cleared the battlements while keeping the lower defenders pinned inside the building. They brought up more of their army and prepared to invade the interior of Whitehall from above.

Emily switched the crystal ball's focus to find Sergeant Harkin. The two Sergeants led the defense of the lower levels, backed up by almost every Martial Magic student in the school. Emily prayed that they managed to hold out. A handful of students used *Berserker*, passing the baton to other students as they tired and crawled back for energy potions that had been prepared by Alchemy students. It wasn't something she'd have thought of them doing; presumably, it was a tactic only used in the direst of emergencies. Using so many energy potions so quickly could be very dangerous for the hapless students. They'd been warned, specifically, never to take more than one at a time.

She looked back at the battlements, just in time to see an Orc pry open one of the doors. A brilliant flash of magic flung the Orc off the roof. The defenders hadn't retreated far at all; they'd set up traps that forced Shadye to expend men and magic to burn his way into the castle. But Shadye seemed more inclined to waste men than magic. Emily watched as the gas-breathing creatures stuck their heads through the doors and spewed green mist into the school. A moment later, one of the creatures twitched and fell over, crushing a pair of Orcs as it hit the rooftop. It took Emily several minutes to work out that someone had cast a botched transfiguration–like she'd done to Alassa–on the creature and killed it instantly.

Shadye drifted up onto the roof, produced a fireball with one hand and threw it down into the building. It was too powerful for the defenders, who stumbled backwards, allowing the monsters to charge into the building itself.

Emily cursed aloud as she saw the Orcs crashing down into the upper levels. She tried to switch the crystal ball around, hoping to confirm that her friends were out of the school. There was no sign of Alassa or Imaiqah anywhere within the crystal ball's range. She hoped they were alive ...

Inch by inch, the Orcs advanced into the school. They ran into all kinds of defenses intended to slow them down and force Shadye to waste power. Suits of armor came to life and advanced towards them with drawn swords. When they fell, they reassembled and continued the fight. When some suits were wrecked completely, their components linked up with others and kept fighting. They had to be reduced to their component atoms to stop them from tearing through more of the Orcs.

If Shadye hadn't been there, Emily would have had no doubts that Whitehall could defeat the Orcs. They were *dumb*; blundering constantly into traps then charging forward in the belief that brute force could clear the way. Keyed transfiguration spells stopped a handful of them dead in their tracks and, when they were pushed out of the way, the second set of spells turned the advancing Orcs into dust. A skilled team of mages would have taken hours, perhaps days, to clear the corridors; Shadye settled for scorching the entire corridor with his magic, wiping out everything that *could* be a threat. His flames even eradicated a handful of his Orcs!

She heard the orders barked through the mirrors the school's defenders were using to coordinate their actions, orders that made no sense to her. But Shadye might be spying on the defenders now that the wards were gone; they used code phases to issue orders to prevent him from taking action to impede the retreat.

Emily looked back at the Sergeants in time to see Sergeant Miles generate a firestorm that swept a dozen Orcs and Goblins out of the building. The remaining students fell back, sealing the doors as they left. Sergeant Miles, breathing heavily and supported by Sergeant Harkin, was the last one out of the abandoned armory. The Orcs would have to crack their way through solid stone to get further into the building.

Whitehall's strange interior started to come into play. She watched as a dozen Orcs advanced into an empty corridor and walked towards the exit ... and walked towards the exit ... and walked towards the exit, not realizing that the interior dimensions had been warped so they were effectively walking in a circle. Three Goblins walked down a corridor when the floor vanished and they fell, plunging hundreds of meters to their deaths. Another set of Orcs walked through a door and found themselves back on the roof, just before their successors pushed them over the edge. Giant statues of famous witches and wizards came to life and directed spells at the invaders, all powered by the castle's interior wards.

They were all buying time, Emily realized, for the defenders to set up interior defense lines.

But Shadye kept coming. He no longer looked human at all and his will was exerting itself on the fabric of the school. Emily could *feel* the school scream in pain as Shadye reached out to impose himself, twisting the interior into something more suitable for his plans. Whitehall was intelligent, in a way, and it could be harmed - or brainwashed into compliance. It struck Emily suddenly that Shadye's ultimate objective wasn't to destroy Whitehall, but to *take* it–and the nexus it used as a power source.

Why destroy the school when he could mould it in his own image?

She flashed back to the nightmarish scenes Shadye had used to push her into destroying the wards. They were going to come true, she realized as the school continued to scream its pain into her mind, into the mind of every magician in the building. Whitehall was going to be shattered, twisted into a foul abomination of everything it had once stood for, and all of the remaining students were going to die to grant Shadye a few extra months of life.

Or maybe he'd do something worse. If he could twist *her* mind–whatever advantages he'd had through her being unique in this world–why couldn't he do the same to others? He could bind and twist the students and turn them into his slaves. What happened if someone was forced to swear an oath to obey at gunpoint? Could Shadye overcome the insistent necromantic infighting by forcing his followers to swear oaths of loyalty?

Emily shook her head, then she felt a dull rumble running through the school. Shadye now clashed directly against the Grandmaster, pressing his will–backed by awesome power–against the Grandmaster's natural supply of *mana*. Emily sought the Grandmaster via the crystal ball and found him stumbling down a corridor, fighting desperately to keep Shadye from turning the school against him.

She knew that the portals leading out of Whitehall had been closed. The remainder of the students and tutors were trapped, unless they managed to flee through the enemy army and escape into the mountains. But one glance at the forces surrounding the school suggested that would be a very difficult task.

How had Shadye managed to slip so many monsters close to the school without being detected? Had he carved hundreds of tunnels into the mountains and hidden his monsters there for months?

Shadye looked up. For a moment, she had the sense that his red eyes were looking right at her, through the crystal ball. She saw him wave his hand in a complicated gesture. Magic burned through the air.

Emily threw herself away from the crystal ball a moment before it exploded, throwing shards of glass everywhere. It was sheer luck that none of them struck her...

... And then she realized the significance of what had happened. Shadye had sensed her spying on him and now he knew where she was. If he still thought she was important ...

The situation had definitely become desperate.

She pulled herself to her feet and ran to the door. Outside, she heard the sounds of fighting in the distance and felt the magic field tingling as Shadye and the Grandmaster warred for control of the school. Glancing over at one of the suits of armor, she removed its sword and hefted it, wincing at the weight. It was too heavy for her to carry easily, but there was no other choice. Looking up into the masked helm, she had the unmistakable feeling that *something* inhuman was looking back at her. She had the feeling of being measured, then she was finally allowed to take the sword and go. Unable to avoid the sense that she had barely escaped with her life, she walked down the corridor, carrying the sword as carefully as she could. The temptation to shoulder it had been almost overpowering.

A roar made her jump as she turned the corner. A trio of Orcs advanced on her–and, behind them, she saw an elderly man carrying a staff. It was Malefic, the Dark Wizard who had kidnapped her as an elaborate cover for stealing a sample of her blood. And, perhaps, the one who had treated it to make it impossible to completely separate it from her body.

She lifted her sword threateningly and readied *Berserker* in her mind. If she was going to die, she would not go down without a fight.

Malefic stopped the Orcs and stepped past them, raising his staff. Emily got her defensive charm up barely in time as a fireball appeared out of nowhere and slammed right into her ward. Flames shimmered in front of her, licking away at her defenses.

She realized, almost too late, that the flames were consuming her power. She jumped backwards and cast a spell on the sword, throwing it at Malefic. The Dark Wizard stepped aside and the sword impaled two of the Orcs, carrying them with it as it flashed down the corridor and crashed into a distant wall. She hadn't told the spell when to stop. Before Malefic could react, she pushed the ward outwards and slammed it into the third Orc. The creature's loincloth caught fire and it turned, running for its life. Emily laughed out loud as it slammed into a wall and collapsed next to its friends.

There was a shimmer of magic. Malefic threw a spell at her she didn't recognize; she quickly jumped aside, cursing her mistake. She should never have taken her eyes off him!

She tossed a fireball back at him, only to see him snap it out of the air with his hand and crush it, as if it were no more threatening than the Mimic she'd conjured up to scare the Orcs. Emily didn't wait for him to throw another spell; she generated a ball of light, a very simple spell, making it as bright as she could. She squeezed her eyes shut as she threw it at Malefic.

The Dark Wizard screamed. He stumbled backwards as the light vanished, grasping at his eyes.

Emily cast a stunning spell and threw it at him, watching as he tumbled to the floor. It looked as if blood was leaking from his eyeballs.

Dear God, how badly had she hurt him?

And yet it was hard for her to care. Malefic had hurt her, and Alassa, and the school. Didn't he deserve a little of his own back?

She froze as she heard the sound of someone clapping, very slowly and deliberately, from behind her. Bracing herself, Emily turned ... because she already knew who was there. Who *must* be there.

Shadye.

## Chapter Forty-Five

EMILY TURNED SLOWLY, RAISING HER WARDS EVEN THOUGH SHE KNEW THEY WOULDN'T stand up to Shadye. All he had to do to overpower her was throw enough magic at her wards to knock them down through simple brute force. He stood several meters in front of her, his face hidden under a dark hood that seemed to swallow all light. He no longer looked human; looking at his robe, Emily had the sense that his body was slowly mutating into something else. A vague feeling pervaded her mind that if she looked too closely she wouldn't be able to look away.

"You have grown, since we last met," Shadye said. His voice sounded inhuman too, a dull rasp that seemed to come out of nowhere. "I expected no less from a Child of Destiny."

Raw power crackled in the air around Shadye, the necromancer who had stamped his will on Whitehall and on the surrounding environment. He seemed to be almost *composed* of magic now, completely dependent on sacrifices to stay alive. Some of the books she'd read had speculated that a necromancer would eventually manage to store enough power to stay alive permanently without requiring additional sacrifices.

Emily found herself silently praying that they were wrong, even as she stood there, trying to fight down the panic that threatened to overwhelm her.

*Distract him*, part of her mind yammered. *Keep him busy while you think*!

She cleared her throat. "How did you manage to control me?"

"Our first meeting in three months and *that's* your question?" Shadye asked. He sounded inordinately amused, as if she'd said something funny. "I have a sample of your blood, remember?"

"But we cut the ties between it and me," she protested. Or the healers had *tried*, at least. "How did you use it to manipulate me?"

Shadye snorted. "You're not from this world. There is no one else like you anywhere in this universe. Your blood is unique. Diffusing the link between you and your blood won't break the connection permanently."

Emily cursed under her breath. It should have occurred to her *before* it was too late, even if it wouldn't have occurred to Kyla or anyone else who didn't know where she'd come from. Shadye was right. She *was* unique. There would be no relatives to make it difficult, if not impossible, to target the spell precisely. Shadye had thought of something completely out of left field, but she should have thought of it, too. All the ideas she'd brought into this world ... but she hadn't come up with the one that would have saved Whitehall from destruction.

Shadye stepped forward.

Emily stumbled backwards, unwilling to be too close to him.

The necromancer stopped in front of Malefic and looked down at the stunned Dark Wizard, his expression hidden by the cowl. He reached down after a moment and cast a spell Emily didn't recognize. Malefic jerked once, then returned to his enforced slumber.

"He failed me," Shadye said. "I do not tolerate failure."

"Of course you don't," Emily said, still backing away. "How did you tolerate yourself when I escaped your clutches?"

Shadye laughed unpleasantly. "Do you really believe that you managed to escape without my permission?"

He continued before Emily could say a word. "I *permitted* you to leave, knowing that you would upset the balance of power in the Allied Lands. And you have played your role magnificently. Political chaos in one of the most important Kingdoms in the world will weaken them to the point where my puppets can take power and shatter the Allied Lands."

His voice darkened. "And I knew that I could use you to bring down the wards protecting Whitehall. You have been my puppet all along."

Emily stared at him, her thoughts churning madly. He was lying. He *had* to be lying. How could he have predicted everything from Void's rescue to her rivalry - then friendship - with Alassa? Or, for that matter, how did he know that she would go into partnership with one of the other girls from the school? Or that she would actually know something of use to this world? Emily had been far from an ignorant girl, like the cheerleaders she'd known from back home, but she'd still found herself having to reinvent the wheel–or the printing press–with only the vaguest knowledge of their principles.

If Shadye had wanted to influence the world, he might have done better if he'd kidnapped a professor of medieval history and the early industrial age, or someone with a background in engineering and chemistry. Emily could have easily failed to introduce anything.

"A Child of Destiny as a puppet," Shadye gloated. "How could I fail to win?"

Cold logic told her that Shadye was lying. She clung to the thought as the necromancer stepped over Malefic's body and strode towards her. There was no way he could have predicted everything, or he wouldn't have needed her to introduce new factors into an already unstable situation. And besides, it was impossible to look into the future and glean anything but the vaguest hints of what might come.

Both science and magic agreed on that point.

But when she looked up at Shadye, she realized that it didn't matter. The necromancer believed every word he said.

She shivered as she backed away, creeping down the corridor.

Shadye had a strong personality; he *had* to have a strong personality, or necromancy would have killed him long ago. But he couldn't allow himself to doubt, or question, for fear of losing himself. And that meant that every reversal he suffered had to be explained, at least to himself, as just another part of his plan. He had to *believe* that he wanted his enemies to score a local victory–and that this victory would lead to their defeat.

Offhand, she couldn't recall if such a scheme had ever worked outside comic books.

*But I'm not a Child of Destiny,* her mind insisted. She could tell Shadye that, but he would ignore her. He took her successes in upsetting the world as proof that she *was* a Child of Destiny.

Besides, what would he do if he ever found out the truth? Would he consider that to be part of his grand plan too?

"Right," she said after a long pause. "And I assume that you're about to sacrifice me to the powers of darkness?"

Shadye chuckled, humorlessly. "I have far more ... interesting uses for a Child of Destiny than just another sacrifice," he said sardonically. "Instead, you will become a necromancer and join me as we crush the Allied Lands."

Emily stared at him in horror. If he truly believed that, maybe he *had* intended to lure Void into rescuing her, knowing she would be his Trojan Horse. But if that was the case, why would he need Malefic to secure some of Emily's blood? He could have taken it from her before she woke up in his prison cell.

*No,* she told herself firmly; he *had* to have improvised a new plan once she'd been plucked out of his grasp. Even Batman couldn't come up with such a plan right from the start and expect it to work.

But Shadye was insane. And therefore unpredictable.

"You want to change things," Shadye whispered. "You are a Child of Destiny, born to change the world. With necromancy, you will be able to change the world in ways beyond your imagination."

*And go insane doing it,* Emily thought.

The awful temptation gnawed at her soul. There was no way she could win a straight duel with Shadye, not one that matched their respective powers directly against each other; he was *vastly* more powerful than any other magician she'd met. If she fought, Shadye would win–and then finish the task of destroying Whitehall. And once she was drained, she would be completely helpless. No doubt Shadye would have some special way to re-educate her if she refused to do as he wanted.

But if she tapped into necromancy herself, she would be as powerful as he–and she already knew she had tricks that no one from this world had ever seriously considered. Using light as a weapon? She could make a laser beam if she tried, one that would go through most wards because they weren't configured to block the light. Or she could transfigure the air around her target into poison gas, or produce hydrogen from water ... she'd even had a half-formed idea for producing *gold* from seawater. She could beat him...

...But if she did that, she'd lose her soul.

No one had *ever* survived contact with necromancy without going mad, often unaware that they *were* going mad until it was far too late. Of course; they had no real way to monitor their own brains for madness. And if their universe was changing and all the tools they had to measure the universe were changing as well?

She believed, firmly, that royal birth didn't equate to anything special, but necromancy could change that opinion ... and she wouldn't even notice.

The temptation danced in front of her, mocking her. There *had* to be another way to beat him, but she couldn't think of anything she could produce quickly enough. If she refused his *gift*, he would take her anyway and then continue destroying Whitehall, sacrificing the remaining students to power his magic. But if she accepted his gift, she would become a worse threat than any ordinary necromancer because of all she knew. And because of her friends. She might end up reprogramming Alassa to deliberately destroy her Kingdom once she assumed the throne.

An idea struck her. "No," she said, hoping that it would distract him from what she was doing. "You will never turn me to the Dark Side. I am a Jedi, like my father before me."

It was a bad example for all kinds of reasons, but it would mean nothing to the necromancer. Luke Skywalker's father had been a Jedi–and a bratty teenager–and he *had* turned to the Dark Side, which made it a very *stupid* example, although it was very dramatic. And in some of the Expanded Universe comics, the ones she preferred to forget existed, Luke had joined his father as a servant of the Dark Side. And she was pretty sure that necromancy was even more seductive and dangerous than the Dark Side of the Force. The Emperor would have been infinitively preferable to a necromancer who had to sacrifice his own people to survive.

Shadye seemed ... surprised. "You were a powerful magician back home?"

"Something like that," Emily lied. She composed the charm in her head. "I come from a place where there were far worse dangers than you."

"I'm sure there were," Shadye said as he took another step forward. "But your father is far from here."

"My father is dead," Emily said. She released the charm. "Die!"

A blazing beam of light tore into Shadye's wards. She felt his power come to life as he attempted to defend himself, even though he might not be truly aware of what she was doing to him. She saw, just for a second, that his robes had blown away, revealing something so horrible that her mind refused to process it properly ...

Then she released the second charm. A direct assault was unlikely to succeed–Shadye had enough raw power to bat away almost anything–but he might not be prepared for something as simple as a practical joke. The hex caused limited forgetfulness, just enough to confuse someone in a duel ...

For a moment, she thought that she'd succeeded.

And then Shadye waved his hand at her, summoned a gust of wind and used it to blow her down the corridor.

Emily grunted in pain as she slammed into the wall next to the Orcs, half-convinced that she'd broken something. Desperately, she pulled herself to her feet -

- As Shadye started to advance on her, his red eyes burning brightly in the darkness of his cowl. Brilliant energy sparkled around his hands–which looked almost like claws now, she saw–and flashed out at her.

Malevolent energy crawled towards her, but Emily managed to throw herself out of the way. The flickering pulses of balefire crawled over the walls, cracking the solid stone and leaving black scorch marks in their wake.

Shadye seemed to have given up on the idea of taking her alive.

"You cannot escape your destiny," Shadye informed her. "You will be mine."

Emily ran.

The corridor twisted around her and she found herself running right *towards* Shadye. *Of course*, her mind noted with an odd detachment as she skidded to a halt. She shouldn't have been surprised. Shadye had forced his will on the castle's very structure. There was no reason why he couldn't force it to keep Emily trapped, or the rest of the students until he needed them.

Shadye reached towards her.

Emily backed off, only to run into a wall that hadn't been there before. The necromancer snickered as she started to press back into the wall, unable to escape.

"You will learn respect for your tutor and master," Shadye said. His red eyes promised no mercy. He would reach into her brain and rewrite it at will. "You will join me."

Desperation gave her inspiration. She threw a hex she'd learned in Martial Magic at Shadye, knowing that he would have no difficulty warding it off. But it gave her time to use her magic to pick up a piece of debris and throw it at him with considerable speed.

The debris struck the necromancer's wards hard enough to send him staggering backwards His wards held, but they weren't able to contain the kinetic force that powered the piece of debris.

Emily took her opportunity and jumped past him, hoping to escape his field of influence before it was too late. She picked up and threw other pieces of debris at him, before almost running right into another stone wall. The corridor had suddenly become a dead end.

What could she do? What else did she know? Nothing came to mind.

A moment later, she felt the strength drain out of her body.

"These games are amusing," Shadye proclaimed, from behind her, "but they are at an end."

Emily felt her body turn around, moving of its own accord. Shadye held a tiny glass vial in one hand, one that contained a reddish liquid. The subtle magic flickering around it was enough to tell her, if she hadn't already guessed, that it was her blood. She'd been asleep the last time he'd controlled her, and she hadn't been able to fight. This time, she was awake—but it made no difference. Her body did as Shadye's will commanded and, no matter how much she struggled, it refused to break free.

The Grandmaster had said he had protected her. But he'd been wrong.

"You *will* become my servant. My slave," Shadye said. He was unmistakably gloating now, enjoying his triumph. "Your unique talents will be bent to serve me. And though you will become a necromancer, you will still be mine. You will never grow to supplant me."

Emily shuddered, remembering the concepts she'd tossed around for a magical processor. It might not have been immediately workable, but Aloha's friends had been making progress—and, at least in theory, a magical processor would be able to process vast amounts of *mana* without going insane. And then there were the inherent possibilities in splitting atoms. If someone could build a makeshift atomic bomb using magic, they could wreak vast devastation on the world.

It occurred to her that she could try to encourage Shadye to build one, in the hope that he would accidentally blow himself up while testing the device, but the plan might not work. If *she* had been controlling another magician, she would ensure that the magician couldn't act, directly or indirectly, against her. She had to believe that Shadye would be equally prudent.

Shadye tossed the vial of blood from hand to hand, taunting her. "On your knees," he hissed. "Show your tutor proper respect."

She struggled, desperately, but knew it was futile. Her body sank to its knees, moving down until her head was touching the floor in full prostration, a position of total submission. Shadye stepped forward and placed his foot on the back of her neck; Emily cringed, expecting him to push down, before he walked away from her. But she couldn't move.

She smelled the Orcs coming up behind her before they came into view and picked up Malefic. The stunned Dark Wizard was powerless to escape. They carted him off to an unknown destination. Emily suspected he would meet his end on the sacrificial table.

"Stand," Shadye ordered.

Emily's body obeyed, even as she searched for ways to beat his control. There *had* to be a way to counter it, or whoever had first invented blood magic would still be ruling the world. *Maybe they were*, part of her mind whispered in a desperate attempt to distract herself; Alassa had mentioned a Royal Bloodline, after all. And there was powerful magic woven into other royal families as well, according to the books. Some of them were even stranger than Alassa's family.

"Follow," Shadye said.

He led her down a flight of stairs and past a small pile of bodies, both human and monster. The defenders had sold their lives dearly, but in the end they'd lost–and died. Emily felt tears welling up in her eyes as she remembered how the scenes of an utterly destroyed school had manipulated her - the scenes that Shadye had made real.

She caught sight of a dead body–a fifth-year student she vaguely recognized–and wanted to be sick. But Shadye's control over her body was so powerful that she couldn't even retch.

*Don't panic*, part of her mind insisted. *Study the problem, find the magic, then counter it.*

But it seemed futile.

The dining hall had been almost untouched by the fighting, she saw, as Shadye led her into the hall. He'd turned it into a prison camp as a dozen students and a pair of tutors were held in chains, guarded by a handful of Orcs. They didn't seem to be resisting, but the Orcs had beaten them savagely anyway. They were wearing anti-magic shackles. Escape was impossible.

And one of the wounded tutors was Sergeant Harkin.

# Chapter Forty-Six

"YOU WILL SACRIFICE ONE OF MY PRISONERS," SHADYE SAID. HIS HISSING VOICE BROKE INTO Emily's panicked thoughts. "His power will be added to your own."

Emily stared helplessly at the Sergeant. Even the thought–the repugnance - of killing a man she respected, even liked, wasn't enough to break the bonds Shadye had put on her mind. And she had a feeling that after she took the first draught of necromantic power, she would no longer want to stop. Necromancers were literally addicted to the surge of power they enjoyed as they killed their victims.

The Sergeant was beaten bloody. One of his arms had clearly been broken, but his one visible eye was bright and calculating. Emily thought she saw understanding, even forgiveness, in his brown eye before he looked up at the necromancer. Shadye didn't seem to intimidate him, even though Shadye was powerful enough to reduce the Sergeant to ashes with a wave of his hand. Or maybe Harkin was just very good at controlling his reactions.

Shadye loomed closer, but Emily couldn't even flinch away as he reached into his robe and produced a stone knife with eerie black runes carved into the blade. Emily felt her hand reach out as he held it towards her. No matter how much she screamed inside, her body was going to take the knife ... her hand closed around the hilt. The knife felt...evil, utterly repulsive, the moment she touched it. It was no ordinary knife, but one crafted specifically for necromancy. The charms on the blade helped to direct the surge of *mana* from the victim into the necromancer.

"Choose one," Shadye ordered, turning to study his captives. "Choose one to die - and the others will live."

Emily found that she could talk again. "You'd let them live?"

"I will not kill them," Shadye said. He looked back at her. "I swear upon my power that I will release them into the forest, free to make their way back into the Allied Lands."

Emily felt cold. *He* had sworn the oath, knowing that once Emily was tainted by necromancy she would want to kill them herself. And even if she didn't kill them, the journey back to Dragon's Den–let alone further north–would be through lands infested with monsters. They might well die anyway, but there would be no deliberate breach of his oath.

A thought struck her. She could tell him about the fairies, deliberately breaking her own oath in the certain knowledge that it would kill her. He wouldn't let her try to kill herself, she suspected, but he wouldn't realize that she'd sworn a binding oath until it was too late. And then he would be deprived of her services ...

She opened her mouth to say it, then hesitated. Suicide would be the end of everything. Even now, she couldn't take that final step.

"Choose one," Shadye repeated. He sounded ... *impatient.* And to think that he'd waited patiently for her to go to sleep so he could manipulate her mind. "Choose one to die and the others will live."

Emily felt her hand shiver where it grasped the knife's hilt, but her hand didn't move. Shadye didn't seem inclined to puppet her body in order to kill one of the captives. This was puzzling until she realized that necromancy was a deeply personal art. If she didn't kill the captive deliberately, of her own free will, the ritual might fail. And who knew *what* would happen then? Maybe Shadye would drain the power himself, as he'd used her body as a weapon, or maybe it would just fade away into the background.

She felt hot tears prickling at the corner of her eye. How could *anyone* make such a choice?

*That's what defines a necromancer,* a voice whispered at the back of her mind. *The decision to put yourself first and foremost, to regard others as nothing more than sources of power or objects to play with as you please. Necromancy is a deeply selfish art.*

"If you do not choose a sacrifice now," Shadye said, "one of these captives will die. And then another, and another, until there are no captives left."

Emily hesitated. One life for the rest of the lives. Shadye seemed to have placed her in a position where killing one person was the moral choice, knowing it would taint her forever to have to *make* that choice. And yet she couldn't see any alternative. She couldn't fight, she couldn't run ... there was nothing she could do.

Sergeant Harkin's chains clinked as he shifted position. "You must use me as your sacrifice," he said. Emily could hear the pain in his voice, but somehow he managed to speak clearly. "It is a small price to pay for allowing the others to go free."

"*Silence,*" Shadye snapped. Behind him, the Orcs stirred angrily. "The choice must be hers."

Harkin smiled, blood trickling down his mouth. "There is no choice," he said. He twisted his head to meet Emily's eyes. "I will die soon without medical attention. The others have long lives ahead of them. Besides, can't you draw more *mana* out of a willing sacrifice?"

Shadye hesitated. "You would willingly offer yourself to the blade to save these worthless lives?"

"*No one is worthless,*" Harkin snapped back. "But I suppose a necromancer wouldn't understand the concept of self-sacrifice. The only reason you'd give someone a helping hand, or a pat on the back, would be to stick a knife in them."

"He wants you to kill him," Shadye said, to Emily. "Kill him."

Emily hesitated. "But ..."

"Do it," Harkin said angrily. "Do you think I want to die slowly of these wounds?" And then he smiled at her, rather tiredly. "You have no choice," he said. "Just ... brace yourself for the power."

Emily stared at him. He was trying to tell her something, but her tired brain refused to process it properly.

She hefted the knife and wondered if she could bury it in Shadye instead before the necromancer could stop her. But when she looked at Shadye she realized that it might not be enough to kill her tormentor. His body was growing into an abomination that might be more terrible than the Faerie of old, something that sucked up life force and would eventually die when it rendered everyone else extinct. He'd start trying to sacrifice animals when the supply of humans ran out, and then he would run out of animals too...

Helplessly, she stepped forward and held the knife above the Sergeant's heart. Up close, she could sense the life energy flaring through his body and knew instinctively where she would have to cut to drain the Sergeant's *mana*, followed by the life energy that kept him alive. There seemed to be no way to drain him slowly, to allow him a chance to recuperate between sessions, or to take his power without killing him -

- In some ways, that was a mercy. If the necromancers ever figured out how to partially sacrifice a person in order to get more and more life energy out of their body over and over again, there would be no stopping them.

"Do it," Harkin hissed.

"*Mana* first," Shadye ordered. "And then you can drain his soul."

Emily closed her eyes and stabbed downwards. The stone knife sliced into the Sergeant's body as if it were cutting through butter - as if it had a mind of its own, eager for the kill. It jerked madly in her hand, but there was no *mana*. Nothing seemed to be happening.

"What?" Shadye demanded. The spell holding Emily in thrall seemed to weaken as the necromancer stared at Harkin in shock. "What are you...? A Mimic?"

Harkin started to laugh, which splintered the last of the control Shadye had over Emily.

The necromancer stumbled backwards.

"You never thought to ask," Harkin said as he coughed up blood. "I was never a magician. No *mana* to drain."

Emily gaped at him, realizing that she'd never seen Harkin perform magic. It had always been Sergeant Miles ... Come to think of it, Harkin had never called himself a combat sorcerer, or *any* kind of magician. And he'd offered himself to the blade knowing that it wouldn't work ...

She twisted suddenly and locked onto the vial in Shadye's hands. The Sergeant had sacrificed himself to give her a chance, and she wasn't going to waste it. There was no point in a direct attack, but if the wards of Whitehall couldn't keep Shadye from manipulating her mind, his own protections couldn't break the link between her and her blood.

The vial exploded in Shadye's hands and he howled in pain, almost as if her blood had turned to acid. It took her a moment to realize that he'd been cut by the fragments of glass.

And then he waved his hands in a complicated gesture and a blast of fire blazed out, scorching Emily's hair as she threw herself to the ground.

"Run," Harkin snapped. "Go!"

Emily ran, through a door that closed rapidly–but not quickly enough to stop her escaping into the corridor. Shadye seemed to be wounded, unable to focus enough magic to manipulate the castle into stopping her escape. But that wouldn't stop him torturing the remaining captives if he figured out a way to break his oath.

Screams followed her down the corridor as she fled, unsure of where she was going. There didn't seem to be anywhere to go, or any way to call for help. The Grandmaster was sealed up in a locked compartment, trying to preserve at least something of Whitehall from Shadye. And there was no way she could call Void, at least not without alerting Shadye.

She thought desperately, trying to find a weapon to use against the necromancer. Nothing came to mind that seemed likely to succeed.

She could feel Shadye's mind reaching out to impose his will on the castle once again. He'd be able to find her soon enough once he gained control of the monitoring spells that kept a careful eye on young students with magic and bad intentions. Unless she could find a way to escape them ... but how?

Maybe she could dismantle the charms using her magic - the talent she was supposed to have - yet somehow she doubted she could do it quickly enough to matter. And if Shadye happened to keep an eye on *which* charms were being dismantled, he'd know *exactly* where to find her.

*The stealth spells,* she thought. The Sergeants–Sergeant Miles, to be precise–had taught her a handful of spells that should help her to hide. They weren't always guaranteed to work against inhuman opponents, but she lost nothing by trying them. She'd also been warned not to use them inside Whitehall, yet she was sure that prohibition no longer applied. The spells fell into place.

She relaxed slightly, before she reached the end of the corridor.

But the corridor was gone.

Emily felt utter despair as she stared at the stone wall. Shadye might not know precisely where she was–assuming the stealth spells were working and not lulling her into a false sense of security–but he'd closed off all possible avenues of escape.

Or had he?

Looking down at where the wall met the floor, she saw a tiny opening, barely large enough to accommodate a rat, or a hamster. The thought came to her before she could think better of it; self-transfiguration was incredibly dangerous, but so was being taken prisoner by an outraged necromancer. Next time, Shadye would rewrite her brain. That would be the end of all hope - or resistance.

The world spun around her as she cast the spell, seeming to grow larger and larger with every second. Emily focused her mind on remembering that she was human as a sudden influx of new sensations flared into her mind. The rat had an excellent sense of smell and better eyesight than she would have believed possible, yet its thoughts were crude, very basic. It wanted to hunt the cheese it could smell in the distance, not follow the demands of a very human brain ...

Somehow, Emily forced herself forward, and into the hole. The rat's mind found nothing wrong with jumping through claustrophobic tunnels and heading downwards, despite the weird flickers of magic that ran through the castle, but Emily found it terrifying–and she didn't dare allow the rat's mind to take the lead. It was quite possible that she would be lost completely if she forgot she was human, or at the very least she might be convinced that she was a rat. Poor Broomstick had been badly traumatized because her roommate had forgotten to include protective wards in her spell. Emily hadn't had time to protect herself against the ratty mind. It was a part of her now.

There were no signs of any other vermin as the rat jumped further down into the castle, something that bothered her. Any large structure should be infested with vermin, from rats and mice to insects and cockroaches, but Whitehall seemed to be immune. And that nagged at her mind. Had someone used magic to make a better mousetrap, or had she missed something obvious?

Actually, what if there *were* people who had been transfigured and forgotten themselves completely? The lower levels of the castle might be guarded by frogs and rats that had once been human.

*Or maybe CT eats them,* she thought. *Or they use them to feed the creatures in the zoo.*

She could feel magic trickle through the air as the rat stopped, right at the very lowest part of the castle. Emily glanced around, fighting to keep the rat's body under control as she tried to determine if she could safely transform back to a human shape. The rat's skewed perception made it difficult, if not impossible, to be certain. *It* saw nothing wrong in a passageway that was little more than ten centimeters high, but Emily knew that she'd be killed instantly if she returned to human form in a space too small to hold her. Shadye would probably sense her death and decide that, too, had been part of his plan.

Eventually, she managed to get out into a giant passageway, large enough to take a human being. The rat's brain fought her as she started to release the spell, either out of self-preservation or because the rat smelled the stench of Orcs with bad intentions. No doubt Orcs ate rats for breakfast ... Emily gagged at the thought as the spell twisted and finally snapped. She flopped against the wall, barely able to hold herself upright. Her mind spun as it struggled to cope with the sudden change, even though the ratty thoughts had faded away into nothingness. But the rat' senses had been better than hers as a human and, oddly, now she was human again she felt blinded.

She took her a moment to gather herself. Then, abandoning the struggle of walking upright, she stumbled down the corridor on all-fours.

*Idiot,* she told herself, when her mind caught up with what she was doing. It had felt natural to move like a rat, natural and right. No wonder Broomstick had been so badly affected, even though a broom shouldn't have had a mind to merge with human thoughts. Maybe she'd just imagined it into existence ...

She shook her head as she heard the sounds of Orcs grunting outside a heavy stone door, the one she'd forced her way into while Shadye had controlled her. A quick glance revealed that there were no less than five Orcs, all heavily armed. She considered casting the Mimic illusion for the second time, but she doubted they would be fooled again ... Of course, they might have released the Mimic from the zoo and left it to dine on unwary Orcs and escaping students.

Instead, she pushed herself into the shadows. There, she created an illusion of herself running around the corner and skidding to a halt when she saw the Orcs. The Orcs howled and gave chase, clearly thinking of the rewards Shadye would bestow on those who took living captives.

Emily watched them go, then stepped around the corner, only to see a short Goblin-like creature standing there. It hissed at her in a language Emily didn't recognize.

"Sorry," Emily muttered, as it advanced towards her with a sword in one hand and a pair of manacles in the other. She hit the creature with a kinetic spell and threw it down the corridor into the wall at terrifying speed, smashing it to paste. Days ago—it felt like years—doing that would have bothered her. Now it was just a way to get through to the nexus itself.

Behind her, there was an angry roar as the Orcs realized that they'd been tricked. They charged back towards the door. Emily had to smile; Shadye wasn't too likely to forgive anyone who messed up, particularly a subhuman Orc. He was unlikely to honor whatever promises he'd made to them. And they were mad enough to kill her rather than try to take her alive.

Desperately, she improvised a spell, scooping up air and cramming it into a very tiny space. The Orcs didn't notice as they advanced, right up until the moment Emily took cover and released the spell, allowing the compressed air to flash out with the force of a small explosion. There was a massive thunderclap, loud enough to damage her ears even though she'd jammed her hands over them.

When she looked back the Orcs all lay on the ground, groaning in pain. Their oversized ears would have been damaged by the sound even if they hadn't been knocked down by the sonic boom.

Bracing herself, Emily pressed her hand against the doorway and tried to open it. A series of powerful charms guarded the room, each one capable of killing anyone who wanted to gain access without the Grandmaster's permission. It was too late to withdraw, so Emily plunged her mind into the charms and worked rapidly to untangle them before they could kill her. The irony struck her as she finished unlocking the final charm. If Shadye hadn't controlled her before, it might have been easier to reach the nexus. The Grandmaster wouldn't have tried to secure it against her specifically.

The door clicked open and Emily stepped through, bracing herself for more surprises. It was unlikely that anyone as careful as the Grandmaster would rely on only one line of defense ...

But she had no choice. There might just be a way to win, but she would need power to use it.

And the only source of power was the nexus.

## Chapter Forty-Seven

THE NEXUS ROSE UP IN FRONT OF HER AS SHE STEPPED INTO THE ROOM.

Instantly, she felt small—and terrified.

There was power all around her, spinning upwards into the school and downwards back into the ley lines, enough power to turn someone into a god. The chamber seemed impossibly vast, like a giant cathedral that reached all the way to heaven. She heard a sound like the beating of a giant heart, the sound of power spinning through the ley lines and echoing all around her. And it reminded her of where Shadye had taken her, the day she'd entered his world. He'd planned to sacrifice her to serve his goals.

*Maybe Void made a mistake*, she thought as she looked over at the towering crystal pillars that seemed to rise up into infinity. *If he had killed me, the Harrowing would have known that I was no Child of Destiny and turned on him. Shadye was saved by Void and he doesn't even know it*!

The thought provided no consolation.

She stepped over to the nearest pillar, wondering if she was out of her mind. If tapping the relatively small amount of *mana* in a magician's body was enough to drive someone insane, who knew what would happen if she tapped into the vast wellspring of power right in front of her? The whole idea of using charmed crystals to control and direct the flow was to prevent someone from having to tap the power directly. It was easy to imagine all the ways it might go wrong.

*I could blow the ley lines*, she thought as she studied the pillar. Even holding her hand near the structure, she felt the power coursing through it. *The school would be destroyed.*

She shuddered. Apart from her, no one in this world had the background to imagine what might happen next. Dragon's Den, ten miles away, might be shattered by the explosion; it would certainly be exposed to hordes of necromancers as they poured through the new pass through the mountains. And that was assuming a relatively *small* blast.

What would happen if the blast was powerful enough to blow the world apart?

Sergeant Harkin had trusted her. He'd given his life to ensure that she had a chance to escape, to meet a destiny she wasn't sure she had. A Child of Destiny should know exactly what to do at any given moment, according to the books, but Emily found herself utterly uncertain of the best course of action. Should she risk merging her mind with the power, knowing that the merest touch might shatter her mind? Or should she try to destabilize it, risking the destruction of everything for miles around? Or should she gamble and hope that her original plan worked?

Bracing herself as best she could, she pressed her fingers against the crystal. Instantly, she felt the power growing stronger, as though it were already coursing through her body. She pulled away hastily, too late to stop some of it from taking root in her mind.

Even after she broke contact, she still felt the school all around her. The Doctor's TARDIS was nowhere near as complicated as the interior structure of Whitehall. She sensed Shadye as he made his unhurried way down to the nexus, and the Grandmaster, as he held the remaining students and tutors safe in a sealed section of the school. All around the latter, there were hundreds of interlocking dimensions, all piled up on top of one another.

Unsure of what she was looking at, she pulled away as she sensed Shadye's sudden alarm. He knew what she'd done - and was coming to stop her.

*Not that he has much choice,* the tactical part of her mind insisted. *Given time, I could turn the school against him. He has to stop me now. Or flee.*

She pulled her mind back to herself and started to concentrate. The power she'd drawn from the ley lines wouldn't match Shadye's power–she doubted she could, unless she was willing to court madness– but it would be enough to keep him busy until she could get him into the right place. At least it would be easier here, in the nexus, than outside in the school itself. There was a risk that Shadye would try to draw the power of the nexus for himself, but–if she was right–the mere contact with it would be too much for him to stand. He'd be convinced he could tame it, right up to the moment when it melted his brain.

The doorway exploded inward with a thunderous crash. Shadye strode into the room, holding up one hand in a defensive posture. He was alone, even though Emily could sense the presence of Orcs and Goblins outside, in the antechamber. Shadye clearly didn't want an audience, or distractions.

Or ... did he fear that his servants might make their own bid for the power? They'd been human before the Faerie started playing with their genes. And she would have been surprised if they didn't trust Shadye any further than they could throw him.

Of course, being Orcs, they could throw him quite some distance.

The necromancer stopped at the edge of the room, almost as if he was reluctant to walk into it any further. His humanity seemed to have completely faded away, his cloak and robe the only thing that kept him even vaguely humanoid.

Emily's enhanced senses saw power coiling around him that wasn't quite visible to the naked eye. Somehow, it reminded her of CT–and how he'd grown additional manipulators at will.

"You have unlocked the power," Shadye said. Emily couldn't tell if he meant it, or if he was trying to play with her mind. "Stand aside and allow me to fulfill my destiny."

"I don't think that would be a very good idea," Emily said mildly. In hindsight, she should have studied acting, as well as engineering, chemistry and a dozen other subjects that would have prepared her for her brave new world. It took everything she had to appear confident in front of the maddened necromancer. "Your destiny doesn't lie here."

"My destiny lies where I say it lies," Shadye snapped at her. He still hadn't moved forward and she took heart from that. "Stand aside."

Emily smiled. "How can you claim that you make your own destiny and, at the same time, call me a Child of Destiny?"

"You *are* a Child of Destiny," Shadye insisted. "You are here to change the world. And it will change, at my hands."

He'd abandoned the idea of converting her to necromancy, it seemed. Or maybe he'd just put it to one side.

Emily studied him and allowed her face to develop the smile that had driven her stepfather into angry fits when she was a kid, waiting to see what he'd do. Shadye might decide to lash out at her, with all of his power, but there was no way to know what would happen if they fought a duel within the nexus. Maybe they would overload it and blow the ley lines accidentally. Or ... once again, there were just too many possibilities.

"Your destiny is to die here," Emily said. She shaped a spell in her mind and readied it for immediate use. "So die."

She tossed the spell at him, transfiguring the air around him to deadly black smoke. For a heartbeat, Shadye was blinded.

It wouldn't take him long to dispel the smoke, but it gave her a moment to cast her second spell. A dozen copies of herself stood around the room, all looking ready to fight. There was so much power flowing through the Nexus that it would be difficult for him to find the *real* Emily among the shadows.

The smoke vanished. Shadye paused, again holding up one hand, then released a blizzard of spells towards her and the duplicates.

Emily jumped in order to avoid some of his tricks, praying that he wouldn't be able to wipe out all of her duplicates before she managed to prepare her next trick.

Shadye seemed to be losing control completely, lashing out angrily towards one of the duplicates. A flash of light powerful enough to blast through stone walls struck one of the crystal columns, only to be effortlessly absorbed into the nexus.

Emily blanched. That could have blown up half the country!

Shadye howled in rage and blasted the column again, but to no greater effect.

Taking advantage of his distraction, Emily created a second set of duplicates and followed her spell up by throwing a hail of practical joke charms at his back. The itching charm, she'd discovered when practicing with Alassa, was actually surprisingly hard to block, even for a skilled magician.

Shadye spun around and unleashed such a blast of fire at her duplicate that the illusion popped like a soap bubble.

Emily jumped back behind one of the pillars, only to find herself staring at black tentacles that seemed to have come out of nowhere. One of them grasped her leg and picked her up, dragging her towards Shadye. His red eyes glared at her as he pulled her closer, one hand holding the stone knife.

*He must be running low on power,* she thought, desperately. *If he wants to drain me, he must be running critically low on power ...*

She looked at the shadow and generated a beam of light, causing the shadow to break apart and merge back into the darkness. But it was too late; a clawed hand caught her and yanked her forward until she was staring into Shadye's glowing red eyes.

Shadye lifted the knife threateningly, ready to plunge it into her chest.

Emily panicked. Raw power lashed out of her with no clear direction, which forced Shadye into a defensive posture. Emily quickly shaped a cutting spell she'd learned from books and aimed it at his arm. The arm disintegrated into nothingness before she dropped to the ground.

Shadye slashed out at her as she fell, barely in time for the blade to miss her skin. She knew *exactly* what would happen if he managed to get his hands on more of her blood.

Shadye bellowed a curse in a language the translation spell refused to adapt for her and summoned more shadowy monsters to his side.

Emily turned and ran. The creatures came after her as she desperately tried to generate another ball of light. But Shadye snuffed her first ball of light out; the shadows fell on her before she could produce a second. A monstrous shape that seemed oddly familiar grabbed her tightly enough to make her cry out in pain. Desperately, she focused her mind, thought of a monofilament blade and lashed out with it. The shadows recoiled, giving her just enough time to pull free.

"There is no escape from the Living Shadows," Shadye informed her. He seemed calmer, oddly; perhaps he thought that victory was within his grasp. "You cannot fight a shadow."

He was right, Emily realized. Laser-like beams melted them, but they reformed with terrifying speed; bright flashes of light dispelled them, yet they returned as soon as the light faded away. She tried to produce permanent globes of light, only to watch helplessly as Shadye picked them off, one by one.

And then the shadow-creatures caught her again and sent her stumbling to the floor.

The chamber shook as Shadye worked his will, summoning a stone table into existence. Emily knew what it was a moment too late. The shadows lifted her up to deposit her on the stone, moving to secure her hands and feet, pinning her. Her magic suddenly seemed to be useless. The stone absorbed anything she did, but it couldn't–didn't - block her link to her prepared spells. She clung to that thought as Shadye advanced on the table, red eyes glowing with bright light. Just a few seconds more ...

"If you will not serve me of your own free will, you will be reshaped," Shadye informed her. He lifted the knife again, moving it to the point where Emily had stabbed Sergeant Harkin and revealed that he had no *mana* to call his own. But Emily knew that Shadye would have no trouble draining her. And then, he'd either feed on her life force or rewrite her brain to suit himself. "I will make Destiny my servant."

Emily wanted to giggle as she released a handful of spells, including the charm keeping her final surprise under wraps.

Shadye held the knife above her chest, his red eyes studying her as if he expected her to surrender and become a necromancer, just before the air started to blow past them. A moment later the knife was yanked out of his hand and spun through the air, finally vanishing into nothingness. Shadye stared at where it had been as the pull grew stronger, tugging at him even as he grabbed hold of the stone table. He started to say something–Emily guessed he was demanding to know what was happening–but it was lost in the noise of the wind. Shadye spun around and threw a fireball at her, but it only made it a couple of inches before the gravity pull sucked it in, too.

The shadows holding her down were coming apart. When they did, the gravity threatened to drag her into the pocket dimension along with Shadye. She grabbed hold of the stone table, praying that Shadye had secured it to the floor, and held on for dear life as the necromancer struggled to find some way to counter what she'd done. Emily hadn't been able to think of anything he *could* do, but Shadye had a great deal of raw power at his disposal - and he was desperate.

For all she knew, maybe he *could* cancel the spells that she'd shaped into creating a miniature black hole leading to a new dimension.

She looked away as his robes were pulled towards the black hole, revealing something so horrifying that she didn't want to look any closer. Whatever he'd become was very far from human, an eldritch horror out of nightmares. Worse yet, his form was threatening to come apart completely.

His eyes glowed bright red as he cast spell after spell in the air, before finally managing to shield them both. Somehow, without quite knowing what he was fighting, Shadye had managed to save his life.

Emily would have been impressed if he hadn't looked as if he was about to forget how useful she could be to him and kill her outright. Dark magic crackled around his one remaining claw and his eyes were bright with hatred and malice.

But he hadn't managed to completely stop the black hole, merely provide some protection for them both. Which gave her hope.

"You will die," Shadye screamed in a cracked and broken voice. Indeed, she was no longer sure if he even had a *mouth*. There were *things* crawling inside his hood. She could sense that it was taking almost all of his magic to keep the protections stable and neglect the black hole. "Child of Destiny or not, you will *die*!"

Emily started to laugh, finally realizing how it felt to know–to truly know–that death was unavoidable. "You were wrong," she said, still keeping a tight hold on the stone table. "You were wrong from the start. My mother's name is Destiny."

Shadye stared at her. It took him several moments to work out what she'd said, and how badly he'd erred right at the start. And when it hit him, he lost control.

The gravity pull reasserted itself. Emily held onto the table, feeling it shuddering under her, as Shadye flew backwards and hit the black hole. For a moment, it seemed that he was just too big to fit *into* the tiny singularity ... and then his body twisted and vanished into nothingness.

Working frantically, Emily reached out and cancelled the spells that had created the black hole. It–and the pocket dimension it led to–simply blinked out of existence, taking Shadye with it.

She rolled off the table and collapsed onto the floor, feeling utterly drained. It felt as if she were alone in the school ... as if she were the last survivor. The sense she'd had of the Grandmaster's presence was gone; she felt too dazed to try to determine if the Grandmaster was dead or if the enhanced awareness she'd been granted of the school was gone, along with the power she had used to make the black hole. Her head spun madly and she felt almost delirious.

When she looked up, she thought she saw a tall man in monkish robes. He carried a huge book and looked directly at her. But when she blinked, he was gone.

Carefully, she pulled herself to her feet and tottered towards the door. It opened at her approach, revealing a dozen Orcs lying on the ground, all dead. There was something wrong with their bodies, something she should have seen at once, but it eluded her. Dazed, she stumbled and would have hit the floor if someone hadn't caught her arm. A tall boy with dark hair looked down at her, his expression unreadable.

After a long moment, he lowered her gently to the floor and walked away. She turned her head in time to see the shadows swallow him up.

The entire building appeared to be shaking madly as the Grandmaster tried to reassume control of the interior dimensions. Emily smiled as she felt his will work through the building, isolating the remaining monsters that Shadye had used to invade the school. She lay back on the ground, too tired to go any further. Her head spun and she blacked out ...

... She must have blacked out, for the next thing she saw were anxious faces staring down at her.

"Rest," a voice said quietly. It sounded like the Grandmaster, but she couldn't tell for sure. "It's all over now."

"The wards need to be replaced," another voice said. Emily felt her head spinning; the wards had fallen because of her unique nature. It had all been her fault. How many had died because of her?

She tried to speak despite the pain in her head. "Grandmaster?"

"Yes," the Grandmaster said. "Rest now."

Something touched the side of Emily's head, and she plunged back into darkness.

## Chapter Forty-Eight

EMILY OPENED HER EYES, VERY SLOWLY.

Her body felt ... weird, almost as if she were lighter than air. It crossed her mind that she might have been dreaming, that she might have had an accident and imagined everything from Shadye's kidnapping to his death ...

... And then she looked up. A ball of light floated high overhead. The Grandmaster sat next to her bed, looking down at her anxiously.

It had been no dream.

"Welcome back," the Grandmaster said. He studied her thoughtfully, his expression oddly familiar. It took her a moment to realize where she'd seen something like it before; on the face of a man studying a new form of life. "You saved the school."

Emily tried to sit upright and failed. "Thank you," she managed to say. Her entire body felt drained, unable to move. "Is ... is he really gone?"

The Grandmaster smiled, but it didn't quite touch his eyes. "I wished to ask you the same question. And I need to know what happened between you and the necromancer before you killed him."

Emily hesitated. Shadye might have been an eldritch abomination, but there had been enough matter left in his body for the black hole to rip him apart before crushing him down to a single point in the pocket dimension, which should then have been deleted from reality. She couldn't imagine how *anything* could have survived that. Even teleportation spells shouldn't have been able to get him out. They were unreliable in pocket dimensions, particularly ones created by other magicians. Even if Shadye had been reduced to a disembodied entity, he should have been deleted along with the pocket dimension. He was–he must be — dead.

But part of her didn't believe it.

"I think he's dead," she said, finally.

The Grandmaster peered down at her, one hand stroking his beard. "And what did you do to kill him?"

The black hole hadn't been a *real* black hole, Emily knew, or she might have had worse problems on her hands than a furious necromancer. But she'd thought of it as a black hole and deliberately set out to create something with a powerful gravity field that could both suck in matter and crush it into a very small space. It might prove to be an ultimate weapon against the other necromancers. Yet, if she introduced the concept of variable gravity fields to this world, who knew how far a curious magician would take the concept? He might produce a *real* black hole, risking the entire planet. Or he might turn it into a new and fearsome weapon. It might be better if she kept her mouth shut.

"I don't think I should tell you," she said, after a long pause. The Grandmaster gave her a sharp look; Children of Destiny were supposed to be enigmatic, but there were limits. "The knowledge would be too dangerous for this world."

"Necromancers could use it," the Grandmaster said. It wasn't a question. "Or are you a necromancer yourself?"

Emily stared at him. "*No*!"

"There are a handful of witnesses who say you murdered Sergeant Harkin to claim his *mana*," the Grandmaster informed her. "Shadye apparently spared them; we do not know why. What happened?"

"The Sergeant knew the ritual would fail," Emily said bitterly. She was no necromancer, but she could see how someone could jump to that conclusion. And if she told the truth about what had happened in the nexus, it wouldn't be long before everyone started meddling with simulated black holes, risking the entire planet. "The Sergeant told me what to do."

"So he did," the Grandmaster said. His eyes never left her face as she puzzled it out. Of course; he would have looked into the witnesses' minds and seen everything. "And in volunteering for death, he helped save the school."

He looked down at the floor, almost as if he were ashamed. "I accept the judgment of a Child of Destiny," he said. His face twisted into a smile. "Or at least that is what I will tell the Council of War, when they finally demand that I tell them what happened to defeat Shadye. But I'm afraid that suspicion will still fall on you. Willingly or otherwise, you took part in a necromantic ritual and may be tainted."

Emily nodded once, slowly. "What will happen to me?"

"You'll be watched," the Grandmaster said. "We've seen too many students become tainted and then fail to purge themselves of the taint before it was too late. Shadye was once a student here, before his interest in the Dark Arts led him to necromancy. Others had to be ... stopped before they could leave the school."

He shook his head. "Rumors are already spreading through the Allied Lands. You beat a necromancer in single combat. You're either inhumanly powerful or you are a necromancer yourself. Neither one is very reassuring to the people in power."

Emily could see their point. A necromancer would be mad, bad and dangerous to know - and would eventually lose all interest in trying to hide it. Someone with vastly greater power than the average magician–without madness–would be a threat to the status quo merely by existing, perhaps a greater threat than a necromancer. And it didn't matter that she had tricked Shadye and defeated him with science, concepts born in her world. If the truth came out, the consequences would be disastrous.

She looked up at him. "How long did I sleep?"

"Nearly two weeks," the Grandmaster said. He didn't quite admit that some people had considered simply slitting her throat while she lay helpless, but Emily heard the subtext and winced inwardly. "It took that long for the Healers to pull you back from the brink of death."

He shook his head. "Whitehall has been badly damaged by the invasion. Upwards of two hundred students and staff are dead, or badly injured. The grounds outside were devastated as the Orcs tore through them and then fled when Shadye was defeated. Luckily, we got most of the younger students out before the wards fell, but our other losses were heavy. If another necromancer had attacked just after Shadye's death, we would have been defeated.

"I managed to get the main wards back up and the Allied Lands dispatched a large army to help secure the school and hunt down the remaining Orcs, so we should be safe for the moment. But in the long term, our reputation for being invincible has been severely dented."

Emily nodded. An invading army had rampaged through the school and forced the defenders to hide in a closed-off section of the multidimensional building. Even though the army had been crushed in the end, it still suggested that Whitehall *could* be beaten. The other necromancers would not fail to take note.

"We will be holding the main funeral rites within a day," the Grandmaster said. "I thought that you might like to attend."

Back home, Emily would never have seriously considered attending a funeral. They had always struck her as pointless affairs. Now, however, she understood the need to say goodbye, to pay her respects to the men and women who had died at least partly because of her. Their so-called Child of Destiny had been responsible for their deaths, as well as Shadye's final defeat. Destiny was very much a two-edged sword.

But then, George Washington had been a great hero to the United States–but the Native Americans had regarded him as a monster.

She impatiently pushed the thought aside. She *knew* that Shadye had messed up the summoning spell; she *knew* that she was no Child of Destiny, except in the most literal sense. And if she started thinking that she couldn't lose, she would lose when she overlooked something important because she was too confident to check on it. She would just have to avoid letting it go to her head.

"I will," she said, and then hesitated. "How many did I kill?"

The Grandmaster looked back at her. "When?"

"Shadye ... manipulated me," Emily reminded him. "I was his puppet and he used me to kill people."

Her memories of sleepwalking, convinced that she was fighting demons that had infested the school, were blurred, but she knew that she had torn her way through everyone who had tried to stop her. And she'd hacked her way into the nexus chamber, even though the defenses had been vastly more capable than anything else she'd ever encountered. How much had been her and how much had been Shadye?

"You cannot be considered responsible for your actions," the Grandmaster said. "I have known more experienced wizards who were ... *manipulated* by someone who secured an undamaged sample of their blood. You were not in your right mind."

Emily managed to pull herself upright to glare at him. "How many did I kill?"

"None," the Grandmaster said.

Emily breathed a sigh of relief.

"But you froze Madame Razz and knocked out seven combat magicians when you tried to enter the nexus chamber," the Grandmaster added. "I suppose Shadye didn't want to risk you becoming aware that something was wrong by killing them outright."

Emily looked down at her hands. "I knocked out seven combat magicians?"

"Shadye did, working through you," the Grandmaster said. Emily wondered, suddenly, if he was lying. She'd thought that she was fighting demons. "It wasn't your fault. They know that."

He stood. "Your friends wish to see you now that you are awake. Would you like me to have them called here, now?"

"I don't know," Emily admitted. She wanted to be alone, even though part of her mind insisted that was the worst possible thing she could do. "Are they ... are they scared of me?"

"I think half the school will be a little scared of you," the Grandmaster said grimly. "But your friends should stick with you. They know the real you."

*No, they don't,* Emily thought. She'd never told them where she really came from, or *why* her morals were so different than theirs. Or, for that matter, why she had insights into magic and science that they found so revolutionary. And she had effectively lied to them more than once to keep her secret.

"Yes," she said finally. She shouldn't be alone. "Call them in."

"One other point," the Grandmaster said. He hesitated awkwardly. "You made a bargain with the Unseelie Court."

Emily froze, expecting her oath to kill her before remembering that the Grandmaster had pulled the information from her mind against her will. She hadn't even *considered* allowing him to learn the answer to his questions by reading her mind, which was probably what had saved her life. It hadn't been her fault.

"I understand why you made the bargain, and that you were given no time to think, but it was not wise," the Grandmaster said. He held up a hand before she could speak. "Say nothing to me, even now. Oaths can be tricky things and this one could kill you. But understand: the Unseelie are *not* human. They may well demand something from you that will cost you everything, perhaps even your humanity."

Emily wanted to point out that the human race used the fairies as potion ingredients and it was hard to blame them for wanting to remain hidden, but she held her tongue. The Grandmaster was right; it had been foolish to make the oath, even though there had been little choice. She couldn't have left the Redshirts to be boiled alive and eaten by the Orcs, or whatever fate their dark master had planned for captured students. They deserved much better than abandonment.

"If their demands are unreasonable, bring them to me and we will try to ... negotiate," the Grandmaster said. "Or you could allow the oath to take its toll."

*And die,* Emily thought, feeling sick.

The Grandmaster bowed to her. "I thank you for saving my school. And I hope that your remaining years will be less exciting."

He walked out of the doorway and left Emily alone.

She glanced around, noting the pile of flowers in one corner of the room and a handful of bottles someone had placed on the table near the bed. It was still hard to move her body without feeling dizzy, but she managed to reach a bottle of juice and take a swig without pouring it down her neck and spilling it on the bed. The liquid was refreshing, enough to make it easier to remain upright without falling back on the bed.

A moment later, the door burst open and Alassa and Imaiqah ran into the room.

"You're awake," Imaiqah said. She threw herself at Emily and gave her a hug. "They kept saying that you were on the verge of death!"

"I felt that way," Emily admitted, unwilling to talk about what had happened. Shadye hadn't just wanted to kill her; he'd wanted to corrupt her, to force her to take up necromancy and serve him as a slave. If it hadn't been for Sergeant Harkin, he might have succeeded. "But I'm getting better."

Alassa took Emily's hand, squeezing it tightly. "You're going to be even more famous, thanks to her," she said, nodding at Imaiqah. "My parents have *insisted* that I invite you back home between terms. I think they want to squeeze some political advantage out of you."

Emily blinked. "More famous?"

Imaiqah reached into her robes and produced a scroll of cheap parchment. "I told my father about what you did, about how you defeated a necromancer in single combat without actually *being* a necromancer and he had it written up for the broadsheet singers," she said. "The news has been spreading through the Allied Lands and everyone *loves* you."

Feeling an odd sense of doom, Emily unrolled the parchment and found herself looking down at a charcoal drawing of her face. It wasn't a bad likeness, although her eyes looked slightly slanted, but it was the caption underneath that caught her eye. It read "Lady Emily, Necromancer's Bane." There was nowhere near as much text below the portrait as there would have been in a newspaper from back home, but the writer had managed to cram a number of exaggerations and outright lies in anyway. It would have been proof that some things were truly universal if she hadn't been so flabbergasted and annoyed.

"You do realize ... " She began, and then stopped. Of course Imaiqah hadn't known how she'd beaten Shadye. If the Grandmaster hadn't known, how could she? "Half of this story isn't true."

She gazed down at the line of text that claimed to be the story of her origin and rolled her eyes. It didn't mention alternate worlds or necromantic kidnappings. Instead, it suggested that she'd been adopted by a farming couple who had found her hidden by the roadside, managing to imply—without ever directly stating it—that she might have aristocratic blood. It also hinted that her parents had been murdered by a necromancer and she had devoted her life to their destruction.

"They'll be expecting me to dress up as a bat next," she muttered as she rolled up the parchment and passed it back to Imaiqah. On the plus side, anyone who actually *believed* that story would prove himself an idiot. And a fearsome reputation would make it harder for established interests to block ideas and concepts she'd introduced into the world. "Or maybe fly through the sky faster than a speeding bullet."

Imaiqah blinked. "You don't like it?"

"It isn't even remotely true," Emily pointed out. It wasn't even the story she'd given them when they'd asked where she'd been born. "They have to know that."

"The common people are fond of believing silly stories," Alassa said dryly. "If they knew little about your origin"—she shot Emily a look she couldn't interpret—"the writers will simply make something up. By now, there will be a hundred different versions of your origin and of how you beat a necromancer. The real necromancers will be unable to deduce the truth from the lies."

"Assuming that one of them doesn't get it right," Imaiqah added. "You'd be astonished how many people have been sending you letters, and presents, and ..."

"Threats," Alassa butted in. "Some people are already hinting that you have already fulfilled your destiny."

Emily opened her mouth and then closed it again, unable to think of a suitable response. She didn't want to be considered a Child of Destiny, or *special.* Or, for that matter, dangerous. But she *was* dangerous to the established order in the Allied Lands, simply by being a font of ideas for Imaiqah's father and others like him. And when she started a bank to reward others with good ideas ... it was going to change the world.

"I wish I knew," Emily said, after a long pause. It was difficult, but she managed to swing her legs over the side of the bed and stand up. "Can you find me some potion for energy and dizziness?"

"You were badly drained," Imaiqah said, carefully. "You really should stay in bed."

Emily shook her head. "I need to find something mindless to do," she said. Everything she'd seen and done was bubbling to the top of her mind, threatening to drive her insane. She'd effectively killed a tutor she'd respected, even admired. And one who had worked at a school for magicians without having any magic himself. She still couldn't believe that no one had realized until it was too late. But then, who would have dared to cast a practical joke charm on one of the Sergeants?

"There are teams sorting through the remains of the alchemy classrooms," Alassa said. She hesitated. "I'd suggest that you got dressed before you went down there."

Emily looked down at her gown and nodded. "Very well," she said. It was difficult to dress herself, even in a basic robe, but somehow she managed it. The more she moved, the more responsive and steady her body became, helped by a potion Alassa found in a nearby cupboard. "Let's go."

# Chapter Forty-Nine

EMILY STOOD ALONE IN THE MIDST OF A VAST CROWD.

The remaining students had been joined by a small army of parents, aristocrats and people who just wanted to be seen there. Emily had donned her training uniform, as instructed by Sergeant Miles, but the crowds had no difficulty in picking her out and pointing at her, as visitors to a zoo might point at a particularly interesting animal. Very few had risked speaking to her and those who had tried to speak with her had made her feel more alone than ever. She wasn't a person to them, just a force of nature that they thought they could bend to their own use.

It made her feel sick.

Sergeant Miles hadn't said anything to her about Sergeant Harkin's death, but she'd overhead whispers from the remaining students in Martial Magic, which probably meant that they were all around the school. They thought that she'd killed him in a necromantic rite; they chose to ignore the fact that he'd *told* her to kill him - and that Shadye had given her no choice. The other students, apart from Jade and the rest of the Redshirts, seemed either contemptuous or terrified of her. They wondered if the school had a necromancer attending classes beside students who would provide an excellent source of power.

Those weren't the only whispers. The Grandmaster had told the school, after Emily had recovered enough to join the rest of the students for dinner in the dining hall, that Emily had defeated and killed Shadye. That was true, as far as it went, and no one disputed that Emily deserved the awards the Grandmaster had given her, but now they were wondering about favoritism. Would Emily be punished if she did something bad? Would the tutors *dare* to punish her if she did something *really* bad? These questions struck Emily as absurd, yet the next two broadsheets she'd read had claimed that she had enough power–naturally–to blink the rest of the necromancers out of existence. Who would dare to try to discipline a walking, talking atomic bomb?

*Maybe I should get myself punished deliberately,* she thought as Sergeant Miles began to bark orders. *Convince them that I am still a normal student. But that only works in sappy novels about boarding schools written by writers who have never attended one.*

She picked up her handle and helped to lift Sergeant Harkin's coffin, carrying it out into the cemetery. The dead students would be buried in their home countries, but the tutors were all going to be buried at Whitehall. She caught sight of the angelic statues and shivered as they moved towards the hole in the ground where Sergeant Harkin would be laid to rest. The whispers only seemed to get louder as the watching crowd realized that Emily was one of the pallbearers. Those who knew that she had killed the Sergeant were shocked, even if Sergeant Miles had been the one who had ordered it.

The Grandmaster stood at the front of the crowd, surrounded by several dozen men and a handful of women in the black uniforms of combat magicians. Harkin would have trained them, Emily realized, wincing at the way they looked at her. She had killed him and some of them - perhaps all of them - would never forgive her for it. They either didn't know what had really happened, like the other students, or they didn't care.

"Lower the coffin," Sergeant Miles ordered quietly. He tapped his throat as the pallbearers obeyed, boosting his voice so he could be heard all over the cemetery. "Sergeant Harkin joined the army as a very young man and served in a dozen battles, earning medals and promotion, before finally being invited to serve as a Drill Sergeant at Whitehall. He shaped the lives of hundreds of students, preparing them for the duties of combat magicians in a time of war. Those who passed his course knew more than just magic; they knew how to *fight*.

"He had no magic, but he never let that stand in his way.

"To be a Drill Sergeant is never easy. Many capable soldiers have failed to train new recruits even if they serve brilliantly in combat, or behind the lines. The Drill Sergeant must *understand* his charges, knowing that they will come to regard him as a sadistic monster. He must push them to their limits, reforming them into soldiers *without* breaking them. He must pretend to be a sadist without actually *being* a sadist. It is not always easy to tell when one is crossing that line.

"Sergeant Harkin never crossed that line.

"Nor did he fall into the trap of going easy on some of his recruits because of their blood, or gender, or age. Those who graduated while under his care have gone on to spectacular careers, defending the Allied Lands against all manner of evil. His legacy lies in those he trained to defend the innocent.

"Like all of us who take up arms, he knew that he might one day die in the service of the Allied Lands. When death came, Sergeant Harkin not only accepted it bravely, but saw a way to turn his own death into a tactical advantage, a tactical advantage that eventually led to the death of a feared necromancer. He chose the manner of his death, knowing that one of his best students would be able to use it to win the day. Very few of us truly manage to die as bravely–and as well–as Sergeant Harkin.

"He was my friend and comrade and I will miss him terribly."

Emily felt tears building in her eyes and tried to blink them away. Miles was right. Sergeant Harkin had known what he was doing, but it didn't make her feel any less guilty. Even the praise she had just received from Miles didn't help, nor would it change any minds. The other students would probably believe that she had killed Harkin in order to steal his life essence and use it for power.

Sergeant Miles stepped forward and threw a piece of earth into the grave. One by one, the pallbearers followed, covering the coffin in soil. Later, she'd been told, powerful charms would be cast on the gravestone to prevent the corpse from being reanimated by a powerful sorcerer or necromancer. And then the body–Sergeant Harkin's body - would slowly decompose into the soil and bring new life to Whitehall.

The rest of the ceremony passed in a blur, ending with a dismissal to their private thoughts. Emily wandered away from the rest of the crowd, heading towards the zoo–or what was left of it. CT moved through the wrecked plant beds, growing new tentacles in an attempt to clean up the mess, but it seemed like the work of years.

Beyond him, the zoo had been completely torn apart. Dead animals were scattered everywhere.

A tentacle touched her shoulder and she jumped. "They found no trace of the Mimic," CT said. His single giant eye peered down at her. "It could be anywhere by now, but they want to search the area thoroughly, just in case. Maybe there will be a clue to its new form."

Emily shivered. A student, or an Orc, could have wandered into the Mimic's range and been sucked dry while the Mimic took on his form and memories. Unaware of it's true nature, it would have wandered out and escaped, only recovering when it ran out of life force and had to resume its true form. It could be anywhere by now.

She found herself looking up at CT and wondering if she was staring at the Mimic, before remembering that CT had been frozen solid by the invading army. The Mimic would have needed to duplicate a more mobile form to escape.

"They also butchered a dozen unicorns and centaurs," CT added after a moment. "You can use their blood and bones in the darkest of arts. I fear we shall see the results of their harvesting soon."

"Yeah," Emily muttered.

The unicorns had been *sweet*, and almost holy. They didn't deserve to be butchered like wild animals. The centaurs weren't so nice–they forced themselves on human women to breed more centaurs, which was why the girls had been warned never to go near them–but they were true to their nature. Even they hadn't deserved to be torn apart by Orcs and have their bodies harvested by Dark Wizards.

But maybe Shadye hadn't sent the harvested items away from Whitehall before he died. There was no way to know for sure.

She thanked CT and walked away from the zoo, unsure of exactly where she was going. The grounds had been twisted somehow, a result of the struggle for control of the school's interior dimensions. One of the *Ken* playing fields had been destroyed; the other had been left largely intact, but damaged to the point where playing a full game would be difficult. Several third-years were trying their best anyway, tossing balls around with spells and tools that reassembled baseball bats. They caught sight of Emily and stared at her before doing their best to ignore her. It would have been funny, Emily decided, if it hadn't been happening to her.

"They are always scared of rogue talents," a familiar male voice said from behind her. "You can't blame them."

Emily jumped and spun around, lifting one hand in a defensive stance. Void stood there, smiling rather thinly as the bubble of accelerated time caught both of them. Emily relaxed–slightly–and looked back towards the third-years. They looked frozen, stopped dead. She knew it was an illusion.

"This can't be good for us," she said carefully. "Aren't we growing older while they remain frozen in time?"

"There was a Dark Wizard who trapped himself in one of these bubbles and aged to death," Void said. "But he managed to bungle the spell. This one won't last long enough for our aging to matter."

Emily shrugged, then waited.

"Shadye's ... brethren have been rather shocked by his death," Void told her. "You're the first person *ever* to beat a necromancer in single combat." He gave her a knowing look. "And believe me, that scares them."

"I cheated," Emily admitted.

"Only way to win," Void said. "But necromancers being necromancers, they are unlikely to believe that you cheated, even if they couldn't imagine you winning *without* cheating. You managed to scare them ... and *that* gives the Allied Lands a chance to rebuild their defenses."

"Someone is going to have to find the tunnel near the Dark City," Emily said. That raised its own problems; someone else might stumble into the Unseelie Court and receive a less friendly reception from the fairies. Maybe the Grandmaster could talk to them and offer to declare the entire area off-limits in exchange for the location of the tunnel. "And who knows how many other surprises they might have been working on?"

"We don't know," Void admitted. His lips twitched into a smile. "And everyone is *still* calling you a Child of Destiny.

Emily groaned. "Am I a Child of Destiny?"

"The perfectly truthful answer would be *yes*," Void pointed out. He smiled at her expression. "But are you a Child of Destiny in the sense they mean?"

He shrugged. "Can anyone *really* answer that question? And does it really matter?"

"I don't know," Emily admitted. "I ... I just feel odd having people either hanging on my every word or being terrified of me."

"Enjoy it," Void advised. "This world is not always kind to the powerless."

"No," Emily agreed. "It isn't."

They stood together in silence for a long moment. "I meant to ask," Emily said. "Can you bring something from my world here?"

"Maybe," Void said, after a bit of thought. "But I'd prefer not to suggest to the necromancers that they can bring items from other worlds. It would only give them ideas."

"I need some textbooks," Emily explained. "There are so many things that would be useful here, if I could only remember how to make them. But I am *ignorant*! I should have studied more at school."

"A very good idea," Void agreed dryly.

He looked down at the ground, thoughtfully. "There are ... *problems* inherent in using entities to bring anything from one world to another," he added, after a moment's silent contemplation. "It may be possible. It may not be possible. I will consider it carefully and contact you when I know what to do."

Emily nodded, suspecting that was all the answer she was going to get.

"Something else, then," she said. "What are *you*?"

Void smirked. "A rogue talent," he said. "Somewhat naturally more powerful than the average magician. There was a ... *disagreement* about how to cope with a situation and I ended up being told that I was no longer welcome at Whitehall. I left, changed my name and became an independent operative. *Someone* had to keep poking and prodding at the necromancers to keep them fighting each other."

He shrugged. "The rest of the story isn't particularly interesting. But I'm sure you will have fun looking through the public records and trying to put it all together."

One finger tapped the bubble around them, which was beginning to flicker. "You nearly killed a Royal Princess, and then you saved her life–and convinced her that she should be a better person. You introduced all kinds of new ideas which will shake up the world, and destroyed at least one guild which held a stranglehold on progress. You were manipulated into allowing a necromancer into Whitehall, the most strongly-warded building in the Allied Lands, and then you defeated him, all on your own."

He smiled. "Tell me ...what are you going to do for an encore?"

Emily shook her head. "I don't know," she admitted. She had ideas she didn't want to talk about, even to Void. "Maybe I don't really have a destiny after all."

Void's smile grew wider. "You know what I think?" He asked, as the bubble began to splinter into nothingness. "I think you've only just begun."

The End

## *About the author*

Christopher G. Nuttall is thirty-two years old and has been reading science fiction since he was five, when someone introduced him to children's SF. Born in Scotland, Chris attended schools in Edinburgh, Fife and University in Manchester before moving to Malaysia to live with his wife Aisha.

Chris has been involved in the online Alternate History community since 1998; in particular, he was the original founder of Changing The Times, an online alternate history website that brought in submissions from all over the community. Later, Chris took up writing and eventually became a full-time writer. *Schooled in Magic* is his first title with Twilight Times Books.

Current and forthcoming titles published by Twilight Times Books:

Decline and Fall of the Galactic Empire SF series
*Barbarians at the Gates*

Schooled in Magic YA fantasy series
*Schooled in Magic* book 1
*Lessons in Etiquette* book 2
*Study in Slaughter* book 3
*Work Experience* book 4
*The School of Hard Knocks* book 5

Chris has also produced *The Empire's Corps* series, the *Outside Context Problem* series and many others. He is also responsible for two fan-made Posleen novels, both set in John Ringo's famous Posleen universe. They can both be downloaded from his site.

Website: http://www.chrishanger.net/
Blog: http://chrishanger.wordpress.com/
Facebook: https://www.facebook.com/ChristopherGNuttall

If you enjoyed this book, please post a review
at your favorite online bookstore.

Twilight Times Books
P O Box 3340
Kingsport, TN 37664
Phone/Fax: 423-323-0183
www.twilighttimesbooks.com/

Printed in October 2021
by Rotomail Italia S.p.A., Vignate (MI) - Italy